NEVER AGAIN

a novel

Harvey A. Schwartz

VIRGINIA BEACH
CAPE CHARLES

Never Again
by *Harvey A. Schwartz*

© Copyright 2018 Harvey A. Schwartz

ISBN 978-1-63393-731-4

This is a work of fiction. The characters are both actual and fictitious. With the exception of verified historical events and persons, all incidents, descriptions, dialogue and opinions expressed are the products of the author's imagination and are not to be construed as real.

Review copy: this is an advanced printing, subject to corrections and revisions.

Published by

◤ köehlerbooks™

210 60th Street
Virginia Beach, VA 23451
212-574-7939
www.koehlerbooks.com

DEDICATION

For Sandra, *merci* for giving me the time, space, love and
encouragement to make it through this process, and for Nana
Ida, who taught me endlessly why "never again"
is so fundamental.

PROLOGUE

Ben Shapiro's flying was sloppy. Downright dangerous. Flying his high-performance sailplane was instinctive, a twenty-first-century remnant of seat-of-the-pants aviation. Sometimes he shut his eyes and imagined his arms spread wide, hands cupped, catching rising air currents under his wings.

Drifting thousands of feet above the ground usually dragged his mind from his Boston civil rights legal practice, from all that was wrong with the world and his life. But not this time.

The sailplane veered side to side as Shapiro floundered through rising air currents. He should have sensed the lift, banked his wings and circled like a hawk. Instead he bumped through the air, consumed by what he'd heard on the radio as he pulled into the Plymouth, Massachusetts, Soaring Society parking lot.

"An apparent atomic bomb has detonated in Tel Aviv, Israel's second largest city." The NPR news reader struggled to speak calmly. "No nation or organization has claimed responsibility . . .

"The mushroom cloud was visible in Jerusalem, thirty-five miles away."

Never even been to Israel, Shapiro thought. *Wonder if I ever will now.*

What he heard next cut deeper.

"Egypt, Jordan and Syria offered to send emergency aid, accompanied by troops," the radio reporter said. "There is no word on deaths, but the population of Tel Aviv is more than 400,000."

■ ■ ■

News analysts speculated that the atom bomb that destroyed Tel Aviv might have been manufactured in Pakistan, North Korea or Iran. Maybe it was smuggled out of the former Soviet Union. It could even have been made in Israel itself and been the bomb the Jewish state secretly traded to South Africa before the Afrikaner government gave way to black majority rule.

American specialists estimated the device was in the twenty-five-kiloton range, almost twice the strength of the Hiroshima bomb. Satellite images showed a crater 370 feet across and nearly 90 feet deep. The detonation ignited a firestorm fueled by ruptured gas lines, gasoline tanks, every object that could burn within a half mile of ground zero.

The enormous fireball, with a surface temperature of 10,830 degrees Fahrenheit, created a glare bright enough to burn out the retinas of people ten miles away. Half a million people, most of them Jews but also tens of thousands of Palestinians, were estimated dead, or they would be within a couple of days. Cool Mediterranean breezes spread the radiation cloud inland and north through Israel's best agricultural region, an area created from desert by generations of Jewish settlers during Israel's brief life span. The bomb split the country in two—literally—creating the next chapter in Jewish history.

Perhaps in a hundred years Jews would memorialize the thousands who died fighting to their last bullet rather than give up their homeland. Or the million who were slaughtered by one uncontrollable army or another. Or the millions more herded into Palestinian concentration camps. If there were Israelis in a hundred years, however, they would be descendants of those who managed to flee to the port of Haifa, where every craft that could float was crammed with hysterical people old enough to remember the last Holocaust or young enough to fear the next. The eastern Mediterranean swarmed with ships with no destination except "away."

CHAPTER 1

Three days after the bomb, only the depths of the Negev Desert remained under Israeli control. A half dozen aging F-16 fighter-bombers provided support for a tank battalion training there. Colonel Gideon Hazama ordered a defensive ring formed around a concrete dome rising out of the desert at a spot known as Dimona, the location of Israel's intentionally worst-kept secret.

Hazama, two air wing commanders, and the minister for cultural affairs, Debra Reuben, who had been on an inspection tour of southern Negev settlements, gathered in a conference room buried fifty feet below the sands.

Reuben looked like she would be staggered by the weight of a well-fed sparrow landing on her shoulder. After surviving fashionable high school anorexia on Long Island in New York, she'd grown into the type of woman who could see where on her hips a bowl of Ben & Jerry's Cherry Garcia took up residence and would then spend the next week exercising it away. Her hair had been colored throughout so much of her life that she'd struggle to name her natural color on the first try. At present, it was a startling red.

Her appearance was deceptive.

Reuben's obsession with Israel separated her from her girlfriends. From her early days attending Hebrew School at Temple Beth Shalom and through her teenage years as president of the Temple Youth Group, the story of young European Jews fleeing oppression to settle in the desert, learning to farm, learning to fight, creating their own government, triggered awe Reuben found difficult to explain. Compared with what she saw in her parents and their friends, with what she saw in herself and her friends, these Israeli Jews seemed larger, stronger, heroic. Mythical super-Jews.

I can do that, too, she'd thought. She was certain her future would be in Israel. Her parents smiled and nodded, confident she would outgrow it if only she'd meet the right boy.

They were wrong. Golda Meir, Israel's first and only woman prime minister, a woman with features so prominent that she looked as if she'd already been carved in stone at twice life size, would have shaken her head in wonder to see tiny Debra Reuben holding the tattered reins of power over the State of Israel. Golda would have smiled, though, to see the stiff-backed soldiers biting any response to Reuben's harangue.

Reuben's rise to cabinet rank was viewed by most Israelis as a fluke, the kind of compromise that pleased nobody but was common in the hothouse of Israeli politics. She'd been a producer for the New York City CBS affiliate until a dozen years earlier, when she vacationed in Israel following a failed engagement to her on-again, off-again college heartthrob. She decided it was time to stop resisting what she'd expected would be her fate all along and stayed in Israel. Reuben found work in Israeli television, where she earned a reputation for integrity with her American brand of investigative reporting.

When a neutral but publicly respected person was needed to round out a coalition cabinet, her name was proposed as somebody few people would object to. To nearly everyone's surprise, she took her new position seriously, worked hard and earned a grudging respect.

She knew nothing about military strategy and in fact would have been hard pressed to load a simple Uzi pistol. But now the fate of Israel's nuclear weapons cache rested with her.

That Israel had nuclear weapons was an open secret assumed by the intelligence services of all the major powers and feared by her neighbors and enemies. Israel's real secret was not that it had nuclear weapons but rather that it had so few. Rather than bankrupt the nation assembling an atomic arsenal, Israel hinted at about a hundred bombs—but stopped at three. Pretend bombs were as great a deterrent as real ones.

Now Reuben played the role of the hard-nosed militant while Hazama and one of the two Israeli Air Force pilots argued against following orders from a nonexistent central government.

"Do I have to repeat the decision made by our government years ago?" Reuben asked the exhausted military officer. "If the end of Israel is inevitable, rule number one is that these weapons must not fall into enemy hands. If all else is lost, they are to be detonated in place. The loss of the Negev is a small price to prevent the future blackmail of whatever Jewish state eventually reestablishes itself.

"Rule number two is that if an atomic weapon is used against Israel, our weapons are to be used, immediately, against the capital city of the country that attacked Israel. And rule number three is that if any devices remain unused, they are to be safeguarded and removed for future use."

"Of course, we know all that," said Colonel Hazama "What we don't know is who is responsible for the Tel Aviv bomb."

The soldiers ached for revenge. Uncertainty about the target for that revenge left them too frustrated to act. The irony that Debra Reuben prodded them to use the bombs, in some way—in any way—was a miniscule component of the desperation of Israel's dying days.

"The country is overrun with Arab soldiers. Palestinians are slaughtering our people. Tel Aviv and who knows how much of the rest of the country is a radioactive wasteland. And you, the lions of Judah, the last remaining arms of the nation, can't decide whether to strike back," she scolded Colonel Hazama.

Reuben was near hysterical from lack of sleep and too much coffee. From the nightmare that decades of Jewish dreams were coming to a tragic conclusion. And that she alone was responsible for Israel's final act.

"One serious attack on our airstrip and any chance to deliver these weapons will be lost," she said. "Another day, maybe two, and we'll all be Egyptian prisoners. Or dead. I am now the government of the State of Israel. As such, I order you to load two devices onto aircraft and drop them on Damascus and Tehran. The planes are to leave in one hour."

Reuben rose from the table and walked across the room, gesturing to one of the pilots, the man who had remained silent throughout the lengthy arguments, to walk with her. She spoke with the man in whispers for several minutes, then she returned to the conference table where Colonel Hazama waited.

She sat, rested her head in her arms. She wanted her father to tell her what to do, her mother to rub her back and say that whatever she did was right. Instead, she fell asleep.

The colonel looked at the two air force commanders. "You, Damascus," he said slowly, as if he were pronouncing their death sentences rather than that of millions of others. "You, Tehran."

And the last one, the little one, we'll hold onto for now, just in case we need it later, Colonel Hazama thought. He left the room to supervise the loading of the weapons.

One hour later he placed his hand on Reuben's shoulder and shook her awake.

"The planes are in the air. May God forgive you. May God forgive us."

Reuben rose from the conference table, feeling removed from herself, as if she were watching from a far corner.

"Let's load the other device into a truck and get the hell out of here," Colonel Hazama said. "A boat is waiting in Elath.

Where it will take us I have no idea, but I have a feeling we are two Jews who will have few friends in the land of Israel for a long time to come."

The two jets took off, one north, toward Damascus. The southbound Israeli pilot, who had not said a word, skimmed just feet over desert dunes until Red Sea waves reached up for its belly, flying ten feet above the water's surface. Rather than turning eastward to cross the Arabian Peninsula, he continued south, following Reuben's whispered instructions.

"Israel will need this weapon later. Later, when we are ready to fight for our land. Not yet, though," Reuben instructed him. "One bomb is enough to use for now," she'd said. "There are still Jews in Ethiopia who will guard Israel's treasure."

■ ■ ■

The United States Sixth Fleet, with the battleship *New Jersey* and the carrier *Lyndon Johnson*, rounded up its sailors from the streets and brothels of Tripoli, cutting short its courtesy visit to the latest Libyan government. The fleet steamed east, breaking out its never-used radiation decontamination equipment, preparing its sick bays. Doctors on board hurriedly read the manuals on treating radiation victims, knowing that by the time survivors would be carried on board the ships, the burn and blast victims would already be dead.

America was on the way, if only Israel could hold out for a few more days.

Damascus was obliterated before the Sixth Fleet arrived. The Tel Aviv bomb horrified the world; the Damascus bomb disgusted it. Israel went from receiving worldwide empathy and support to being demonized.

A dozen organizations jostled to claim credit for bombing Tel Aviv, but no one boasted about bombing Damascus. No one needed to claim credit. No one but Israel would have or could have done it.

American Jews made little effort to justify Israel's conduct. The Damascus bomb was seen an act of desperation, a drowning nation seeking to take an enemy—any enemy—down with it.

Hearts hardened. It was one thing for a crazy religious fanatic suicide terrorist to use an atom bomb, but another for a government to choose to do so. Even American Jews conceded that Israel went too far this time.

■ ■ ■

Tel Aviv no longer existed by the time the Sixth Fleet arrived. The fiercest fighting was between the Syrians and the Egyptians, each claiming sovereignty over what had been Israel. Palestinian refugee camps in Lebanon, Gaza and the West Bank emptied as four million people thanked Allah for the miracle and rushed to claim what was theirs by divine right. Or at least as much of it as did not glow in the dark from radiation.

The Sixth Fleet was met by an Egyptian patrol boat whose nervous captain politely informed Admiral Jameson Barons on the *Lyndon Johnson* that the situation was well in hand, that the best medical teams were on the scene and that while the American offer of help was appreciated, the situation was not nearly as serious as first thought. So many armed groups were on the scene, however, that it would be best for the fleet to withdraw before a tragic accident took place.

Admiral Barons, who had lost his son, a Marine lieutenant, in Afghanistan, and his daughter, a Navy SEAL, in Yemen, waited for orders from Washington. He was commanded to exercise restraint and to act in his best judgment based on the local situation.

Enough young deaths, Barons thought. *Enough Americans dying in wars where we can't tell the good guys from the bad guys.* The Americans withdrew.

CHAPTER 2

The white glider banked steeply, its forty-five-foot, carbon-fiber right wing pointing at Plymouth Rock 6,000 feet below. Ben Shapiro lay under the blue-tinted canopy nearly flat on his back, craning his head for the telltale wisp of forming cloud that indicated a thermal, warm air rushing upward, that would float his engineless aircraft higher yet.

Good lift over the shore would make this flight a special one. Shapiro needed a special flight to take his mind off the events in Israel.

He'd spent the morning sitting in front of the television monitor in the conference room in his Boston law office, staring at coverage of refugee ships forced out of harbors in Greece, Italy and Albania. Europe had learned that once such refugees enter, they never leave.

From Israel itself there was no coverage. Newscasters speculated about what was happening when four million vengeful Palestinians backed by three armies swarmed over the sick and dying remnant of those Jews who had neither the will to resist nor the strength to flee. The total ban on foreign journalists—for their own safety—by the occupying powers fueled the worst fears. Al Jazeera's Damascus coverage showed children's burned corpses, block after block of leveled buildings, demolished schools and hospitals. In contrast, it reported that bomb damage to Tel Aviv, although serious, was miraculously limited to Jewish neighborhoods. Troops provided relief aid to the Jews who had wisely chosen to remain in Palestine.

Shapiro prepared for the next day's deposition of a Raytheon sales manager who'd fired his administrative assistant after she refused to go to a motel with him. But the case seemed silly now in contrast to the news from the Mediterranean. Maybe a million Jews dead. Maybe two million. Another million in the camps and tens of thousands more in the ships.

Shapiro knew he had to do something to take his mind off the news, something that would take all his concentration. That's what his sailplane was for. No matter how much a next day's jury argument consumed his thinking—so he could not take a shower without the words of his closing argument forming silently in the back of his throat—he knew that once he strapped himself into the sailplane and wiggled the rudder to signal the towplane pilot he was ready to be pulled into the sky, his mind would focus on nothing except the aircraft and what was happening to the air around it.

"Good to see you again, Ben," Willy, the glider club's towplane pilot, said when Shapiro pulled up to the club hanger. Willy was a retired commercial pilot, never having made it to a major carrier before mandatory retirement. "Too bad what's happening to your people over there. Who would have thought somebody would be crazy enough to mess with an atom bomb? Must have killed himself, too, don't you think?"

Shapiro gave Willy a nod, then a second quick look, surprised but not upset about the "your people." He'd never discussed being Jewish with Willy, or hardly anybody else for that matter. For him being Jewish was more a fact of life, like being six feet tall. It wasn't as if he ever went to religious services or bought Kosher meat for any other reason than that it seemed healthier. Shapiro referred to himself as a "gastronomic Jew," not a religious one.

"Yeah, too bad, too bad," Shapiro muttered. "How's the lift today, Will? Been up yet?"

"It's developing," Willy answered, looking up at the puffy white cumulus clouds, a sign of rising air currents. "A hell of a lot of traffic out of South Weymouth, though. Never seen it so busy there."

South Weymouth Naval Air Station was a recently reopened Navy Reserve air base a dozen miles north of Plymouth from which the Massachusetts Air National Guard flew F-15s up and down the northeastern seaboard.

Military traffic complicated the basic rule of safety in the sky—the rule that said, "Don't worry. It's a big sky and you're in a little airplane." Gliders were a special problem.

The largest piece of metal in Shapiro's glider was the thermos bottle he carried his Gatorade in. The German-built, fiberglass-and-carbon-fiber sailplane, with its wings only inches thick and its smoothly curved body, was a better stealth aircraft than the hundred-million-dollar fighters the Air Force was so proud of. The glider returned a radar echo about as well as a hawk with a bottle cap in its mouth, and its circling flight, searching for the same rising air currents as the birds used, was a perfect imitation of a lazy bird of prey.

"Your tax dollars at work, Willy," Shapiro said. "If those Reserve pilots are up on a Wednesday, you can bet they're getting time and a half."

Shapiro walked slowly around the glider, mentally ticking off each of the twenty-seven items on his preflight check list, then kicked the wheel centered under the cockpit and gave each wingtip a good shake, just to prove once again that the plastic plane would stay together when he hit the turbulence that marked entry into strong lift.

He opened the rear canopy in the two-person glider and checked that the safety harness straps were buckled, holding the seat cushions in place so nothing could get loose in the rear cockpit and jam the controls.

Some glider pilots would chat away while going through the preflight ritual. Shapiro, Willy learned from experience, treated each stage of the inspection like a surgical procedure, counting the number of threads showing beyond the safety nuts on each connection. This attention to detail paid off in the courtroom and carried into every aspect of Shapiro's life, including what was supposed to be recreation. His wife joked that he planned their vacations down to making reservations at gas stations every 375 miles, knowing his car got 400 miles to a tank.

To a woman who never turned off a light or closed a drawer, who tossed away the cap when she opened a new tube of toothpaste, this seemed to be a foible she categorized as one of those "Jewish things" about him caused by a compulsive mother, things she sometimes found enchanting but usually put aside with a laugh. In Sally Spofford's childhood in the big house on the rocks overlooking the ocean on Boston's North Shore, there was always somebody else to worry about the details, to turn off the lights, to make sure the gas tank was full.

The tow pilot walked over to Shapiro's glider.

"Let's go up to three thousand feet. A tourist flight today," Shapiro said.

Shapiro squirmed into the front seat in the glider, lying back with his head held up by a small adjustable support. The shape of the glider was designed to minimize air resistance, with the smallest frontal area the designer could devise and still fit the pilot. Shapiro buckled all five straps, one from each side around his waist, one over each shoulder and one coming up between his legs, the "aerobatic" strap designed to keep him from sliding under the instrument panel when he turned the plane upside down. He closed and latched the hinged plastic canopy, put his feet on the rudder pedals and gently grasped the control stick, projecting between his legs, in his right hand.

The tow pilot attached the towrope to the release mechanism

in the glider's nose, tugged to confirm it held tightly, then walked the 200-foot length of the rope to the towplane and started his engine.

Shapiro breathed in, filled his lungs with air, held his breath, then released the air slowly. Chanting his "rope break" mantra of "stick forward, land straight ahead, stick forward, land straight ahead," the action to take if the towrope broke in the first 200 feet of flight, he stepped down hard on the right rudder pedal, then hard on the left, wiggling the plane's rudder from side to side to signal the tow pilot he was ready.

He heard the towplane get full throttle, and the next second he was moving along the grass field the gliders used. In thirty yards he had enough speed to ease back on the stick and lift the glider five feet off the grass, holding it there until the towplane rose from the ground. Carefully duplicating each movement of the towplane, wings banked right, then level, then left, then level, the two aircraft rose into the sky, linked by a rope umbilical.

At 200 feet his mantra changed to "sharp turn to the left, stick forward," knowing he had to act instantly should the rope break above 200 feet of altitude, turning the glider back to the airfield before it ran out of altitude and hit the trees at the end of the runway. The rope had never broken, but some day it would. Shapiro got through life knowing that even though the odds against disaster were a thousand to one, if you did something a thousand times, disaster was a certainty. He expected the towrope to break on every takeoff, just as he expected the arresting police officer to lie at every trial. In both cases, if the expected didn't happen, he was pleasantly surprised.

The towplane circled and crossed the duck-shaped pond southeast of the grass field that marked the IP, the interception point, where gliders entered the landing pattern for that runway, just as the altimeter needle touched 3,000 feet. As the glider passed over the pond, Shapiro took the yellow release handle in his left hand and gave it a strong pull, then another to be sure the towrope released. Two tugs on the release were standard procedure. Just in case. Following the prearranged pattern, the towplane banked sharply to the left and the glider gently to the right.

Pointing the plane's nose into the wind coming from the ocean five miles to the east, Shapiro slowed the plane to forty-seven miles an hour, its minimum sinking speed. Although almost all glider competition was in smaller one-person aircraft, Shapiro preferred his two-seater. Few things impressed clients more than a glider ride. Besides, it got them used to being in a position where their lawyer was in complete control of their fate.

Shapiro's glider was, for the moment, state of the art, delivered from Germany the previous winter. With its ninety-foot wingspan, wings smoothed to a tolerance of a thousandth of an inch, and the latest high-tech tubes and turbulators designed to squeeze every ounce of available lift out of the air, the plane had a glide ratio of seventy-five to one, meaning it went forward seventy-five feet for every foot it dropped. From 6,000 feet up, that meant the plane could glide for seventy-five miles even if it found no lift.

The glider could carry a 200-pound passenger in the rear seat. Shapiro had flown two 500-mile cross-country flights in it already, and he was still learning how to press the plane to its limits.

The glider floated over the moored sailboats and fishing boats filling Plymouth Harbor. He spotted the canopy over Plymouth Rock and pictured the crowd of disappointed tourists surrounding the rock, expecting something like Gibraltar and finding an ordinary boulder with a crack down the center.

He gazed at Cape Cod hooking out into the ocean, its tip swirling around at Provincetown like a cat's tail curled up for the night. To his left he saw Boston, a layer of smog hugging the ground for a thousand feet above glass towers reflecting sunlight. He flew silently for two hours and let the altitude and solitude disconnect him from whatever was waiting for him on the ground—anxious clients, an increasingly distant wife and a marriage that seemed to have passed its expiration date, law partners worrying about collecting fees. Shapiro sometimes wished he could fly off and never land, impossible as that was. Eventually, as always, he steered for the interception point and flew the landing pattern.

Willy helped him pull the glider into the club's hanger, next to the custom trailer Shapiro used for towing his disassembled plane to other flying areas.

Shapiro, his mind eased by the medicine of the sun, the wind and the sky, opened his car door, sat down, started the engine with its reassuringly powerful Mercedes turbo hum. He rolled down his window, not yet ready to give up the feel of the wind for the sterile coolness of the air conditioner.

As the electric antenna whirred up, the radio came on.

"Two ships carrying thousands of Jewish refuges illegally entered Boston Harbor early this morning," the radio announcer said. "The Coast Guard ordered the ships quarantined. President Quaid personally directed that nobody be permitted ashore. Spokesmen for the Jewish community in Boston expressed outrage."

I'd better stop by the office on the way home, Shapiro thought.

CHAPTER 3

Three weeks after the Tel Aviv and Damascus bombs, the anchorage area in Boston Harbor next to Logan Airport's runway 4R/22L sat empty as Boston went to bed. By dawn two elderly freighters, Greek-owned but flying the Israeli flag, the *Iliad* and the *Ionian Star*, swung from their anchors a thousand yards from Downtown Boston.

The ships arrived with between 1,500 and 2,000 passengers each. Their cargo holds, ventilated only when the overhead hatches were left open to the rain and spray, were filled with miserable people, cold, wet, hungry, using buckets for latrines and seawater for washing. The decks, too, were crammed with people lying on every horizontal surface, crowding the railings for fresh air and a place from which to vomit from seasickness, bad water, spoiled food.

The captains had listened to radio reports of countries throughout the Mediterranean blocking their harbors to Israeli refugees. They'd decided to head directly for the United States, one country where they felt sure of finding a welcome.

The ships were immediately quarantined, supposedly for health reasons, in the anchorage area adjacent to the runways of

Logan International Airport. They sat at anchor, the miserable, exhausted people on board not understanding why America, a country of immigrants, barred its door to them.

The ships presented a problem—not because America could not absorb three or four thousand refugees, but because it did not know if it wanted to.

By 2021, years of massive budget deficits, soaring oil prices and healthcare costs, and record-high immigration from Mexico, Central America and Asia brought the US to its knees. Wall Street was a wreck as banks again collapsed and real estate values crashed.

Congress responded by demonizing newcomers, in much the same way Hitler blamed Jews for Germany's economic hardships after World War I. Turning their backs on the Statue of Liberty and egged on by the former president, Congress passed the American Pride Identification and Display Act, a law that created a national identification card program, a law aimed at identifying the millions of Mexicans, Haitians, Salvadorians, Nicaraguans, Thais, Chinese, Nigerians, Somalis, Cambodians, Vietnamese, and other people who had come to the country by one means or another for thirty years.

"Americards" were issued to every person who could show proof of citizenship: a birth certificate, a passport, naturalization papers. Within a month, some 275 million Americans were registered. At least thirty million others—people who could not prove citizenship or legal residency—were not and could not be registered. Like credit cards, Americards included a computer chip encoded with the person's name and registration number, plus physical data such as height, weight, eye and hair color and, most powerfully of all, a digitized photograph, fingerprints and a retina scan.

The enforcement phase took longer, but the public was behind that effort, too. Employers were required to print workers' registration numbers on their paychecks. Paying workers in cash was prohibited. Employees with no registration number were not allowed to be paid. Payroll checks with no numbers could not be cashed. Employers hiring unregistered workers were fined. Repeatedly.

Welfare workers were required to verify that recipients were registered. No Americard, no welfare.

Schools checked students' registration, with the threat of having federal subsidies cut off if they refused. Unregistered students could not attend school. The law's intent was brutal and obvious: to ostracize immigrants and starve them out of the country. No work, no food, no housing, no education, no health care. The system worked. The cards were issued in January 2021, and by May the nation's workplaces, schools, welfare rolls and most public places were purged of illegal aliens.

The backlash stunned people. News stories told of immigrant families hiding in their apartments, of mothers, fathers and children slowly starving to death; of mothers walking the streets as prostitutes because that profession did not require registration cards; of shoplifting arrests in supermarkets. Crime, always an alternative way to get by, became the only way for millions of people locked out of the American dream to feed themselves and their children.

That wave of crime, of course, created yet one more backlash. Get these people out, send them back where they came from. The deportation planes and ships left New York, Miami and Los Angeles daily. The overcrowded, impoverished countries these people fled from were forced to reabsorb them.

Then the *Iliad* and the *Ionian Star* limped into Boston Harbor and became the focus of national debate.

"Let them in. These people are different; they are victims of war," some said. "They are good refugees, not bad ones— not Salvadorians, Nicaraguans, Vietnamese, Cambodians, Mexicans." "These refugees are Jews, like so many powerful and famous Americans." "America has always accepted Jewish refugees," the historically ignorant said.

"They are our brothers, our family," cried American Jews.

Even former president Donald Trump weighed in, tweeting that the Jews sitting on ships in Boston Harbor should be allowed to join the Great Society because they share America's Northern European heritage and values. "They look like us, they think like us, they contribute to our society instead of milking it like other groups," Trump said. Liberals backed by immigrants' rights groups, youth, aging progressives, church groups and some power nonprofits blasted Trump and Jewish sympathizers for their hypocrisy. No special treatment for anybody. "That would be wrong," they said. Especially wrong for the murderers of Damascus.

So the ships sat in Boston Harbor. Surrounded by America, floating in American water, watching Americans cruise the harbor in their sailboats, watching American airplanes thundering over their heads to land at the nearby American airport, watching American cars drive on American streets. Surrounded by America but not allowed in.

CHAPTER 4

The ebonized cherry table in the conference room at Shapiro, McCarthy and Green felt freshly oiled but of course left no residue on fingers rubbing across its surface. The table, the conference room, the art on the walls and the entire office were on the top floor of a former Howard Johnson's chocolate warehouse on Boston's now fashionable waterfront. The conference room was where lawyers from other firms sat during depositions, where they sized up the firm, estimating where their opponents placed in the pecking order of Boston's legal community. The conference room was where clients were introduced to the firm's three partners and where fees were first discussed.

The firm's three partners were Jewish, Irish and black, former assistant district attorneys who had to take second mortgages to meet their first year's overhead. They had grown the business and now employed eight associates.

The three young men sitting at the conference table across from Ben Shapiro were obviously impressed—and uncomfortable—not knowing what to do with their hands or whether they could put their elbows on the table. They had not spoken except to mumble a barely audible greeting. The middle-aged man with them didn't share their problems. He sat back. Listened closely to Shapiro.

"Your first problem is a legal doctrine called standing," Shapiro said, speaking to the older man but occasionally glancing at the three others, noting that every time he looked at them they looked away.

"What this doctrine means is that not just anybody can walk into court and say a government action is unconstitutional. Only people directly affected by a law can challenge it. You can't challenge a law setting the drinking age at twenty-five if you are thirty years old because that law doesn't affect you. Before we can challenge what the government is doing, we have to show that somehow, even in a minor way, it affects you."

"What does that mean?" the older man asked, seemingly annoyed. "Do these boys have to say they are Jewish, or that they lived in Israel, or that they are American citizens? I'll have them dance the hora in court if you think it would help."

"No. They are going to have to say, under oath, that they escaped from the ships in the harbor. And then they'll face the consequences." Shapiro spoke bluntly, testing to see how serious they were about this lawsuit. "As an officer of the court, I'm not supposed to advise you to break the law, but you do realize, don't you, that now that you are off the ships, you could disappear into this country, even without legit ID cards."

"The organization I represent went to considerable effort to surreptitiously remove these men," the older man said. He pointed at the three young men, who remained silent and seated. "These men are soldiers. Their families were murdered. They came here for sanctuary. They should live with dignity, not hide in the shadows like common criminals. They deserve to be treated with dignity. I want them here legally."

Shapiro thought a moment. All that the old man said was true, but the case was a loser. No judge would grant asylum in direct defiance of Congress and public opinion. But perhaps the case would garner sympathy and rattle America's anti-immigrant hysteria.

"This kind of lawsuit can be awfully expensive," Shapiro said, speaking only to the older man. "We'll need high-powered experts. They won't come cheap. Even with them, chances are we'll lose at the trial level and have to work our way through the appeals courts. You're probably looking at $400,000 in legal fees and another $40,000 at least, in expenses."

"It's not the money that matters," the older man said. "An important principle is at stake here."

"The money matters if you don't have it."

"Rest assured, counselor, we have it. How much of a retainer do you want?"

"Just to clear up one point. Will you all be parties to the case?" He locked eyes with the older man.

"These men are your clients. I am their, shall we say, benefactor."

Alone in the conference room after the men left, Shapiro took a deep breath and sat looking out the window at Boston Harbor. He pictured the thousands of frightened people on the two ships.

I guess I took the case, he thought. *I don't expect we'll win. I wonder what else will have to be done to save these people.*

CHAPTER 5

A Hinckley Bermuda 40 yawl is the ultimate New England cruising sailboat—the kind of boat that turns heads, the kind pampered by its rich owners. A blue water boat built with a tile fireplace as standard equipment, the Bermuda 40 *Swift* looked as incongruous tied up stern-first among the fishing boats in the tiny harbor on Xanthos as would a camel in the Alps. The rocky Greek island off the west coast of the Peloponnesus between Greece and Italy saw few yachts, and fewer built by dour Maine boatbuilders as family heirlooms for wealthy Yankees.

Lt. Chaim Levi, former first officer on an Israeli Navy coastal patrol boat, could have cried when he saw the Hinckley's long, blue hull, the roller furling jib and the stowaway main and mizzen sails, designed so the boat could be sailed singlehanded in the roughest of weather. The boat had been unattended for weeks.

With this boat I could sail anywhere in the world, he thought. *With this boat, I could go to America.*

Levi's Israeli Navy patrol boat had spent three days escorting freighters and fishing boats, yachts and ferry boats, anything that could float and could carry people from Haifa Harbor westward into the Mediterranean, getting them away from the coast and the hastily armed fishing boats manned by Palestinians who'd spent three generations trying to force Jews from Israel but were now doing their best to keep any from escaping what they saw as Allah's punishment.

Finally, out of torpedoes and ammunition for the twin 50-caliber machine guns, with his captain dead from a knife wound to the chest when the boat was boarded at night, Levi knew the remaining fuel was down to a few hours. When his sole crewman spotted a wooden boat powered by two huge outboard engines and crammed with gun-waving men, Levi knew this would be the last engagement for his tired vessel. The Israeli fishing boat he was escorting was loaded with elderly people and children, one of the last boats to escape from Haifa before Lebanese soldiers, Israel's former Christian allies, roared through the streets looting shops and raping women.

Levi stationed his patrol boat between the Palestinians and the crowded fishing boat. He and his crewman had their handguns and nothing more. Engines full forward, he drove his vessel straight at the bow of the Palestinian boat, playing chicken with the armed men the way he used to race his little outboard head-on at friends when he was growing up in the small coastal resort town where his father managed a hotel for American tourists and Levi gave sailing lessons.

This time, as he had so many times with friends, Levi swore he would not swerve. The two boats rammed into one another, the steel bow of the patrol boat driving through the wooden hull. Locked together, the two boats sank.

Levi threw the inflatable life raft off his vessel's stern seconds before the boats collided. The raft inflated automatically when it hit the water. Levi splashed in behind it, climbed into the raft and paddled desperately with both hands away from the glossy film on the water. As he feared, the fuel ignited, sending yellow flames and black smoke into the blue sky, roasting the men thrown by the collision into the water.

Fortunately for Levi, a stiff breeze from the southeast drove his rubber raft out into the Mediterranean, away from what would, in other circumstances, have been the safety of the Israeli shore. Two days later he was picked up by a Greek fishing boat. The captain, no friend of Turks or Arabs, spent an evening in his cabin with Levi and two bottles of ouzo. He left Levi on the stone pier when the boat returned to Xanthos a week later, taking Levi's worthless shekels in exchange for euros, both of them knowing the exchange was a gift, not a business deal.

The captain's parting present to Chaim Levi, one Levi never learned about, was the bottle of ouzo the captain left with his cousin, the corporal of the port police, Greece's equivalent of the coast guard, with a request that Levi be left alone. This was a man who'd suffered enough, and Greeks could sympathize with suffering, the captain told his cousin. The corporal nodded and carried the ouzo into his tiny office on the stone quay. He passed the word among the fisherman that Levi was approved, and Levi found work cleaning fish and helping to mend nets. He slept on an old fishing boat too leaky to take to sea, run aground at the edge of the harbor.

Chaim Levi introduced himself to the corporal, pronouncing the *CH* in his name with the full Hebrew guttural sound, as if he were clearing his throat before getting to the rest of his name. That pronunciation was beyond the Greek's abilities. Levi was known among the fisherman as "the Jew."

Levi's eyes were on the Hinckley, standing empty at the pier. "That is a fine boat," he mentioned casually to the port police corporal as the two walked the fifty-meter length of stone pier that made up the town's waterfront. "Maybe it is owned by a wealthy fisherman."

"A wealthy fisherman? There is no such thing," the corporal laughed. "There are poor fishermen and there are old fishermen and there are tired fishermen and there are dead fishermen, but there are no wealthy fishermen. That fine boat is owned by an American whose wife had the misfortune to step on a bed of sea urchins. I myself offered to piss on her feet to soften the spines. I told him to soak her feet in lemon juice so the spines would not cause infection. He tried to pull them out himself, though, and of course they broke off in her feet, dozens of them."

Levi nodded as an idea formed in his mind.

"He spent an hour on the telephone at the post office and they flew away in an airplane that landed right in the harbor on the water, the first time such an airplane has landed here," the corporal said. "The great tragedy of it all is that he only paid his docking fee for two nights. He owes me twenty-five euros for each night for the past two weeks. That is a serious amount of money."

"Maybe somebody should move the boat from the dock and anchor it. That would give more space at the dock for the working boats," Levi said.

The corporal nodded and held both hands in the air, palms upward.

"Who in this village knows about American boats, how to raise the sails or start the engine?" the corporal groused.

"I've sailed such boats when the Americans visited my country," Levi said. "I'd be pleased to help you after all the kindness you've shown me. I'll do it this afternoon. Where should I move the boat? It must be someplace safe, someplace sheltered from the winds to ride unattended at anchor."

The corporal told Levi about a cove a few kilometers down the coast. Nobody lived there. Steep rock walls protected it from the prevailing east winds.

Levi topped up the water tanks in the sailboat's bilge and pondered whether he should fill its diesel tanks, too.

That would be too risky, he decided. *How would I explain that?*

During the next week he spent his mornings riding a borrowed bicycle over the hills to nearby villages, where he bought all the canned goods he could afford and stashed them on the shore of the cove. Every afternoon, he rowed to the cove in one of the fishermen's skiffs on the excuse that he wanted to make sure the boat was doing well unattended. He took fishing gear with him, telling people the small cove was the best fishing spot he'd found. Instead of fishing, though, he ferried supplies to the Hinckley.

His body ached after six days of bicycling over the hills in the morning and rowing down the shore in the afternoons, but the boat was crammed with an unappetizing collection of canned goods.

"I am sure the American will pay you well for all the care you have taken of his boat," the corporal told Levi a week after the boat was removed from the pier. "I received a telegram from him saying he will return in two days."

"Two days?" Levi asked. "When was the telegram sent?"

"It was sent yesterday and sat in the post office all day. The lazy postmaster was too involved in gossip to even send a boy to let me know it had come," the corporal replied angrily. "I should get more respect. What if it had been something important? An important message should not sit overnight in a village post office, not with me a short walk away."

The corporal calmed down as a thought crossed his mind.

"Perhaps, though, we should return the boat before the American arrives. He does not need to be worried about what might have happened to his boat since nothing did happen to it. Do you think he should have to worry about such a nothing?"

"I agree with you, my friend," Levi said. "There is no need to worry the American about a problem that never happened."

As Levi and the corporal walked to the rowing boat, Levi looked at the trees blowing in the strong east wind and calculated how far he could sail before the American arrived.

"I think I'll spend tonight on that boat. I've grown fond of it and I want everything cleaned and polished when the American comes."

"That should get you a nice tip," the corporal said.

"Goodbye, my friend," Levi said, taking the corporal's large hand in both of his. "You were a friend when I needed one. In this world at this time, a Jew appreciates kindness."

"What do you mean, goodbye?" The corporal eyed Levi strangely. "Do you expect the American to give you enough money to leave this island? Where would you go? A Jew will not have many friends right now. Stay here where you are welcome."

"Oh, the American will be good to me," Levi said. "I know he will."

He waited until dark to raise the anchor, pulling the thirty meters of anchor chain hand over hand, not wanting to use even the small amount of diesel fuel the engine would consume to run the electric windlass that would have raised the chain. He unrolled the sails and drifted away from the island in the night breeze.

I can reach Crete in two days, Levi thought. *And then it will be decision time. Continue on to what is left of Eretz Yisrael, or head west for . . . whatever? Maybe one final raid on whoever is in Israel now.* As an officer on the coastal patrol boat, he'd studied the methods used by Palestinians to run ashore onto deserted Israeli beaches. *The Palestinians were caught more often than not because they never learned from their mistakes*, Levi thought. *So, maybe I'll be the one who learned something.*

Jews made good terrorists once, against the British—at least that's what the old men used to brag about. Stealing this wonderful boat and leaving Greek friends who'd opened their hearts to him in a time of need would be Levi's first act of terrorism.

He frowned—frowned knowing terrorists left few friends in their wake; frowned, knowing how effective, but how unloved, a terrorist is.

CHAPTER 6

The hearing was in what locals called the New Courthouse building, which meant it was the half of Boston's main courthouse that was built in 1938 rather than the half from 1893. In the eight decades since the two halves were mated, nobody bothered to change the room numbers, so those unfamiliar often got lost or went to the wrong half.

That probably explained why Ben Shapiro's clients had not yet shown up for the hearing on the preliminary injunction he was seeking, a court order he hoped against hope would allow the passengers of the two ships to come ashore. *Maybe they're lost,* he thought. *Or maybe they took off.*

The suit was titled John Doe, John Roe, and John Coe vs. Lawrence Quaid, President of the United States of America. Each man had to stand before a judge and admit he'd escaped from the ships. Without that admission, the case would be dismissed for lack of standing. Shapiro had prepared each client to make these admissions.

Normally, a case against the United States government would be brought in federal court, not state court. Shapiro realized, however, that this case did not stand a chance of winning in the federal court system, in which almost every judge right up to the Supreme Court had been appointed by increasingly conservative Republican presidents, Donald Trump being the standard bearer. Cutting-edge civil rights decisions these days came from state courts, interpreting state constitutions, often in a more liberal manner than their federal counterparts. Massachusetts had led the way by legalizing gay marriage, a decision based entirely on the Massachusetts constitution, a document predating the US Constitution. It was a creative but risky legal maneuver.

The instant Shapiro learned which judge had been assigned to the case, he realized his roll of the dice had come up with legal snake eyes—a loser.

Superior Court Justice Francis X. O'Sullivan, despite his ranting about cameras invading his courtroom, loved nothing better than to strut back and forth behind his desk and lock eyes with the cameras swiveling to remain centered on his startling white hair while he glowered down at an attorney. He had been called back from retirement to temporarily fill a vacancy on the bench. He enjoyed reminding young attorneys that he'd been wearing a black robe when they wore diapers.

Shapiro sighed with relief when his clients appeared at the end of the corridor. The three young men were dressed in nearly identical new navy-blue suits. He ushered them into the courtroom and sat them in the first row of wooden benches.

At precisely ten o'clock the court officer rapped his hand three times on the wall and read from the same wrinkled card he'd been reading from for ten years, "Hear ye, hear ye, hear ye. All persons having business before this Honorable Court come forth and you shall be heard. God save the Commonwealth of Massachusetts."

Shapiro wondered, as he did nearly every time he heard those words read, why there was not a court officer in the Commonwealth who seemed capable of memorizing that short speech.

All five foot two inches of Judge O'Sullivan stood behind his chair, the famous, custom-made low-backed high-backed chair. After a glance at the cameras to assure himself there were no technical problems, he pointed his right arm, palm down, fingers outspread like a biblical prophet, and glared at Shapiro, completely ignoring the assistant attorney general representing the Commonwealth.

"Mr. Sha-pie-ro, Mr. Sha-pie-ro," O'Sullivan boomed in a shockingly deep baritone. "I take it you were so enwrapped in your legal research that you did not have time to peruse this morning's newspaper."

The judge unfolded the Boston Herald and waved it back and forth in front of his chest, careful not to obscure his face from the cameras.

President Boots Jews covered the front page of the tabloid.

"Mr. Shapiro, you want me to disobey my commander in chief?" He threw the newspaper onto his desk. "You may not appreciate that I am a veteran, Mr. Shapiro."

"With all due respect, Your Honor, my clients have constitutional rights that not even the president can take from them."

"Who are your clients? Mr. Doe. Mr. Roe. Mr. Coe. Moe, Larry and Curley? I've read their affidavits. Oh, I have read them very carefully. Where are these men, these men who drop atom bombs on innocent Syrian children?"

The judge stood on his toes, scanned from side to side, his palm over his eyebrows, like Tonto searching for his *kemosabe*.

"Stand up if you are here. Stand up. Stand up."

With a deep breath, Shapiro turned to the three men in the front row and motioned them to rise, noticing the cameras swivel toward them.

"For the record, Your Honor, my clients are before the court."

O'Sullivan snatched his newspaper and held it at arm's length in front of his mouth, as if it would somehow ward him against contact with the men.

"Are you the plaintiffs in this case? Did you sign those affidavits? Answer me. Answer me each of you one at a time. For the record. For the record."

Again Shapiro nodded to them.

"Yes, Your Honor," each man said clearly, one after the other. The men remained standing silently.

O'Sullivan took a step backward as if struck by a sudden gale-force wind.

"Mr. Court Officer," he intoned. "Take these men into custody. I have already called the Coast Guard to escort them back where they came from. And for God's sake, be careful, be careful. Don't let them escape again."

When O'Sullivan turned his back to the courtroom, the court officer looked at Shapiro and shrugged. The three men filed out of the courtroom, meekly following the court officer.

When they were gone, O'Sullivan turned again to face Shapiro. "I would no sooner prohibit the forces of our government from taking any step necessary to safeguard our homeland than I would order the Lord to stop the flowers from blooming.

"Mr. Shapiro, you yourself should ponder long and deep what you were about to ask this court to do and what it would have meant to you had I not taken this matter from your hands. Ponder, Mr. Shapiro. This is no time for your kind of fish to swim against the tide."

The judge pivoted so quickly that his black robe swirled around him. He walked straight to his chamber door, leaving the courtroom in silence until the reporters surrounded Shapiro, asking if he would appeal the decision that was apparently made before he'd spoken a word in defense of his clients.

Ben Shapiro struggled to maintain his composure. He'd won cases and he'd lost cases and he accepted that was how the law worked. What Shapiro could not accept was when prejudice conquered reason, when the law became a cudgel for beating people down rather than a scalpel for excising what was wrong.

What did the *tzadik,* the righteous man he yearned to be, do when his hands were tied, Shapiro had begun to ask himself. Shapiro had not found an alternative to the legal system, but he reluctantly suspected that such an alternative existed.

CHAPTER 7

The Spofford family joked that they had lived in poverty in this country for three generations. The first three. The succeeding five fluctuated between comfortable and wealthy.

Marrying a Jew was not quite the social suicide it would have been two or even one generation previously, especially since Sally Spofford had inherited a Bohemian reputation from Grandmother Bo Peep, a name earned at prep school when her girlfriends followed her like sheep. And Ben Shapiro wasn't too Jewish. He looked almost British sometimes, dressed the right way. And he was a Boston lawyer. Not an ambulance chaser or divorce lawyer. Most of Sally's family wasn't quite sure what he did except get his name in the *Boston Globe* once in a while for representing a criminal. It was assumed those were charity cases he took to please a judge.

Sally was not especially charmed when she'd first met Ben. President H. W. Bush was gearing up to invade Iraq. Ben was against the war. They met when Sally almost stepped on him lying on the ground, blocking the entrance to the student union building at Wesleyan University. Sally was late for an interview for a summer position with publisher Houghton Mifflin and gingerly stepped on Shapiro's chest to get by.

Raytheon Corp. was interviewing for summer interns too, prompting the anti-war student protest. When Sally emerged from the interview, Ben was being dragged away by campus police. Their next encounter was some days later. Sally was sitting by herself reading when Shapiro sat next to her.

"Are you going to apologize to the babies your new employer bombs?" he asked. "Or didn't you get the job?"

"What in the world are you talking about? And who the hell are you?" Sally was used to boys trying to pick her up. Her long, straight blonde hair and athletic build burdened her through adolescence with the problem of which boys to go out with and which to turn down. "A book publisher burning babies?"

They'd spent the rest of the evening arguing, he trying to condense a complete history of America's foreign policy toward developing nations, she defending this country as the freest and finest place on earth and why didn't he leave if he felt America was so awful. They continued the argument over pizza at midnight and scrambled eggs in the morning.

They were married the September following graduation. She proofread historical novels at Houghton Mifflin in Boston while he attended Boston University Law School. He worked for a small general practice firm after graduation. It was two years before he earned as much as his secretary. He grabbed the opportunity to work for the district attorney's office when a new, surprisingly liberal district attorney was elected. For the first time, he would be earning a salary at least at the bleacher level of the ballpark of what a lawyer was expected to earn.

It was four years before Sally's *Adventures of Ish the Fish* series was published. Six books later, her income did not quite match his, but it was enough so that she was satisfied with herself and content with her life, except for one thing. Despite years of writing for children, it was not until she was forty-two years old herself, and long after she'd given up hope of having a child, that miraculously, or so it seemed, Adam was born.

They sold their city condo and bought a small house in a seaside town north of Boston, tucked at the end of a dead-end street, their backyard abutting a salt marsh divided by a tidal creek winding out to a beach and the sea. They agreed Adam would go to Hebrew school when he was older, that he would celebrate Christmas and Easter now and that they would worry about the problem later. Sally ate buttered bagels religiously on Sunday mornings, although she could never get used to the concept of having smoked fish for breakfast.

To her, Ben's being Jewish was one more odd fact about their relationship. It didn't hurt anything and it didn't really make much difference. That was why she was so surprised to see him consumed by the tragic events in Israel. He was aroused by America's initial openhearted reaction, and without even asking her he wrote a check in an amount far greater than she would have approved the night of the All-Star Fundraiser for Israel. After the Damascus bombing, she listened to him scream at the television as American hearts hardened and the tide of public opinion turned against Israel.

Is being Jewish keeping him from seeing the burned Syrian babies? she wondered.

Sitting on the floor in their living room, with Adam coloring dinosaurs nearby, she saw the fire from his college days rising again in her husband and knew she had long ago outgrown that kind of passion in herself.

"Turn off the TV," she said hopefully.

"No, you go ahead," Shapiro replied, without looking away from the television. "I want to watch CNN a bit more. Can you believe we aren't sending troops? We invade every two-bit country on the planet. Why don't we send troops when millions of Jews are dying? Where are the Marines when we need them? And those ships in Boston harbor. I'm going to lose that case. Why don't we let those poor people come ashore?"

She carried a drowsy Adam up to his bedroom, smiling to herself at her husband calling for the Marines, remembering the man she'd walked over to get to a job interview, a man who would sooner have called for help from a magician than the United States Marines. *Has he changed that much,* she wondered. *Or is it me?* Being married to a Jew had been a quirk, she realized, with very little downside to it. She feared that was about to change, and she did not know how she would react.

She put her son to bed, then went to bed herself, ducking her head under the pillow to cover the sound of CNN.

CHAPTER 8

Chaim Levi's plans to return to Israel were cut short when he saw more Egyptian naval ships in Israeli waters than he thought were floating on all the world's oceans. Instead, he came up with a new plan to sail *Swift* west "into the sunset." Or "to America and freedom." Maybe the Caribbean, maybe New York, maybe Miami Beach—mystical places he'd heard about from American tourists.

He knew his time in Marbella, on the southern Spanish coast, was limited. Eventually an inquisitive police officer would wonder about the American boat tied to the pier and would realize that it had not always been there and that he should look into it. Levi's paranoia notched upward when he'd returned to the boat from a grocery expedition and found the cabin subtly rearranged, as if somebody had been on board.

The sail from Greece to Spain was easy enough, stocked with cans of Greek provisions and the water tanks topped off. The boat had charts covering the entire Mediterranean and, while Levi's navigation was rudimentary, he knew that if he sailed far enough west he would reach Spain, and he was not too particular as to where in Spain he wound up. Besides, with the global positioning system on the boat, navigating did not involve much more than moving a cursor across the screen to set his course.

Tied to the pier in Marbella, sitting in the boat's cockpit, sipping a vodka and orange juice and studying a *World Book Atlas* he'd found in a secondhand book store, Levi suddenly looked up when he became aware of a woman standing on the pier, blocking the sunlight.

The sun behind her turned her red hair into a blazing halo and obscured her face completely.

Levi smiled tentatively.

"Shalom," she said.

"Shalom," he answered automatically, then realized what he'd said. Heart beating rapidly, he considered diving overboard and swimming for his life, or leaping to the pier and running.

She was alone, he observed, or at least he did not see anybody with her. *Play it cool*, he thought. Lifting his glass, Levi said, "Would you like to come aboard? For a drink? Or a chat? Or whatever?"

As she climbed over the stern railing into the cockpit, he saw her face for the first time.

I've seen her before, Levi thought with relief. *The hair is different, but the face is familiar.* He watched her hop from the dock onto the boat's deck. He smiled. *And the body. I should remember that. She knows me; we've met before.* What he'd first seen as a threatening situation was a familiar problem he'd lived with as long as he could remember.

Levi had no memory for faces. Shopping for clothes, Levi was always startled to see himself in the full-length mirrors. Not tall, not short. Thick, dark curly hair. Always tan from being on the water. Good build. Big Jewish nose. *Not a bad-looking guy*, he thought. *Is that really me?* Levi knew he'd recognize the redhead eventually. He guessed she was probably in Spain on a two-week vacation from Chicago or someplace. *Her name will come to me*, he thought. *Probably someone I gave sailing lessons to.*

"Imagine us meeting again," he said, smiling at the woman as he stepped onto his boat. "It seems like such a long, long time."

"We've never met," she said, the smile dropping from her face, her eyes narrowing. "Save the charm for someone else. But we have business to discuss. Does this boat of yours have a cabin, someplace private?"

"Sure, welcome aboard," he invited.

Sitting facing each other on the cushioned berths inside the boat's cabin, surrounded by New England craftsmen's woodworking, the teak and holly cabin floor, the white pine cabin walls, the tiled fireplace, Levi waited anxiously for her to speak first.

She looked around the cabin slowly and spoke for the first time in English rather than Hebrew.

"You've done well for yourself since the death of Eretz Yisrael, haven't you, Lt. Chaim Levi?" she said slowly as her eyes swung to meet his. She noticed the shock in his face, all pretense of suave confidence evaporated.

Her right hand came out of her pants pocket and she swung his gold-colored dog tags on their chain in front of his face.

"Lt. Chaim Levi of the Israeli Navy. Do you call this vessel a motor torpedo boat, or is it a submarine? I'm afraid I have not kept up with the state of the art of Israel's warship industry."

"Okay, okay," he muttered, avoiding her eyes. "Who are you? What do you want? You're an American, so what are you, a private detective? Is that what you are? The American wants his boat back? Fine. Take it. It's in better condition now than when I borrowed it."

"Lt. Levi, I'm not a detective and I'm not, or at least not any longer, an American. I am, in fact, your commanding officer." She tossed the dog tags into his lap and laughed. "Just when do you think you were discharged from the navy?"

She fixed her eyes on his, watching for the man's reaction.

"Certain people working with me have had their eyes on you here. They searched this boat of yours. If you want to get rid of your identification tags, you'll have to find a better place to hide them than under your mattress. Lieutenant, your country still needs you." For the first time she smiled and leaned back on the berth, "and you seem to be captain of the entire Israeli naval war fleet. By the way, my name is Debra Reuben."

"Do I salute you or kiss you?" Levi asked. He looked at her closely. "Reuben? I know you. The one from the television who went into the government. I thought you did things with artists or tourists or something like that, not with the navy."

"Today," she said, "we do what we can."

"With what?" he asked. "Our country is gone. Our people have been exterminated. We have no navy, no air force, no troops. Fight back with what?"

"With what we have," she said slowly, looking him squarely in the eyes. "We could start World War III, and then get our land back."

As she explained a carefully redacted version about Dimona and what was stored in the warehouse ten miles up the Spanish coast, Levi realized with a stunning certainty that his plans for drinking piña coladas on Caribbean beaches would be put on hold for a while—a long while.

CHAPTER 9

The decision was made at the highest levels of government. No exceptions. Not for any refugees. Not even for Jewish refugees. The two ships were ordered to leave. They would be escorted by an Egyptian warship on a visit to New York back to the new nation of Palestine.

Before dawn the next morning, two rocket-propelled grenades dashed from the *Iliad* and three from the *Ionian Star*, turning both Coast Guard thirty-eight-footers into flaming wrecks that quickly sank to the bottom of the harbor, killing all ten on board the two boats.

Dozens of small boats—even canoes from the Charles River—dashed out from the nearby shore. The boats filled with people jumping into the water from the ships' decks. Once loaded with wet passengers, the small boats disappeared into the darkness. Fireboats speeding out from the inner harbor to help the Coast Guard vessels ignored the dozens of small boats, which the firefighters assumed were shoreside residents out to search for survivors.

By noon, the *Iliad* and the *Ionian* Star were empty, even their crews deciding perhaps this was a good time to look up relatives in Chicago.

Newspaper accounts of the attack on the Coast Guard boats and the escape of the refugees used a new phrase to define America's latest enemy. *JEWISH TERRORISTS KILL 10 ON COAST GUARD SHIPS, PASSENGERS ESCAPE INTO HIDING,* the *Boston Globe* headline said.

JEWS KILL AMERICANS was the *Boston Herald* front page, implying there was a difference between the two groups.

■ ■ ■

Howie Mandelbaum did not think of himself as a violent criminal. Neither did his fellow residents of the Charles Street Jail, a Dickensian building leaning against one of the outbuildings of the Massachusetts General Hospital. The jail was a model penal institution when it was opened in 1857, shaped, as were classic cathedrals, like a cross. The central vault was an open space, 100 feet long on each side, five stories tall. The four stubby arms of the cross were short, U-shaped hallways open to the central vault. In turn, the hallways were lined with row after row of steel bars separating the hallways from the cells.

The benevolent theory, at least in 1857, was that each cell was open to the central vault so that every guard could see into every cell and every prisoner had the benefit of the light and fresh air from that central vault. What that also meant was every inmate could see every other inmate. No cell was separated from any other cell by anything but steel bars and open air. All that prevented any of the 687 inmates of the jail from speaking with any other inmate was the strength of his lungs and his ability to make himself heard over the roar that reverberated through the central vault. On top of the inmates' shouting were the shouts of guards telling prisoners to shut up, and radios and televisions turned to maximum volume to be heard at all.

The cells were meant to hold one inmate. Despite the order of the United States District Court for the District of

Massachusetts enforcing that intention, Mandelbaum shared his accommodations. His roommate found Mandelbaum's whimpering funny.

"Never heard of a Jew being anything but a bookie, Jew Boy," said Sean Connery, like the James Bond guy. "And you don't look like no bookie. What happened, pretty boy, get caught with some coke on the front seat of your Bimmer when you ran a red light?"

Connery was interrupted by a banging on the cell bars.

"He came on the Jew boats. He was fished out of the hahbah." Bobbie Flynn, a corrections officer, came from the same Charlestown project as Connery. "But leave him be, lad. This here is a foreign agent who came to our country and is committing crimes, serious crimes, before he even steps foot on American soil. He's facing murder charges, ten murder charges. Ten dead Coasties in Boston Hahbah. This must be one big tough Israeli Jew boy.

"Your lawyer's here to see you. Come with me," Flynn said to Mandelbaum.

Flynn escorted Mandelbaum to a small room on the ground floor. The young man sat in one of two chairs in the room—chairs abandoned from some Boston public school, writing platforms on the right armrests. Years of initials and obscenities, from bored high school students and terrified jail inmates, covered the writing platforms. Ben Shapiro sat in the other chair, his briefcase open.

"If you are the court-appointed lawyer the judge said I'd get, you might as well leave," Mandelbaum told Shapiro, speaking in the same tone he'd use with a surly waiter. "My father is hiring me the best lawyer money can buy."

Shapiro looked up slowly, then held his hand out without rising from the chair.

"I was hired by your father," he said. "I don't know if I'm the best. I'll tell you one thing, though. I'm not bought by anybody. And I'll tell you another thing. You better understand that you are in the deepest hole of your lifetime, and it goes downhill from here. I'm walking out in an hour and going home to my wife and son. You are going to be behind bars tonight. You are most likely going to be behind bars when you are sixty years old."

Another one, Shapiro thought. *If only I could have a case without a jerkball client. Hundreds of clients, and still barely a handful I'd invite for dinner. And here was jerkball number 1,001.*

Mandelbaum sat facing Shapiro.

"What is this shit case? I didn't kill anybody. All I did was jump off that stinking boat when they told me to jump. How can they charge me with killing anybody?"

"What you are charged with, sir, is conspiracy to commit murder." Shapiro looked through his papers. "This is the charge—actually one of ten charges, all the same, one for each dead Coast Guardsman."

Shapiro read from the document in the sing-song rhythm legal pleadings seemed to call for.

"You have been charged with conspiring with other unknown persons to illegally enter the United States and in furtherance of that conspiracy to commit acts of violence, to wit murder and assault with intent to commit murder, and that in furtherance of this conspiracy you or others with whom you acted in concert did commit acts of violence including assault with intent to murder and murder in the first degree."

He looked up at his new client, searching for any sign Mandelbaum appreciated that he'd come to a fork in the road of his life and was heading down the wrong path.

"You had the misfortune, Mr. Mandelbaum, of being the only person from either ship who Boston police managed to retrieve from the harbor. I expect that the other four thousand people will be difficult to hide for very long and that you will soon have company. But for today, at least, you are the test case. Tell me, Mr. Mandelbaum, how did you come to be on that ship?"

"I didn't come to be on the ship," the young man said angrily. "I got on that ship to stay alive. The fucking Arabs were killing people all over the place. I was lucky as hell to get on that boat. Wait, before I answer your questions, you tell me first, how can they do this to me? I'm an American. Why didn't the Marines come to save me? Why did I have to spend three weeks on that ship like some kind of refugee?"

"From what your father told me, you moved to Israel and you became an Israeli citizen. And you were in the import-export business there? Is that correct?"

"Sure I moved there, but I was born here. I'm an American, dammit, I went to school here, I watched *Sesame Street* as a kid, I know all about Homer and Bart, I cried when John Kennedy Jr. got killed in the airplane crash. I saw all those dumb Disney movies when I was a kid. My dad even voted for Reagan once. Listen to me, don't I sound like an American? Look, I grew up in Fair Lawn, fucking New Jersey. What is this foreigner crap they keep calling me?" The young man paced around the small room, working himself into a rage. "I'm as American as you are, right?"

He stopped talking and sat in the chair, all evidence of cockiness evaporated, the enormity of his situation slowly sinking in.

"They'll kill me in this jail. Get me out of here. Get me out of here before they kill me. Or worse."

His head fell to the armrest. Shapiro watched the young man's body shaking, heard him crying, gave him a few moments to regain control, placed his hand on the young man's shoulder and shook him gently.

"I only have an hour with you. We have a lot of ground to cover. Let's get to work."

■ ■ ■

Within minutes of leaving the jailhouse, Shapiro was confronted by eager news reporters. Shapiro didn't mind; in fact he reveled in the attention. News coverage was good for business, and certainly for his ego.

"Mr. Shapiro, do you have any personal hesitation about defending a foreign national who killed American servicemen on American soil?" The reporter attempted to inject a sense of righteousness into her questions about Shapiro's representation of the only person—so far— arrested for escaping from the two ships.

"It has not been established that my client killed anybody." Shapiro looked directly at the camera, not at the reporter holding the microphone in his face. He knew to look directly at the camera; the camera was the audience, not the interviewer.

That evening at dinner, Sally Spofford Shapiro turned off the TV. She usually liked her husband's celebrity, but not this time. America was threatened by intruders, by murderers of the ten coastguardsmen and her husband was representing the worst of them.

"Please, Ben, please. Can't you skip this one, just once, for me? I've never asked this before."

"I don't see why this case is any different," he said. "I've represented unpleasant folks before. What's the big deal this time? What I said on TV was true. I'm a lawyer. Sometimes I represent people who have done bad things. That's my job. It gives me the greatest stories to tell at parties." He smiled at her.

Sally stood, looking down at him. "This is different," she whispered. "Different. It feels un-American. Yes, un-American, Ben. I've never asked you this before but . . . but this time this is important to me. Please, once, this time, let another knight slay this dragon."

She sighed, exhaling like a balloon deflating. Those were her best shots, and they'd missed.

Ben looked at his plate, chasing cherry tomatoes with his fork while he searched for the right words. Or for the right effect. Sally knew her husband, knew he was always performing. In the midst of a fight with a courtroom opponent. In the midst of a fight with her. He lived his life onstage—at least, in his mind he did.

"You're right," he finally said, speaking without raising his head from the plate. "This one is different. This one I can't refuse."

"Because they are Jews?" she whispered.

He looked up. "Because I'm a Jew," he said. He stood up and held both hands out to her. Reluctantly, she played her part, held her own hands out to him, then leaned her head against his chest, feeling his arms wrap around her, feeling one hand slide down to her buttock and squeeze. It had been a while. Her head dropped to his shoulder. He pushed her out at arm's length.

"Let me tell you about the SS *St. Louis*," Shapiro said slowly. "You know about Kristallnacht?"

"Of course I've heard of Kristallnacht. Some Nazi thing, wasn't it?"

"Yeah, some Nazi thing," Shapiro replied. "After Kristallnacht, the handwriting was on the wall for German Jews. They knew they had to get out, but getting out had gotten harder, and, it turned out, getting into any other country also became harder.

"The *St. Louis* was a German passenger ship. Nine-hundred-thirty-seven Jews managed to bribe their way on board. The ship sailed to Cuba, where the Jews expected to wait until they could get into the US.

"But it didn't work out that way. The Cubans wanted half a million dollars to let the Jews off the ship. They couldn't raise the money and the ship sailed for Florida, a ship with nearly a thousand Jews, old people, women, children. Things were so desperate the passengers formed a suicide committee to keep people from killing themselves, they were so afraid of being sent back to Germany. Remember, this is 1938. Franklin Roosevelt, the great liberal, is president. So guess where the *St. Louis* landed in the United States."

"Stop. Enough," Sally said, her voice rising. "I don't want to hear about Nazis. Nazis have nothing to do with what's happening now. This is America. There aren't Nazis here. Nazis were history. I don't know where the ship landed, Ben," she said, acid slipping into her tone, "but I am sure you are aching to tell me, so go right ahead."

"Nowhere. That's where in the United States of America the *St. Louis* passengers got off that ship. Nowhere. We shut the door. Wouldn't let them in. The *St. Louis* sailed back and forth near Miami and we sent the Coast Guard to make sure nobody tried to swim to shore. So guess where the thousand Jews went? Back to Europe. The *St. Louis* delivered its passengers right back to the Holocaust. To the camps.

"Two years later Congress voted to change the immigration laws to allow twenty thousand additional people into this country. Guess who they were. Jews? No, they were twenty thousand English school children sent here by their parents to keep them safe. Don't you think the *St. Louis* passengers could have used a good lawyer?"

She knew better than to answer. She turned her back and walked away from her husband, leaving him alone in the living room, thinking he'd won another argument.

CHAPTER 10

How many "cousins" paying surprise visits, "cousins" who spoke little English, could suburban Boston accept? Four thousand frightened people could not be hidden for long, no matter how quixotic their rescuers hoped to be. The cleverest ones landed on shore and never stopped running, catching planes and trains and buses heading anywhere, ducking police and immigration authorities as best they could. Most of the people off the two ships, however, were smuggled into finished basements and attic bedrooms in houses in Boston suburbs.

These houses were not fitted with secret doors and hidden rooms like Anne Frank lived in. No underground railroad had been established to smuggle illegal Jewish immigrants. Instead, Jewish doctors, lawyers, businessmen, woken from their beds by late-night telephone calls, had to make snap decisions.

"Can you take somebody in?" the caller would ask. "Just for a day or two until we sort things out. There's really no risk to you. Nothing will happen to you. Don't worry."

How could they refuse, just for a day or two?

Cold, wet, terrified, hungry people, sometimes an entire

family, were dropped at nice houses in nice neighborhoods, 4,000 people scattered and hidden before the sun rose the next morning. They were treated not quite as guests, not quite as fugitives. They weren't foreign exchange students, an accepted category of foreigners who showed up once in a while. They certainly weren't au pairs; neither were they foreign business visitors. They certainly couldn't be fugitives from the law. Good people would not hide criminals.

People didn't know how to handle these sudden visitors. Could the neighbors be told or not? Did they distinguish between Jewish neighbors and non-Jewish neighbors? Were they only staying at Jewish homes? Suddenly the distinction between Jewish friends and non-Jewish friends took on a new significance.

■ ■ ■

Roselyn Lowenstein was called to the principal's office at Swampscott High School the day after the escape from the ships.

"Roselyn, I have some serious questions to ask you," Principal Warren said.

Roselyn was a National Honor Society member and co-captain of the school's state championship debating team. Principal Warren knew Roselyn and her parents well. Roselyn was never called to the principal's office for causing trouble. This time, however, she was nervous, fidgeting while Principal Warren spoke to her.

"Roselyn, somebody told me you were talking at lunch about visitors at your house. I'll be blunt with you. I heard you told people you have a family from those ships hiding at your house. Is that true?"

For a seventeen-year-old girl who should have been worrying about whether she should apply early decision to Harvard because, after all, it was Harvard, or to Columbia, because imagine going to the Columbia School of Journalism, hiding illegal refugees was the last problem Roselyn Lowenstein expected to have to face. She did not want to deal with it now. In fact, she did not want to give up her bedroom for four people who barely spoke English. And Mr. Warren wasn't the enemy. He was okay. He'd promised to write a great college recommendation letter for her.

"It's a secret. We're not supposed to tell," she whispered, laying the drama on thickly.

Warren removed a yellow filing folder from a desk drawer. Peeking, Roselyn could see her name was typed across the tab.

"I have a very important letter to write for you," the principal said, looking closely at the young woman. She stared at him for no more than five seconds, then glanced again at the file folder.

"Okay. It's only for a few days. Maybe the school newspaper should be covering this. Lots of other kids have them at their houses, too, you know." He could hear the excitement in her voice.

Warren watched the local TV news while eating breakfast that morning. He watched the bodies of young coastguardsmen lifted from the water. He watched footage of the flaming remains of the two patrol boats. Like many people, he was ambivalent about letting the refugees off those two ships. Sure, they needed someplace to go, but hadn't the US just deported all those South Americans and Haitians and Asians? You couldn't start making exceptions for white people; fair was fair.

And now ten Americans were murdered by these Jews. That sealed it for Warren.

When Roselyn left his office to return giggling to her Spanish class, where she huddled with half a dozen friends who also had instant relatives at home, Warren searched the telephone book for the Massachusetts State Police number, picked up the telephone and dialed quickly.

"I don't know how many other families are also hiding people," he told Detective Lieutenant Francis O'Brien, "but there is an awful lot of whispering in the halls, and it's mostly the Jewish kids doing it. I suspect there are a lot of them in town, a lot of them. So what are you going to do about this?"

CHAPTER 11

Lt. Chaim Levi applied the last brushstrokes of WEST System epoxy to the water storage tank under the main cabin settee, then scrambled up the cabin ladder into the boat's cockpit, drawing deep breaths of fresh air after inhaling epoxy fumes in the closed cabin all morning. He regretted losing the forty gallons of water storage from the starboard water tank; he'd have to find someplace to put collapsible plastic water bags for the crossing, but he was terrified of what filled the tank now.

This warhead, alone among Israel's diminutive nuclear arsenal, was designed for use by a commando squad, perhaps one infiltrated into, say, Tehran. In a truck. The tube-shaped warhead was three feet long and eighteen inches across. He'd cut the water tank open, then sealed it with fiberglass and epoxy. It held water again, but Levi did not want to drink it. He was careful to leave no inspection port in the fiberglass. The tank would have to be cut open to find the warhead inside. Levi expected no customs inspector would be willing to do that much damage to such an expensive boat.

Before sealing the weapon inside the water tank, Reuben and Levi spent a morning with a young man whose English and

Hebrew were equally interrupted by fits of nervous coughing. This man, a physics graduate of Hebrew University whose newly sunburned face was the recent payback from years spent mostly underground at the Dimona facility, carefully explained the workings of the arming device and the detonator. He was obviously proud.

"Even a child could use it," he said. "It was my design the government selected as the standard detonator for nuclear field munitions."

"Field munitions?" Levi asked. "What are nuclear field munitions?"

The technician gave Reuben an exasperated look.

"Are we really giving this man access to the device?" he asked. She nodded.

"Nuclear field munitions are small nuclear devices designed to be carried by jeep, boat or helicopter," he explained slowly, as if speaking to a child. "There are unique problems in designing the detonator for field munitions."

"Why not just a simple clock?" Levi asked. "Or a button to push while you kiss your ass goodbye. Why are these any different from detonators for normal bombs?"

"Do I have to go through this with this man?" the technician asked Reuben.

She waved her hand, her impatience showing.

"Because," he said, "with nuclear devices you only want them to detonate when you want them to detonate. There is always the possibility, slim as it might be, that these devices could fall into the wrong hands and then—"

He stopped in mid-sentence, realization clouding his expression as he recalled what happened to Tel Aviv.

"I suppose we might not have made the security quite as good as necessary."

Levi looked at the young man and shuddered. *Scientists like this one made the bomb they used in Tel Aviv*, he thought.

"Air-dropped bombs have fail-safes so they only detonate

under specific conditions of acceleration and altitude, conditions that don't apply to field munitions," he said. "So on this device the timer can be set anywhere from one hundred hours to one second. Two arming codes must be entered on the keypad first, followed by the time setting, followed by the timing code. That sequence sets the trigger. Reentry of all three codes in the proper order stops the timer and disarms the device.

"Of course, you have to first insert the authorization card before entering the codes." He looked at Reuben as she removed a Chemical Bank of New York Visa card from a chain around her neck.

Reuben looked at Levi, then at the scientist. She inserted the Visa card into a slot. Levi placed his hand on her wrist and held it away from the keypad.

"Now what would happen," he asked with a smile, "if you have a heart attack after you entered the codes and before you have time to reenter them? Where would that leave me?"

Reuben smiled. "It would leave you to join me in heaven," she answered. "Only I know these codes. It's going to stay that way."

She armed the bomb and disarmed it, twice, confirming that the detonator activated each time.

"Load it into the boat," she told Levi. "And your job is done," she told the scientist. "Give me your card."

He handed her a Visa card identical to the one dangling from the chain around her neck.

"Remember, this never happened," Reuben told the pale man. "You never met me. You will tell no one. If you do, we will find you. Not every member of Mossad was in Tel Aviv."

Reuben and Levi watched the scientist leave. She climbed down the companionway into the boat's cabin and emerged with a bottle of Bacardi rum, a glass and a bowl of ice cubes. Levi looked at her and frowned.

"It isn't even lunchtime yet," he said. "Sure you want to start that so early?"

Reuben didn't know whether to be angry with the man or not.

"If anybody on the face of this planet has earned the right to a drink in the morning, or any time of day, or any time of night, as many drinks as she goddamn well wants, that person is me," she said, looking vacantly at the floor of the boat's cockpit as she drained her glass and then poured another over the unmelted ice.

Levi stared at the woman. In the week they had spent preparing the sailboat to hide the bomb and getting ready for their voyage, the two of them had had few serious conversations. She'd explained to him what the tube-shaped device was, in general terms, and she'd told him a carefully edited version of how she'd come into possession of such a lethal object. But Reuben had avoided any discussion about either the Tel Aviv bomb or the Damascus bomb, two blatantly obvious subjects for people who had a close relative of those two bombs in their personal custody. Levi sensed Reuben was struggling with something in her recent past, but he chose to wait for her to put it on the table. Whatever it was, certainly every person who'd escaped from what had been Israel had horrors behind them. Levi did not discuss the bodies he'd watched sink beneath the burning sea when his patrol boat met its end, nor did he dare to mention the family and friends he expected to never see again. Knowing who Debra had been in Israel and obviously aware of the object she'd delivered to what he viewed as "his" boat, he suspected she was connected in some way with the Damascus bomb. He had not dared to raise the topic. *She'll talk in her own time, in her own way*, he decided.

He also sensed that there was a strength in this woman he had not yet seen displayed—that she was more than a beautiful woman with a weight on her shoulders. Levi was not used to dealing with women with either strength or substance. Superficial women had suited him just fine so far. That seemed about to change. Of the many words that could describe Debra

Reuben, ranging from "troubled" to "intense," "superficial" was not among that vocabulary.

Reuben lifted her gaze from the cockpit floor, drained her glass of rum, poured another one, and smiled gaily, falsely, at Levi.

"I feel like a sea voyage," Reuben said. "Let's discover America.

■ ■ ■

Sailing across the Atlantic Ocean ahead of the trade winds from east to west was no longer the epic adventure it was when Columbus first journeyed. The trip had been made by a German paddling a kayak in the 1930s, a fourteen-year-old English boy sailing alone, and, of course, by countless private yachts.

Being lost was no longer an option. The planet was circled by an armada of global positioning system satellites that transmitted to GPS receivers giving latitude and longitude to an accuracy of ten feet. The Hinckley Bermuda 40, being top of the line itself, carried a state-of-the-art Magellan GPS and chart plotter, a high-powered computer display with digitized maps for the entire planet stored in postage-stamp-sized memory cartridges. Levi could determine the boat's position as easily as he could locate a bar of soap in a bathtub.

It would have made the vacation of a lifetime, sailing from Spain to the Caribbean, then north to New England—an idyllic eight weeks at sea, well before the hurricane season. Maybe even a honeymoon. *She isn't at all bad looking*, Levi thought, checking out Debra Reuben for the umpteenth time. She was lying on the foredeck, the forward area of the sailboat she'd claimed as her own space. *I'm checking her out, and nothing more.*

If she'd only loosen up a bit, he thought, *this trip would be a lot more interesting. I'm the only guy within a hundred miles and, hell, we both have nothing to lose from a little companionship.*

He'd tried being soft and gentle, listening for hours as she finally told him about Dimona and the air force pilots. She explained again and again that she had no choice about sending the jet toward Damascus. It wasn't her decision at all, in fact, since she was just following orders, she'd told him. He'd decided not to point out the irony of her excuse, "just following orders"—especially for a Jew, and especially for a Jew responsible for what was already being called the Islamic Holocaust.

He'd tried being domestic, whipping up the last of the fresh meat into a beef Wellington that would have impressed the guests at his parents' hotel. He tried being the tough soldier, telling her tales—mostly true—about manning the inshore patrol boat, dropping commandos on the beach in Lebanon.

But all they'd done was talk. He talked. She listened. She talked. He listened.

Levi was surprised during the first three weeks of their crossing at the amount of rum Debra put away. She drank without pleasure, as if she were taking medicine. Some days she started at breakfast and kept a glass going through the entire day, like a chain-smoker lighting one cigarette from the previous one. Levi assumed this drinking was something new to her. *She can't have drunk like this for many years*, he thought. *Not while maintaining her appearance, her health, her sanity.*

It came to a head after three weeks, when Reuben stormed on deck swearing.

"Where the fuck is that second case of Bacardi," she screamed at Levi. "I bought two cases. I told you to load them into the forward cabin. The first case is gone and I can't find the second fucking case. I need it. Now. I need it."

"There was only room for one case," Levi answered. "It was that or the carton of extra provisions, and I made a decision. Hey, look, I never thought we'd go through even the first case of rum."

Levi's answer did not satisfy Reuben. She tried to speak, tried to yell, but only sputters came from her mouth. Instead, she stormed to the bow of the boat, stamped her feet on the deck and lay down, rolled into a ball, hugging her knees, rocking slowly from side to side.

Levi chose to leave her alone.

■ ■ ■

That evening, over dinner in the cockpit—a bluefish he'd caught with the trolling rod he left dangling from the boat's stern rail—she tried to speak to him, failed, was silent, then sobbed. Levi rose from his seat and sat next to her, his arm around her shoulder. Debra leaned into him, her head against his chest.

Without the alcohol to dull her pain, to kill her thoughts, she ceased fighting and gave in to the fist that had been clamped on her stomach since she awoke at Dimona with the planes gone. Levi held her tightly as her body shook, sometimes softly as the pain drained from her, sometimes so violently he feared she'd fling herself over the side of the boat. He did not know what to say, so, uncharacteristically for him in such a situation with such a beautiful woman, he said nothing, just held her as the sun splashed into the western sea and the boat, guided by the autopilot and leaning gently with the wind in its sails, followed Columbus's wake toward the sunset.

Eventually, her body and mind both tired. He carried her to the bunk in the forward cabin she had claimed for herself and, for the first time since he'd met her in Marbella, she slept through the night. He chose not to wake her for her late-night watch and remained in the cockpit himself until dawn.

Whether it was that night or the missing second case of Bacardi, Reuben seemed eased the next morning. Neither acknowledged what had happened the previous night, although both realized they had shared an intimacy more intense than simple intercourse would have been. Nonetheless, despite Levi's hints, Debra rebuffed any further steps toward physical closeness. Levi felt like a teenager, taking pleasure from accidentally brushing against Reuben in the cramped cabin, thrilled by a goodnight peck on the cheeks from her. He sensed that she was not rejecting him, she was rejecting life itself—rejecting it as a gift she did not know if she deserved after what she had done.

So she claimed the foredeck during the day and the forward cabin at night. He ruled the cockpit. Inside the boat they were each shielded by an invisible zone of protection that the other was forbidden from entering. In that way, they sailed across the Atlantic Ocean, more like brother and sister than two young, healthy people, people who had lost important parts of themselves, he his country and his family, she her belief that she was a good person.

Their first landfall was the tiny island of Jost Van Dyke, a speck of land north of Tortola in the British Virgin Islands. They tried to blend in with the fleet of bareboat charters filled with idling Americans trading several thousand dollars for a week of sunshine and warm breezes, beach bars and snorkeling. Levi and Reuben inflated the dinghy and rowed ashore, where they stretched their legs on the walk to the only grocery store in the small harbor, buying overpriced apples, oranges and potatoes shipped in from Florida. Before rowing back to the Hinckley, Levi persuaded Reuben to sit with him under a palm-frond umbrella at Binky's Peace and Love Beach Bar.

"At least have a piña colada with me to celebrate our transatlantic crossing," he urged. "This isn't something you're going to do every day." He knew she would not refuse the alcohol.

"Okay," she said warily, looking at the group of Americans at the next table glowing red from days of tropic sun blasting on their winter-pale skin. "Ply me with rum." Maybe she was a bit severe with him. After all, the man had just brought her —and a tactical nuclear weapon—safely across the Atlantic Ocean. She smiled at him. "And sing the Banana Boat song to me."

Levi grinned. *It took long enough. But then, patience is a virtue*, he thought, appreciating once again the power he had with women, with all women.

Four piña coladas later, he really did stand in front of her and warble, with not a hint of any accent heard on any Caribbean island, "Hey, mister tally man, tally me bananas." Reuben looked at him softly, smiled to herself, smiled at him and said slowly, "Lets row back to our boat, banana boy. It's feeling crowded here."

Before she could stand up, however, a loud, grating voice reached from across the thirty feet of sand and six tables making up Binky's Peace and Love Beach Bar.

"Debbie Reuben. My gawd, is that Debbie Reuben from Great Neck? Wait till I tell yaw motha where I saw you I haven't seen you in ye-ahs and ye-ahs come and give me a great big hug."

Reuben turned and saw a vaguely familiar woman, hidden behind yard-wide sunglasses, head wrapped in a yellow scarf, bathing suit covered by what looked like the greater portion of a white parachute. Rising from her table and flapping her arms out wide, surplus flesh palpitating below her arms, this apparition from her Long Island childhood stood waiting for Reuben to cross the hot sand.

"Debbie Reuben, I haven't seen you since you were in that wonda-ful high school play I forget its name with my daughta Miriam. You look older but not so much is that yaw husband sitting there with you invite him ova."

Miriam Babinsky's mother, Reuben thought. *Funny, I never would have thought of her as a sailor.* She started walking toward the woman.

Levi leaped up on suddenly wobbly legs and mumbled loudly to Reuben, "Honey, I don't feel so good. I think I drank too many piña coladas. I think I'm going to be sick."

He sat back down with a thump, dropping his head to the table. Reuben did an about-face, running thankfully back to Levi.

"You don't look well, dear," she said a bit too loudly. "I'd better get you back to the boat."

She dragged him to their dinghy.

"Goodbye, Mrs. Babinsky," Reuben shouted to the woman,

still standing at her table, who'd watched this scenario in shocked silence. "Good to see you again."

"Good to see you, Debbie. I never see yaw motha anymaw since we moved to Syosset but if I run inta her at the mall I'll tell her I saw you hee-yah."

Please don't do that, Reuben prayed to herself. *I'm ready to deal with the United States Coast Guard or even the Egyptian Navy if I have to. But please don't start my mother looking for me.*

The last email Reuben sent to her mother from Spain hinted vaguely at a long trip through Europe with a "very interesting man I just met, more later."

"Thanks," Reuben said to Levi as they arrived at the Hinckley waiting quietly at anchor for them. "That was quick thinking."

The incident evaporated any trace of Jamaican rum from her brain. Reuben was back to all business.

"Let's get out of here right now, before they decide to drop by for a visit to see how my husband is doing so they can gossip about the lush I married."

Levi stood at the boat's bow, his foot holding down the button that operated the electric anchor windlass as the anchor chain noisily wound up from the water and down into its storage locker in the boat's bow.

"Anchor's up. Let's go," he shouted to Reuben, standing at the wheel. She pushed the engine shifter forward, engaging the gears and driving the boat forward around the point of the harbor entrance.

"What's our course," she asked. "Find us a course well clear of everybody, and far away from Long Island, New York."

"Swing us north, due north," Levi said, climbing out of the cabin into the boat's cockpit. "Eight-hundred-and-twenty-two"—he stuck his head into the cabin for a second glance at the GPS—"point three miles due north is Bermuda. We'll head that way and decide what to do before we get there. We can't risk any more chance meetings with ladies from Long Island."

He raised the main and mizzen sails, unrolled the genoa jib, and the boat heeled over in the warm trade wind breeze. Levi connected the autopilot, dialed in the heading and sat back in the cockpit.

■ ■ ■

Two days later, as the boat continued to sail under blue skies before moderate trade winds, Levi climbed up the ladder from the cabin, where he'd been perched at the chart table working with the computerized plotter for most of the past two hours.

"Here's what we'll do," he told Reuben, who was stretched on one of the cockpit benches as the autopilot steered the sailboat. "We're going to sail one straight shot up the whole East Coast, no stops, no islands. I've plotted a course that takes us past Bermuda. From Bermuda we'll sail due north and land somewhere on the American northeast coast. This will take us two weeks of straight night-and-day sailing. We'll be staying out of the shipping lanes on most of this course."

"You're the great sailor, buddy. I don't care how you do it. Just get us there," Reuben responded.

"I'll get us there all right," he answered. "But what happens then? When do you fill me in on your plans for that deadly toy we have hidden away? Even after what happened at home, I have limits as to what I'm willing to do." Levi laughed nervously. "I won't blow up New York City, you know."

"Blow up Noo Yawk?" Reuben laughed too, putting on her best Long Island voice. "Blow up Bloomies? Blow up the Central Pok Zoo? Blow up, oh my God, Saks Fifth Ave-a-noo? I may be desperate, may be a bit crazy, but I'm not sick."

She dropped the accent.

"I don't know what I'm going to do when we get to shore," she said. "I'm hoping there will be people there—Jews, American Jews—who'll take us in, take that thing off our hands. I don't want to have to decide what to do with it."

She paused, her eyes taking on a faraway look.

"I did enough during those days in the desert. If what I've done becomes known, I've already earned a dark place in the history books. I expect millions of people hate me already."

Nobody had ever hated her before.

She stopped speaking suddenly; her eyes clouded, her breath stopped, her shoulders shook. Levi looked at the woman, opened his arms wide, and she flung herself against his chest, sobbing. His arms surrounded her, pulling her close, tight against his chest, as her body shook with her heaving sobs.

After several minutes with no words exchanged, Reuben pulled back and looked Levi in the face. She spoke quietly.

"I'm a mass murderer. I am, right? I sent that bomb to Damascus. A billion Muslims believe if they kill me they go straight to heaven. Right?"

Levi did not respond. She made a fist and pounded on his chest.

"Right? Right? They kill me and they go to Paradise. I know that, at least I know they think that. Why do you think I stay awake all night and drink myself unconscious all day? I don't know what we are going to do with that thing." She pointed into the cabin. "I don't know what we'll do with it. But it's the property of the State of Israel—the property now, I guess, of the Jewish people. It's better to still have it than to have lost it to the fucking Arabs, right?"

She looked at him, waiting for a response. He nodded, barely moving his head. That wasn't enough for her, he sensed. He spoke up, in a whisper first, then repeating himself firmly.

"You did the right thing, Debbie. You followed orders. You had no choice. And this one"—he nodded toward the boat's cabin—"this one will be somebody else's choice. We'll hand it over and be done with it. We won't do anything stupid with it."

His words comforted her, whether or not he believed what he was telling her. Reassured, she smiled at Levi. "New York? Blow up Lord and Taylor? My mother would kill me. She'd have to go naked the rest of her life."

The autopilot whirred as Levi loosened the main sheet to ease the sail as the wind veered slightly. They sailed onward toward New England, the three of them: the last sailor in the Israeli Navy, the last member of the Israeli government, and the most powerful weapon in the arsenal of the (former) State of Israel.

CHAPTER 12

"Harry, we can't say no," Myrna Blumberg had shrieked after hanging up the telephone at two in the morning. "Everybody is taking them. We can't be the only ones to say no."

"Myrna, they're criminals. It's against the law to hide them. We'll get arrested," Harry, her husband, begged.

"Arrested *shmested*. What are they going to do, arrest every family on the block? Harry, do you want to be the only family at synagogue to say no? I'd be so ashamed. Besides, they said it's only for a day or two until something more permanent comes up."

The decision was made the way most decisions in the Blumberg family were made. Harry never actually agreed to take the Gorinskis into their house. He'd just stopped saying no.

The Gorinskis—father Oleg, mother Karin, and daughters Olga and Petka—were a nice enough family. They'd been in Israel all of two years after moving from Moscow. Oleg was a computer programmer who was fortunate to have obtained Russian exit visas for his family, since he worked on air defense radar software. He quickly found work with an Israeli electronics business. The two daughters were excited to be in

America, where they wanted to move in the first place, but were most excited about finally getting off that horrible, stinking ship. They fought over who would get the first bath in the Blumbergs' jacuzzi.

"No more than two days" turned into a week. The Gorinskis remained inside the house, as instructed. The Blumbergs' fifteen-year-old son, Sam, was sworn to secrecy, which lasted almost halfway through homeroom the following morning at school, where the teacher, aware of the rumors circulating among Marblehead High School's large Jewish student body, came right out and asked for a show of hands, asking who took in refugees in the middle of the night. As hands were slowly raised, a good third of the students responded. Then, one after another, rather than raising their hands, they stood up, beaming, as their classmates applauded.

Helping refugees was a good thing, right? They'd be heroes. The kids who didn't have refugees show up during the early morning felt as if they'd done something wrong.

All efforts at secrecy ceased within days of the sudden appearance of thousands of new cousins, uncles and aunts. Warnings to keep the new visitors hidden indoors began to seem pointless. A quick trip to the mall couldn't hurt. After all, these people needed clothes, didn't they? And maybe a nice meal out, and a movie—how could a movie hurt?

Jewish families that turned down refugees, families that said no or slammed down the telephone when asked to take people in, had second thoughts. What kind of examples were these parents to their children, especially when it seemed that all of their friends had said yes? Refugee families quickly became commodities, transferred from house to house as offers came in volunteering to share the burden.

Secrecy dissolved. The *Salem Daily News* ran interviews with Israeli refugees living in North Shore homes, changing names and addresses to protect the "secret locations" at which they were living.

A fundraising rally to aid refugees was organized five days after the escape. A Jewish community shell-shocked at the destruction of Israel, ashamed that their government did nothing to stop it and appeared to be buckling in to the demands of the triumphant Arab states, opened their wallets as they'd opened their homes.

A long-range resettlement committee was formed. It appeared that the escape of the passengers of the *Ionian Star* and the *Iliad* was a fait accompli.

Until the protests began.

The tone of newspaper editorials gradually changed from "The government must seek a long-term solution to this tragic problem" to "We cannot let one group take the law into their own hands and accomplish by lawlessness and violence what they could not accomplish by government action." Boston's Haitian community, stung by raids by Immigration and Customs Enforcement agents, decimated by deportations of longtime but undocumented residents, led the first march on the John F. Kennedy Federal Building at Government Center in Boston.

Deport White Illegals, Too, the largest banner read. Henrique Depardieux, the chairman of the Massachusetts Haitian Rights Committee, made his point clearly.

"ICE knows where these people are staying. It knows they are here with no papers. It knows they broke the law to enter this country. Yet we see these people on the news every night being taken to shopping malls to buy new clothes. We see the Jews raising millions of dollars to give to these people. Why doesn't the government round them up the same way they rounded up my brothers and sisters?

"We will return here every day until every one of these white illegal immigrants is placed on the same airplanes that took black refugees away from us. We will not be stopped. We have suffered. Now it is time to prove to us that our suffering was not in vain, that this country treats blacks and whites alike."

A half dozen uniformed storm troopers from the United

Nationalists Movement drove through the night from Mississippi to parade in front of the Kennedy Building. Swastika-adorned flags straddling a banner declaring *Jail the Jews* were broadcast on TV news.

By the third day of demonstrations, the Haitians were in the minority. Mexicans, Salvadorans, Guatemalans marched with them. They, too, had lost family members to deportation. A South Boston Irish contingent joined the demonstration, as did a small group of Chinese.

The South Boston group carried a different banner. They, of course, could not complain about different treatment for whites. Their uncles and aunts, cousins, nieces and nephews who came to Boston from Cork and Galway, from Dublin and Donegal, looking for work after the Irish economic bubble burst, only to be rounded up and sent home when their tourist visas expired, were as white as the Jews from the two ships. The South Boston banner said, *No Special Treatment for Jews.*

While these events took place, Howie Mandelbaum, the only person arrested the night of the sinkings, remained in the Charles Street Jail. He would not be alone for long.

CHAPTER 13

At five seconds per channel, it took Adam Shapiro three minutes to flip through the circuit of cable TV selections. It drove his father crazy. It was a skill Shapiro's generation lacked but his son seemed to have been born with, just as his son could carry on a conversation with his parents while at the same time slaying enemy soldiers on his Nintendo. Cartoons, movies, talk shows, commercial after commercial cycled past on the screen, all while Shapiro hoped to spend some time with his son. TV time together might not be "quality" time, but it was time together.

Shapiro lost patience.

"Okay. Enough. Stop that," he barked. "Why don't we look at the listings and decide what we want to watch."

"That's not how I do it, Dad. I have to see what's on before I decide," Adam responded. "It just takes a minute."

"All right, but come on, make a decision," Shapiro said, only half paying attention to the TV, fascinated by his son's intense concentration on the screen, eyes pinched together, analyzing each five-second segment and literally making instant thumbs-up or down calls.

"Call me back when you've decided." He walked toward the

door of the room they called "the TV Room," much as Shapiro disliked that label.

Just as he reached the door, a phrase caught Shapiro's attention. He swiveled around.

"Punish the so-called Chosen people for spitting in God's face," he heard a voice say from the TV as the channel flipped to a Toyota commercial. "Zero percent financing . . ."

"Wait," Shapiro told his son. "Flip back to that last one. I want to hear what he's saying."

"Dad, no. It's some God show or something."

Before Adam could say anything more, Shapiro grabbed the remote and toggled the channel button to return to the previous show.

"What I am saying, in plain American English, is that God wants us to round up the Jews in this country. Time to take our country back."

Shapiro saw two men in dark suits standing in front of what looked like a living room set—two comfortable chairs and a coffee table. The man speaking was being ejected from the set, none too subtly. A young blonde walked on, smiling and excited, bouncing up and down in her enthusiasm, her hemline demurely below her knees, two breasts that someone other than the Lord gave to her bouncing to a rhythm of their own. The show's host, however, took a couple of seconds to recover before greeting the woman with a broad and perhaps overly enthusiastic hug.

"Why does that man want to round up all the Jews, Dad?" Adam asked. "I don't understand what he's talking about. I thought that was something they did back in history. I don't understand."

Shapiro saw the tentatively fearful expression on his son's face. *This will be a quality parenting moment after all*, he thought.

Shapiro had never directly experienced anti-Semitism. Adam, who liked to boast that his Dad was Jewish, his mother was some kind of Christian, and he would decide what he was when he grew up, never felt shunned because of his father's heritage. He'd learn about the Holocaust in school, of course, just as he'd learn about the Civil War and the Great Depression, but at his age historical events did not seem any more real than *Star Trek* or *The Lord of the Rings.* That stark brand of "round up the Jews" talk was entirely new to him.

"Dad, what kind of jerk was that guy? How come they let him say that on TV? Americans don't hate Jews, right? That's some German—or Arab, I guess—kinda thing, right?"

"Actually, Adam, this country has its share of that, too, and not too long ago. There used to be the same kind of preacher on the radio. Father Coughlin was his name. He was a Catholic priest with his own radio show. Millions of people listened to him every week. And he used to say the same kind of stuff about Jews, the same kind of hate talk. He went on for years.

"And plenty of people agreed with him. Hey, Charles Lindbergh, the first guy to fly across the Atlantic Ocean, he used to talk about a worldwide Jewish conspiracy to get us to fight in World War II. Even some presidents have talked that way. Harry Truman, you know, the guy who took over after President Roosevelt died, he said something like the Jews are all selfish and they are as cruel as Hitler and Stalin when they get any power."

The six-year-old's puzzled look reminded Shapiro that his son's knowledge of American history included George Washington, a cherry tree and some vague knowledge about Abe Lincoln freeing the slaves.

"You've never experienced anti-Semitism yourself, but it has been a part of America right from the beginning." Shapiro put his arm over his son's shoulder. "Sorry about going on like that," he said sheepishly to his six-year-old.

Adam looked puzzled.

"Hey, buddy, forget about it. I don't expect this will ever be a problem for you." Shapiro rubbed the top of his son's head. "So, what's on TV?"

"It won't be a problem for me if I don't decide to become a Jew, right, Dad?" Adam asked, not quite willing to drop this topic. "And if it became a real problem, you could decide not to be a Jew anymore, so there isn't anything to worry about. How's that?"

Shapiro turned to look at his son.

"Adam," he said. "I can't ever stop being a Jew. And I wouldn't if I could. And you know, Son, with me as your father, I don't know if you can help being considered a Jew no matter what you want. And since most everybody is going to think Adam Shapiro is Jewish, no matter what you decide, you might as well get the benefits of being Jewish. Hey, who knows? There might be some girl someday who wouldn't think of bringing you home to meet her parents unless you were Jewish. It could come in handy."

"Dad, stop that," Adam moaned.

He went back to the remote and found a *Mork and Mindy* rerun. Father and son sat side by side on the sofa, watching Mork from Ork consider what a strange place planet Earth is.

Shapiro agreed.

CHAPTER 14

President Lawrence Quaid was sprawled on the sofa in the Oval Office. Sitting in chairs facing him were Robert Brown, his chief of staff; Senator Grant Farrell, Democratic minority leader; and Quaid's wife, Catherine.

Sen. Farrell broke the silence.

"The law is clear, Mr. President. You can't be faulted for enforcing the law. These people entered the country illegally. They used violence, military weapons, to kill American military personnel. They're flaunting their presence in Boston, not even trying to be subtle about it. They are daring you to do something. They don't believe you have what it takes to take them on."

"Easy now, Grant," Brown said. "This isn't a test of the president's manhood."

"The president is man enough. I'll swear it under oath," the First Lady said. "We are not going to make this decision based on whether my husband is going to back down in front of a dare. According to a story he told me when we were courting, the last time he accepted a dare was in junior high school when a friend dared him to piss on an electric fence. That's a lesson he won't ever forget, right, dear?"

"It was certainly a shocker," Quaid responded. "If only this dare were as easy as that one."

"We go back a long way, a long way, and I know in all that time your heart has never steered you wrong." Brown spoke as much to Catherine as to the president. Brown and Catherine met in their junior year at Cornell University. After two dates, both realized there was no chemistry between them—friendship perhaps, but no chemistry. When Catherine asked Brown whether his roommate was seeing anyone, he'd known where the chemistry was. She and Quaid married shortly after graduation and had a marriage people didn't think happened anymore. Faithful, sharing equals, either could have been elected president and the other would have been there in support. Quaid relied on Catherine to steer him toward deciding what the right thing was and then convince him to do it.

"The United States of America cannot deport Jewish refugees to a country in which they will be placed in camps, subjugated and, quite possibly, exterminated," Brown said sharply. "You do that and you will earn a place in history, all right, but you won't like it."

"Just a minute now, Bob," Farrell interrupted before Quaid could respond. "Don't you think maybe you've got a bit of a personal bias on this issue? You know, Mr. President, maybe it would look better if Bob stepped aside on this issue and let the rest of us make a decision. It doesn't look right having him here right now. Word could get out and there'd be hell to pay."

Quaid shot from the couch to stand over Farrell.

"Grant, are you saying what I think you're saying?" Quaid asked. "Hell, I've known Bob since college and I'll bet I've been in more synagogues than he has since then. I'd guess Bob's just about forgotten he's even Jewish, right, Bob?"

Brown rose from his chair to stand beside the president, both of them looking down on Farrell. Catherine Quaid beamed at her two men.

"I wouldn't go that far, Mr. President, not these days.

Evidently others haven't forgotten the fact that my parents happen to be Jews. Just for the record"—Brown stared at Sen. Farrell—"I haven't been to a synagogue since I was bar-mitzvahed at thirteen years old. Neither of my sons had a bar mitzvah. I don't belong to any Jewish organizations and, as you've scolded me several times, Mr. President, I go to work on Rosh Hashana and Yom Kippur every year. Despite that, lady and gentlemen, I am most certainly a Jew, if that makes any difference."

Catharine applauded, got up from her chair and gave Brown a hug.

"That is why we love you so much, Bob. You are the heart and soul of this presidency and we won't forget that either."

"Heart and soul is one thing, Mr. President, but politics is something entirely different," Farrell said, remaining seated while the president walked to the three windows facing the South Lawn and the Washington Monument in the distance. Quaid stood staring out the window, his back to the others in the room. Farrell continued speaking.

"You might not have to run for office again, Mr. President, but the rest of us Democrats still do. Now, I don't know what you're going to decide on this issue, and I suspect you don't know either. But if you allow the country's most powerful Jew, with all due respect to your chief of staff, to influence your decision, that decision won't get much respect. This has to be your decision, not influenced by a Jewish insider in the White House.

"I tell you this for your own good, and for the good of the Democratic Party. This issue has disaster written all over it. There won't be much of a national Democratic party without Jewish support. I know that, even if I don't especially like it. But if it looks like we're knuckling in to Jewish pressure, then this party will only have Jewish support and nothing else."

Sen. Farrell looked back and forth between the president and his chief of staff. Farrell knew he didn't have the same history with Lawrence Quaid that Brown had, but it was Farrell's job to look out for the party. Brown's job was to look out for Quaid.

"We have to watch ourselves on this one, Mr. President," Farrell continued. "Make the right decision, sir, whatever that is, but be sure to make it in the right way, in a way the rest of the party won't have to explain in Congressional hearings someday. I don't want to be placed under oath and asked what role Mr. Brown played in this decision. For the good of the country, for the good of the Democratic Party, I suggest that Mr. Brown voluntarily absent himself from this discussion."

President Quaid continued staring out the windows. Before he could say anything, his wife spoke up.

"Larry, you tell Bobbie to leave and I'm walking out with him. He's your best friend and most trusted advisor. He won't do anything to hurt you. The three of us are the home team, remember, the three of us. We're the good guys. Lose one member of this team and I swear you'll lose the other one, too, at least on this issue."

President Quaid spun around.

She stared him directly in the eyes until he looked away. The president walked to his wife and took both her hands in his.

"Catherine, the last time I disagreed with you was when I wanted to buy a bass guitar and you said it had four strings and I only knew one note. I bought it anyway and never got past the first string."

Quaid stared silently at the ceiling, paused, then turned back to his wife.

"What Grant says is right. We both know it is. This is the toughest issue of my presidency. How I handle this will define me. This is my moment in history. The way I handle it is as important as the result I achieve, or don't achieve. It can't appear that any decision I make is a payback for Jewish support, especially for Jewish financial support."

Quaid turned to his chief of staff. "Bob, I think it would be best for all of us if you would decide that your presence is needed elsewhere. I'm sorry, but that's the way it has to be."

Brown stood, looked at Quaid, shook his head in disbelief

and walked from the room. The door swung shut.

Catherine walked to the door without looking at Quaid. It slammed behind her, loud enough to startle the Marine guard.

"Now let's do what has to be done, Mr. President," Farrell slowly said.

"Okay," Quaid replied. "But this better be worth it. I'm paying an awfully heavy price for following your advice."

■ ■ ■

The five men met in the family quarter of the White House: the majority and minority leaders of the House and Senate, and President Quaid. No staff. No record was kept of meetings in the family quarters, unlike in the Oval Office, where every visit was tape-recorded for history. Their conversation was unofficial, off the record, not for repetition outside the room.

"The problem," Sen. Farrell began, "as we well know, is that the real minority in this country is those of us not identified with any minority. Add up all the blacks, Latinos, and Asians and collectively they outnumber ordinary white folks in this country. Throw in the whites who identify with some ethnic or religious minority and you've got a small group of what would be called traditional Americans. Now, Mr. President, I'm not saying there's anything particularly wrong about this, but, well, it sure is an eye-opener when you think about it."

"And it has potentially unpleasant implications for the current situation," House Majority Leader Frent Gastly added. "I don't see that we've got much of a choice on this Jewish refugee business. We can't make exceptions for these Jews. We do that and every city in the country will be up in flames."

"And don't forget the oil problem. It could be a damn cold winter in New Hampshire," said Senator Wayne Giddings, the conservative New Hampshire Republican majority leader. Giddings' state had shivered through a winter that saw oil prices nearly double. He wasn't about to go through another such winter, with even higher oil prices caused by an Arab oil boycott. One more winter like the last one and his free-market preachings would ring on cold ears.

Congressman Gastly joined in.

"I've been speaking with some leaders of my evangelical base," he said. "They've been stronger backers of Israel than even most Jews. Second Coming and all that. Every person I spoke with, half a dozen or so, made just the opposite choice our Jewish citizens seem to be making. When Israelis start killing Americans, especially American military, especially in America, well, American Christians are putting the America first, to coin a phrase. American Jews seem to put Jew first, American second. The *born-againers* are waving their flags and turning their backs on Israel."

"It's more than just these two ships, Mr. President," Sen. Farrell said. "We let these people in and the doors are flung open. There are how many million Jews left in Israel? They damn well all need someplace to go—those that are still alive, those that are allowed to leave. We aren't going to send in troops to get their country back—need I say that *Iraq* word, sir—and we just can't take them all in here."

"We've got to find every damn person who came on those ships and boot them out, turn them over to somebody, anybody but us. But that's only half of it," Giddings continued, locking eyes with the president. "A crime has been committed, hell, five thousand crimes. What made thousands of Americans do what they did, kill ten coastguardsmen, sink two ships, hide all those escapees? Who knows? Whatever made them do it, they're criminals, too. Criminals who have to be arrested. Tried. Punished. There's no getting around that, sir."

"I hear what you are saying. I see the inevitability of what we have to do," Quaid said. He shook his head. "Damn, but it feels wrong. Look, my wife and my oldest friend are barely speaking to me over this. They know what I'm going to decide and they don't like it. Don't like it is putting it mildly. I'm having some pretty chilly nights myself, gentlemen."

They all smiled.

The First Lady had announced she was going to visit their daughter at Harvard, and while she was in Massachusetts she might attend a fundraiser for Israeli refugees.

Quaid walked to a window. The illuminated spike of the Washington Monument drew his eyes toward the sky, where the first stars were becoming visible. *There'll surely never be a Quaid Monument,* he thought. *I'll be lucky to escape as a historical footnote. Damn those Jews and Arabs, all of them.*

"Look," Quaid said, turning to face the two Republican leaders. "If I do this, if I round those people up and prosecute them, I want your complete support. I'm not going to hang myself on the line for every liberal to take shots at if I've got to worry about being kicked in the butt by the Republicans. I'll do this, but only if you sign on all the way. Otherwise, hell, otherwise I don't know what I'll do, but I'm not going to have to duck for cover from both the left and the right on this one. Do I have your words on that? No half-hearted support, either. I want you right there in front of the cameras with me when this gets announced."

"We've discussed this with our folks already," Sen. Giddings said. "You arrest those people, try them, send the illegals back where they came from and throw the book at everybody involved in killing those ten Coasties, and we'll stand side by side with you. If ever there was an issue that actually did rise above politics—and I'll admit I haven't seen one yet—this could be it."

"Same goes for me," Gastly said. "My people are behind you on this one. You won't have to watch your back. We'll protect you there. Just do it firmly and quickly. Don't get cold feet halfway through."

"Well, I hope God and history will forgive me, but I'll do what has to be done," Quaid said softly. "May Catherine forgive me, too. I'll speak with the attorney general first thing tomorrow morning. She won't like doing this, but I'm not giving her any choice."

■ ■ ■

Attorney General Maryellen McQueeney, "the Queen" to friends and enemies, had an uncomfortable feeling when she was summoned to the White House for an early morning meeting with the president the next day. He'd been right. She didn't like what she heard from him. She asked for more time, a week or so, to study options.

"You have no options, Queen," Quaid told her. "This decision has been made. You are going to implement it. There may be a high price to pay for what we're about to do. I'm willing to pay that price. You won't have to. This is my decision, not yours, and people are going to know that. Your job is to do your job. I suggest you fly to Boston and tell your people what they are going to do. I want this kept quiet until you have all those people in custody, then I'll make the announcement myself."

The attorney general nodded, looking grim.

"One other thing. I don't want some Jewish Assistant US Attorney in Boston deciding his loyalty is to other Jews and not to the United States. This will work if we do it quickly, with surprise, with no advance warnings. I don't want this to turn into a months-long nationwide manhunt. I want it over with, quickly and cleanly. Be careful who is on the case and who is off the case. Keep it subtle, but let's not be stupid on this one."

"Mr. President," the attorney general said. "I most respectfully disagree with what you are asking me to do. Please, let's give this a bit more thought before we start down a road without knowing where it will end. Please, sir, don't ask me to do this thing."

"I'm not asking you to do anything," Quaid huffed. "I am telling you to do this. I am ordering you to do this. And you will do this. You will not resign, at least not until this is over. You will do this. I will have your support and your loyalty. Do you understand me?"

McQueeney stepped back. She had never seen the president like this. She had been a judge on the federal Ninth Circuit Court of Appeals in California and had been drawn to Lawrence Quaid because of his unflinching ethical record. She had felt like a colleague to Quaid—until now.

"Yes, sir," McQueeney said with a faux salute. "I'll follow orders. I won't publicly disagree with you. I won't embarrass you. And when the job is done, you can look for a new attorney general."

She walked to the door, reached for the doorknob, then turned to face Quaid.

"Mr. President, I'm not the first good soldier to agree to follow orders to round up Jews. I hope history is more kind to you and me than it was the last time this happened. Good day, sir."

■ ■ ■

McQueeney was on a plane and in her Boston office that afternoon. It was unusual for the attorney general to visit a field office. If the Queen wanted to speak with her subordinates, they were usually summoned to Washington. She ordered the staff assembled and wasted no time getting to the point.

"This decision regarding the Jewish refugees comes direct from the president," she told the assembled attorneys. "I won't say I played no role in the decision, but it was apparent to me that the president's mind is made up. Some of you are not going to be pleased by this decision, but I am sure you will each do your jobs. Or if you feel you can't do your job, then resign effective immediately. There are no other options, no other choices. There will be no free passes on this one."

Still, it was not as simple as that. Arresting Israeli soldiers, or even all the Israeli civilians from the ships, was something she could live with. More difficult was the decision about who should be arrested from the thousands of local families who sheltered these people.

McQueeney did not want the US citizens arrested, she told the Boston staff. Her preference was to issue summonses ordering these people to appear in court at a later time, a time she hoped could be postponed enough so some new crisis would draw the public's attention and she would not have to prosecute generally law-abiding citizens, prosperous citizens, for doing what she felt in her heart she would have done had she been in their shoes.

She decided to modify the president's order. Only one adult member of every household that harbored refugees would be taken into custody. Each household would decide who would take responsibility and who would stay behind.

"And no children, no teenagers," she told her subordinates. "Not even if they want to go, not even if they ask to go."

CHAPTER 15

Judy Katz broke her widowed grandmother's heart every day, torturing the woman who raised her after her parents were killed in an automobile accident when she was six years old. Judy barely remembered her parents and knew little of their history, how they'd met, why they'd married. She retained no memory of her life with them. Her grandmother rarely spoke about her dead son and daughter-in-law, and never spoke about her own husband, who Judy only knew had died long before she'd been born. Judy had no family besides her grandmother—no cousins, no uncles or aunts.

They'd lived in an old woman's apartment in which fresh air was prohibited and the sofa was covered in plastic except when company was present, in the same Queens, New York, neighborhood where her grandmother moved on her arrival in the US after the war.

The only hint about her family history came once when Judy was watching *Schindler's List* on HBO, pretending to be able to sip Manischewitz concord wine, a slightly alcoholic grape juice. Halfway through the movie, with Judy in tears, her grandmother turned toward her and, in a voice as casual as if she were discussing chicken breasts going on sale tomorrow, said, "I was there, you know."

A stunned Judy Katz listened to her grandmother describe how she had lived in Warsaw, Poland. When the Germans invaded, all the Jews were imprisoned behind walls, the Warsaw Ghetto. The greater shocker was that Judy's father had been born there, in the midst of the ghetto. Her grandfather, who she learned for the first time had been a tailor, smuggled his wife and newborn son out through sewer lines that led under the walls. Once his wife and son were outside the ghetto, the tailor had returned—returned to fight the Nazis. They killed him. No other family member survived the war.

Her grandmother never mentioned that history again, waving her hands and poofing at "history-schmistory." It never left Judy, though. *I am a child of death and destruction, the offspring of tyranny and war,* she thought.

Her grandmother was less lyrical. She was devastated that her granddaughter was thirty-one years old and not married, not even seeing anybody "serious."

But that wasn't the biggest disappointment. After putting her granddaughter through Amherst College, then Boston College Law School—"A Catholic law school," her grandmother would say. "What kind of law can nuns and priests teach?"—Judy clerked for a federal judge and then was hired as an Assistant US Attorney in Boston. She was assigned to the organized crime strike force and was eventually tapped to head it. Katz had a knack for chasing and prosecuting bad guys. Even more surprising to the five-foot-four-inch attorney was the almost sexual thrill she felt locking eyes with the third-generation Boston Irish and Italian hoodlums as they stood silently before the magistrate judge at their arraignments.

She prosecuted them for criminal conspiracy, loansharking and mail fraud. She also enjoyed mixing with the similarly third-generation Boston Irish and Italian FBI and DEA agents she worked with and then hung out with several nights each week.

"No husband material here," she often joked.

Katz heard about the attorney general's visit and was shocked that she was excluded. As she was stewing, a colleague stuck his head into her office.

"We're having lunch today, Judy," Bob Shaw, head of the Antitrust Division, told her. "You can't say no. You can't ask why. Just meet me at the Sultan's at noon. Bye."

The Sultan's Palace was a Turkish restaurant across the footbridge from the courthouse. It was popular but a bit expensive for lunch. Nonetheless, there was always a line.

Shaw was waiting for her.

"So, what's the occasion for this unexpected lunch?" Katz asked, walking up to him and taking a seat at a corner table.

"Judy, my father is Jewish," he said slowly and almost at a whisper. "Most people don't know that. It's not that I have anything to hide, but, well, he wasn't around all that long and my mother was pretty serious about raising me as an Episcopalian and all and, well, I guess you're the first one in the office I've ever mentioned that to."

"So, why the big confession now?" Katz asked.

"I owe it to you. There was a meeting this morning."

"I know. I wasn't invited," she said. "Were you there?"

"I was there. We were all there, all the department heads. And FBI, DEA. ATF. US Marshals. Even ICE. Even Jed. Jed was there."

Jed Delaney was deputy chief of the Organized Crime Strike Force. Katz was his boss.

"Jed was there?" she whispered. "Why wasn't I there? Bob, is something going on?"

"Listen, Judy. Nobody can know I'm telling you this. Understand? I'm willing to do the right thing, but I don't want to pay the price for the rest of my life for this. Okay? Agreed? I need a promise from you. Nobody ever knows. That means not even if you are under oath. Can you agree to that?"

"Should I agree? You're asking me to promise to lie under

oath. I can't agree to that, Bob. That's too much to ask. I send people to prison for that, Bob. Bob," she said slowly, almost in a whisper, leaning forward, close to him. "Bob, are they setting me up for something? Does this have anything to do with why I wasn't at that meeting this morning? Holy shit, Bob, was I not invited because I'm under investigation? Is that why I wasn't there, Bob?"

Shaw put both elbows on the table, cupped his hands and spoke slowly.

"You weren't at the meeting—not because you're under investigation, Judy. It's because you're a Jew . . . because you're Jewish. That's why . . . I've got to go. Judy, I'm sorry. It isn't right and I couldn't let it happen and not tell you. Don't burn me, Judy. Please. I did this to help you. Don't burn me now."

Shaw stood and walked away between the crowded tables, not looking back at the frozen woman sitting alone, still leaning forward as if ready for a kiss, unable to move.

CHAPTER 16

The North Shore Jewish Council coordinated housing of the refugees and planning to relocate people around the country. Lists were drawn up—lists of refugees, lists of families housing them, lists of financial contributors. The database was kept in the office of the emergency coordinator at the Jewish Community Center of the North Shore, in Swampscott.

The inevitable next step on the path from secrecy to media blitz took place. A press conference was called. Moishe Cohen, the emergency relief coordinator, was the chief executive officer of Winston Mills, one of Massachusetts's last remaining textile manufacturers. Cohen stood before a bank of television cameras, reading from a prepared statement. He spoke with the barest trace of his childhood German accent. At his sides stood rabbis, a state senator, business leaders and the inevitable musician, the interim conductor of the Boston Pops, the first Jew to hold that position since the death of Arthur Fiedler.

"First, and most importantly," Cohen began, "let me fervently emphasize how seriously the entire community regrets the tragic loss of life that was unintentionally inflicted in this act of liberation. Those of us involved in the planning of this action share all Americans' shock and horror at this violence. We did not plan on using physical force and certainly never anticipated that such weapons would be used."

Cohen looked up at the row of television cameras directed at him.

"We were told by certain professional persons who accompanied the passengers that the Coast Guard boats would be disabled and distracted. We did not anticipate the means they would use. For that, we apologize. We will offer financial compensation to the families of those who were lost, at the same time appreciating with all our hearts that money cannot make up for their tragic losses."

"You're damned right that Jewish money can't pay for murdering Americans." A man standing at the rear of the hall was grabbed by two uniformed security officers and ushered out the doors.

"I appreciate that there are hard feelings, angry feelings," Cohen said. "But let there be no mistake. What was done by this community was what had to be done. It was the right thing. What this nation is doing, what this nation is continuing to do, is wrong. We will continue to protest and we will continue to resist when this great nation hides its head in the moral sand and does what all of us, what all of you, know in your heart of hearts is wrong."

Cohen halted. He appeared confused, confused that his audience was not cheering what to him was obvious.

"Israel was established as a sacred home for the Jewish people. That home has been stolen from us by force. We demand that our government, the United States government, use all means available, all means, to restore the Jewish people's homeland.

"A million people—" Cohen paused to wipe his eyes with the backs of both hands. He fought for control, overwhelmed by the concept of a million—another million—dead Jews. The room was silent. The audience, the Boston press corps included, held its collective breath. He continued.

"A million Jews have died already, from the bomb, from the armies, from the Arabs. There are concentration camps, Jews in concentration camps, in the Holy Land. We will do everything, everything in our power to convince the United States, President Quaid, to do what is right and just in this horrendous situation."

His back straightened as the elderly man found his strength.

"In what we have done already and in all future endeavors, one ideal will guide us. One phrase will determine our actions. What words guide us, you may ask. What words?"

He stopped speaking, struggling for control of his emotions. His head rolled back as he gazed at the ceiling, as if by doing so his tears would be hidden. Both hands clenched the podium to support him under a weight of memories.

The room hushed, even the veteran reporters did not know what to expect next but knew, too, they had the lead story on that night's broadcasts.

The cameras remained locked on the thin, white-haired man at the podium, his head now dropped onto his chest, too heavy for him to hold up. His eyes were closed as he fought for inner strength. Reporters wondered whether his knees would buckle under his invisible burden.

Barely in control of the tears that ran freely from both eyes, Cohen straightened his back, lifted his chin and ever so slowly unbuttoned the cuff of his left shirt sleeve. Standing upright now, he shoved the sleeve up toward his left elbow, exposing his forearm. He lifted that arm in the air, fingers spread wide, above his head. The small row of tattooed numbers was visible in the glare of the television lights.

"What words?" Cohen whispered.

His voice rose to a shout.

"*Never again. Never again. Never again. Never again. Never again.*"

He walked from the podium, followed by the other men, leaving the room in silence.

That afternoon all six US magistrates—the lowest-level federal judicial officers—spent hours signing search and arrest warrants based on the information already made public, names and addresses collected from newspaper accounts, from local police reports and from simple observation. The first search warrant was for the Jewish Community Center of the North Shore.

The Relief Committee took all the proper safeguards to protect its data from accidents, such as making duplicate backups of the database so the information would not be lost. It did not occur to anybody to set up a system where the database could be quickly and permanently destroyed.

FBI agents entering the Jewish Community Center at ten that night found the lights on and a meeting taking place about relocation efforts with representatives of Jewish communities from across the country. Computers were seized, along with all discs and backup drives. The agents left within a half hour, leaving an ominous silence behind them.

Still, the arrests later that same night were not expected. Also not expected was the visit to Verizon Communication's North Shore business office by the FBI. The agents displayed a most unusual court order: telephone and Internet service in seven towns north of Boston was to be disconnected from ten at night until six in the morning—no questions asked, no options available. Similar court orders were served at the business offices of cellular telephone providers north of Boston. All cell towers were to be shut down as well. By the time the telephone companies' attorneys could protest the court order the next morning, it was history and phones were back in service.

The seized computers were carried to the Winnebago used by the FBI as its mobile command center. The database of households and refugees was quickly found and sent by secure wireless email to Camp Curtis Guild, a Massachusetts Army Reserve base outside Boston, and to the federal courthouse. The data was merged into more than 5,000 arrest warrants, all quickly signed by the half dozen magistrates.

Attorney General McQueeney had insisted that the raids be polite and low key. No doors were to be knocked down, no weapons were to be displayed, no shouts, no force, no helicopters and, hopefully, no news media.

Teams fanned out through suburban neighborhoods, followed by hastily requisitioned school buses. Agents knocked on doors and displayed arrest warrants. No shouting. No guns. Lots of "sirs" and "ma'ams." But arrests were made, and arrests meant handcuffs, fingerprints, mug photos and detention, one person per household.

■ ■ ■

"David, I hear the doorbell. Wake up. There's somebody at the door."

Estelle Rosen shook her husband, thankful at least that she could stop his snoring. Twenty-two years of marriage and she never got used to it.

"David, wake up. See who's at the door," she said, shaking him, wondering for the thousandth time how he could sleep through his nasal thunder.

Pulling on a bathrobe, Rosen walked quietly down the stairs, trying not to wake his daughter or the Moscowitzes sleeping in the guest room. The pounding got louder, more insistent. He turned on the porch light and opened the door. Two men in dark suits stood there, holding flashlights.

"David Rosen?" one man asked.

"Yes, that's me. What's wrong? Has something happened?"

"You have people staying here with you, Mr. Rosen? Arnold, Greta and Carol Moscowitz?" the other man asked, consulting a piece of paper.

"Who are you? Why do you want to know this? Why are you here so late? Come back in the morning." Rosen moved to close the door.

A hand went to the door, holding it open. The paper was

displayed. It was hard to read by the porch light. All Rosen saw was the large type at the top, *United States District Court for the District of Massachusetts*. And one other word in large black letters: *WARRANT*.

"Can we come in, sir? We have something to discuss with you."

Rosen nodded numbly. Estelle stood at the top of the stairs, looking down.

"David, who are these men? What is it? My God, David, has something happened? Is it my mother? Please God, not my mother." Her voice approached hysteria.

"No, Estelle. Mother is fine. Everything is fine. Go back to bed, dear. I have to speak with these men."

"Actually, Mr. Rosen," the second man said, consulting his list. "It would be best if Estelle came down here. But first, Estelle, could you ask the Moscowitzes to join us, too."

In minutes, Estelle, joined by sleepy Arnold, Greta and Carol Moscowitz, came down the stairs.

"What is it David? What do these men want?" Estelle asked.

"These men are from the FBI," Rosen said, looking at his wife and Arnold Moscowitz, a short, dark man. Moscowitz was born in Milwaukee and emigrated to Israel immediately after college. He owned Israel's largest chain of photocopy shops. At least, he used to. Now he owned the clothes he wore and little else. He hoped to find a cousin in Milwaukee, the only family member he'd remained in contact with after his parents passed away.

"Let's get this over with, sir," the first man said. "Here's how it is. We have an arrest warrant for you and for an Estelle Rosen. You are charged with aiding and abetting a whole list of crimes, ranging all the way to murder of a federal officer and—"

"Oh my God." Estelle, all color drained from her face, slumped soundlessly to the floor. Rosen knelt beside her, patting her cheeks.

He looked at Carol Moscowitz.

"Get a wet cloth. Quickly. Help me," he begged.

Estelle opened her eyes and sat up.

"I'm so sorry. That's never happened to me, ever," she said, surprised, then embarrassed. She slowly, carefully got up from the floor and stood eye to eye with the man holding the warrant.

"Do you really think you are going to charge me and David with, my God, with murder? That's the most ridiculous thing I've ever heard. David, call the lawyer. Don't say a word to these men. Don't say a word. Get on the phone. Call the lawyer, what's his name, we used him when we bought the summer house."

She turned back to the two men.

"This is all a mistake. Get out of my house. Come back in the morning. You can't take anybody until my lawyer gets here. This is crazy, crazy."

"Ma'am, I'm afraid there is no mistake," one of the men said. "We have a warrant and we're under orders. Here's how it's going to work. These folks are coming with us. Their names are on the list and they have to come. You folks"—pointing at David and Estelle—"only one of you has to come; the other gets this notice. One comes. One stays here with your daughter. Makes no difference to us who comes, who stays. Just decide right away. We've got a busy night. Who's it going to be?"

"Can I get dressed first?" Rosen asked, taking Estelle's hand. "Just let me get some clothes on, okay?"

"Certainly, sir," the second agent said. "But please hurry. And you people"—looking at the Moscowitzes—"you'd better get dressed and get whatever things you have together. You won't be returning here. Whatever you want to keep, better take it with you."

Minutes later the three Moscowitzes, Rosen and the two men stood on the porch. A yellow school bus was parked down the street. Rosen saw other groups of people standing motionless on the sidewalk, waiting for the bus to slowly roll down the street to them.

He turned to his wife.

"I'll be home soon. This is all a mistake. Call the lawyer, Estelle." He turned to walk away. "Estelle." He turned back and held both her hands. "This was my decision, not yours. We did the right thing. Estelle, I love you."

Estelle immediately ran into the house and picked up the telephone receiver, dialing for directory assistance. She held the phone to her ear, puzzled. The telephone was dead.

CHAPTER 17

Jonathan Kantor had not left his house since the bomb destroyed Tel Aviv. One thought ran through his mind like a Motown song, repeating constantly. Without control.

I should have been there. It should have been me. I should have been there. It should have been me.

Kantor's wife, Elaine, and their twin daughters, Rachel and Rebecca, were visiting Elaine's parents in Israel. Jonathan had planned to join his family on the three-week vacation until his boss, a partner in a premier patent law firm in Boston, struck a tree on his mountain bike and ended up flat on his back for weeks. Kantor was at his desk when his wife and children were incinerated in her parents' Tel Aviv condominium.

I should have been there. It should have been me.

Kantor's Bushmaster semi-automatic rifle lay on the kitchen table, looking as out of place as a dog turd on a Persian rug. Kantor bought the gun three years earlier after two men jimmied a living room window and crept into the house while he and Elaine were sleeping, only to run from the house when a police car drove by with its siren blaring. The weapon had never been fired. Having it was enough for Kantor. It went into the bedroom closet, bullets in the clip, ready to fire the next time there were late-night footsteps on the stairway. That was all he wanted. He was satisfied.

The weapon was moved from the closet to the kitchen table a week after Tel Aviv.

Kantor watched television news, absorbing everything he could from Israel—or what had been Israel. When word reached the leadership of the North Shore Jewish Council that Elaine and the Kantor girls had been in Tel Aviv, calls were made to Kantor. He was invited to memorial services, to substitute funerals. He was urged to join others in grieving.

He stayed home thinking for the first time in his life of what it meant to him to be Jewish. It had not meant anything in particular—until now. Blatant anti-Semitism was something that happened in other times. In other places. To other people. Years ago. In Europe. Not here. Not here in America

Kantor and his family, like most American Jews, had been untouched by anti-Semitism. Now, all he could think about was how the Jew-haters and killers could get to him, too. They took his wife, his daughters.

When the phone call came asking if he could put a few people up for a few nights, the words went in one ear and out the other. Kantor did not remember how he answered. But his name had made a list, a list of people called for help. And next to his name, next to *Jonathan Kantor, 26 Endicott Drive, Peabody, Massachusetts* was a check mark.

Kantor slept in front of the television, listening for footsteps. Some nights he sat at his bedroom window and stared at the dark street until the sky lightened.

That was what Kantor was doing when he tried to comprehend what was happening on his street. Black cars, no police markings but lots of radio antennas, stopped in front of houses. Pairs of men in dark suits rang doorbells and went inside. At one thirty in the morning, at two. Not all the houses, just a few. And then people came out their doors, neighbors, some people he knew well, some he barely recognized. And with them were other people, families it seemed—people Kantor did not recognize. They were led to the sidewalk and placed in clusters, standing there until a yellow Peabody school bus appeared and rolled slowly down the street, stopping at each cluster for the people to get on board, then rolling on to the next group of people, where they, too, got on.

All in silence, all without Kantor hearing a word spoken. All up and down quiet Endicott Drive. Kantor was stunned and could not figure out what was happening or even whether he was so sleep-deprived that he was hallucinating.

Then he understood which houses the men were going to, which people were being led to the yellow bus. "They're rounding up Jews," Kantor said out loud. "They are skipping the Christian houses. They are rounding up Jews. They're arresting all the Jews in Peabody . . . I'm next."

He looked out the window. A black SUV stopped in front of his house. Two men got out and walked toward his door.

Am I hallucinating? Is this real? he thought.

POUND POUND POUND.

It sounded like a hammer on his front door. Kantor stood. Looked around frantically. He looked at the window. *Should I jump out and run away?* The window led to the garage roof. He took a step toward the window and stopped.

POUND POUND POUND.

If they're waiting in front, they'll be waiting in the back. He looked toward the hallway door, half expecting two men to walk into the bedroom.

Then Kantor's eyes slowly moved toward the bedroom closet, where his carefully pressed suits and polished black shoes were lined up. The bedroom closet where he kept his gun.

Kantor's legs buckled as he realized there was no gun in the closet. The gun was on his kitchen table.

POUND POUND POUND.

Kantor raced from the bedroom and down the stairs, almost

falling over his feet as he hit the bottom landing and turned toward the kitchen, running inside his own house faster than he had since the day he and Elaine moved in. He heard a jiggling, clinking sound from the door jimmy the men used to force the lock as he reached the kitchen and snatched the Bushmaster from the table, reaching forward to slam the fifteen-round ammunition clip home.

He turned and faced the front door as FBI agents William Moriarty and Angelo Ansella threw the door open and walked slowly into the dark entryway.

"Is anybody home," Moriarty yelled. "Is Jonathan Kantor here?"

They know my name, Kantor thought.

Kantor did not wait for the two men to see him walking from the kitchen into the front hallway. As soon as he saw the men, Kantor raised the rifle, jerked the trigger again and again and again until the two men lay on the floor, motionless.

Then Kantor sat in his living room and waited for the other men, the ones he knew would still come to round up Jews.

Fifteen minutes later, tear gas canisters crashed through windows from all sides of his house. Kantor ran out the back door, firing the Bushmaster without aiming until he ran out of ammunition. He was lifting it over his head to demonstrate that it was empty when bullets from three sharpshooters' rifles pulverized his skull.

Kantor had time for one last thought.

It should have been me.

CHAPTER 18

Monhegan Island appeared as a blur on the horizon as the fog lifted and the boat sailed on the morning breeze. Levi and Reuben had spent hours debating where to make their landfall. There hadn't been a whole lot to talk about on the three-week nonstop sail from Jost van Dyke to Maine. When the wind increased, the boat sailed faster. When the wind slowed, the boat slowed. Levi was scrupulous about not using the engine, saving what little diesel fuel the boat had on board.

With one exception, the weather had been favorable—generally soft winds, increasing during the day, lessening at night. Once in a while, the wind disappeared entirely and the boat flopped from side to side, motionless, making no forward progress at all. When that happened, they waited, as sailors have waited for the wind to return for thousands of years. And as it did for thousands of years, the wind always returned and their forward journey resumed.

Once, however, Reuben yelled to waken Levi, who was sleeping in the main cabin. A black line of cloud squatted on the horizon directly in front of the boat, barely visible at first as nothing more than a pencil line where sky and water met. The cloud raced toward the boat, flashes of lightning visible within its mass, illuminating it from within.

"Quick, get the sails down."

Reuben rolled the jib, the big sail in the front of the boat, and tied it down. Levi dropped the other two sails and wrapped ropes around them.

"That's the best we can do for now," Levi said. "Now we go inside and wait it out. We are going to bounce around a lot."

The black clouds brought what sailors called a line squall— fierce winds that went from almost calm to near hurricane force in seconds, churning the water into short, steep waves that washed over the boat from all sides at once. Levi and Reuben were snug in the cabin, holding onto whatever handholds were available. It was terrifying at first, but after fifteen minutes of feeling as if they were inside a washing machine on spin cycle, it became obvious they were not going to die and they both sat in silence, side by side on the bench seat, holding on and waiting for the storm to pass, Levi's arm around Reuben's shoulder, offering what protection he could.

Something on deck rattled ominously after a wave crashed on top of the cabin. Another wave and the rattling became a deep thump sounding as if it were trying to crash through the roof under which Levi and Reuben huddled. Another wave. The thump was louder still. Reuben watched the blood drain from Levi's face.

"I've got to go out and see what that is," Levi said, putting on foul weather gear, waterproof bibbed overalls, and a jacket with seals at the neck and wrists. He opened the cabin door and stuck his head into the cockpit, only to be drenched by a wave breaking entirely over the boat. He pushed through it, thumped to a seat in the cockpit, glanced forward at the top of the cabin, then poked his head down into the cabin.

"Not too bad," he told Reuben, who was curled on the cabin floor, wondering now whether she really would survive this voyage. "The life raft is loose. Waves must have broken the bracket holding it to the deck. I'll cut it free and carry it inside. Hand me that big knife, will you, and the vise-grip pliers from the tool box."

Minutes later the cabin door flung open, letting in a spray of water. Levi entered carrying a white fiberglass canister, three feet by two feet, obviously quite heavy.

"Here is the raft," he said. "I hope we won't need it. I'll find a place to store it where it will be out of the way."

Levi carried the heavy canister into the boat's forward cabin, where there was a V-shaped berth Reuben usually slept in. He pushed the canister as far forward on the berth as it would fit, right up into the pointy front end of the sailboat.

"You'll have to sleep with your legs bent," he said, smiling, then added, "or you could sleep with me in the main cabin."

The storm blew itself out as quickly as it arrived, and within the next hour the sails were back up and the boat continued its northerly course. Levi and Reuben resumed their debate about where in America they should make their landfall.

"Right into New York Harbor," Reuben said. "Then we tie up or dock or anchor or whatever it is that boats do when they get to the land. I climb off this stinking thing and never get on another boat for as long as I live. I can't say I know what I'll do when I get to shore, but whatever, it will be better than this. I've had it with this fucking boat. Goodbye ocean."

She was reaching her limit. What had looked luxurious tied to the dock in Spain was taking on the feel of a damp pup tent. Worst of all was the constant movement. Reuben expected the rocking to continue for days after she reached shore. The storm had terrified her more than she wanted Levi to know.

"No, not New York. Not a city," Levi responded. "Someplace small. Someplace where nobody is looking out for anything. Someplace where the government is not on watch for terrorists sailing in with a bomb on their boat."

Levi's knowledge of American geography was a bizarre mix of what he'd figured out from hearing stories about the hometowns of American tourists in Israel, what he'd seen in American movies, and what he'd studied in the few books left on board the sailboat, including *The Cruising Guide to the New England Coast*. That book, the classic bible for Yankee sailors entering new ports, described useful details of every cove, marina, harbor and island from New York to the Canadian border.

"I want a place with no Coast Guard station, no military base, with no police department, if there is such a place in America," he said. "I want us to sail in as if we're stopping by for lunch, a loving, sailing couple on vacation on their beautiful sailboat. I want someplace with lots of other sailboats, lots of other couples on sailboats, where we are just like everybody else, nothing special about us. Who goes to New York City in a sailboat?" Levi asked. "You grew up there. Does anybody sail into New York City harbor?"

"Well, nobody I knew actually sailed into the city. That was what the Long Island Rail Road and the Long Island Expressway were for. People kept their sailboats at yacht clubs, on the sound, Long Island Sound," Reuben answered. "But cruise ships go there, and ferry boats. Maybe no sailboats, though."

She paused, thinking.

"Okay," she continued. "I see your point. We'll sail this boat where other sailboats go, and I agree it should be somewhere quiet and out of the way. We don't want anybody snooping around this boat."

The *Cruising Guide* was open in Levi's lap. "Not New York. We are sailing to Brooklin," he announced.

Levi was shocked at Reuben's reaction. She cracked up, literally falling out of her seat in the boat's cockpit and rolling on the cockpit floor, laughing so hard she gasped for breath.

"Brooklyn?" she shouted at last. "Brooklyn? You don't want to go to New York, so you go to Brooklyn instead? I've got to get off this boat before I get as crazy as you are.

"For your information, Captain or Lieutenant or whatever you claim to be, Brooklyn is part of New York, one of the five boroughs of New York. Brooklyn is where my bubba, my grandmother, lives right now. Great plan, oh fearless Sabra. A couple of Jews try to sneak oh so quietly into the United States, which has ringed its coast with the Navy, with the Air Force, with the Coast Guard and probably with Boy Scouts in kayaks. All looking out for bad guys trying to sneak in and do bad things in America. And where does the great Jewish warrior decide we should go? To Brooklyn, New York, the same place in America where a million other Jews went from Poland and Russia and who knows where."

Levi stared at her. She couldn't stop mocking him.

"They have the best bagels there, you know. And knishes. We'll step off the boat and ask the first cop we see where the best potato knishes are sold. Maybe I'll ask him in Yiddish, so we'll blend better. That's what you want us to do, isn't it, to blend? Right, we'll blend in Brooklyn."

"Are you finished," Levi said. He turned the book in his lap toward Reuben. "Not Brooklyn, New York. Brooklin, Maine. Population eight hundred and forty-one. And, I'll bet, not a single Jew among them."

■ ■ ■

The week after the storm provided pleasant, straightforward sailing under clear skies. Levi glanced at the glowing GPS screen showing a map of the Maine coast with a blinking dot next to an elongated island. Monhegan Island, their destination, was dead ahead. He looked over the boat's bow at the lighthouse on the island's southern shore.

"You know," Reuben said, staring at the rocky island covered in pine trees, a few scattered rooftops showing, "I think I went there on vacation with my family when I was a kid. I thought it was way out in the middle of nowhere. I never thought I'd be so happy to see it again. I am so sick of this boat and so sick of this ocean. And so sick of—"

"Don't say it," Levi interrupted. "I'll admit I can be difficult to live with, and I'll admit, too, that you are the first woman I've lived with for more than a month but—"

"You asshole," she shouted. "Don't you dare call what we've been through *living together*. You damn well better get your head clear; our Ken and Barbie days are over. We'd better get real serious real quick or we are going to spend the rest of our lives looking back fondly on this little sea voyage as we make license plates or break rocks or whatever it is they do in federal prisons."

"I know all that. But, Debra . . . before it all changes, I want to tell you how much I respect you for what you are doing. I admit that you give a first impression like a Jewish-American princess, and I've seen my share of that form of royalty, but you know that I know what you did."

Levi saw the dark cloud cross Reuben's face, although he didn't know whether it was the precursor to anger or tears. He quickly corrected himself.

"I mean, what you had to do before you left Israel. I was just trying to tell you that deep down, you are one of the toughest Jews I've ever come across, and I've seen some pretty tough Jews in Eretz Yisrael."

She just nodded at him, perhaps in thanks.

"Time for some real navigation," Levi said, trying to hide any hint of nervousness from his voice. He guided the boat down a wide bay between pine-covered islands, surrounded by other sailboats, fishing boats, lobster boats and scattered ferries. The GPS directed them toward their destination.

The boat rounded the lighthouse at the western end of the oddly-named Eggemoggin Reach. Levi steered down the center of the long, narrow channel, heading for the middle of the Deer Isle Bridge, with the town of Brooklin a few miles beyond.

"Okay," Levi said. "We will be there in an hour. Remember, we are a lovely couple on vacation on our lovely sailboat. Use your best American when you talk to people. I'll get us there. But once we get there, you are in charge. I assume, although you sure have not told me, that you've got this all planned out for after we arrive. You know what we are going to do, right? I expect that you have it all arranged for people to meet us and hide us and take care of us, right?

So, isn't it about time you let me know the plans?"

Levi looked at Reuben expectantly. She shook her head.

"To be perfectly honest with you, I don't have a clue what we are going to do. I'll be goddamned happy to be home in America. Maybe I'll call my mother and tell her I'm alive. Maybe I'll forget about being the warrior queen of Israel and find some nice doctor to marry and move to Long Island and have a couple of kids. Maybe I'll take you to McDonald's. Maybe we'll just, as you say, blend, maybe forever, maybe nice and quiet and blending will be what I do from now on. I'm so tired of excitement. All I know is that I want to get off this boat in the United States of America."

Levi was silent, staring at the coast, at the huge summer cottages on the shore they sailed past, eyes on the sails, trimming them in and out as needed. After ten or so minutes of silence, while he struggled to come to terms with the realization that she had no secret plans for what they would do next, he looked into Debra Reuben's eyes.

"Go ahead and rest, Debra. Eat your McDonald's. But do not forget who we are. Do not forget what we left behind us. Do not forget a million dead Jews behind us. And, Debra, you want to blend? You want no excitement? Do not forget what is sitting inside that water tank, what you have been living with and I've been sleeping on. We can make more excitement than this country has ever seen, Debra. We have serious decisions to make, responsibilities. Debra, your family is here. I have no family."

Levi paused, eyes closed.

"My family *was* there. You may be able to forget. I want to remember."

In all their weeks alone together, Levi never mentioned having family in Israel. Reuben felt terrible to realize that she hadn't ever thought to ask. He was right, she knew. She had responsibilities—to herself, to a million dead Jews, to the Land of Israel, to history. It was her responsibility, she knew, because history had, for some bizarre reason, given it to her. She also knew that she already had a place in history—a place called Damascus.

"You're right. We have responsibilities," she said. "And I agree. We blend, that's our first job. Inconspicuous. Don't stand out. Let's enter America. And once we get there, we'll figure out what happens next."

The GPS indicated less than a mile to the harbor at Brooklin. Levi spotted a dozen sailboats swinging at moorings ahead and to the left. He dropped the sails, rolled them neatly over the boom and started the engine to motor into the harbor.

Inconspicuous, he thought. *Don't stand out.*

The modern fiberglass sailboat puttered into Brooklin Harbor and anchored in the middle of the fleet of classic, white-painted wooden boats moored in front of a dock with a large sign declaring, *Brooklin, Maine, home of WoodenBoat Magazine.*

CHAPTER 19

Ben Shapiro listened to WBUR, one of Boston's two National Public Radio stations, as he drove to his office wondering for the hundredth time why he bothered to pay for the upgraded sound system in his car when all he ever listened to was either news or talk stations. Mention of Boston on the national news broadcast caught his attention.

"President Quaid said he regrets having to take this action against American citizens in the Boston area," the announcer reported. "Nonetheless, he said at last night's midnight news conference that he refused to stand idly by while a virtual insurrection took place in New England that resulted in the deaths of ten American military personnel, and two additional federal officers last night.

"Those taken into custody in last night's roundup included approximately seventeen hundred American citizens who harbored refugees from the two ships in Boston harbor, and an additional thirty-two hundred persons who fled the ships. Tragically, two federal agents were murdered last night when a man being arrested resisted and opened fire. The man was killed by the FBI. The names of the victims are being withheld.

"President Quaid said there are at least a thousand people from the two ships still at large. He said a manhunt on an unprecedented scale is in effect for those people and anybody harboring them."

Shapiro was so distracted by this news that he swerved into the adjacent lane, correcting himself quickly.

"The president said he expects arrests to continue for the next few days. The midnight press conference was called with only thirty minutes' notice as word of the roundup spread through the Internet. The president said he expects to make further announcements during the day today."

Shapiro turned down the volume on the radio and dialed his office. He first left voicemail messages for his partners telling them he'd be tied up at least all morning and didn't know if he would be at the office at all. They would have to tap-dance him out of a ten o'clock deposition in an age discrimination case, call opposing counsel to reschedule. He wouldn't be making friends by doing that, but Shapiro sensed where his priorities would be today, and for many following days.

Next, Shapiro dialed Aaron Hocksber. Hocksberg was an attorney with a large Boston firm known as much for its political connections and lucrative public-bond-offering representation as it was for the opulence of its new offices on the continually developing South Boston waterfront. Hocksberg was the fundraising chair for the Anti-Defamation League. He and Shapiro had served in the district attorney's office together. While they weren't close friends—moving in decidedly different legal circles in their careers— they got together for lunch every few months.

Hocksberg had recently urged Shapiro to take more of a role—actually, to take any role at all—in the ADL. Shapiro begged off, claiming that his involvement with the ACLU took up all the time he was willing to devote to such cases, which usually took on lives of their own, lives that went largely uncompensated. If anybody was wired into this whole refugee business, Shapiro knew it would be Aaron Hocksberg.

Rose Hocksberg, Aaron's wife, answered the phone on the first ring.

"Hello, Rose, this is Ben Shapiro. Sorry to call you so early, but I need to speak with Aaron. Has he left for work yet?" Shapiro said into his car's speakerphone.

"Oh, Ben, I've been trying to reach Aaron's law partners all night but the phone was broken and it just started working a few minutes ago." Her voice, while not quite hysterical, was well down that road. "Ben, you have to help us. They took Aaron away last night. Two men came and took him. I don't know where he is. I haven't heard from him, and it's been hours and the phone hasn't worked all night."

"Calm down, Rose. Who took Aaron? Did they say who they were?" Shapiro asked calmly.

"They wore suits. They had some legal papers. They knew his name. They knew my name. They took those Israeli people who were in the boys' room. They left me and our girls at home. And the phone has been dead all night. I didn't know what to do. Will you find Aaron and get him back to me, please, Ben?"

"I'll do everything I can, Rose, I promise," Shapiro said. "Stay home. I'll call as soon as I know anything. Stay in the house. I promise I'll call."

Shapiro pressed the steering wheel button that terminated the call. He had not expected to get his first new client that quickly.

■ ■ ■

Ben Shapiro also had not expected to have so much difficulty locating his new client, Aaron Hocksberg. He got nowhere with state authorities, calling district attorneys' offices for counties around Boston. All he'd learned was that whatever happened the prior night in the suburbs north of Boston, it was entirely federal. No state prosecutors involved.

At nine thirty in the morning, nobody who was anybody at

the United States Attorneys Boston office was there. They were, he was told, universally "unavailable," probably meaning the entire crew was awake through the night and were all home sleeping.

"I don't think any of the assistants are in yet," the phone receptionist said. "Oh, wait just a second."

The voice on the phone became muffled. Shapiro could barely make out what was said.

The secretary came back on the line.

"Assistant United States Attorney Judith Katz just came in. She said she can speak with you. I'll put her right on."

Shapiro had never met Judy Katz, although he'd read about her in the newspapers. Shapiro intentionally avoided representing the kind of persons Katz was building a career prosecuting. Nonetheless, Shapiro expected Katz had heard about him.

"Mr. Shapiro, this is Judy Katz. How can I help you?"

"Ben, call me Ben, please, Judy," Shapiro said, trying to balance between sounding firm, sounding friendly, and sounding like a "senior" member of the bar due some deference by a young Assistant US Attorney. "Judy, I have a client who was taken into custody last night by federal agents for some unknown reason and I'm trying to locate him and return him to his moderately hysterical wife. Do you suppose you could punch his name into whatever computer system you folks have for locating missing arrestees? I'd greatly appreciate it."

"You've reached the wrong person. I'm just about the only one around the office right now, and I'm also probably just about the only one in the office who has absolutely no idea about what seems to have happened last night." The exasperation in Katz's voice was obvious. "Um, maybe you could tell me what you know about it. I went to bed early last night, worked at home for a few hours this morning and just walked in the door here myself, and half the support staff and almost all the attorneys are not around. I'm sort of wandering around right now."

Judy Katz had a strong suspicion that whatever was keeping people away from the office had something to do with the Queen's visit the previous day.

"Judy, I'll be blunt with you," Shapiro said into the telephone. "I've been retained by Aaron Hocksberg. Do you know him, from Rudnick, Fierstein? No? Well, actually by his wife. It seems he was arrested last night, or at least that he was taken into custody."

"What makes you think my office has anything to do with it?" Katz asked. "Do you know what he was charged with?"

"Well, Judy, I suspect that he was part of that thing last night, that roundup thing that is all over the news," Shapiro said.

Katz was puzzled.

"I don't know what you're talking about, Ben. I haven't listened to the news today."

"Judy, my understanding is that the Department of Justice took hundreds of people into custody last night from homes all around communities north of Boston. My further understanding, from what his wife told me, is that Attorney Aaron Hocksberg is among those taken into custody. I've been trying to locate him all morning. Obviously he's being held somewhere, but everybody who is around this morning knows nothing about it, and the people who do know, people I expect work in your office, are, I'm told, universally unavailable.

"I have to tell you, Judy, that I am having considerable difficulty believing that somebody who is the head of a criminal division in the US Attorneys office is totally unaware of a major criminal operation conducted by that office."

He waited for a reaction. Hearing none, he continued.

"Look, Ms. Katz, I realize we've never had a case against one another before, but as you know, Boston is an extremely small town and what goes round in the legal community comes round someday. I don't take well to being fed a bowl of bullshit by another attorney. I have a client to represent and I want to know where he is, right now."

"Look yourself, Mr. Shapiro. I am not feeding you bullshit, or feeding you anything at all. You seem to know a lot more than I do about what might or might not have gone on last night. I don't know anything about any sort of roundup of criminals by my office, and I can assure you that as the head of the Organized Crime Strike Force in the office of the United States Attorney, I would have been told about any such major operation."

She decided to try the silent treatment herself, but after hardly more than a moment she relented, feeling guilty that her first conversation with a lawyer she respected, from a distance, had gone badly so quickly.

"Ben, really and truly, I don't know anything about what you're speaking about. Tell me what you know."

"Okay, Judy, I'll accept what you're saying, although I've gotta tell you, I'm surprised." Shapiro's tone, too, was conciliatory. He didn't enjoy hearing himself speaking sternly to a young lawyer, especially a young woman lawyer. "Judy, I didn't say there was a roundup of criminals last night."

"Well, if they weren't criminals, Ben, who were they? Who else but criminals would be rounded up by the government?"

"I'm shocked that you, you of all people at that office, don't know about this. And, come to think of it, the fact that you don't know anything about this is damned frightening to me."

"Enough, Ben," Katz interrupted. "Tell me, if we didn't arrest criminals, who did we arrest?"

"Jews, Judy, Jews. It's all over the news. Hundreds, actually thousands of Jews were taken into custody last night and are being held. Not criminals. Jews were arrested."

Shapiro's words were beyond comprehension, as if he spoke in Swahili. Then Judy remembered her odd lunch the day before.

"Oh my God, Ben," she said, looking around her nearly empty office. It suddenly dawned on her that the man she was speaking with was himself a Jew and a civil rights lawyer. "Ben, I think it's time we met. Can I come by your office sometime soon? No, come to think of it, I'd rather not meet at your office, just in case. Can we casually just happen to both have lunch around noon tomorrow? I have something to talk about with you. Okay?"

"Sure, Judy. Meet me at the Sultan's. Do you know that place?"

"I've heard of it. See you there."

CHAPTER 20

President Quaid showed his agitation as Attorney General McQueeney and two deputy attorneys general walked into the Oval Office. Quaid gestured for them to sit. He remained standing, glowering, hands on his hips as he looked down at McQueeney. She was exhausted. Awake all night through the arrests, she'd flown to Washington at dawn when summoned by the president for a nine o'clock meeting.

"Dammit, Queen. What the fuck happened out there? How the hell did those agents let themselves get killed like that? Aren't they trained better than to walk through a door at two in the morning without even carrying their weapons? Whose fucked up idea was it that the agents wouldn't carry weapons? I want that guy's head."

"Well, that guy was me," McQueeney said. "And as you know, Mr. President, I offered you my head, and my job, before this operation even started. I wanted nothing to do with it. You gave me no choice, sir."

"You know better than that," President Quaid barked. "When I give you a job to do, your job is to do it, and do it right. Right now I've got two dead FBI agents to add to the body count from the dead Coasties. This is starting to look like a brand-new Boston Massacre up there, and we're the ones getting massacred. My problem right now is the muttering I'm hearing about who is doing the killings. I don't like it one bit. I don't like what I'm hearing."

"The bigger problem we've got, sir, is that we took almost five thousand people into custody last night and we have no way to handle them. This whole thing was put together in such a rush, and in so much secrecy, that we didn't have time to think through the details, sir, details such as are we going to hold all these people or release them on bail? The Boston people we can take care of; they won't go anywhere if we let them out on bail. But all those people off the boats, they have nobody here, nothing to their names. They can't afford to hire lawyers, and there aren't enough lawyers in Boston to appoint to represent them all—not ones who know what they're doing in a case like this."

"Dammit, Queen, don't bother me with details. Figure it out."

"What are we going to do with these people? They're families mostly, husbands, wives, children. Do we separate the husbands and wives in detention, or do we leave them together? If we separate them, what happens to their children? The Massachusetts Department of Social Services head just laughed when I asked her if she could take custody of nine hundred kids tomorrow. What are we going to do with these people? If we book them and release them, you know we'll never see these people again. And, Mr. President, don't you dare suggest we put the children in cages like you-know-who did with other refugee kids."

Quaid was taken aback by that.

"We don't release the Israelis, Queen," the president said. "What kind of fool would I look like going to all that trouble, and losing two FBI agents? We go through all that to round these people up, only to let them loose the next day. They'd disappear on us for sure. I'd look like a horse's ass for sure, now wouldn't I? Queen, you are going to hold onto those people—grandparents, parents, children and Chihuahuas—until we find someplace to put them. Do you understand?"

"Sir, Mr. President, with all due respect, how are we going to charge these people? I certainly appreciate that there are dead coastguardsmen and two federal agents. The district attorney in Boston is holding a guy from the ships in the county jail. They got him because he swam to the wrong shore and into the hands of the Boston cops. The DA's charged the guy with ten counts of first-degree murder.

"There is nothing that makes him any different from the other people we rounded up. If the state charges him with conspiracy to murder, then they all are murderers. If we let everybody else go, then I'm going to be faced with one angry district attorney whose murder case will go down the tubes." McQueeney glared at the president. "Please, sir, don't ask me to charge five thousand people with murder and expect those charges to stick. That just isn't going to happen."

The two deputy attorneys general who'd accompanied their boss to the Oval Office watched silently, their heads turning in unison from one speaker to the other, like front row spectators at the Olympic ping pong finals.

"Nobody from the ships gets turned loose, Queen," President Quaid said sternly, standing directly in front of the seated attorney general, his legs spread apart, his hands on his hips. His initial frenzy had subsided almost to a monotone.

McQueeney was undeterred. "We're holding these people at a basketball stadium at Boston University, and we have that only because the stadium was built on the location of a former National Guard armory and somebody inserted some bizarre language into the purchase agreement that the government can preempt any other use of the stadium in a time of national emergency. So we're holding five thousand people in a basketball stadium for today.

"But that won't last long. The TV crews are having a field day there, interviewing Jewish grandmothers who came off that ship, spent a few days in suburban land visiting shopping malls, and now find themselves crammed into a domed stadium wondering if they are going to be shipped off to Syrian concentration camps. It's going to make great copy. Remember Katrina and the Superdome? Think Jewish instead of black. That's tonight's news, sir."

Before President Quaid could reply the telephone on his desk rang.

"Good, send him in," he said. "Grant Farrell is here. I woke him this morning with the news of the roundup last night, and I asked him to spend the morning speaking with folks on the Hill. I want to hear what he has to say."

Grant Farrell, Democratic minority leader of the Senate, entered. He did not look pleased.

"Mr. President, Madam Attorney General."

"So, how are folks taking the latest news, Grant?" the president asked.

"Not well, sir, not well at all. Each and every senator I spoke with this morning—and I got to people on both sides of the aisle, Mr. President—the first thing every single person said was about the two dead agents, not about what a good job we did rounding people up, not about what a difficult decision this must have been, not even, as I would have expected, some song and dance about civil rights after we dragged a thousand citizens from their beds and hauled them off. No sir, it was all about the dead agents."

The president glared at his attorney general.

"Let me tell you what Senator Jackwell said; you know, Jake Jackwell, Wisconsin, as screamer of a liberal as we've got on board. Well, Jake dragged me off to the side of the senators' locker room this morning when I was only halfway into my workout gear and said—here's as good a quote as I can give you, sir, and these are his words, not mine—he said the score seems to be Jews twelve, Americans zero. Then he asked me, when do we start to even things up?"

The president, staring at his feet, listening, raised his head.

"Jake Jackwell did not say that, did he, Grant?"

"Those are as close as I can get to his words, sir. Losing those FBI agents last night has people awfully angry. It's as if we're being gunned down by foreigners who came to our country armed and ready for a fight, and all we're doing is threatening to give them speeding tickets. People are angry, Mr. President. There are two more bodies to be buried. That makes two heavy media events we've got to get through. What are you going to do, Mr. President?"

Before President Quaid could answer, McQueeney spoke.

"That's not fair, Senator, nor is it accurate. Those FBI agents were shot by a US citizen, by a man who thought he was defending his home from what to him could have looked like a break-in in the middle of the night. There were no armed foreigners involved in that shooting. At least get your facts right."

"Stop thinking like a lawyer, Queen," Quaid said. "You're letting the facts get in the way. I'm afraid, Queen, that Jake Jackwell is closer to the general public than we are on this one. He doesn't see any difference between the foreign citizens on those two boats and the US citizens who got them off the boats, at least not when it comes to taking shots at US agents."

"With all due respect, sir," McQueeney retorted, "he's wrong then."

"No, he's not wrong, Queen," the president answered, making no effort to conceal his impatience with the attorney general. "That guy, whatever his name is, who killed the agents is going to be viewed as much as a foreign agent as the people from the boats. Those new deaths make even the US citizens involved seem like . . . somebody give me some sort of legal term to use, like . . ."

"Enemy combatants, sir. That's what they all are. Enemy combatants, if I may, sir," interjected one of the two deputy attorneys general.

"Enemy combatant? Does that have some specific legal meaning?" Quaid asked.

"Enemy combatant has a very specific meaning, Mr. President," the deputy said, seeming to gain confidence with each word. "The Al Qaida detainees at Guantanamo Bay were classified as enemy combatants. That shoe bomber who tried to blow up a flight from London to Boston was called an enemy combatant. The Supreme Court said even US citizens could be labeled enemy combatants. It didn't matter where they came from, citizen or not. They all got the same label: enemy combatant."

He looked at his boss, seeking approval to continue. McQueeney sat motionless, exhausted, ignoring him, ignoring the president. The deputy continued.

"Legally, Mr. President, you have the power to label anybody an enemy combatant and no court in the land has jurisdiction to hear any challenge to that designation by you, sir. No judge has the power to hear or decide any case brought by an enemy combatant, thanks to our wise Congress."

"How can that be?" Quaid asked.

"Mr. President, the defense appropriation act of 2005 stripped the federal courts of jurisdiction to hear any legal proceeding, including an application for a writ of habeas corpus, brought by any enemy combatant detained by this country at the Navy base at Guantanamo Bay, Cuba.

"A few years later, after some clever lawyers were able to file their habeas petitions within hours of their clients being taken into custody in Afghanistan, before they actually arrived at Gitmo, Congress extended that stripping of court jurisdiction to all cases brought by all persons declared by the president to be enemy combatants. Once you put that label on him, whether he is an Afghan bomb thrower or a Cleveland Boy Scout, he lives outside the laws of the United States of America. He has no rights, or, more accurately, he has all the rights every American has, but he has nowhere to go to enforce any violations of those rights. Congress shut the courthouse doors to everybody who you, Mr. President, declare to be an enemy combatant."

The President glanced at McQueeney, waiting for her to contradict what the deputy just said. She said nothing.

"Okay," President Quaid said. "I've got the picture. Queen, I hear what you are saying. Young man, thank you for your legal insight. Grant, let's talk later this afternoon. Keep speaking with people, then give me a call. Me, I have some serious thinking to do. For now, Queen, keep those people fed and comfortable. See what you can come up with for them. And try to keep the news media away from them. I'll talk with you first thing tomorrow morning."

After the Oval Office cleared out, the president asked his assistant to locate the First Lady.

Catherine, my love. Don't abandon me now, of all times. I need you more than ever right now, here with me, Quaid thought. *And Catherine, maybe you ought to bring that bright son of a bitch Bobby Brown back here, too.*

CHAPTER 21

Debra Reuben spoke sweetly into the telephone, shivering in the damp air, using the pay phone outside the Brooklin, Maine, post office. She'd almost forgotten what it was like to speak to another adult; it had been so long since she'd spoken with anybody but Levi, the Mossad men in Spain or the hard-eyed soldiers in the desert at Dimona, putting aside that little incident at Jost van Dyke.

"Sarah, this is Debbie, Debbie Reuben. I know it's been a while . . ." Reuben tried not to sound too desperate. Sarah Goldberg, now Sarah Goldberg-Goldhersh, was Reuben's sorority sister at Delta Phi Epsilon at Syracuse University. They stayed close for several years after graduation but drifted apart when Sarah became involved with Abram Goldhersh. He'd dragged her, reluctantly at first, then deeper and deeper, into right-wing Jewish politics. Goldhersh was a supporter of Amana, the West Bank settlement movement in Israel. He'd helped found a settlement on the Golan Heights itself but was delegated to return to the US where he was born, to recruit and fundraise. Reuben kept abreast of her friend's exploits, but only remotely over websites.

Sarah and Abram were carried on the payroll of Abram's uncle's jewelry business in Portland, Maine, but few employees there would have recognized them. They crisscrossed the country raising money for the movement. Sometimes, they purchased supplies that not even the government of Israel was anxious for the settlers to have.

Goldhersh became skilled at negotiating the clandestine weapons markets in towns outside American military bases—places where soldiers could make beer money, and more, by smuggling items off the bases. That was one of the other reasons he'd returned to Portland. It was an old seaport. Not too large, not too small. International freighters called regularly, delivering containers from around the world, leaving with containers of American goods. Once in a while, a freighter left for the eastern Mediterranean and Goldhersh could ship a cargo container with "farm supplies" for his former settlement on the Golan. Goldhersh also had access to warehouse space along Portland's waterfront.

Homeland Security monitored shipping containers entering American ports, but who cared what was shipped out of the country?

Sarah knew most of what her husband did. More often than not, she joined him on his cross-country shopping trips. As they were more and more successful in purchasing such "surplus" military equipment, they cut ties to people outside the movement, partly for security reasons but mostly because they had little time for anything but their work. Debra Reuben had only an inkling of what her former roommate and her husband were doing. They had not spoken in half a dozen years.

On the telephone, Sarah was cold at first; then an incredulous tone came into her voice.

"Debbie," she said. "I thought you were in Israel, that you moved there, lived there permanently. I've been wondering about you, and, of course, about all the other poor Israelis we knew, but I really have been wondering whether you were okay. Debbie, you did live in Tel Aviv, didn't you? To tell you the truth,

I assumed you were dead. I've included you in my prayers. I said your name when I lit the candles. Debbie, it's nice, nice to hear your voice."

"Sarah, it's nice to hear your voice, too. You can't imagine how nice it is to hear a familiar voice. And yes, I am alive. It's a long story, a very, very long story. I can tell you most of it but not all of it. Yes, I was in Israel. I was there pretty recently, when the, you know, thing happened. And, obviously, I did escape. But there is so much more to it than that. Sarah, I'm in Maine. I looked at a map. I'm on the coast north of Portland by probably a few hours' drive.

"Sarah, I know it's asking a lot and I know I am the one who stopped calling you, but, Sarah, this is so important. Could you possibly drive up to where I am? I don't have a car. I don't really have a place to stay. Please come, and I'd like it if Abram could come, too. I'm in a small town called, of all things, Brooklin, near Blue Hill. Do you have any idea where it is?"

"I know where it is, Debbie. Abram and I attended a fundraiser at somebody's vacation house there. It was somebody important. Not the kind of somebody you'd expect to find in a little town like that in Maine, but you'd be surprised who vacations around here sometimes."

"Sarah, what I have to discuss is important too."

"Look, I'd like to see you, but Abram and I are very busy with what's going on in Boston. They're rounding up our people and jailing them like war criminals. It's frightening. I never thought I'd see this in the United States."

"Sounds horrible, but this is important for our cause and our people. Please, just trust me."

Sarah told Reuben to hold on so that she could consult with her husband. A couple minutes later she said they would make the drive.

"Debbie, swear to me that you're not a government agent. Swear to me this isn't some sort of setup."

"I swea, Sarah. We're on the same side now," Reuben said.

■ ■ ■

Reuben and Levi sat inconspicuously at a corner table at the Brooklin Inn. Both felt disoriented. For one thing, the table was not rocking from side to side, and they had an actual wine list to choose from.

"How we gonna pay for this?" Levi asked.

"No worries," Reuben said. "I have this." She flashed an American Express Card. "And I have these." She opened her purse. At the bottom were gold coins.

"Those aren't shekels," he said.

"Krugerrands," she answered. "Gold coins. Part of the national treasure of Israel, I suppose. There was a box of them back at . . . at that place I left. I took a few just in case."

"How many makes up a few?" Levi asked. "And what are they worth in real money, in dollars?"

"As many as I could stuff into my bag. That's why my duffel was so heavy. As to what they're worth, to tell you the truth, I've got no idea. I expect Abram Goldhersh will be able to tell us what solid gold goes for now, being in the jewelry business and all."

They sat nearly an hour, sipping on wine and apologizing to the waiter. Finally, Sarah and Abram arrived.

Reuben leaped to her feet. Levi rose slowly, hesitating about whether it was proper.

"Sarah. Abram. How wonderful to see you."

"Sorry," Sarah said. "Turns out Brooklin was a bit farther away than I remembered. But here we are."

"Hello, Debbie," Abram said flatly. He never was a great fan of his wife's former college friend—not when Reuben was a TV reporter in New York and not even after she'd moved to Israel. In fact, once she turned up as a member of a coalition Israeli government, a coalition not fully supportive of the settlements in the West Bank, Abram was ashamed to tell friends in the movement that he knew her.

The Goldberg-Goldhershes waited throughout dinner for

any explanation of why they were summoned. In fact, besides introducing Levi as "my friend," Reuben said almost nothing about the man she was obviously closely involved with. Abram puzzled over Levi's accent. His English was excellent, almost good enough to pass as an American, but there were occasional hints that Goldhersh recognized as Israeli.

Sarah, who after two years sharing the same sorority room truly did know Reuben well, could not figure out what the involvement was between Levi and Reuben. They touched, seemingly by accident and only occasionally, but when they did they lingered, if only for the barest hesitation. Sarah guessed, accurately, that Debbie herself did not know where the relationship was or where she wanted it to go.

Mostly, they talked about what happened in Boston, about the ships, the refugees fleeing in the middle of the night, and then about the arrests, thousands of refugees and thousands of American Jews rounded up in the middle of the night and taken into custody.

Reuben was incredulous, not having been privy to the news while at sea.

"Wait a minute, just hold on. Haven't we, I mean hasn't the United States, sent, like relief ships and medical aid and troops and billions of dollars to Israel to help those poor people? I don't understand. Are you trying to tell me America was going to send those ships full of people where? To Palestine—God I hate saying that name—with an Egyptian Navy ship? Honestly, Sarah, I just don't believe it. There has to be more to it than that." Reuben looked at her friend, waiting for an explanation.

Instead, Abram responded.

"You are demonstrating how naive you are, once again. You and that whole government of cowards you got dragged into as a little showpiece. Jews should know better than to count on anybody else to protect them when the tide turns against us," Abram said, speaking in a whisper. "Sure, for a few years or even a few generations they let us blend in, they let us believe everything is different this time. But then something happens, or some crazy leader comes along, and it starts all over again. What do you think was more important to these Americans? What was more important when it came to choosing between sending doctors to treat dying Jews or getting cut off from half the world's oil? Tough choice, right? Not for this country, it seemed."

He looked Reuben straight in the eyes.

"How do you think German Jews felt in 1938 when their neighbors, neighbors who they thought viewed them as good Germans first and as Jews second, stopped talking to them, and then started turning them in? And that was far from the first time. What about the Spanish Jews? The Inquisition ring any bells for you? Don't you think Spanish Jews felt as comfortable, as much a part of their country, as American Jews feel now? Don't you think some Spanish Jewish banker told his wife not to worry, nothing bad can happen to us here?"

Levi interrupted, speaking for the first time after he was introduced.

"What are you talking about in Spain? I was there just two months ago. Nothing happened in Spain with the Jews."

Goldhersh glared.

"I'm talking history. Jewish history. Don't they teach Jewish history in the public schools in Eretz anymore?"

The conversation paused as all four realized they were getting heated and loud. After a few sips of wine, Reuben continued.

"Abram, Spain, Germany, they were abominations, horrible, but certainly they were exceptions," she said. "Jews have been accepted in plenty of countries. England, Holland. France. Okay, I know Russia was bad, Poland, too. But please, Abram, is that what's really happening here in the US?"

Goldhersh started to stand up, throwing his hands over his head, then looked around the restaurant and restrained himself. He sat back down.

"Why don't people study history? How can Jews forget their own history? Where do you think the Spaniards learned about expelling Jews, Debbie? I assume you are not acquainted with the Jewish Expulsion from England in 1290? Well, good King Edward ordered all the sheriffs of England to serve writs on every Jew in the country, and there were plenty of Jews in Jolly Olde England then. Jews were craftsmen, teachers, rabbis, active in government, politics. The writs ordered them to pack up and leave . . . Want to hear a few more dates, Debbie? How about the Expulsion from France in 1182? At that time almost half the property in downtown Paris was owned by Jews. Think they felt secure? Sure they did, about as secure as a Jewish doctor living in Brookline, Massachusetts, does right now."

"Abram, enough, stop it, right now," Sarah barked.

Goldhersh rested his head in his hands.

"How many Jews were turned to dust in Tel Aviv?" he whispered. "Dust. Dust, like in a crematorium. Tell me, Debbie, tell me, Chaim Levi, do you suppose the Jews of Spain, the Jews of England, the Jews of France, the Jews of Germany, those of them that survived, vowed that it would never happen again? How could they not have done so? That is what frightens me more than anything else—that the first words on my lips when I wake, the first words when I go to sleep, are never, never, never again, not here, not now. What frightens me is that no matter what I do, it is going to happen again, like it has always happened before. Why do people think it is impossible here, now, when it has always been possible everywhere else? Why does God do this to his Chosen People? Why?"

Sarah turned to Reuben.

"Debbie, I apologize for Abram. It's been difficult. He's so tired. We're all tired. But, Debbie, you still haven't said a word about why we had to get together. It's your turn. Tell us what is going on with you"—she gestured toward Levi—"with both of you."

"Not just yet," Levi interjected. "We have to be careful. We'll go for a walk after dinner. Then we'll talk. Now, let's eat."

"And drink," Debra said, finishing her rum and coke and

picking up the wine list. "We need two bottles, don't we?"

The rest of the dinner was spent reminiscing about Sarah and Debra's college days and how much their lives had changed since they were sorority sisters. Levi listened patiently. Goldhersh sat silently, simmering.

When the table was cleared, the waiter placed the bill, inside a leather folder, in the geographic center of the table. Abram waited to see if anybody would move first. He cleared his throat and sat motionless. Reuben spoke.

"Abram, we have a little problem about money."

"Ah, now we get to the truth." He smiled at Reuben. "Tell me about your money problem and how much you want from me, Debbie."

"Well, Abram, for reasons that you will soon appreciate, I don't want to use this." She showed him her American Express card from her wallet. "And I have a whole bunch of these, but I don't know what they're worth and I don't think they'll take them here."

She slid open the top of her purse and tilted it toward Goldhersh. His eyes widened. He reached inside and removed one shiny coin, cupping it in his hand so only he could see it. He returned it quickly to the purse, where it made a dull thunk when it slid into other coins.

"A Krugerrand. You don't see them much anymore. They went out of style when Nelson Mandela was released from prison," he said. "What an odd currency to travel with, Debbie. I assume there is a story that goes with that coin, and it sounds as if that coin may have some company."

"Oh, there is certainly a story," Reuben responded. "But for now, tell me, Abram. Is that worth anything? Is there some way to turn it into real money?

"It certainly is worth something, Debbie," Goldhersh said. "I'd have to check where gold is floating today, but I'd say that coin is worth about twelve hundred dollars. And it is gold. Solid gold, South African gold. Gold can always be turned into money.

That is what gold is all about. I can do that for you easily enough. Tell me, Debbie, how many of these do you have?"

"Well, there was a box of them, a pretty big box. I couldn't carry them all, but I took some in a bag. I haven't counted them, but it's awfully heavy, maybe twenty or thirty pounds I'd guess."

"In that case," Abram said, smiling, "I'll spot you for dinner, and I can be generous with the tip."

He paid the bill, in cash, Levi noticed, even though he had a wallet full of credit cards. *A cautious man,* Levi thought, *who does not want to leave a trail. I like that.*

All four pushed their chairs back and stood up.

"Let's take a stroll down by the water," Levi said, taking command of the conversation. "We have a story to tell you."

■ ■ ■

The two couples got into Abram Goldhersh's Nissan Pathfinder and drove to the waterfront area near where the sailboat was anchored. Levi had not decided whether he was ready to tell the Americans about the bomb hidden in the sailboat's water tank. The decision was taken from him when Reuben took his hand, leaned close and whispered in his ear.

"Don't tell them about it," she said. "Not yet. I have more thinking to do first."

Levi nodded.

"That's our boat out there," Levi said, pointing at the Hinckley riding calmly at anchor a hundred yards or so from the shore. "Home sweet home for the two of us."

He placed his arm around Reuben's waist and drew her closer to him, emboldened perhaps by the wine, by her whispering in his ear or just by the expectation that she would not pull away in front of her friends. Levi was surprised when Reuben did not resist but, instead, leaned her head to rest momentarily on his shoulder. *She barely smiles at me when we're living in a box together for two months; now we get on shore and she acts like my girlfriend,* Levi thought. *Well, I like it better this way.*

"Debbie, I can't believe you came all the way from Israel in that tiny boat," Sarah said. "Weren't you frightened to death?"

"Actually, I was surprised at how comfortable it was, once you got used to being stuck in such a small area," Reuben said. "I suppose we were lucky on the weather. Everything was great, until the Bacardi ran out."

"Quite a voyage, all the way from Israel," Abram said.

"We didn't quite sail all the way from Israel," Reuben replied. "We met in Spain."

She told them that Levi was in the Israeli Navy and how he escaped in a naval vessel.

"As for me, I was with the government. Luckily, I was away from Tel Aviv, in the Negev in fact, when the bomb went off. I was with some, well, some military people and they helped me get out of the country. I am the only surviving member of the prime minister's cabinet, which I suppose makes me the highest ranking official of the government of the State of Israel. I suspect there are a lot of people from other governments who would like to question me."

Reuben took a sip of her drink, paused. Goldhersh, looking awestruck and angered, launched into a tirade.

"They sure would like to find you. They haven't found anybody to hold responsible for Damascus, not that I think anybody needs to be held responsible for it. In my mind, whoever did that should receive Israel's highest decoration. My regret is that since Israel had a hundred atom bombs, why did we only use one. Why didn't we blast every Arab village back to the Stone Age where they deserve to be?"

Reuben was frightened to see how little control the huge man had over his anger.

"Debbie, I don't know if you had anything to do with Damascus—after all, I kind of doubt whether the minister for tourism was given the code for launching the missiles or fighters or whatever," Goldhersh continued. "But it seems you're the only person still alive who could be blamed for that decision. You'd better be plain Debbie Reuben, or chose some other name, while we see which way the wind is blowing."

Reuben smiled and nodded.

"We're in agreement on that," she said. "Just being Debbie from Long Island sounds pretty nice to me right now."

"Oh no, no no," Abram started. "That's not what I'm saying at all. This is no time for any Jew, especially an Israeli Jew, to look for rest and quiet. We have serious work to do, perhaps dangerous work, especially after what happened to all those Jews in Boston. I'm not saying to run away. I'm saying be careful, that's all."

"I know, I know," Reuben said. "Forgive me a passing fantasy. That's all that was."

"So," Levi interrupted. "Tell us all about what happened in Boston. And tell us what people, what Jews are doing about it."

"We're organizing a massive demonstration, a march on Washington," Sarah said, unable to hide the excitement in her voice. "We want to get media coverage across the country to shine a light on what our government has done. I'm organizing the Portland contingent."

Reuben recalled how in college Sarah could organize a march on almost anywhere over almost anything in almost no time at all. She had a way with slogans and chants and signs.

Nothing ever came of them, though, Reuben thought.

"And I'm organizing a different kind of demonstration," Goldhersh added. "I have a warehouse full of little items that were waiting for shipment to Israel. I expect we'll find a use right here for all my goodies. Sarah can march and carry the most clever of signs as long as she wants to, but this country's government was the first to use force against Jews. The government can't expect force to be met only with words and songs. After all, we didn't conquer the West Bank with words, except maybe the words of the tank commanders to move forward and fire accurately."

He tapped Levi on the shoulder.

"Lieutenant Levi, I have some things that will get President Quaid's attention. I would not be surprised if other people have attention-getters of their own, would you, Levi?" Goldhersh asked.

"Not in the least, Abram," Levi replied. "Not in the least."

CHAPTER 22

The federal justice system was well on the road to recovering from the overload following the arrest of nearly 5,000 people. The Israelis seized from hundreds of homes were taken to the Agganis Arena at Boston University, an indoor stadium where the BU Terrier hockey and basketball teams played. The stadium had seating for more than 7,000 spectators. With guards posted at all entrances, the detainees were given free run of the confined area.

McQueeney returned to Massachusetts, making her fourth round-trip flight between Boston and Washington in a Justice Department executive jet in three days. She sat at the head of a table in the conference room at the US Attorneys office in the federal courthouse. Seated around the table were Arnold Anderson, the US Attorney for Massachusetts, and his top staffers. Although no one mentioned it, each was aware that their colleague Judy Katz was again not present.

Her absence, and their individual assumptions for why she was not asked to attend, caused varying degrees of embarrassment and anger. Nobody raised the topic that she was Jewish.

"As far as I'm concerned, this situation is out of control,"

McQueeney said, looking around the table. "I hate to use the phrase, but I ordered this whole roundup because I was following orders. I have never, ever spoken badly of my boss, but I feel that I owe a duty to each of you to be as blunt as possible before any of you go any further down this path. My boss gave me no choice. This may shock you, but I am being candid. I offered to resign rather than do what we are doing. The boss wouldn't let me resign—at least, not yet."

There was shocked silence around the table. The Queen continued.

"I don't want any of you to justify what you are about to do by saying you were following my orders. I am not ordering anybody to do anything. Any of you who wants out of this operation can get up and walk out of this room, now, without retribution from me. I was not offered that choice. I'm not the first attorney general ordered to do something she believed was wrong. In 1973, Eliot Richardson, the man who held my job, a man from Massachusetts in fact, was called into the Oval Office. His boss, Richard Nixon, ordered him to fire a fellow named Archibald Cox, a special prosecutor who was investigating Nixon.

"Richardson refused. So he resigned. Nixon then turned to the deputy attorney general, Bill Ruckelshaus, and ordered him to fire Cox. Ruckelshaus resigned, too. Nixon finally found somebody in the chain of command who would do his bidding—Robert Bork. Bork fired Cox and, perhaps not too coincidentally, fourteen years later Ronald Reagan nominated him to the Supreme Court, but I'm sure you know how badly that nomination failed.

"So why this history lesson when we're all so busy? Because I want each of you to know that sometimes the honorable thing, the downright right thing to do is to refuse to follow orders. I can tell you that I am ashamed of myself for not doing what Eliot Richardson did. I've got my reasons—maybe because with nuclear bombs destroying cities and armed attacks on Coast Guard ships in our own harbors we live in a less innocent time. But I can't tell you that what we did was the right thing to do. And I can tell you that what we are about to do is the wrong thing to do."

Again she looked around the table.

"Anybody leaving? Nobody! Well, damn you all then. And damn me. So let's figure out what we're going to do with this mess."

■ ■ ■

Anderson had accepted appointment by President Quaid as US Attorney for Massachusetts because he saw the position as a stepping stone to other, higher state office, such as senator or even governor. He appreciated that despite his basic agreement with the Queen on this issue, ducking out of it would be political suicide. An astute student of Massachusetts politics, Anderson knew that regardless of Eliot Richardson's status as the hero of Nixon's Saturday Night Massacre, Richardson's later effort to be elected US senator from Massachusetts came to a dead end when he was defeated in the Republican primary by a political nobody.

"The big problem, boss, is that about four thousand of the detainees came off those ships. No question they are in this country illegally. The trouble is, we can't deport them back to Israel because, well, there isn't any Israel left to send them to." Here even Anderson was hesitant. "We don't want to turn them over to the Arabs, do we?"

Like everybody else in the room, Anderson had seen clandestine surveillance footage from the refugee camps set up by the Palestinians for those surviving Israelis who failed to escape the invading armies. It was worse, far worse, than Guantanamo Bay. Palestinians were the world's leading authorities on inhumane detention camps, having lived in them for generations.

McQueeney interrupted.

"We're not going to have to worry about those people, the people from the boats. The way the president was talking yesterday, I think he's come up with his own solution for dealing with them. A military solution that won't involve the criminal justice system and therefore won't involve us."

She looked around the table, from face to face.

"What are we going to do with the other ones? The Boston people we're holding? As I was reminded by my boss, more than once, ten Coasties are dead and somebody is going to pay for killing them. Suggestions, anybody?"

"Conspiracy to commit murder," one attorney said.

"Harboring fugitives. Or maybe obstruction of justice?" said another.

"Catch and release," a third suggested. "Just like striped bass. We caught them, we taught them a lesson they won't forget, now we slap their wrists and send them home, that's what I say. We can't charge a thousand people with murder."

McQueeney turned to Anderson.

"Arnie, what do you say?"

"Split the difference," he said, looking for the political compromise. "We've got open-and-shut cases on harboring fugitives. After all, we took those boat people out of each of their houses. Charge them for harboring, let them plead out, and fine them a thousand bucks each. There's nearly a thousand of them. That'll be a million bucks, which will just about cover all the overtime for this whole deal. That's what I say."

McQueeney sat back in her chair, tilted her head to look at the ceiling and stared silently for a minute. The president would not be happy with this solution. *Well then, Quaid can go fuck himself,* she thought. *I'm the chief law enforcement officer of this country. He's commander in chief of the military, not commander of the Justice Department. This is my call, not his.*

Maybe now he'll accept my resignation.

McQueeney leaned forward and looked Anderson in the eyes.

"I like that. Make it happen. Make this all go away."

"Will do, boss," Anderson said. "But this one isn't going to go away."

CHAPTER 23

Moishe Cohen felt obligated to take in a family from the ships. He lived in a large waterfront house in Marblehead, a yachting community north of Boston that had a substantial population of substantial Jews. Cohen thought many times about selling the house after his wife, Zelda, passed away from breast cancer three years earlier. He'd remained there more from inertia than for any other reason.

There was plenty of room for Walid ben Mizrachi's family in the nearly empty house. The three teenagers spoke English well, having attended Israeli schools their entire lives. Their parents, however, struggled to learn Hebrew after their arrival from Yemen. Their English was limited to a few phrases they'd heard in movies.

Cohen had toyed with the idea of asking them to remain at the house, of taking on their adoption to America as a mitzvah—a good deed. They'd lost everything they owned in Israel and barely escaped with their lives. It was nice having children around the house, nice to take them in wide-eyed awe to the shopping mall. And he could find a place for Walid in the business.

Watching the startled ben Mizrachi family carted off by

federal agents in the dark of the night was more terrifying to Cohen than even his own arrest had been. He did not expect to see them again. Ever. Like so many other Jews who'd been taken to camps and were never seen again.

Cohen had been placed on a yellow school bus filled with men pulled from their homes. Frighteningly, the bus was driven by a uniformed soldier. Cohen had watched dozens of yellow buses rendezvous at some sort of military camp in nearby Reading, Camp Curtis Guild. He'd never heard of the place and, in fact, did not know there were military camps in Massachusetts. But, then, what did he know of such things?

The buses had parked in a large open area, engines were shut down, and then nothing happened. The men had to use a porta-potty next to the driver's seat, in plain sight of all the others. Cohen was too embarrassed to use the device. The ache in his bowels only added to his discomfort.

Some men dozed as the night wore on. Cohen had been unable to sleep. He recognized a few faces from synagogue and nodded to them. The man sitting next to Cohen made an attempt at conversation.

"I told Nadine we shouldn't have gotten involved," he said. "Taking in fugitives. Hiding them in our house. And then when I saw on TV about those people being killed on that Coast Guard boat. I told Nadine we had to get rid of these people, we had to. But would she listen to me? God knows, does she ever listen to me? No way. So what does she do? She takes them shopping. To the North Shore Mall, of all places."

Cohen nodded, saying, "Good shops there, but expensive. I haven't been there since Zelda, may she rest in peace, passed."

He paused. Smiled. Remembering.

"No, that's not right. I took the kids there last week."

"Nadine grew up around here and she grew up surrounded by Jews," the man, Harry Mason as he'd introduced himself, continued. "I told her, I don't know how many times, Nadine, I said, when you grow up the only Jews in a small town in

Pennsylvania, like I did, you know better. I told her, Nadine, Jews better not rock the boat. I told her, Nadine, when Jews rock the boat, Jews are the first ones who fall in the water. That's what I told her, but did she listen? Never. So what do you think they're gonna do with us?"

Cohen shook his head. He had no idea why he'd been arrested, or even if he was arrested. He pretended to sleep.

An image surfaced in Cohen's mind of a similar journey he took when he was nine years old, in Poland. Rather than a bus, he'd been on a train, a freight car. And rather than being surrounded by men, the freight car was filled with families, old, young, children, men, women, girls, boys, strong, weak, healthy, sick, frightened. All frightened. All Jews. He'd spent a week in that freight car, a week with only the food they'd brought with them, a week with only the little water they'd brought in jars, a week using a pile of straw in one corner as the communal toilet.

He'd been with his mother, his father, his grandfather Shmuel, Shmuel his hero, and his two little sisters, Emily and Sarah.

Finally, the train arrived at its destination, a railroad station in what looked like a small town. There were buildings in the distance and one tall smokestack, belching black smoke—the darkest, blackest smoke Cohen ever saw.

As the people stumbled from the freight car, soldiers lined them up and they passed in front of a table at which two men sat, one in a German officer's uniform, one wearing a white coat, like a doctor. When the Cohen family stood at the table, the officer gestured at Cohen's mother and sisters. Soldiers dragged them off to the side. The doctor glanced quickly at Cohen, his father, and his grandfather.

"Take the old one, too," the doctor barked, and the soldiers took Shmuel, Cohen's grandfather, and dragged him to where his mother and sisters stood trembling.

Cohen and his father were taken through a door and eventually to a wooden barracks. His father lived five weeks and then did not awaken one morning. Cohen persisted. And persisted.

Cohen never saw his mother, his sisters or his grandfather again.

His eyes opened quickly and his head jerked forward as he suddenly came awake. The images were so real. He'd seen the faces of his family and heard the cries of the people around him. Most frightening, however, he'd smelled smoke, a smell he'd inhaled every day for two and a half years in that camp.

Sitting in the yellow school bus as the eastern sky gradually lightened, surrounded by terrified Jews, Cohen smelled the smoke again and trembled. *Shmuel, my hero.*

This time, he thought, *this time I'm the old man. The very old man.*

Meals were distributed to the men, some sort of military food in packages marked *Meals Ready to Eat.* Cohen's bus was sent to the Rockingham County Jail over the border in New Hampshire. The men were ushered off the bus and into several group cells, ten or twelve to a cell.

Nobody told the men what was to happen to them. It was not discourtesy; it was just that nobody knew.

As the day wore on Cohen became increasingly confused, unable to nap as most of the men were doing. His mind raced, jumping randomly, faster and faster from one thought to another as he lost all conscious control of his own thoughts.

I was a mensch, he thought. *I survived for a reason. My life's goal was to do good, to treat people the way God wants people treated. When other fabric mills left Massachusetts and moved to Carolina, to Alabama, to China, I stayed. I paid my people well. I provided health insurance. I produced good products, not schlock. I supported the synagogue. I gave money to Israel. I've lived to be such an old man. Why am I here? Why, after all these years and all I have done, why am I locked up surrounded by Jews who are locked up?*

Cohen sat on the concrete floor and looked at his left forearm, at the row of numbers there. He smiled as he recalled the speech he'd given at the press conference a few days earlier. He recalled the words that brought a room full of news reporters, cameras, television lights and all, to absolute silence.

"Never again," he mumbled out loud. "Never again, never again."

Moishe Cohen closed his eyes, rolled his head back so his shut eyelids were facing heaven and silently asked Zelda what he should do.

"Not again, Zeldala. I can't go through it again."

Cohen stood, then slowly walked among the men to the far corner of the cell, where the toilet was located beneath a barred window. His trousers dropped to the floor. He knotted one pants leg into a loop and quietly placed it over his head. Climbing on the toilet seat, Cohen reached up on his toes and tied the other trouser leg to the window bars as high as he could reach.

Taking one last look at the men in the cell, dozing or talking softly among themselves in groups as far from the smelly toilet as they could get, Cohen whispered the prayer that had comforted him through his years in the German camp.

"*Sh'ma Yisrael Adonai Elohaynu Adonai Echad.*" Hear, Israel, the Lord is our God, the Lord is One.

Moishe Cohen, millionaire industrialist, stepped off the toilet seat in the drunk tank of the Rockingham County Jail and dangled from his knotted pants. He'd stopped breathing by the time anybody noticed the old man in the corner.

CHAPTER 24

Abram and Sarah Goldhersh got a room at the Brooklin Inn and stayed overnight. The next morning at breakfast they still could talk about nothing but the events in Israel and Boston. Levi's mind drifted. After three days in Brooklin, Levi was concerned they would soon attract unwanted attention. He wanted to find a place to stay on shore, and he wanted to remove the object from the boat and find a safe place to hide it.

Abram Goldhersh would not stop talking. He grew increasingly more excited.

"They've jailed thousands of Jews, thousands of Israeli citizens, and all you want to do is march around carrying signs saying 'Let My People Go,'" he said, speaking to his wife, Sarah, in a tone so exasperated he sounded like a teenager whose voice was cracking. "Sarah, you know what sort of things I've been running around the country collecting the past few years. I've done that because Jews, at least Jews in Eretz Yisrael, learned that carrying a sign gets attention, but carrying a gun gets results."

"That is Israel and this is America," Sarah said to her husband. "You walk around Boston with a gun now and you'll wind up behind bars and that won't do anybody—*anybody*—any good, will it, Mr. Shoot-em-Up? We have some very prominent people coming to this march— politicians, actors, business people. Besides, those poor people have been in that stadium for almost a week now. They have to let them out. What else is the government going to do with them?"

Debra Reuben interrupted. "Sarah, I understand all that, but Chaim and I have a more immediate concern. We can't stay on that boat much longer; at least, I know that I can't stand it. We need someplace to stay. Do you have any suggestions?"

Levi interrupted before Sarah could respond.

"And it has to be someplace, can I use the phrase, 'out of the way.' There is a slight chance that the government may take some interest in us," Levi said. "I assume that an Israeli naval officer and a former cabinet minister aren't high on America's invitation list right now. I myself would rather not be locked up in any stadium."

Goldhersh looked at the former Israeli naval officer closely. Reuben had been part of an Israeli government that Goldhersh viewed as weak, as far too willing to compromise with Arabs. Here she was now, though, with an in-the-flesh member of the Israeli military. He placed an arm on Levi's shoulder.

"Well, Chaim, I'd like to have you not too far away," Abram said. "I was never in the military, you know, and I wouldn't mind having somebody look at my warehouse who knows something about weapons and explosives. I got quite a deal on some drums of something labeled C4. I know that's an explosive, but that's about all I know."

"C4? That sure is an explosive," Levi answered. "We trained with that for commando operations in the navy. Half the C4 in the world is manufactured, or was manufactured, in Israel. It is a magnificent weapon as long as you remember that it packs a bigger bang than TNT. You can mold it like modeling clay. You can drop it from the roof and it won't go off, but use the right detonator and its child's play to make a big boom with it.

"I set off some great bangs in training. We'd leave our patrol boat at night, run a rubber boat up a beach and rush ashore to the target—all in training, never did it for real—stuff it with C4 and set the detonators, then run for the rubber boats." He looked at the other man oddly. "How in hell did you get that stuff, Abram?"

"Let's just say that I spent a lot of time hanging around Army bases. I got to know some gentlemen marketing heroin. Once they learned how much more I'd pay for toys like that C4, they started taking payment from their soldier customers in goods rather than cash. That way they made money from both ends of the deal. It was all in a good cause," Abram said. "I doubt the Army knew what it was missing."

"Stop that kind of talk," Sarah said, looking at her husband with a not-very-loving expression. "Boys and explosives and guns. Stop it."

The huge man obeyed his wife's command, for the moment. Levi saw Abram's eyes light with excitement—not uncontrolled anger—when he talked about the drums of explosives in his warehouse. *Drums of C4*, Levi thought. *That will get some attention.*

Sarah interrupted Levi's reverie.

"Debra, Chaim, I have an idea about a place where you two could stay. I'll have to make a phone call first, but I think it could work out very well. Remember, Debbie, I told you that I knew somebody with a vacation cottage here in Brooklin? Well, she's Nancy Lowenstein, married to Arthur Lowenstein. He's the CEO or the chairman or something of KGR Insurance, that big insurance company that advertises all over TV and the newspapers. They have a summer cottage here on the water.

"I know Nancy from a fundraising campaign she and I managed together for Ethiopian Jewish children. It was so beautiful; those children are so beautiful. Imagine, black Jews. We raised over five million for them. Nancy broke her back working so hard, and broke her husband's bank account. We had an event at their house here. Nancy told me they'd had their caretaker come by to turn on the water and electricity because they hadn't been to the house in two years themselves."

Sarah smiled at a memory.

"Nancy was so excited to do something for Israel. And she was charmed by an Israeli man who hinted that the money was not going to be used entirely to help poor black Jewish kids. Nancy thought he was involved with the Mossad—you know, the Israeli secret service?"

She looked inquisitively at Levi and Reuben.

"We've heard of Mossad," Levi said dryly.

"Well, she just loved the whole cloak-and-dagger aspect to it. I'll ask about opening her house to help some secret friends from Eretz. I'm sure she'll go for it."

"The sooner the better," Reuben said. "I want to sleep in a bed that doesn't move."

"And I want to move something off that boat. The sooner the better," Levi added.

Abram gave Levi an odd look after that statement but chose to go no further, for now.

■ ■ ■

The Lowenstein house was far more than a summer cottage. Besides the six bedrooms and the sauna, exercise room, media room, and sauna, what made the house most attractive to Levi was the long dock that extended on stone pilings into water deep enough to motor the sailboat to the float.

He'd spent the better part of the afternoon cutting away the fiberglass covering he'd built over the starboard settee water tank, careful not to let his battery-powered circular saw come anywhere near the metal shell surrounding the device inside the tank.

The boat's cabin was filled with dust and shards from the

cut fiberglass, but the metal cylinder, eighteen inches across and three feet or so long, lay on the cabin berth across from where Levi was working. It was still sealed in the clear plastic he wrapped around it in the hope of keeping the device dry when he filled the tank with water. He left it wrapped. It looked less ominous that way, like some sort of kitchen trash can still in its bubble wrap after being lifted out of the shipping box from Amazon.com.

Besides, Levi liked the idea of having something, even if it was just a few layers of clear plastic, between the device and his hands. He had no idea how much radiation leaked from the thing.

I suppose that is the least of my worries, he thought. *I've been sleeping on top of it all this time.*

It was getting dark as Levi finished his efforts inside the cabin. He walked up the dock and into the house, looking for Reuben. What he saw stopped him in his tracks.

"Nancy Lowenstein and I must be the same size," Reuben said, smiling. "Although her tastes are a bit flashier than mine. She has most of the Victoria's Secret catalog in her closet."

Reuben looked well scrubbed, well manicured, and, to Levi, sexy. She wore an extremely short and tight black skirt. Her stomach was bare. She wore a black leather halter top that tied in the rear, leaving most of her back bare. Her red hair shone and smelled faintly of an organic herbal shampoo.

"It is so wonderful to get off that boat," she said. "I felt like dressing up. Sarah and Abram stocked up the fridge before they left, and the Lowensteins have a pretty impressive wine collection. Why don't you clean up—you're filthy—and we'll celebrate our first night on shore."

"Not yet," Levi answered. "I have a bit of heavy lifting to do first. I'll feel better with that thing off the boat and stashed away on shore. I'm going to carry it into the basement and leave it there tonight. We'll find a place for it tomorrow, and then we'll figure out what to do with the boat."

"As far as I'm concerned," Reuben said, "you can take it out and sink it. I'm ready for a long break from the deep blue sea."

"That's not a half bad idea," Levi said. "We've got to get rid of it somehow. You start on dinner. I'll be back in a few minutes. Then I'll clean myself up and we can really and truly celebrate." He laughed. "Get a couple of bottles opened. We deserve it."

Debra lifted a tall glass half filled with white wine. She pointed at a bottle on the counter, which Levi noticed was more than half empty.

"Way ahead of you on that, sailor," she said, grinning.

Forty-five minutes later, the cylinder, still wrapped in plastic, lay on the basement workbench. Levi scrubbed his arms and hands with extra energy in the shower, hoping to wash away any radiation his body had absorbed. While Arthur Lowenstein's clothes were too small for Levi, he was surprised to find that Reuben had laundered the few clothes he'd brought in from the boat. He appeared downstairs for dinner, dressed in cleaned khakis and his one collared shirt.

A huge pot sat on the stove, steam billowing as the water inside reached a boil. On the counter lay two two-pound lobsters, their claws wrapped in wide, yellow rubber bands. Their antennae waved from side to side and their fantails opened and closed. Two ears of fresh-shucked corn were in a ceramic bowl near the stove.

Two bottles of Meursault stood upright in a bucket of ice, two wine glasses next to it. Diana Krall sang "I'm Thru With Love" on the best stereo Levi ever heard.

Reuben stood behind the kitchen island, her arms spread wide, her hands on the counter, leaning forward toward Levi, her cleavage enhanced by Victoria's Secret's best engineering. She smiled at him and said softly, "Well, sailor, what do you think?"

Levi struggled to bring his eyes up to her face. He, too, smiled.

"To quote Richard Thompson, whose songs made it all the way to Eretz Yisrael, red hair and black leather is my favorite color scheme," he said. "I think I just might be able to forget about the atomic bomb in the basement for a little while."

CHAPTER 25

B en Shapiro thought that with all the craziness—he remembered his Nana Ida's complaints about *mishegas,* Yiddish for craziness—with all the *mishegas* in the world and in Boston, why was his house, too, turned on its head? He'd spent the past two nights sleeping alone in the guest room on a lumpy futon rather than the Swedish foam mattress he was used to.

"You are totally and completely obsessed with this thing," Sally screamed earlier that week at dinner. "It's all you talk about and, it seems, all you are doing at work. What about your other cases? Who's working on them, on the cases that actually make us some money?"

"My partners understand how important this case is to me. They're covering me," Shapiro said. "I'm not obsessed with this. It's just that this is important, extremely important, maybe the most important thing that has happened in my entire life."

"I thought I was the most important thing in your life, or at least that Adam was," Sally said flatly. "Remember, Adam, your son?"

"Yes, of course you are, both of you, but I mean in my work life. No, not just my work life—my other-than-my-family life."

Shapiro was fed up with his wife's complaining about something that he acknowledged had taken over his thoughts and time.

"Look, honey." He saw her eyes go wide. She was in no mood for sweet talk. "I mean, listen, I've spent my whole life, my whole life as a lawyer at least, taking on case after case to protect peoples' rights. And who have I represented? Gay people, women, poor people, black people, pornographers, Nazis, goddamn Nazis who wanted to hold a goddamn Nazi parade in Boston. And who have I never, ever represented? Whose rights have I never defended? Jews. That's who. Well, now is the time. You know Primo Levi's question, his book title, *If Not Now, When?* I keep thinking that if Ben Shapiro, the great civil rights defender, won't take a stand for Jews now, when will I? When should I?" Shapiro glared at his wife.

"You Jews have a fucking famous saying for everything. I'm sick of it all," Sally said. "You know, Ben, there comes a time when you've got to decide whether you're a Jew or an American. Sometimes you can't be both. I agree these are difficult times, but, Ben, look, there were enemy soldiers on those boats, not just refugees. Soldiers. And they fired weapons at Americans, at the Coast Guard. And they killed them, they killed every one of them.

"I can't stop thinking about the mothers of those poor kids on those boats, killed right in Boston Harbor, where you'd think your son or daughter would be safe. It could have been Adam on those Coast Guard boats. And for you to be defending the people who did that killing, I can't understand it, Ben. I simply can't understand it. What would you say to the mother of that girl who was killed, the one in the Coast Guard?"

He looked at her, assuming her question was rhetorical and that there was more of the same to follow. *More likely*, he thought, *it could have been Adam on those refugee ships.* He didn't dare say that to her. Sally went on.

"My God, Ben, what if you win? You're such a good lawyer, you always win. What if you win? What if you get these killers off? What will people say? How will we live with that? What about me? What about Adam? Have you thought about any of that, Mr. Civil Rights?"

Shapiro's normal means of dealing with his wife's anger was to give in. That tactic didn't leave him satisfied, but it brought their conflicts to an end. Submission squirmed in his belly. He resisted. *Not this time,* he thought.

Sally usually won. If she outlasted him. She fired her next salvo.

"It's already happening, you know. You are just so caught up that you are oblivious to what is happening, happening even to your own son, you know?"

"What do you mean," he asked. "What's happening? Did something happen to Adam?"

"Yes. Something. Happened. To. Adam," Sally said, pausing between each word. "You were on the news again the other night. I know you say you don't watch yourself on the news because it's no big deal. But you were on the news a few days ago, another story about you defending that Jew who murdered the Coast Guard people. And they said you said it was all a misunderstanding and your client had nothing to do with anything.

"Well, there was a memorial service at Adam's school for the Coast Guard people who were killed. And the principal, Mr. Williams—remember him? You once said he was a wonderful principal. Well, Mr. Williams gave a speech. And he said that the lawyer for the murderers said it was just a 'misunderstanding.'" She lifted both hands in the air, two fingers extended to place quotation remarks around the word.

"And then the principal said that anybody who defends a murderer of Americans is as guilty as the murderers themselves. Well, after that some of the kids started talking about how Adam's father was the lawyer defending that murderer Jew. And I guess they started pushing him around and he got pushed to the ground and somebody kicked him and he came home from school with his clothes all torn, and he was crying like I've never heard him cry before. He said they kept calling him a Jew. That is what you are doing to your family. And you didn't even know about this because you came home so late we were in bed."

She glared at Shapiro. *Scored some points with that one,* she thought. *If he doesn't care about hurting me, he stills cares about his son.* Sally Spofford was not a woman to stop when she was winning.

"And, well, I wasn't going to tell you this, but some of my friends have been talking, too. You know the Rodger's dinner party we were supposed to go to next weekend, their anniversary party that they made such a big deal about?"

"Yes, what about it?"

"Janice Rodgers called me and, oh so politely of course, you know how totally proper Janice is, suggested that perhaps it would be a good idea if we skipped the party. Because of all that's happening, she said, as if that's supposed to explain everything."

Shapiro pushed his chair back, walked to the other side of the table and opened his arms to invite his wife to hug. She remained seated, folded her arms across her chest and shook her head from side to side.

"I'm sorry, Sally," Shapiro said. "I didn't know about any of this. Why didn't you tell me about Adam, or about that party? I know how much you were looking forward to that party. You bought a new dress and everything."

Contrition got him nowhere.

"I didn't tell you about Adam because this is the first night since it happened that you've come home before I went to bed. You may have noticed that we haven't seen much of each other recently. In fact, when is the last time you saw your son awake? And I didn't tell you about the party because"—she hesitated, then continued—"because what Janice actually said was that it might be a good idea if you—you, Ben—didn't come. She said that of course I was still welcome. I haven't decided what I'm going to do. At least I hadn't decided until right now. I just decided that

I am going to the party. By myself. I'll expect you to be home to babysit your son."

"If that's what you want to do, then go ahead and do it," Shapiro said. "I can't say I understand, but I guess there isn't a whole lot I can do about it."

He turned his back to his wife and started to walk from the room. She spoke to his back. He stopped and turned.

"Ben, what I don't understand is how this one case, this one client, is taking over your life. Can't you please back off from this case?"

Shapiro hesitated, stared at the ceiling.

"Actually, Sally, it isn't just one case," he said, instantly realizing that he was opening the door to another storm. "I'm representing a few other people, too, some people who were arrested that night from their homes. There's a legal committee that was formed to defend all those people who are in custody."

Her reaction was what he'd expected, a flash of lightning followed by dark clouds.

"A legal committee? So what if there is a committee of some sort?" Sally asked. "Are you involved in that, representing all those Israelis, the soldiers who were on those ships? No, no, no, tell me you're not doing that, Ben."

"Actually, they asked me to be the head of the defense committee. And I agreed to do it. That's what's kept me so busy the last few days, and nights. Honey, a *tzadik*? You know, a truly righteous man—"

She jumped to her feet, waving her hands in front of her face to cut him off.

"I can't take this. I'm going up to read. You can do the dishes. Good night."

When Shapiro slowly climbed those same stairs two hours later, he found the door closed and his pajamas on the floor in the hall.

■ ■ ■

As he pulled into his parking space in the garage next to the John F. Kennedy Federal Building in downtown Boston the next morning, Shapiro recalled that he was scheduled to meet Judy Katz for lunch that day. He was intrigued by the idea of meeting the young woman who he'd read about in the newspapers but never run into. He laughed at himself when he thought that from the photos in the newspapers, she was a real hottie, at least for a lawyer.

He was surprised at how disappointed he was to find an email from the young Assistant US Attorney saying she was going to take a few days off. Could they meet for lunch next week, she asked.

CHAPTER 26

Nancy Lowenstein's suspicions that something deliciously mysterious was up with the people staying in her Brooklin cottage increased when Sarah Goldberg-Goldhersh called to ask Nancy to have the boatyard launch her thirty-two-foot motor boat for her guests to use.

"They only need it for one night," Sarah said. "But please have the boatyard fill the fuel tank and make sure the engine is okay."

Lowenstein, sure by now she was part of something clandestine, called the Brooklin Boat Yard as soon as Sarah hung up.

The next day, Levi and Abram Goldhersh powered up the twin 250-horsepower Honda outboards on the Lowensteins' Boston Whaler Outrage and motored away from the boatyard at little more than an idle. Goldhersh had never been on a boat, any boat. Levi gave him a crash course in boat handling.

"You will follow me the whole way," Levi said. "I'll be in the sailboat going about six knots. This boat can do six knots while it's still tied to the dock. The hardest thing for you will be going slow enough so you stay behind me. Steering is easy, just like a car. Here, give it a try."

"First, you've got to tell me how fast is a knot. This whole adventure will be a lot easier if you talk in English."

"I get it. Keep it simple," Levi said. "Assume a knot is the same as one mile an hour. So we're going to be zooming around at just about a fast walk. Does that make you feel better?"

"Actually, it does. That's pretty slow," Abram replied. "I can handle that—a fast walk? I can do that."

It was not quite like driving a car, at least unless the car was driving down a road a hundred yards wide and negotiating a slalom course from one side to the other. After a while, however, Abram learned that a little turn on the wheel went a long way toward turning the boat.

"What about navigation?" he asked, looking blankly at the bank of electronic instruments behind the steering wheel.

"Don't worry about it," Levi said. "I'll be right in front of you. I'll do all the navigating. All you have to do is follow me. If you get lost, I'll show you how to call me on the radio, but I'd rather not use that. We're on a mission, remember. A secret, quiet mission. I expect that people around here listen to the marine radio for entertainment. I don't want anybody wondering why we're going on a pleasure cruise in the middle of the night."

Once Levi was satisfied that Abram could point the powerboat in the direction he wanted it to go and could control the engine speed, he had him take the boat up the long, thin body of water on which the Lowensteins' house was located, the same Eggemoggin Reach he'd sailed down when he and Reuben arrived a week and a half earlier.

"I'll take over here," he said as the boat approached the Lowensteins' dock. Levi steered the boat next to the dock, quickly reversing the engines to drive the rear portion of the boat lightly against the float. He jumped out and secured the mooring lines to the float.

Reuben walked down the dock from the house when she saw the motorboat arrive. She carried a backpack.

"I've got a thermos of Starbucks for you, and a couple of tuna sandwiches, and a bag of chocolate chip cookies," she said.

"Chocolate chip cookies. How American I'm becoming," Levi said, laughing. "Thank you, Debra. I appreciate your thoughtfulness in making this for us."

Reuben had difficulty believing that the present person who called himself Chaim Levi was the same surly sailor she'd spent two months with cramped on that sailboat, which was tied on the opposite side of the dock from the powerboat.

Maybe he's a nicer person when he's on land, she thought. *Or maybe it was Victoria's Secret.* Reuben, after months of grubbiness on the boat, was working her way through the collection and enjoying it thoroughly. Apparently, so was Levi.

Tonight, though, the two men were going to get rid of the sailboat. Levi saw the boat as his last link with Israel. He planned on sinking it to the bottom of nearby Penobscot Bay. While Abram fiddled with the motorboat, Reuben took Levi aside. She handed him something from her pants pocket, two gold-colored metal tags on a linked chain.

"My dog tags," he said. "So you've had them all along. I wondered where they'd gone. Why give them to me now?"

"Lt. Levi of the Israel Defense Forces, I thought since you were getting rid of our boat, maybe you'd also want to get rid of this," she said. "I don't see them being much good to you here. Maybe they'd better go down with the ship."

"Thank you, Debra," he said. "I appreciate that. Of course, you're right."

He looked at the glittering gold objects in his palm.

"I'll miss this, but you're right." He put the dog tags in his pocket. "I'm going to turn off all the navigation lights," Levi explained to Goldhersh. "I'm hanging this one little light from the back railing. It's not too bright, but you should be able to keep it in sight. Stay close, not too close, but close enough so you can see the light. If you get lost, if you lose sight of me, just stop. I'll circle back and find you. I'll be going as fast as this sailboat can motor, which means you'll be using one engine and not getting it much above an idle. Got all that?"

"Yes sir, Captain. I'm on your tail the whole way." Abram tried to hide the nervousness in his voice. It would soon be fully dark on a moonless night. He could not believe he was about to be out on the ocean in this darkness, all by himself in a boat he could barely control.

Levi climbed into the motorboat, fiddled with the controls, and one of the two large outboards roared to life.

"She's all yours. Stay close to me."

Levi leaped from the motorboat to the dock, untied the docking lines and pushed the boat from the float. He then walked quickly to the sailboat, where the diesel engine was idling. He'd plotted his course fifteen miles out to the middle of nearby Penobscot Bay, where the chart showed a depth of 135 feet. The course took him from one lighted buoy to the next and the GPS showed exactly where the pair of boats was.

Two and a half hours later, Levi waved to Goldhersh to cut his engine. The powerboat drifted up next to the sailboat and Levi tossed a line from his vessel around a cleat on the powerboat, tying the two boats side by side.

"Now we play *Titanic*," he said to Goldhersh.

With Goldhersh standing by in the Boston Whaler tied to the sailboat's side, Levi went into the forward head, the boat's bathroom, and moved a device called a seacock lever to the open position. He'd removed the rubber hose from the seacock to the boat's toilet. Moving the lever let off a geyser of freezing seawater. He watched the water shoot four feet toward the cabin ceiling. He backed out and climbed up to the cockpit. In a few minutes he looked into the cabin and saw the wooden floorboards begin to lift and float out of position.

Levi fought an urge to wade forward through the icy water and close the seacock, regretting how he was paying back this beautiful vessel, this wonderful work of craftsmanship that safely carried him and Reuben from a world of troubles to this peaceful corner of the world. Then he realized what could happen to them should this boat be discovered and traced back across the ocean.

As the boat settled lower into the water, Levi climbed across to the Boston Whaler. He reached for the rope tying the two boats together, then paused.

"Wait a minute," he said. "I almost forgot something."

Levi climbed back onto the sailboat and stepped down into the cabin. The water was already above his bare feet and ankles. His eyes settled on the navigation table, where he'd spent so many hours in the transatlantic voyage. He reached in his pocket and carefully placed the dog tags in the center of the tabletop. He stood, saluted, and quickly climbed up and back to the motorboat.

He watched the boat slowly sink below the ocean surface.

"Let's go home," Levi said as he started the second outboard and pushed the twin throttles forward.

As the sailboat settled toward the ocean bottom, at a depth of fifty feet, a glass vial on the automatic inflation system of the life raft jammed into the forward compartment burst, as it was designed to do. The inflation valve on the compressed air cylinder was triggered. The raft instantly inflated, filling the forward cabin. The additional buoyancy was enough to stop the boat's descent and slowly return it to the surface, masts waving in the air.

■ ■ ■

The two brothers who co-owned the lobster boat *Robin Mary Joseph Warren Katy* were out on Penobscot Bay just before sunrise, motoring at full throttle toward their lobster grounds, 400 pots to pull that day. Their view of the mast and partially submerged bow of the Hinckley drifting dead ahead of them was blocked by the rising sun. The lobster boat was almost on top of the hulk of the sailboat before they saw it. They cut their engine and slowly circled the sailboat, looking to see if anybody was on board.

Not seeing anybody, they radioed the Rockland Coast Guard station and reported what they'd found. The Coast Guard ordered them to stand by the vessel until assistance arrived. Lobstermen being lobstermen—no great fans of authority or the Coast Guard—they radioed the GPS coordinates of the boat and took off once again at full throttle.

The Coast Guard's 110-foot Island-class coastal patrol boat *Wrangell* was returning to Rockland after a one-week VBST, vessel boarding and security team, patrol off the Maine coast, inspecting container ships bound for Portland and Boston. The radio operator at Coast Guard Station Rockland diverted the *Wrangell* to the coordinates given by the lobstermen.

It took the patrol boat, traveling through the flat water near its top speed of twenty-nine knots, less than an hour to reach the Hinckley. The captain ordered three men to lower a rigid-bottom inflatable boat and inspect the sailboat. Arriving alongside, two of the men hopped into the sailboat's cockpit, which was full of water. The men were thankful they wore full immersion suits in the cold water. Clipped around their waists were utility belts with the full VBST pack of equipment they wore when boarding suspicious boats, including their sidearms.

Looking into the boat's cabin, they observed one end of the life raft coming from the forward cabin.

There was three feet of air space beneath the ceiling in the main cabin. The two men climbed into the cabin, intending to inspect the boat for survivors, hoping they would not find any bodies. The main cabin and the forward cabin were both empty. One man forced open the door to the head compartment, where the toilet was located, and glanced inside. Nobody was there. He did not notice the open seacock beneath the water.

The men were puzzled but relieved that they'd found nothing especially gross, no decomposing bodies, to report. Looking around the cabin, one man noticed that the cushion on the starboard settee had floated free. The top of the settee looked as if it had been ripped open, exposing the water tank beneath.

On closer inspection, he saw the top of the water tank had been smoothly cut out.

"What do you suppose caused that?" he asked his buddy, who shook his head and leaned forward to look into the opening. As he did so, a loud bleeping filled the cabin.

"What the hell was that?" the other man asked.

The first coastguardsman reached toward his belt and lifted a small, rectangular black device on which a red light was flashing and from which the *bleep, bleep, bleep* sound was coming. He unclipped the device from his waist and held it close to the opening in the settee. The sound increased and the red light flashed more rapidly.

"Holy fucking shit," he muttered, holding his Polimaster personal radiation monitor, the device coastguardsmen used to check cargo containers for signs of hidden radioactive material. A red LED on top of the device was flashing rapidly and the device emitted a continuous *bleep, bleep.*

The man leaped from the cabin into the sailboat's cockpit and screamed to the third coastguardsman waiting in the inflatable boat alongside.

"Call the captain. Now. Quick. We have a situation here."

CHAPTER 27

Enclosed stadiums, fine as they were for sporting events, don't work as detention centers. That lesson was learned in New Orleans. The Agganis Arena, to put it bluntly, stunk. There were no showers. The miasma of 4,000 people living together twenty-four hours a day, cooking food on hotplates when they tired of trying to eat what was trucked in to the concession stands, settled down from the domed ceiling like a fogbank over the surface of the ocean, gradually lowering until it hovered just over the heads of the people on the floor, engulfing those families who'd staked out higher sections of the seating area.

Something has to be done with these people, thought retired General Hutchings Paterson, director of the Department of Homeland Security. Gen. Paterson was responsible for housing the Israeli detainees. He knew he had a problem but was at a loss with what to do with the people he was holding. There was not enough prison space in the Northeast to house them, even if prison were the solution. After all, they had not been charged with any crime. From what he'd heard, they would be dealt with by the military, not the criminal system, not even by Immigration and Customs. That was fine with him. He just wished somebody would come up with a bright idea. Soon.

Harry Wade, the wonder-manager recruited from Honda Motors USA to revitalize the moribund Federal Emergency Management Agency, had won wide praise the past year for FEMA's response to what was dubbed the Twin Hurricanes, which resulted from Hurricane Jack branching into two separate cells tracking side by side. This had never happened before. Because Hurricane Karla was already forming, claiming the *K* name, the twin cells were named Hurricane Jack and Hurricane Jill. The storms struck southern Florida from both the east and west simultaneously, causing record property losses and loss of life. Wade telephoned Gen. Paterson.

"General, I understand you have a few thousand people on your hands in Massachusetts and no place to put them," Wade said. Problems, to Wade, were like daisies on the lawn—something to be dealt with, plucked and displayed.

"Nice to hear from you, Harry," Gen. Paterson said into the telephone, signaling his first assistant director to pick up the extension next to the sofa in the director's office. "Haven't spoken with you since that reception at the British Embassy, when the prince introduced the new wife, that third one. Let's hope he got it right this time, them being our one and only ally in Europe."

"His problem isn't in outliving his wives," Wade joked. "His problem is that it looks like his mother is going to outlive him."

Gen. Paterson laughed politely.

"I'm calling about your situation in Boston, General. You've got thousands of people trying to live in a basketball stadium, with more being arrested every day."

"Yes, Harry, it was my people who stopped that Amtrak train heading to Montreal and checked Americards. We picked up a dozen Israelis trying to get out of Boston."

"And what a good job that was. But where are those people, General? Cooped up in that basketball stadium at Boston University. That's a problem." Wade had a solution. "Here's my suggestion. You can't take all those Jews and hand them over to the Arabs, like the Arabs want us to do. Not after the TV coverage of those camps over there. Wouldn't look good. Time for that is past. Agree with me so far?"

"The president tried getting those ships out of our hair and he failed," Paterson said. "We've lost the option of returning these people to their homeland, like we did with all the other illegals in the past, since their homeland no longer exists—at least, as their home. So go on."

"General, FEMA's got access to a former military camp with housing for five thousand people in more comfort than any other federal detention facility," Wade said happily. "It's right in Massachusetts, a military place with loads of security, but a place with enough comforts so the liberals won't scream too loud. We just removed the last of our Jack and Jill refugees from Camp Edwards at Otis Air Force Base on Cape Cod. Great facility. We left it all spiffed up. Why don't you ship 'em down there, General?"

"What about security, Harry?" Paterson asked. "Your hurricane folks weren't trying to escape."

"No problem with security. The Air Force stored nukes there. Best security in the world. Triple razor wire fences all around, guard towers, the works. If it was good enough to keep terrorists out, it's good enough to keep terrorists in. Right? So, what do you say?"

Gen. Paterson paused to think. Any place was better than the basketball stadium. Then he pictured the military base, coils of barbed wire. Old women, children inside. He looked at his assistant. The man's eyes were closed. All color had left his face. Paterson knew why. He picked up the phone again.

"I can't make a decision like this on my own, Harry." He paused for an acknowledgement. Hearing nothing, he continued. "I don't have to tell you that shipping Jewish refugees to a military detention camp surrounded by barbed wire has a pretty bad historical precedent for some people."

"General, I'm well aware of historical precedents, but we live in the present. We have people in our custody, people who just happen to be Jews. We're not holding them because they're Jews, we're holding them because we can't do anything else with them. Which do you think would cause more of a fuss? Handing a bunch of Jews over to the Arabs or moving them into comfortable housing on Vacationland Cape Cod?"

"Agreed, Harry. I've gotta tell you, though, I get a sick feeling with the idea of me being in charge of a military detention camp filled with Jews. There are going to be photos of Jewish kids staring through barbed wire, American barbed wire. You know that. I don't want to be America's Adolph Eichmann."

"You don't want to be Jimmy Carter, either, General, wringing your hands and complaining that we've got a problem we can't solve. This decision is in your hands because these people are in your hands. So, what's your decision?"

"My decision is to run this by the president and let him decide. This is too big for me on my own."

Gen. Paterson hung up and looked across the office at his assistant.

"So?" Paterson asked.

Harris Rosenberg turned and walked out, slamming the door, thinking of his grandfather, a sergeant in the US Army's First Infantry Division, who was captured by the Germans two weeks after landing at Omaha Beach, held in the Berga slave labor camp for Jewish-American soldiers and haunted the rest of his life with dreams that left him screaming at night.

"What was that?" the assistant yelled at Rosenberg as he stormed past her. He turned his head without stopping and said as he continued down the hall, "That was my resignation."

CHAPTER 28

The crew of the *Wrangel* made short work of refloating the Hinckley yawl with inflatable salvage bags. The sailboat was towed to the Coast Guard station at nearby Rockland. A Department of Homeland Security Gulfstream 550 jet landed at Owl's Head Airport near Rockland within two hours. The four members of the Nuclear Emergency Support Team, a NEST team, hurried to the Coast Guard minivan waiting to drive them to the sailboat. The team members carried innocuous-looking backpacks, but when the Coast Guard driver offered to help the one female member of the team with her bag, she angrily pushed him aside, then reacted to his hurt expression.

"I'm sorry, sailor," she said. "This isn't feminism; it's just that what's in this bag is very expensive and very fragile. If anybody is going to drop it and get in trouble, I'd rather it be me."

Chief among the devices was a ten-pound battery-powered instrument called a Cryo3. It looked like little more than a shiny brass coffee can with legs on the bottom and a handle on top. In reality, the device was a sensitive radiation monitor developed by scientists at the University of California at Berkeley's Lawrence Livermore National Laboratory. The unit contained an extremely high-purity germanium crystal designed to absorb energetic photons emanating from radioactive isotopes. Germanium is sensitive to radiation only at extremely low temperatures. The scientists who designed the Cryo3 used a cooling system originally built for cell phone tower equipment to deep-freeze the germanium crystal. Analysis of the machine's readout could pinpoint both the quantity and type of radioactive material present.

Arriving at the dock, the team leader climbed onto the sailboat carrying his Cryo3 and disappeared into the cabin for five minutes. When he emerged, his face was ashen. He sat in the boat's cockpit and looked at the anxious faces of the NEST team members.

"What is it, boss?" the woman team member asked.

The team leader looked up and spoke quietly.

"U-235," he said. "A clear, strong indication of U-235 and nothing else. This is it. The real thing."

He stood.

"Get me the radio," he said. "Things have to start happening, fast."

As one team member handed the team leader a high frequency satellite phone, equipped with a sophisticated scrambler, the Coast Guard driver standing next to the woman turned to her with an inquisitive look on his face.

"What does that mean, U-235? Are we all hot or something, hair gonna fall out, or worse than that?" he asked with a worried tone.

"No, nothing like that. We're not in any danger, at least not from radiation," the woman answered. "U-235 is a radio isotope. That means it is a material that is radioactive, that emits radiation. But U-235 is a fairly low-level emitter, not all that dangerous to handle. It can be blocked by something as simple as aluminum foil."

"Oh, so that's a good thing," the sailor said. "How come all the long faces, then, if this is the good radioactive stuff?"

"It isn't all that good," she answered. "Most radioisotopes have lots of different uses—for medical devices or scientific instruments, for example. U-235 is different. It has only one use. That's the problem we have here."

"Why," he asked. "What the hell is the stuff used for?" The sailor laughed. "What, they make bombs from it or something?"

The woman looked at him with a deadpan expression. "You've hit it right on the nose, sailor," she said. "The only thing U-235 is good for is making bombs, very powerful bombs. Think Hiroshima. What was on board that boat was either enough U-235 to make a bomb or, God forbid, an atomic bomb itself."

"How can you tell whether it was a bomb or just some material?" the sailor asked.

"Easy. Either when we find it," she answered, "or when it goes bang."

NEST could call on four helicopters and three fixed-wing airplanes—a King Air B-200 twin turboprop, a Citation-II jet, and an ancient Convair 580T—all equipped with advanced radiological search systems. These aircraft could sweep a fifty-square-mile area in a matter of hours. Airborne detection of atomic radiation was a tricky business, however. U-235 was almost impossible to detect from the air unless the substance was lying on the ground in the open. Just a few inches of concrete or a solid substance like granite could totally block the radiation. Maine islands provided most of the granite used for centuries of public buildings across the United States.

The team leader had little expectation that the material, or the bomb containing it, would be found from an aerial search, but he had to try nonetheless.

More likely to be successful was an old-fashioned detective investigation. That began with tracing the history of the sailboat. The Coast Guard's Vessel Documentation Office collected registration and home port information for every American boat about thirty feet. Documentation numbers were required to be engraved into a structural portion of the hull.

The NEST team leader crawled into the forward compartment in the boat and searched the ceiling beams there for the documentation number. He found the requisite three-inch Arabic numbers on a beam running crosswise at the aft end of the cabin.

As soon as he finished his confidential report to Washington on the encrypted high frequency sat-phone, the team leader called the Vessel Documentation Office in Falling Water, West Virginia. An official there came on the line immediately.

"This is Commander William Jameson responding to your code-word-THOR call. To whom am I speaking, please?"

"This is Robert Rhymes, team leader for a National Department of Energy Nuclear Security Administration Nuclear Emergency Support Team presently located in Rockland, Maine."

"That's quite a mouthful of a title," the Coast Guard officer responded. "But a very impressive mouthful. What can I do for you?"

"I need to find the owner of a boat, a sailboat, immediately. It is without question a matter of great national security and I ask that you devote your entire resources to this. Can I have your agreement to do so, sir?"

"Sure thing, buddy," the officer responded. "No problem. But this won't take anybody's entire resources. Give me the documentation number and I'll punch it right into my computer here. You could have done this from any computer on the Internet, you know. It's no big secret. What's the number?"

"The number carved into the boat's main beam is 1129082."

"Fine, hold on one second," the officer replied. "Okay, here it is. The boat is owned by one William Appleton of Seal Harbor, Maine. That's just down the road from where you are in Rockland. Served up there myself. Breathtaking scenery, though cold as . . . cold as, well, you know what, in the winter."

The team leader wrote down that information, along with the telephone number for William Appleton listed in the Coast Guard records. He thanked the officer and hung up, then dialed Appleton's number on his cell. His fingers were crossed.

"Appleton residence," the voice answering the phone on the second ring said. "Abigail Appleton speaking."

"Ms. Appleton," the team leader said. He was instantly interrupted.

"It is Mrs. Appleton, please."

"Mrs. Appleton, my name is Robert Rhymes. I am with— well, I am with a very important government agency and we are having something of an emergency. It is of the utmost importance that I speak with your husband. Is he available, please?" His tone of voice could not be more deferential.

He heard the woman choke for a moment. It was several seconds before she replied.

"I'm afraid that is not possible," she said. "You see, my husband passed away, two weeks ago. Two weeks tomorrow, actually. I can refer you to my attorney, who is handling all of my husband's matters. He is in Boston. If you'll hold on for a moment, I'll get his phone number."

"Wait, Mrs. Appleton. Look, I'm so sorry about your loss, but I don't think your lawyer will be able to help. Maybe you can. I'm calling about your husband's boat, his sailboat. It's named *Swift*. Can you tell me who has been using the boat recently?"

"Well, that I can help you with, young man," she replied. "Our son, William, he's actually William Junior, had been living on that boat for more than a year, doing that instead of working if you really want to know. He sailed it all over, across the ocean to England and around France and Italy and all. Then he met up with some woman. He said we'd love her and he loved her and all that trash and he couldn't wait for us to meet her.

"He'd finally agreed to come home, to sail the boat home and settle down, when all of a sudden we got a phone call from him that he was in some hospital in Athens with this woman. She'd been bitten by a poisonous fish or something and almost died. So he'd left the boat on some Greek island and flown with this woman to a hospital.

"A week later he called and said the boat had been stolen.

He flew home right after that, with that tramp he'd met. They're married now. We don't speak often. His father owned that boat for twenty years. He was heartbroken at its loss. I told my son the loss of that boat undoubtedly contributed to his father's heart attack. He was completely unapologetic."

Rhymes was shocked to hear the boat was so close to the Middle East.

"Did he mention the name of the island?" he asked.

"Yes, he did, and I wrote it down so I could look on the National Geographic world map we have and find where he had been. I circled it on the map. It was the tiniest dot . . . I have the map in a cabinet in the next room. William and I always mark our travels on it, or we used to do so. Wait one moment."

The woman came back on the telephone.

"The island is called Xanthos. That is *X-A-N-T-H-O-S*. Have you heard of it?"

"No, ma'am, I haven't," Rhymes responded. "But I expect I will learn quite a bit about it shortly. Thank you. You've been extremely helpful."

"Wait," she commanded in the same tone of voice she probably used with her servants. "The Greek police have been most boorish about their efforts to recover the boat. We don't believe in paying good money for insurance, my husband and I. Insurance promotes poor seamanship, he used to say. I demand that the government find my husband's boat. It has immense sentimental value."

"I will be absolutely certain that gets done, ma'am," Rhymes said before hanging up.

Rhymes consulted his notebook, then dialed another telephone number.

"CIA, how may I direct your call?" the answering voice said.

"This is a THOR call. I need to speak to the director," Rhymes said flatly.

"Yes sir."

A moment later a voice came on the phone.

"This is the deputy director. The director is unavailable. To whom am I speaking?"

Rhymes identified himself and briefly explained the situation. The voice on the phone was just as abrupt.

"Thank you, Rhymes," he said. "I'm on it. I'll have our man in Athens get to that island immediately. Who gets the information?"

"For right now, I'm in charge at the scene," Rhymes said. "But I expect to be replaced as the person in charge. You'll know who to call. This is big and I expect you folks will be brought in soon. And, Deputy Director, I've been in this business for twelve years. This is for real—very real. I feel that in my bones and I'm scared shitless."

■ ■ ■

Even though it was three in the morning in Athens, the agent in charge answered his phone on the second ring. At first light a seaplane took off from nearby Piraeus Harbor with the agent on board. The aircraft became the second plane to land in the harbor on Xanthos. The agent quickly found his way to the small building on the quay where the port police office was located. He held a photograph of the *Swift* emailed to him overnight.

"I'm trying to find this boat," he told the corporal. "You've seen it before."

"Oh yes, the American boat," he replied. "What a beautiful boat. What a tragedy happened to it. I could not believe it myself. My own trust and good judgment had been so wrong about that man. What a shock. People are still talking about it."

"The man, what man?" the agent asked. "Who are you talking about?"

"The man who stole that beautiful American boat," the corporal said. "He just got on the boat and sailed away, gone, over the horizon and gone."

"What man? Who was he?"

"The man from the Israeli Navy. The Jew; that's who took

the boat. Don't know his name. We just called him the Jew."

The agent reported to the deputy director, who then called Rhymes. He was surprised by Rhymes response.

"I expected something like that," Rhymes said. "Not that exactly, of course, but something like that."

"I'm sorry we couldn't come up with a name," the deputy director said. "We'll keep on it. He must have given a name to somebody. We'll stay at this. I fully understand how important it is to identify that man."

Rhymes interrupted him.

"I appreciate your efforts. But you needn't bother. I know exactly who the Jew is. I just needed confirmation."

"Well, then let's cut the crap, Rhymes. What is this guy's name? Who is this Jew?"

Rhymes jiggled the gold-colored dog tags he'd found lying on the navigation station of the sailboat. "His name is Chaim Levi. Lieutenant Chaim Levi of the Israel Defense Forces."

CHAPTER 29

Sam Abdullah and Alfred Farouk had been close friends since they met at the Boston Islamic Society day care center fifteen years earlier. The boys were born in Massachusetts and raised in comfortable suburbs just west of Boston, where both their fathers hopped from one high-tech corporation to another. They'd resisted spending time at the Islamic Center, tired of stories from old men about how things were so much better "over there" and criticism about the evil of Americans here. Eventually, the boys' parents relented and sent them to public schools, Sam in Framingham and Al in nearby Natick.

By the time they were teenagers, they struggled to conceal their Muslim identity. America had hardened to Muslims in the wake of Bin Ladin, the Iraq War, terror bombings and the country's seemingly lost cause in Afghanistan.

Sam was the first to begin, ever so gradually, to swing back toward embracing his culture and religion. He grew tired of the taunting, hard looks and racist rants on social media. Sam found himself drawn to a website called American Mujahidin as if it were pornography. He checked it daily, sometimes first thing in the morning before he went to school, reading commentaries on the day's news or inside information telling him which TV shows were controlled by Jews, which clothing designers were Jews, which store chains were owned by Jews. The website portrayed America as a nation owned and operated by wealthy Jews who controlled the way Americans dressed and thought and entertained themselves. Sam introduced Al to the website.

The two spent much of their weekend time, especially through the cold Massachusetts winter, surfing the Mujahidin site and others to which it was linked, joining chat groups connected with the site and messaging with Muslim teenagers across the country.

They absorbed the website's concept that they could be good Muslims and good Americans at the same time. Their task was to save America from the Jews who had taken over the country's business, cultural and political life. By any means.

They argued about whether they had the balls to blow themselves up as their peers in Palestine had done for decades. They discussed what they'd say in their farewell videos, what their school friends would think of them afterwards. They agreed it would be "the coolest thing in the world," in Sam's words, to be the first Americans to sacrifice themselves.

Al said, "My father's construction company uses TNT all the time to blast rock ledge to dig foundations for new houses. I even got to set off a blast when I worked for him last summer. He's got boxes of the stuff in a little steel building at his business, way out back."

"Yeah, but isn't that stuff all locked up?" Sam asked. "Nobody's going to leave TNT lying around."

"It sure is. There's a big combination lock on the door and no windows," Al replied. "It's locked, but my dad uses the same password all over the place—on his ATM card, on his computer and everywhere. I'll bet he set the combination on the padlock to the same code."

"Do you know it?" Sam asked excitedly.

"Sure, it's the birthday of his oldest son, me, 5-28-04. I'll bet anything that's the combination. You know, just for fun, we ought to go there some night and try it, just to see."

"I'll do it if you'll do it," Sam said.

"Yeah, well, I'll do it if you'll do it."

Despite the solemn nature of their dare, they didn't attempt the padlock on the explosives shed. Fantasies about suicide bombers remained just that—fantasies.

All that changed with the bombing of Tel Aviv, followed by the destruction of Damascus. The website contained graphic photographs from Damascus showing bodies burnt to cinders and entire blocks of buildings leveled to rubble.

A new video appeared on the website, on the password-protected section, showing a sermon by a man identified as Mullah Abu Hamzah. He spoke in a rapid, singsong Arabic translated in English captions flowing across the bottom of the screen. He swayed from side to side as he spoke, his words hypnotic.

"The battlefield has moved to America itself," the mullah said. "Allah gave us victory over the infidel in the Holy Land. Only the Great Satan America can snatch that victory from us. But the Great Satan is also the Great Coward. We must encourage fear in the American cowards. We pass the sword to our Muslim brothers in America to fight against the Jew infidels in their country, to take action to turn the cold heart of the Great Satan against the Jews in its midst.

"For this reason I issue a fatwa for our American brothers. Listen to me, brothers. I teach to you that it is allowed to jeopardize your soul and cross the path of the enemy and be killed, if this act of jeopardy affects the enemy, even if it only generates fear in their hearts, shaking their morale, making them fear Muslims. Only if it does not affect the enemy, then it is not allowed."

The two teenagers debated the meaning of Mullah Abu Hamzah's sermon, especially the meaning of his fatwa. Finally, Sam put an end to the discussion.

"I can tell you what it means," he said. "It means we can stop saving for the airfare to Israel. The battle is here, in this country. We need to save America from the Jews. That is our battle."

Al looked at his best friend with a startled expression as he realized that what he had viewed as a fantasy, as role-playing, his friend was deadly serious about. He felt a cold sweat on his forehead as the image of the two of them wearing the belts they'd viewed on the website came into his mind—belts covered with what looked exactly like the sticks of TNT he knew were stored in wooden crates at his father's business.

"Hey, hold on, man. Are you really serious about all this stuff? I mean, is this really for real for you?" Al asked incredulously.

Sam turned to look at his friend. His eyes were cold, hard, mature. Different. "I understand that Allah placed us here as Muslims in America for a holy purpose," he said. "With one action we can do the work of Allah as good Muslims and do the work of America, as good Americans. We can steer our homeland from the course of evil and snatch it from the grip of the Jews."

"Man, you sound like Mullah Abu Hamzah," Al said.

"I don't know what our action will be, but I know that our path will be shown to us. We will each have to decide whether to follow that path or whether to turn away in fear. I know I have courage and faith. Do you, brother?"

Al hesitated. "I'm not sure," he said softly. "I think so, but I'm not sure. I need more time to think."

"The time for action is near," Sam said. "We only have to wait for that action to become clear. But while we are waiting, now is a good time to test the combination on that padlock at your father's business. Will you take that first step with me, or should I go alone?"

"Okay, I'll do that," Al replied cautiously. "When do you want to go there?"

"Tonight."

"Okay, tonight, but just to test it, not to take anything."

"Deal. We don't take anything. Not tonight."

CHAPTER 30

Levi and Reuben sat on the cottage's porch overlooking the water, watching the parade of lobster boats, sailboats, motor yachts sailing past, traveling from one end of Eggemoggin Reach to the other.

"I feel better that the boat is gone," Levi said. "And that *thing* is hidden until when, or if, we need it."

Levi had noticed a low wooden door in a basement wall and was curious to see where it might lead.

The door was locked. Ten minutes of yanking and prodding with a crowbar and the door opened. An overhead light revealed a twenty-foot-long chamber with walls, floor and ceiling of solid granite, a tunnel blasted into the bedrock. Lining the sides of this tunnel were wooden racks, from floor to ceiling. The racks held wine bottles, hundreds of them. The air inside the tunnel was moist and chilly. *There must be twenty feet of granite above the far end of this fancy wine cellar,* he thought.

Levi walked to the workbench where the nuclear device rested. It had an aura about it—the souls of thousands of innocent people, available for the taking at any instant. *It is an evil object. It deserves to be locked away in a cave,* he thought.

He was about to lift it when he paused. *Perhaps I've been too cavalier with this thing.*

He looked around the basement and found a pair of thick gloves covered in hard rubber tossed into a plastic milk crate containing the mixings for epoxy resin. They were bright orange and came halfway to his elbow. The label identified them as Nitrile Chemical Gloves.

"Just in case," Levi said to himself, donning the gloves before he lifted the bomb and carried it to the far end of the wine cellar.

Later, sitting with Reuben on the porch waiting for sunset, Levi sucked down his third Tanqueray and tonic so quickly that Reuben stared at him questioningly.

"Something bothering you," she asked. "Or just thirsty?" She was used to outpacing him, two drinks for each of his.

"Nothing special," he answered, looking out at the water. "This place is so peaceful I sometimes forget why we're here and what we left behind." He pointed at the water, at the horizon to the east.

"I know what you mean," Reuben said. "I forget sometimes, too, but not for long. Not when I turn on the television and see what is happening in Israel—I mean, I guess, in Palestine. Do we have to start calling it that?"

"Never," Levi retorted.

Reuben looked closely at the man in the wooden rocking chair. *I've hardly been out of his sight for two months, yet I know almost nothing about him,* she thought. *Nothing except that he carried me across the ocean and that I feel safe when I am with him.*

"Tell me about what you left behind," she said softly.

Levi turned toward her, startled. Despite all the weeks they'd been isolated with only one another for company, Levi had barely opened up about himself.

Maybe he is just shy, she'd thought. *Maybe, perhaps, when you've lost everything in life, it's too painful to think about, much less to talk about loss.*

"My *eema*—my mother—and my *abba*, my father, met on a kibbutz in the Galilee. They were both orphans, their parents were killed in the 1948 war. They never talked about their childhoods. I used to wonder why they never spoke. Now I know why. The dead are dead, gone. Speaking about them won't bring them back."

"Are you sure they are dead?" Reuben asked, desperate to keep him speaking.

"Sure? I don't know. I had breakfast with them a week before the bomb, before I returned to duty. I saw a photograph in a news magazine in Spain. It was taken from an airplane. It showed the bomb crater in Tel Aviv. It showed the shorefront. It showed rubble where my parents' hotel had been."

"Do you have brothers, sisters?" she whispered.

"My sister, Leah, was supposed to visit them that week, with her baby, with six-month-old Aaron."

"Maybe they survived," Debra said, looking at Levi, struggling to see if he held any hope.

"No. I know they are gone, all of them. I hope it was fast for my sister. She would not do well in a camp. She would not have done well being raped by Arabs, watching her son being slaughtered. I am all that is left of my family, and I am alone in a strange land."

Debra had been so consumed by her own guilt over Damascus that until that moment she had not thought about Levi's loss. He was so strong, so impenetrable. Suddenly, his loss put a face for her on what all Israel had lost. She shot from her chair and turned her back on him, then spun around to stand facing Levi.

"I get so fucking angry at America I can hardly control myself," Reuben screamed. She turned her head from side to side, then hurled her glass. "Look, this is where I was born, where I grew up. For as long as I've been alive, America sent soldiers all over the world for the dumbest reasons imaginable. What the hell do we have to do to convince this goddamn government to do something to put Jewish people back in control of the only place on this entire planet where we can be absolutely certain we're safe? One little tiny bit of real estate on the face of the whole planet is all we want. What the hell is wrong with those idiots in Washington?"

"Evidently, even that one place was not safe," Levi said. He turned when he heard a car on the dirt drive leading up to the cottage. He walked to the end of the porch. "Sarah and Abram," he said to a worried Reuben. Her face cleared. "I expect they'll have some ideas about how to attract the attention of the president of the United States."

"A march," Sarah said. "Just about every congregation in the country will be sending people, some of them busloads. There are six million Jews in America. It's beginning to seem like an awful lot of us are going to be in one place at one time. I can't tell you how excited I am."

THWACKA-THWACKA-THWACKA-THWACKA.

"What's that?" Levi asked, interrupting Sarah. He looked up. A helicopter hovered directly overhead, then disappeared from sight. "I don't like that. There have been airplanes and helicopters flying around the past few days. Something is happening."

"It can't concern us," Abram said as he joined them on the porch. "I don't see how it could."

"I don't either," Levi said. "But it is odd. Maybe I'm just imagining."

CHAPTER 31

The White House Situation Room was in the basement of the West Wing. The president sat in the middle of the long cherry table that dominated the room.

"Here is what is troubling me the most, keeping me awake through last night, to be perfectly frank," Quaid said. He reached into his jacket pocket and dropped a handful of gold-colored objects on the table. Each was a flat metal plate, two inches wide by four or so inches long, containing a Star of David, the letters *IDF* and some writing in Hebrew.

"These are twenty Israel Defense Forces dog tags. Divers salvaging the two Coast Guard boats that sank in Boston Harbor recovered these from the bottom of the harbor underneath where those two freighters were anchored," the president said. "Quite obviously, they were thrown overboard by people on those ships, military people, almost certainly the people who fired the rocket-propelled grenades that sank our two Coast Guard boats. Twenty Israeli military commandos—special forces, probably. And they are in this country. Somewhere. We have no idea what weapons they took with them off the ships."

"Mr. President, chances are we have them in custody right

now, sir, along with all those other people we grabbed from the ships, right?" Attorney General McQueeney said.

McQueeney was unsure where the president was heading with this meeting. She'd learned that he'd met for hours with his own counsel, Carol Cabot. What worried McQueeney more, however, was that she'd also learned that her deputy, Wilson Harrison, had met privately with the president too. That troubled her the most. At a minimum, it was a breach of White House etiquette.

"Well, dammit, Queen, we don't know that, now do we?" the president retorted. "We don't know who we have in custody, and we don't know who is on the loose from those ships. And we certainly don't know if any of the people we have in custody are the military people who sank our Coast Guard boats.

"All we know is that at least twenty members of a foreign military snuck into this country, armed to the teeth, it appears, and killed Americans and attacked our military vessels. And we've done squat to either retaliate or protect ourselves. Now doesn't that make us look like a fine collection of horses' asses? Anybody disagree with that analysis?"

There was no comment from around the table.

"Well, gentlemen and ladies, that isn't the half of it. General, give everybody the bad news."

Paterson, head of the Department of Homeland Security, stood and reached into his pocket and removed a single gold-colored object and tossed it on the table.

"That is one more IDF dog tag, identical to the ones recovered from Boston Harbor," he said.

"Tell everybody where that came from, General. But let me tell you, folks, as scary as the first set of dog tags is, this one is going to make you wet your pants," Quaid said. "Go ahead, tell them everything. That's what we're here for."

"This dog tag was recovered from a sailboat in Maine—a sailboat that somebody intentionally scuttled in the middle of Penobscot Bay. Whoever sank the boat bungled the job. A life raft inflated automatically and provided enough buoyancy to float the boat. A couple of lobstermen spotted it and called the Coast Guard."

"So we've got twenty-one Israelis rather than twenty running around," McQueeney said. "What's so significant about that?"

"What is so significant is that the Coast Guard found that the top of a water tank on the sailboat was cut open so something inside the water tank could be removed. Somebody rigged up the water tank to hide something.

"Now, what is so scary about all this is that whatever was inside that water tank, whatever was recently removed from that water tank was a strong emitter of U-235, a radioactive isotope of uranium. There is only one use for U-235, which is damned near impossible to manufacture. It is the primary ingredient in atomic bombs, right from the bomb dropped on Hiroshima up to many of our present bombs. We don't know whether what was in that boat was a functional bomb or enough U-235 to make a bomb. Either way, this is a serious problem.

"If it is only the U-235, then it could make a dirty bomb using conventional explosives to spread radioactive material for miles in some city center. If it is an operational bomb, all bets are off. For the first time, we have confirmed evidence that an enemy of this country has managed to smuggle nuclear material across our borders. We've dreaded this day coming. Well, it's here."

The Situation Room was silent.

Air Force general Ricardo Cruz, chairman of the Joint Chiefs of Staff, nodded to his adjutant, who sat with an open notebook computer in his lap. A greatly enlarged photograph of the IDF dog tag appeared on a screen covering one wall.

"The dog tag recovered from the sailboat belongs to an Israeli Navy lieutenant named Chaim Levi," Gen. Cruz said. "We know absolutely nothing about his military service or training. The Israeli military is, or was, exceptionally secure about identifying individual soldiers. They had to be careful, considering that their enemies' families could have been living down the block from their soldiers' families. We do know that when he wasn't in the navy, he worked at a beach resort. He was a sailing instructor, among other things."

"How in the hell did you learn that?" Quaid huffed. "You can't tell me whether this guy was a nuclear spy, but you know he taught sailing,"

Cruz whispered with his aide.

"Evidently, sir, we googled him."

President Quaid slammed his hand on the table.

"Well fuck me to high heaven," he said. "How many trillions of dollars have we spent on intelligence gathering and all we can do is the same thing a twelve-year-old would do. Let's keep this bit of information to ourselves. Is that understood?"

"Uh, Mr. President, we do have a photo of Levi," Gen. Cruz said. "The hotel was affiliated with a Swiss hotel chain and they never removed it from their website." It showed Levi on the beach, sailboats visible over his shoulder. He was smiling and tanned, and wearing the skimpiest of bathing suits. The photo caption identified him by name.

"That is our nuclear terrorist?" Quaid said. "He looks like he'd be happier on a surfboard than a warship. Okay, we know the guy's name. We know what he looks like. Let's find him and question him. Gen. Paterson, I take it you are about to take this man into custody."

"Actually, Mr. President, if he is on US soil, jurisdiction belongs to the FBI, not Homeland Security. We'll fully brief them."

"Okay, Mr. President," McQueeney said. The FBI fell under the Department of Justice. "We'll get started immediately. It will be massive, Mr. President. Unprecedented."

"Good. What about the rest of the Israelis, the ones we're holding?" Quaid asked.

Gen. Paterson spoke. "We've located a facility, Camp Edwards on Cape Cod. Just cleared out the last hurricane refugees. It's a fully secure facility. Otis Air Force Base there used to stock nuclear weapons. It's tight, sir, triple razor wire circling the entire installation. Just waiting for your go ahead."

"You've got it. Is there any indication the military from the two ships hooked up with this Levi guy or with the bomb?" Quaid asked.

"No proof, sir," Gen. Paterson said. "Actually, we don't know one way or the other since we don't know who they are or even if we are holding them. I can tell you that nobody we have in custody matches any of the names on the dog tags we recovered from the harbor."

"With all due respect," Gen. Cruz interrupted, "is there some rule that says spies have to give their real names when they are captured? Of course these people won't voluntarily tell us who they are, especially if they're involved with a nuclear bomb being smuggled into the country. We're going to have to get it from them through interrogation, which is one more reason to have them in military rather than civilian custody."

"That brings me to my next point," Quaid said. "I've received legal guidance from people I trust on this point."

The attorney generaland Carol Cabot glared at each other, each suspecting the other. Both were wrong.

"Immediately after this meeting I will be issuing a presidential finding and directive that the people taken from those two freighters are declared to be, uh, enemy combatants. Every one of those people joined an operation that included taking up arms against the United States and killing US military personnel. They are each to be considered enemy combatants and to have only the rights of enemy combatants. They are now under military jurisdiction. Not the immigration service. Not the Justice Department. Is that clear?

"And one more point," the president added. "Based on the legal advice I've received, I will be submitting a request to Congress tomorrow for legislation affirming the revocation of federal court jurisdiction for all claims brought by enemy combatants, confirming that the law that brought to an end all those lawsuits by Guantanamo detainees years ago applies to present enemy combatants, too."

Jewish grandmothers are now enemy combatants locked behind razor wire, McQueeney thought. *What comes next?*

CHAPTER 32

No buses this time. The 1164th Transportation Company of the Massachusetts Army National Guard pulled up at the loading dock of the Agganis Arena with its fleet of five-ton trucks, plus three tractor trailers. With barely a half-hour's notice, the 4,000 people who inhabited the basketball stadium picked up what few belongings they had, mostly items purchased for them by host families in their brief period of freedom, and were loaded into the trucks.

The job was a simple one for the seventy-five Guardsmen. They were trained to move thousands of soldiers across long distances. This time, their drive was just an hour and a half to Camp Edwards on Cape Cod.

The camp commander was Army lieutenant colonel Ted Dancer, who served briefly as deputy commander of the detention facility at Guantanamo Bay. After the last truck was unloaded, an announcement over the public address system said there would be an assembly of all detainees on the parade ground at four that afternoon.

People interrupted their settling in process to attend the meeting. It was a warm, sunny day. Breaking surf could be heard above the slight breeze. Children were anxious to explore along the shore. The former passengers of the *Iliad* and the *Ionian Star* were relieved to move from the oppressive stadium. They were anxious about what would come next.

They noted the rows of freshly-painted barracks buildings, the mess hall, and the collection of buildings surrounded by barbed wire fencing. This facility had a distressing sense of permanency to it.

That fear was driven home by the camp commander.

"Ladies and gentlemen, by order of the president of the United States, you have each been declared to be an enemy combatant subject to the exclusive jurisdiction of the United States military," Dancer announced. "It is the intention of the United States to detain you in this facility, or any other facility the United States so desires, for the duration of the present hostilities, however long they may last.

"You are entitled to all of the rights of persons holding the status of enemy combatants. Those rights include the following:

"You have the right to receive reasonable meals sufficient to maintain minimal good health.

"You have the right to reasonable medical care for life-threatening illness and injuries.

"You have the right not to be subjected to life-threatening torture or mistreatment."

A murmur started up from the rear of the assemblage. Someone near the front of the crowd began shouting.

"Ah'm not doing shit until ah see mah lawyer," a man shouted, his Southern accent out of place. "Ah demand to see mah lawyer, now."

The crowd became louder, others joining the man in the front demanding to meet with their lawyers—not that they actually had lawyers.

BANG!

The crowd was startled into silence by the shot fired into the air from the pistol in the camp commander's hand.

"Let's get something clear from the start," Dancer said into the microphone. "This is a military camp, a detention camp. You people are military detainees. You don't get lawyers. You don't go to court. You don't even dream about suing me or anybody else. You don't like how we treat you, then tough fucking shit. The president declared you enemy combatants. He did that because you killed American military personnel. And sank our vessels. And then ran into hiding. You are enemies of the United States of America. You will be treated like enemies.

"Get used to it. That is how life is going to be. This meeting is concluded. Troops, see that this crowd disperses to their barracks."

Dancer stepped down from the platform and walked to his office, accompanied by his second in command.

"I thought that went quite well," Dancer said.

"I was not briefed about carrying firearms, sir," the second in command said. "It certainly did get their attention, though."

"There will be no firearms carried. I wanted to make a point, that's all. We won't need firearms to keep these people under control. Didn't carry firearms at Gitmo and we had some tough people there—some of them, anyway. We worked things out on our own." He smiled, as if remembering his introduction to detention of enemy combatants fondly. Dancer placed an arm around the young captain's shoulder. "Let me tell you about *E-R-F*-ing, Captain. Do you know what ERFing is?" Dancer saw the puzzled look on his assistant's face.

"A little method we came up with at Guantanamo. *E-R-F.* Emergency Reaction Force. Pick the ten biggest goons we've got. Dress 'em up in black, from ski mask to boots. Give 'em body armor, the full suit, and Kevlar shields, helmets, batons. They'd scare the shit out of a sumo wrestler. Ten of them come screaming into a room, waving their batons, clanging on their shields, the detainees shit their drawers, they do. That's ERFing. Pick the men. I'll train them myself. And if our guests don't like it, let them cry to the lawyers they won't be meeting with."

"Guantanamo? That must have been quite an experience."

"That's one way of putting it. But I learned some lessons there. Kind of ironic, though. Arabs there. Jews here. Will be interesting to see if there's any difference between them. My money is on them all being the same."

CHAPTER 33

Abram Goldhersh sounded excited on the telephone. "Chaim, we need to meet, right away. I'm sending somebody to pick you up. His name is Mr. Gimel. Remember that. He won't introduce himself. You ask him his name. He'll say Gimel. If he doesn't, don't get in the car."

Levi told Debra Reuben about the telephone call.

"Where are you going?" she asked.

"I don't know," Levi answered.

"How long will you be gone?"

"I don't know."

"Who will you be with?"

"I don't know."

"Why does he need to see you, at least?"

"Debra, I just don't know. I don't know anything more than I've told you. Please, enough with the questions."

"If you don't know anything, why are you going away? I don't understand. It could be dangerous for you out there." Levi sensed the concern in her voice. He answered carefully.

"First, it isn't dangerous for me. I'm nobody out there. Nobody has the slightest idea who I am. What I am. Why I'm here. It's perfectly safe for me to leave this house.

"Second, why am I going? Because I'm bored out of my head sitting around here all day watching television and waiting for something to happen. At least other people are doing things, even if they are childish things like parades that will be forgotten in a week. Debra, with all that's happening, what are we doing? Bubkes, that's what."

She smiled at the Israeli's use of the Yiddish word for "nothing." Secular Israelis avoided Yiddish just as African-Americans avoided Amos-and-Andy-isms like "massuh." Reuben enjoyed dropping the occasional Yiddish into her speech. It reminded her of her grandmother.

Levi must be softening up.

"Okay," she said. "Maybe I'm paranoid. But be careful. Anyway, I've been thinking of going to Washington with Sarah." A smile spread across her face. "It's going to make history. A million American Jews in one place. What a trip it would be to be there."

Levi looked at her. Stunned.

"Forget that," he said. "Look, I'm going out in secret, quietly, making no fuss. Nobody in this country has ever heard of me. You're different. Don't forget who you are. You were on TV, here and there. You were in the government. You have a face people don't forget. You're beautiful."

Chaim thinks I'm beautiful.

"What will you do when they point you out, Debra?"

Reuben frowned.

"Actually, Sarah is on the steering committee for the march. She's going to be speaking. She asked me to think about speaking. I'm a representative, maybe the only representative, of the government of Israel, you know." Reuben pictured herself addressing a crowd of a million Jews gathered in Washington.

"You'll be in handcuffs before you say three words," he said. "When they hold Israel responsible for Damascus, who do you think they'll arrest first?"

Her face paled. "Nobody knows I did that," she whispered. "Nobody but you, and me." She stepped to Levi, throwing her arms around him, clutching him tightly, dropping her head to his shoulder. He held her for several minutes, softly rubbing her hair, holding her tightly against his chest. Her breathing deepened, then slowed, as she absorbed his strength, flowing from his body to hers. *This man has enough strength for the two of us,* she hoped.

Levi gently pushed her away.

"Debra, they don't have to know they picked the right person. They'll take whoever they can get. Do you think you can stand up, identify yourself and then walk away? That won't happen."

"They won't know it was me," she whispered. "And we had the right to defend ourselves. We didn't drop the first bomb. People will understand. We were defending our country. Who could hold Israel, or me, responsible for that?"

"Shall we start a list?" Levi said. "Maybe a billion or so Muslims who believe that taking your head off buys them a ticket to paradise. Maybe the United Nations. Or how about the World Court? Feel like standing trial in Brussels for murdering a hundred thousand people in Damascus? Or maybe even your own United States. Remember what you told me about five-dollar-a-gallon gasoline? Think turning you over for trial in Syria might buy a few million barrels of oil?"

He placed his hands on her shoulders. Looking her full in the face, he continued.

"The name of the game for you is invisible. Low profile is too high. Your days of giving speeches are over. You made that decision months ago."

Reuben was stunned. She'd never truly comprehended the global implications of her role in the Damascus bombing. She'd considered it her personal demon, the tormentor who would never let her forget what she had done. She'd punished herself. She hadn't considered that other people, millions of people, would want to join in. She broke into tears, quietly at first.

Louder and louder until she lost all control as she struggled for breath.

"The best hope we have is finding somebody who can give us new identities, and maybe new faces to go with them," Levi said. "So, no Washington? No speeches? You'll watch it on TV, okay? And I'll be back soon. I promise."

■ ■ ■

A car pulled into the driveway, a Honda Accord sedan. A man in his early twenties behind the wheel. A yarmulke on his head. He remained in the car as Levi walked up to the driver's door. The window rolled down.

"And your name is?" Levi asked.

"Gimel," the man answered. "Shalom. Get in the car."

Debra Reuben let the curtain fall back over the kitchen window as she watched the car drive away. *Be careful, Chaim,* she thought. She poured Bacardi over three ice cubes in a tall glass. She'd stopped adding Coke.

Gimel headed south down the Maine coast toward Portland, Maine's largest city. Neither spoke for the first two hours. Finally, as the car drove through Freeport and Levi craned his neck to stare at the complex of buildings that made up the retail store for L.L.Bean, which even he'd heard about in Israel, Gimel could no longer contain himself.

"I hear you're IDF," he said excitedly. "From Eretz Yisrael."

Levi nodded but said nothing.

"Abram said you're going to train us, teach us," the young man continued. "That's why I'm taking you there. We must do something; we just have to. And we have to do it soon."

The young man turned his head to look at Levi.

"I'm willing to give my life for Israel," he said.

"Keep your eyes on the road," Levi barked. "How much longer until we're there, wherever there is?"

"I'm sorry," Gimel said. "I know. Don't talk. Silence. I can keep secrets, military secrets. We're almost there, maybe another half hour."

The remainder of the drive passed in silence until the car left the highway and drove through a waterfront industrial area with aging brick warehouse buildings set back from the water. They stopped in front of a brick building no different from dozens of others along the docks. The two men entered an unmarked door.

Inside was a small office with a single desk. The desktop was empty. No papers. No lamp. Not even a telephone. There was no chair behind the desk. Abram Goldhersh sat on the desk, eating a sub sandwich, his beard smeared with tuna and mayonnaise.

"Ah, Levi, welcome to the world headquarters of Maccabee Trading Corporation," he said. Turning to the young man, he asked, "No problems getting here, right? Nobody following you?"

"No problems," Gimel replied. "Are the others here?"

"They're inside, with the equipment," Goldhersh said. "Come on, Levi, let me show you our product line, this business of mine."

The three men entered the cavernous interior of the building. Dim light seeped through dirt-encrusted windows high on one wall. The space was gloomy, chilly, damp. A bare bulb illuminated two men sitting in folding chairs next to three metal drums, the size of fifty-five-gallon oil drums.

The two men appeared to be in their early twenties. As with Gimel, both wore small yarmulkes on their heads. Except for that indicator, they were dressed as indescribably as most members of their generation—jeans baggy enough to conceal a brick in their pockets, shirts that looked as if they were purchased for a dollar at the Salvation Army store hanging outside their pants. They stood when Goldhersh and Levi approached. Goldhersh spoke first.

"This is the man I told you about," he said. "He can be trusted." He turned to Levi. "This is Aleph." Goldhersh gestured toward one man, who nodded silently. "And this is Bet."

Levi nodded.

"This"—Goldhersh pointed toward the three steel drums—"is what I was telling you about. What I managed to obtain and was prepared to ship off to Israel. I take it you know what this is, right?"

Levi walked to the drums and inspected writing stenciled on the outside.

KAI ZE QIEN GO INDUSTRIAL CO., LIMITED, Jinan City, Shandong, China 250000.

CAUTION.

MilSpec: MIL-C-45010A

HSE Serial number: 32-A-68450

RDX content: 91 ± 1%

Polyisobutylene plasticiser: 9 ± 1%

Moisture: 0.1% max

Velocity of Detonation: 8092 ± 26 m/s

Density: 1.63 g/cm3

Colour: Nominally white

TNT equivalence: 118%

Chemical marking for detection: Marked

Shelf life: At least 10 years under good conditions.

The top of one barrel was pushed partially to the side. Levi lifted the electric light, held it over the drum and looked inside. He whistled quietly.

"You could do damage with this," he said to Goldhersh. "Of course, without detonators, it's just modeling clay."

To demonstrate, he reached into the barrel and scooped out a handful of light-gray material the consistency of putty. He molded it between his hands like a snowball, something he'd heard of but never actually seen.

"See," he said, tossing the ball from hand to hand. "I trained with this stuff. It's practically inert." He spread his hands and let the ball fall to the concrete floor. All three young men cringed as it splattered on the floor with a thud. Goldhersh was unmoved.

"I know that," he said, speaking to Levy. "I wasn't able to obtain military-grade detonators. You'd think they would be easier to buy than the explosive, but I tried and couldn't get any. I must have tried twenty blasting supply companies, but they all wanted to see my explosives permit."

One of the young men, Mr. Aleph, interrupted. "I told Abram I could take care of a detonator," he said, with a slight smile. "All it needed was a lot of heat in a little space in a very short time. It didn't take me long. Abram was looking in the wrong stores. I just went where I go shopping for everything else. The mall."

He removed a box that said *Blast Off Flight Pack* from a shopping bag labeled *Mostly Maine Hobbies*. Dumping the box on the lid of one of the sealed drums, two dozen small cylinders rolled out, each about four inches, made of rolled brown paper. They had hard clay caps at one end and an odd, cone-shaped indentation at the other, with a small hole through the center of the indentation. They looked, to Levi, like unusual shotgun cartridges.

Estes Industries Model A8-3 Model Rocket Engine was written on the side of each cylinder. The box also contained short lengths of wire bent into *U* shapes with a bit of some material at the bend of the *U*. Finally, the young man removed a small, black, plastic rectangular box with two wires ending in alligator clips coming from one end. A label said *Estes Industries Electron Launch Controller*.

"Cost me almost fifty dollars," he said, beaming. "These are model rocket engines. The wires are electrical igniters. Stick the wire in the hole at the end of the engine. Hook up a battery and the igniter wires to the controller, push the launch button and, boom, the engine ignites and hot flames shoot out the end. There are your detonators."

Goldhersh turned to Levi.

"Will it work?"

Levi recalled the digital electronic detonators he'd trained with in the navy in mock raids in rubber boats. These toys were far from the sophisticated devices he'd used. Nonetheless, he was impressed.

"They'll work," he said. "The C4 will explode. But you've got one extremely serious problem." He moved his gaze from Goldhersh to the three eager young men clinging to each word coming from a real member of the IDF.

"There is no timer," Levi continued. "You press this button"—he gestured at the Electron Launch Controller, with its red button labeled *LAUNCH*—"and the C4 explodes. Whoever presses the button will be blown to small pieces before his finger gets off that box."

Goldhersh spoke first, seeing each of the men nod. "We appreciate that quite well. These three heroes appreciate that. How many millions of Jews have already been killed, by that bomb, by the Arabs, by disease or starvation or torture in those camps? What are three more deaths if they are in a good cause?" He turned toward the young men. "Do you agree?"

"Of course."

"Do you think only Arabs have the courage to kill themselves?"

"It is God's will."

Levi said nothing but walked off by himself into the darkness inside the empty building. After a few moments, he called out.

"Abram, can I speak with you for a minute?"

Goldhersh joined Levi. They stood in the dim light, barely able to see each other as more than a shape.

"Abram, I take it you are serious about this, about setting off that explosive?" Levi asked. "Three drums of C4, Abram, that's like a bomb from a B-52. That will kill an awful lot of people, a lot of Americans. Are you really planning on doing that, Abram? That is a serious action."

"Aren't these serious times?" Goldhersh answered. "Has any time been more serious for the Jewish people? An atomic bomb has killed Jews, who knows how many Jews. Once again, Jews are put into camps, camps in the Holy Land and now camps even right here in America. Camps, Levi, camps. Does that sound familiar? Do you remember what happens to Jews in camps, Levi? I do. Those boys do."

"But, Abram, bombs?" Levi asked. "Terror. Killing more people. Will that accomplish anything?"

"I need an Israeli to ask me whether terror works," Goldhersh laughed. "Were you sick the day they taught Israeli history in school? You remember the Haganah? The Irgun? The Stern Gang? They were the so-called terrorists who drove the British from Palestine and let us create our own nation. They were called terrorists. They set off bombs. They killed people. And they won. Terror worked."

"But Jews have been on the receiving end of more terror than we've dished out over the years," Levi answered.

"That we have. That we have," Goldhersh said. "Black September. The Munich Olympics. The Intifadah and all those public bombings, buses, cafes, shopping centers, flaming kites, for God's sake. But you know what, Levi? You know what? Those bombs worked, too. Do you think that coward Sharon would have handed over the West Bank to the Palestinians, that he would have dragged our own settlers out of Gaza, if it hadn't been for all those bombs they set off? I don't think so. Why do you think I got all this stuff in the first place? It was to give to the settlers so they could set off bombs of their own.

"Terror works, Levi. History proves that. Look what crashing those planes into the World Trade Center did to the United States. Everything changed that day. Nineteen men willing to die changed everything."

Levi's thoughts wandered to the wine cellar under the house where Debra Reuben was at that very moment. He considered for a fleeting second whether to tell Goldhersh what was in that cellar. *Not yet*, he decided, *and not without talking it over with Debra first. It's the government's bomb, and she is the government.*

"So, where are you going to use that stuff, Abram?" Levi asked. "What's the plan?"

"Come with me," Goldhersh said, taking Levi by the elbow. They walked to a far corner, near an overhead garage door leading outside. A large object was covered with a blue plastic tarp. Goldhersh took one corner of the plastic and pulled. Under the tarp was a white Chevrolet van with the words *National Park Service* painted on the side.

"Young Aleph and Bet paid a visit to Acadia National Park last week," Goldhersh said. "Actually, it was more of a shopping trip. They brought this back. Do you suppose our product will fit in the back of that van?"

"Of course it will," Levi said. "But I don't understand. You are going to blow up Acadia National Park. What will that do, kill a few bears?"

"No, my friend," Goldhersh said. "Wrong national park. Wrong place. Wrong message. We want to get the attention of the government, the United States government. Well, where is that government? And what park service is in charge of all the parks there? We're going to have our own march on Washington this weekend, Levi."

CHAPTER 34

After six nights of sleeping alone, Shapiro found the bedroom door ajar. He'd undressed in the dark and climbed into bed as quietly as he could, not knowing if his wife was really sleeping or just pretending. In either case, they spent the night back to back, the gap between their spines either three inches or two feet. It did not matter, Shapiro realized. It might as well have been a brick wall—possibly permanent.

Sally pretended to sleep, her mind racing. Just as Shapiro could not understand his wife's rejection of him, she could not understand how a man who had not been inside a synagogue in ten years, a man who knew maybe six words of Yiddish, a man who laughed at her when she'd suggested they vacation in Israel rather than go on a bicycle trip in Scotland, as he planned, how that man all of a sudden became the Head Jew leading a crusade.

After so many years of marriage, they now seemed so wrong for each other. Thinking back to her college years, she wondered whether her friends were right when they warned her he was too different, that it could not work in the long run. Sally remembered how popular she'd been in college until she became inseparable from Ben Shapiro. *How different my life would have been if I'd never met him, if I'd ended up with somebody more like me . . . I never signed up to be a Jew. Or to have my son treated like a Jew.*

Shapiro had made one more effort to talk with Sally earlier that evening, leading to a discussion that ended after five minutes with her swearing at him for the first time in perhaps a decade, after he'd asked her to join him in going to Washington for the huge march.

"No, absolutely not. There is only one fucking Jew in this family," she shouted, leaping to her feet. "And it certainly is not me, and neither is it Adam."

She thundered up the stairs and slammed the bedroom door. He'd been surprised to find it ajar later.

■ ■ ■

Shapiro's problems at home mirrored his problems with the two cases dominating his work life. The good news was that by the time Shapiro located Aaron Hocksberg, still his only client from among the local Jews arrested at their homes the night of the roundup, Hocksberg had been taken before a federal magistrate, charged with harboring fugitives and released on his own recognizance. All that happened before Shapiro could even meet with his client. The chief judge decided it took less resources for the six federal magistrates, who handled such minor criminal matters as arraignments of arrested persons, to be shuttled from county jail to county jail than it did to transport all the defendants to the federal courthouse.

US Attorney Anderson's press conference, announcing that all of those arrested would be charged with harboring fugitives and in return for guilty pleas his office would request fines and suspended jail sentences, went a long way toward defusing what had the potential to be an explosive situation in Massachusetts.

Attorney General McQueeney's judgment on that issue

proved correct. Despite early threats from defense attorneys to fight every arrest, it appeared that all those charged would escape jail sentences and would have to pay a not-too-significant fine. Samuel Cohn, a senior partner at Goldman Sachs, immediately wrote a million-dollar check to the United States Treasury to pay all the fines.

"These people are heroes," Cohn said. "Given the opportunity, I would have done just what they did. Doing the right thing shouldn't cost them a penny."

Shapiro was not so lucky with his other client, the one charged with state criminal violations. Howie Mandelbaum remained the only person from the two ships taken into custody by state law enforcement officials rather than the feds. Patrick McDonough, Suffolk County district attorney, was infuriated that the US Attorney had wimped out.

McDonough was a proud son of South Boston. He could smell the waterfront from his boyhood home. The idea that foreign forces sank military vessels, even if they were just Coast Guard, and killed military people, including that poor girl, within sight of his own mother's living room window drove McDonough nearly crazy. He didn't care what the feds were doing. He had one Jew in his custody and he intended to throw the book at the young man.

Shapiro returned to his office from a meeting with McDonough gravely concerned for his client. He had assured Mandelbaum's father, who seemed to have something technical to do with stock trading in New York as far as Shapiro could quickly determine, that the feds would take over all the cases and the state charges were likely to be dropped.

Now he'd have to call the senior Mandelbaum and admit he'd been wrong. The only plan Shapiro could come up with was to slow the criminal process and hope public opinion would ease and McDonough would back down.

The Camp Edwards detainees were the third hot potato Shapiro was juggling. He'd enthusiastically volunteered to head the legal defense committee for those detainees, a decision he was beginning to regret. The defense committee was being coordinated through the ADL, the Anti-Defamation League. Dozens of lawyers—not all of them Jewish, Shapiro was pleased to see—volunteered to represent individual detainees. The ADL set up what they hoped was a secure extranet website to coordinate the cases that were soon to be filed. The website included a list server that allowed each participating attorney to send and receive confidential emails. Guantanamo defense attorneys had used a similar arrangement.

Shapiro's inbox was flooded with back-and-forth emails among lawyers on the defense team and new lawyers joining up, it seemed, by the hour. It would be a full-time job just reading all the email. One stood out, though, with a subject header in all capital letters saying *EVERYBODY READ THIS ONE.*

It was from Shapiro's client, Aaron Hocksberg. He was incensed by the arrests in general and by his arrest in particular. The partners in his primarily Jewish law firm voted to devote a don't-worry-about-the-budget effort to representing detainees. The email contained a draft of a petition for a writ of habeas corpus that the firm prepared as a model for all the cases. It was twenty-five pages long.

This is good, Shapiro thought, *this is very good. I wouldn't want to guess how many associates have been awake for the past couple of nights pounding this out.*

The petition traced the history of the writ of habeas corpus back past the founding of the United States and through English history. It referred to a case brought in 1627 by Englishmen jailed by King Charles I. The king locked them up without charge for failing to assist England's war against France and Spain. The prisoners sought writs of habeas corpus, arguing that without specific charges, they should not be imprisoned. The king's attorney general replied that the Crown's interest in protecting the realm justified suspending the ordinary judicial process. The king prevailed, but there was such outrage that Parliament responded with the Petition of Right in 1628, which prohibited imprisonment without formal charges. The petition said that Parliament next passed the Habeas Corpus Act of 1679, which required the government to bring formal criminal charges against any person held in custody within three months of his arrest, bringing to an end the process of arresting people and holding them indefinitely without criminal charges.

That's what they are doing with our detainees, Shapiro thought.

The petition then crossed the Atlantic and emphasized that the only individual right included in the original United States Constitution, even before the Bill of Rights added the first ten amendments, was the right to petition a court for a writ of habeas corpus. The petition pointed out that all other individual rights, such as freedom of speech and religion and the right not to be deprived of life or property without due process of law, were all added later, starting with the Bill of Rights. The Founders felt that only the right to habeas corpus was vital enough to be included in the body of the original constitution.

This is powerful legal argument, Shapiro thought. *Fundamental to our rights as a free nation.*

Shapiro read the remainder of the petition, which read like a historical tour through colonial and Civil War America. He skipped to the bottom line, to the *Relief Requested* portion.

Wherefore, the Petitioners demand that this Court declare that the Petitioners are being deprived of their liberty by the United States without Due Process of Law, without formal charges having been brought against them and in violation of their rights as protected by the Fifth and Fourteenth Amendments to the United States Constitution. Petitioners further demand that this Court issue preliminary and permanent injunctions prohibiting the United States from further holding said Petitioners in custody.

I like that, Shapiro thought. *That's legalese for Moses's message to the Pharaoh another time Jews were held in captivity without cause. Let my people go.*

■ ■ ■

The iCal reminder message beeped at Ben Shapiro. *Lunch with JK*, it said. Judy Katz. *Shit,* he thought. *I'm late.* Shapiro leaped from his desk, grabbed his suit jacket and jogged out the door. He arrived at the Sultan's Palace right at noon.

Shapiro scanned the people standing in line outside the door without recognizing anybody. As he moved forward to look inside the restaurant, he felt a tap on his shoulder. He turned and felt a charge race through his body. Standing in front of him was a stunning young woman with long, full black hair swept back from her face and falling beyond her shoulders. Her dark eyes were clear and intelligent. Her coal-black suit was certainly businesslike, but it did little to hide her figure.

"Ben Shapiro?" she asked.

"That I am," Shapiro answered. "I take it you are Judy. Nice to finally meet you. I've followed your exploits in the *Globe*. I've gotta tell you, I enjoy it when a young attorney kicks butt—especially, and I'm not being chauvinistic here but maybe a bit paternalistic for an old man like me, I enjoy it when a young woman attorney can kick butt in court in front of a jury. There's nothing like that thrill when you know the jury is buying your act, right?"

She gave him a puzzled look. "Are you this candid this quickly with everyone you meet?" she asked.

"No, sorry, look, I apologize. One of those mornings so far, I guess. No, what I meant to say is that good trial lawyers are rare, and from all I've heard and read about you, you are a good trial lawyer." He was surprised to feel the rush of a blush come to his face. "That was an awkward effort at a compliment, I suppose."

She smiled. "Compliment accepted then. I agree." She leaned close to him. He smelled a fresh, outdoor smell from her hair, her skin perhaps. Not flowery—more like an absence of odors than any particular smell at all. She put her lips close to his right ear, glancing at the backs of the people in line in front of them. He heard her whisper, "I know what you mean. Hearing that word, *guilty*, from the jury foreman is as close as I've come to having an orgasm with my clothes on," she said.

"Never quite gone that far myself," Shapiro said quickly, standing straight, pulling his head away from her.

After five minutes they came to the head of the line and placed their orders, which they carried to a table on the second level. She glanced at Shapiro's left hand, confirming that the gold band was a wedding ring. That was disappointing but not totally disqualifying.

"So, wonderful as it is for us to meet, I assume there was a specific reason for this get-together," Shapiro said as they finished their lunches.

"Yes, there certainly is," Katz said, businesslike and much less flirtatious. "I want to know whether you would be willing to bring a religious discrimination lawsuit against the United States Attorney."

Shapiro sat back in his chair, hand on his chin, looking closely at Katz to see whether she was joking.

"I'm not afraid to sue anybody. I've certainly taken on bigger fish than Arnie Anderson," he said calmly. "I assume you are the plaintiff."

She nodded.

"And I assume you are Jewish."

She nodded again.

"So you want to sue Arnie Anderson because he did something to you at work because you are Jewish? Is that what you are saying?"

"That is precisely what I'm saying," Katz said. "Let me tell you what happened." She described the recent events to him, leaving out only her lunch with Bob Shaw, honoring her promise to keep that confidential. She owed him that much.

Besides, it was a promise.

She finished her recitation with a question, the question clients always ended their recitations with. "So," she said, "do I have a case?"

Shapiro respected her for not asking the other question clients always asked: "What's it worth?" He paused to draw a deep breath, then let it out slowly.

"Yes, technically you have a case. You were treated differently in the terms and conditions of your employment because of your religion. That violates Title VII, the federal employment discrimination statute. You're a federal employee, so you have to jump through a few more procedural hoops than if you were a private employee, but you do have a valid, legitimate, even winnable claim."

She smiled. Relieved.

"But, Judy, it isn't a case I'd be interested in bringing. There is so much more going on that concerns me, concerns me as a lawyer but mostly concerns me as a Jew. You're looking at probably five years of litigation. You have to go through the Justice Department human rights office first, then through the Equal Employment Opportunity Commission process, all before you, as a federal employee, get to first file suit in court. I think five years would be quick.

"In five years Arnie will be gone, either in the statehouse where he wants to be or in some big firm, where he's more likely to be. You won't be doing what you are doing now. That lawsuit would kill your career. And all for what? What damages could you expect? You aren't out of pocket a nickel. I assume you didn't have any nervous breakdown and wind up committed to McLean Hospital. That's what it takes to get big bucks for emotional distress. You could win and get twenty-five grand, and I'd get an award of attorney's fees and make ten times what you get from the case, and neither of us would see a penny of that for five years. I wouldn't do it if I were you, and I won't do it myself."

She sighed. "How did I know you were going to say that?"

"Because you're a trial lawyer yourself," he said. "A real trial lawyer."

"So, I'll quit then," she said suddenly, waiting for him to tell her how wrong a move that would be.

"I would if I were you," he answered, surprising her. "I'd quit any government job these days. This is not a government a Jew should be affiliated with. I'm fighting against this government. That's what you should be doing, too."

Shapiro paused, rubbing his chin and looking at Katz carefully. Then he smiled at her.

"So, Judy, how are you fixed for money?"

"I'm comfortable," Katz said. "I sure haven't spent much over the years, and my parents left me, well, something. They had life insurance. It paid into a trust fund—not a real huge trust fund, but enough to live on, the way I live. Why do you ask?"

"I'll tell you in a moment," Shapiro replied. "One more question. Do you have a security clearance?"

"You'll have to explain what significance that has before I answer," she said, a tinge of coldness coming into her expression.

"Ok, fair enough," Shapiro said, smiling at her, encouraged by her caution. *This woman is the kind of lawyer I like*, he thought. "I know an organization looking for a good trial lawyer. I don't know how much it pays or even if it pays at all. The ADL, Anti-Defamation League. I'm working with them, along with what seems to be half the Jewish lawyers in town, on habe petitions for the people being held on the cape. It's already out of control. There could be four thousand separate lawsuits the way it's shaping up. We need somebody to coordinate it all.

"I'm in charge of the committee that is supposed to be running the whole show. About two minutes ago I appointed myself head of the hiring subcommittee. In that position, I'm offering you the job of head coordinator of the habeas corpus litigation team. What do you say?"

"Whoa, let me catch my breath here," she replied. "There

are going to be petitions for writs of habeas corpus filed for all the people, Jews, held at that Army base, or whatever it is, on the cape. The argument is that they are being illegally detained because of their religion. On the other side the government would be defended by"—a smile crossed her face—"by the United States Attorney for the district in which they are detained, which would be Massachusetts. Arnie Anderson. Is that right, Mr. Shapiro?"

"Ben."

"Yes, of course, Ben. That sounds an awful lot like what I wanted to talk with you about in the first place. I'll do it. And I'll enjoy doing it."

Shapiro thrust his hand across the table. She placed her hand in his and squeezed, firmly. He was slow to let go. She was even slower. The tips of their fingers dragged against one another as they withdrew their hands.

This is going to be interesting, Shapiro thought.

"I'll resign this afternoon," Katz said. "I don't feel like I've got to give Arnie more notice than that. He's already told me in the best way he can he doesn't want me working for him. So, what happens next?"

"Come to my office at eight tomorrow morning. You'll work from there. I'll find a space for you," Shapiro said. "We'll try to get something done tomorrow. I leave for Washington pretty soon after that. I can't miss the march."

"You're going to that big march in Washington," she said, laughing. "Of course you would go. You're one of those 1960s-wannabe guys, aren't you, civil rights and marches and all that." She looked him in the eye and spread a mile-wide smile at him. "I just love '60s guys."

This woman is so young, Shapiro thought.

"Are you planning on going?" he asked.

"My grandmother asked me to go with her. Her entire canasta club is going; actually I suspect her entire congregation is going. Nana told me to go. You have to fight the Nazis, she told me. Even should they kill you, you fight them, she said. I was shocked. My nana telling me to fight. I didn't know how to respond. I told her I couldn't go, blamed my job."

Her next words chilled the smile from Shapiro's face.

"She was in the Warsaw Ghetto," Katz said, surprised at the pride in her voice. "She escaped. Her husband, my grandfather, died fighting."

Shapiro did not know what to say. Judy continued.

"I hadn't even thought about going. Didn't seem like a good career move for an Assistant United States Attorney, but that isn't my career anymore. I suppose the head habeas coordinator really should be there. Sure, why not? Sure, I'll go. I'll make reservations this afternoon."

Shapiro shook his head. "I'm pleased you're going, but there are no reservations to be made. Every flight is booked. The trains are booked. I even heard the Greyhound buses are booked. Most people are going on charter buses. Do you belong to a synagogue? I'm sure it has a bus or two going."

"No, I'm not much of a joiner," she said sheepishly. "How are you getting there?"

"I waited too long, too. That's how I know there are no reservations. I'm driving, although I don't know what I'll do with the car when I get there, or where I'll be staying. I expect all those details will work out. The important thing is being there."

"Could you fit a passenger?" Katz asked, looking him in the eyes.

"Sure," he said softly. "Big car, lots of room."

"And if we can't find a place to stay we can always camp out in the car," Katz said. "Your car has a back seat, doesn't it?"

"Sure does," Shapiro answered. "A big soft one."

"Great," she answered enthusiastically. "One thing, though. What was that about a security clearance?"

"Just the Justice Department jerking us around," he said. "You know how that's done, I'm sure."

She nodded. "I wrote the memo on jerking around defense counsel."

"They've told us no lawyer goes to Edwards unless he's got a top secret security clearance, just like at Guantanamo," Shapiro said. "And the screening process takes six months. I'll pay a bonus on top of the pro bono salary you won't be getting if you've got a security clearance."

She nodded. "No problem on that. Let's just say," she said, glancing at his left hand, "the United States government certifies that I can keep a secret."

CHAPTER 35

The Jewish March on Washington was all over the news. Boston stations reported that local synagogues had chartered virtually every available bus. Sam Abdullah and Alfred Farouk watched the news in Sam's room, when Al supposedly came over to work on a history project.

The ABC News reporter described the security precautions in Washington as "unprecedented."

"The FBI is saying that as many as a million American Jews are expected to descend on the city this weekend," the carefully coifed reporter said with a concerned expression. "And other law enforcement sources predict that several hundred thousand counter-demonstrators may attend, angry that there have been no prosecutions for the murders of ten Coast Guard officers and two FBI agents by Jewish terrorists in the Boston area. The law enforcement presence here is overwhelming."

Al jammed his thumb on the remote control to turn the television off.

"A million Jews all in one place," he said. "Imagine what a little bit of bomb would do there. There'd be Jew-meat splattered all over the place."

"Yeah, but it doesn't sound like there's any chance that's gonna happen," Sam responded. "It looks like every cop in the world is gonna be there to protect the Jews. Wouldn't you know it, they're the ones who killed people and yet it's our taxpayers' dollars that keep anybody from getting back at them. It shows that no matter what the Jews do, they get away with it, no matter how bad it is. They can do anything."

"You're right, man," Al said. "Just let some Muslim set off a bomb or highjack a plane and they get the Special Forces and all after them. Jews set off an atom bomb in the middle of a Muslim city and we still let them all get together for the biggest picnic in the world on the front lawn of the fucking White House. What does it take before this country gets pissed off at Jews for a change?"

The two young men sat in silence for several minutes, infuriated at the waste of their tax dollars, neither acknowledging that they had yet to actually earn enough money to have to pay any taxes.

Sam spoke first.

"What if the Jews did something bad this week, just before their big march, something that really got the government down on them? Wouldn't that screw up their march?"

"Probably. Maybe," Al responded cautiously. "But that would be pretty dumb of them, right before they hold what they say is gonna be a super peaceful demonstration, to do something that would get people pissed at them. One thing everybody knows is that Jews are smart. It would be dumb to fuck around right before they go to beg the government for sympathy. They're not that stupid, man. But it would be cool if they were."

"It sure would be cool. It would be better than cool," Sam said. "It would totally mess up their peaceful giant march. Mess up that march, man, and there's no way even that Jew-lover Quaid is gonna go into Palestine and bail them out."

"Yeah, yeah, man, but like I said, Jews are smart. They aren't gonna do anything like that, not now," Al said.

Again, the two sat in silence. Again, Sam broke the silence.

"What if people thought it was Jews who did something really bad? Wouldn't that do the same thing? It doesn't really have to be Jews who do it, not as long as everybody thinks it was. Am I right or am I right?"

"I guess you're right." Al Farouk sensed, again, that his friend was serious; this was more than playing fantasy games. "Man, are you, like, for real about this, about doing something, and not just talking about how cool it would be to do something?"

Sam paced the room. He pointed toward the computer on which they'd spent so many hours visiting the American Mujahidin website.

"Serious?" he asked. "Of course I'm serious. Don't you think those guys we read about in Palestine, all those martyrs, were serious? Not just guys. Girls. Girl martyrs over there, man. They aren't any better than us—no older, no smarter, no braver. If they could do it, why can't we? If they can die for Allah, why can't we do it, too?

"Just think what a difference we could make. We stop the United States from bailing out the Jews in Palestine and the whole world is different. If we could do that, just us, a couple of ordinary guys here in Massachusetts, if we do that, they'll write poems about us around the world, sing songs about us. How cool would that be?"

"Yeah, that would be pretty cool," Al replied. He was catching his friend's enthusiasm. "Yeah, pretty fucking cool. Heroes around the world. Pretty cool. I could get into that. So we die. Big fucking deal. We know what happens to martyrs when they die. I could dig that."

He was talking more to himself than to his friend—talking himself into doing something he would not do but for all the hours of listening to Mullah Abu Hamzah, months of discussions with his best friend about martyrs in Palestine, young men who looked not unlike the two Americans, young men who were also in high school, who also left family behind. Talking himself into something that without that preparation he would view as just plain stupid.

Now, though, watching the news, listening to Jewish leaders predict they would get all the support they asked for from Washington, now it sounded more like a spectacular way to pole-vault himself into history.

"What do you have in mind?" he asked Sam. "Because whatever it is, I'm in it with you."

"We do something big, really big. Lots of people die. And we do it so people think it was Jews who did it. They blame the Jews for it. Cool, right? Right before their big peace march the Jews kill a shitload of Americans. Make killing those Coast Guard guys seem like pissing in public."

"Yeah, I see it, man. People are pissed off at the Jews enough for killing the Coast Guard guys, and that girl Coast Guard, too. And the FBI guys." Al was getting excited. "So what are you thinking?"

"We can't do it in DC," Sam said. "Every cop in the world is gonna be there, and besides, we don't want to kill Jews with this."

"Well, duh, we do want to kill Jews," Al interrupted, then thought for a moment. "Just not this time around." He paused again. "Oops," he continued. "Guess this thing will be our only thing. Guess somebody else will have to kill Jews. Our thing is to kill Americans and make everybody think the Jews did it. Right? That's the game plan?"

"That's the game plan," Sam said. "Okay, we gotta get that TNT from your dad's shed. You sure were right about the combination. So what do we do with it? Blow up a school like those Chechen guys did in Russia? That got people pissed off."

"I don't know if I want to kill kids," Alfred said. "How about if we do grownups, adults? Kids is pretty heavy duty. Besides, it could be hard to get into a school if you don't go there."

"We could do our own schools," Sam speculated, then backed away. "No. Don't want to do our own friends. Some of those kids are okay. Besides, that might seem like a Florida kinda thing—what was that school?"

"Parkland," Al said.

"Right, Parkland. They'd probably make us seem like loser types doing our own school. Okay, not a school. How about some sports event? Too bad it isn't Super Bowl time."

"Think, man, that doesn't work. We've gotta do it this week. There won't be any big sports events this week. Besides, there's security at those things. I saw it on TV. They check everybody coming in and they've got dogs and sniffer machines and shit. No, man, it's gotta be someplace where lots of people go all the time, even during the week. Someplace where there's shit for security."

"But there's gotta be cameras, security cameras so everybody knows it was Jews that did it, right? Where do people hang out all the time, with no security except cameras?"

They thought for no more than thirty seconds before Al smiled broadly.

"The mall, man. The fucking mall. It's perfect."

"Fucking A, you're right," Sam said. "But not one mall. There's two of us. We'll do two malls."

"Two malls. Okay. Let's make a pact, a pact before Allah." Al Farouk's tone of voice changed from the near hilarity with which he and his friend were speaking as they exchanged ideas. Now, he was on board, committed. Neither of them spoke about Allah in jest.

"I vow before Allah that I will do this deed," Al said. He looked at Sam.

"And I vow before Allah that I, too, will do this deed."

"Good," Sam continued. "Let's go to your dad's place tonight and get the TNT."

"And the blasting caps," Al added. "We need the blasting caps and the six-volt batteries there. We can skip the fancy box they use to set it off. Just touch the two wires together and boom. That's all it will take."

"Boom. That's all it will take," Sam echoed. "We skip school tomorrow and put the belts together. Nothing to it. Just duct-tape the TNT around us, hook up the wires and the blasting caps, connect it to the battery and boom when the wires get touched together. Right?"

"Right," Al said. "We do it tomorrow night, three days before the big Jew march on Washington. So, man, what's your favorite mall?"

Sam thought for a moment. "North Shore. The food court. Love that Japanese chicken thing they sell there. And you?"

"Burlington Mall," Al replied. "Yeah, the food court is the place to do it. It'll be packed around, say, six thirty, everybody eating their mall food."

Sam looked at his friend.

"We are going to do this, right? We vowed before Allah. No backing out?"

"Hey, we vowed. We can't back out now," Al said. "Tomorrow night. I'll meet you in Paradise."

"Yeah, Paradise," Sam said, shaking his head. "Do you suppose that shit with the virgins and all really happens when you die a martyr's death?"

"I don't know," Al said. He smiled at his friend. "I guess we'll find out tomorrow night."

CHAPTER 36

Robert Jordan was head of the White House Secret Service detail. Unlike two other presidents he'd guarded, Jordan both liked and respected President Quaid. Jordan's job was protecting his boss from physical threats. And because he liked President Quaid, he thought it proper to tip him off to a political threat, too.

"Mr. President. I just spoke with Joe Bergantina. Joe's in charge of the First Lady's detail. Joe wanted to brief me about the First Lady's travel plans for tomorrow, sir."

"I appreciate the call, Bob," President Quaid replied. "But the First Lady makes her own travel plans these days. In fact, she makes her own plans for pretty much everything these days. We've decided not to coordinate our schedules anymore."

There were no secrets from the Secret Service. The First Lady was referred to in the Secret Service radio code as "Fox," a corollary to her husband's code name of "Wolf," which he claimed derived from the way he could make a roast beef sandwich disappear in fifteen seconds. Agent Jordan knew Fox had not spent a single night in what the detail referred to as the Wolf's Den in several weeks. The Lincoln bedroom was no longer available for overnight guests because Mrs. Quaid claimed it for herself.

"Okay, Bob, just out of curiosity and not because I seem to have any say in the matter, go ahead and tell me. Where is my wife going tomorrow?"

"She's informed her detail she'll be traveling to Massachusetts tomorrow. She will be flying on Air Force One. She said she will be traveling with a delegation."

"So she's going to Boston on Air Force One. What's the big deal?"

"Well, sir, that's the problem. Mrs. Quaid isn't flying on Air Force One to Boston. She is flying to Otis Air Force Base on Cape Cod. That's where that detention camp, Camp Edwards, is. The one where the Jews—I mean, the Israelis are being held. She's flying with a delegation of Jewish leaders. She told her security detail that there should be trucks standing by at Otis to transfer supplies. Actually, the term she used was 'relief supplies,' to the detention camp."

President Quaid glanced at the ceiling, considering his response.

"You did the right thing by sharing this, Bob. This isn't something I'd want to find out from the six o'clock news. Tell me, Bob, do you have a wife?"

"Yes, sir, I do. Three of them, in fact. All ex-wife types, though. Nobody on board at the moment."

"Sometimes, Bob, I think an ex-wife could be the best kind to have. But keep that one under your hat, will you please?"

"With everything else, sir. With everything else."

■ ■ ■

Lawrence Quaid prided himself on his moral compass. Patted himself on the back for knowing right from wrong. For doing right, opposing wrong. Quaid had become increasingly concerned in recent weeks that this moral compass had not been in his hands all those years but had rather been held by his wife. That she, rather than he, was the good person. That her role was to guide him down the right path. Away from what was expedient but wrong.

This time, though, he was lost and alone.

And it didn't help when his chief of staff Bob Brown bailed out, either. Quaid corrected himself. *Brown didn't really bail out*, he thought. *I booted him out. Come to think of it, Catherine told me which way to go on that decision, too. I chose not to follow her.*

President Quaid picked up the phone and asked to have Gen. Cruz located. As it turned out, the chairman of the Joint Chiefs of Staff was in the West Wing and came to the Oval Office at a brisk walk.

"Mr. President," he said, slightly out of breath.

"General," Quaid said. "I am extremely upset to hear about the mechanical problems that grounded Air Force One."

General Cruz looked at the president with a puzzled expression. He said nothing, waiting for Quaid to continue.

"The First Lady planned on flying to Massachusetts tomorrow, to deliver supplies, relief supplies, to Otis Air Base. General, you can imagine how upset I am that she will be unable to make that trip, can't you?"

The general nodded, understanding.

"Yes, sir, I'll apologize personally to the First Lady. The Air Force prides itself on maintaining Air Force One scrupulously. Unfortunately, Air Force Two is also undergoing service. This is a major blunder and I take full responsibility for it, sir."

"No apology necessary, General. Better safe than sorry, to be trite. So how long do you expect the plane—any plane, in fact—to be unavailable for the First Lady's use?"

"Mr. President, for just as long as you say so, I expect."

"Thank you, General. I see we understand each other."

CHAPTER 37

The Camp Edwards detainees were sorted into categories. Families were moved to barracks where they could remain together. Some even included a small kitchen. That portion of the base was called Camp Foxtrot. Those age fifty and above were in Camp Alpha, with unmarried men and women in separate buildings. Residents of both camps could visit one another, and they ate in a communal mess hall.

At the far side of Edwards was Camp Echo, named nostalgically by Base Commander Dancer after the Camp Echo at Guantanamo, where the least cooperative detainees were housed. The residents of Camp Echo were all between eighteen and forty-nine and all potential members of the Israel Defense Forces. Camp Echo was surrounded by a wire fence topped with coiled razor wire. A second identical fence stood a dozen yards outside the inner fence. Wooden guard towers stood at each corner.

The barracks at Camp Echo showed their hasty and recent renovation. Plywood partitions created a series of separate rooms, each ten feet by eight feet. Windows were covered by plywood. Air circulated from ceiling vents. No light entered from the outside. Each room had a single wire-covered fluorescent fixture. There were no light switches in the rooms, no electrical outlets of any kind. The lights were never turned off—never during the day, never at night.

Each room had a loudspeaker mounted high on a wall. There were two plastic pails in each room. One held drinking water. The other was the toilet. A plastic pad served as a mattress. Detainees were issued plastic foam blankets that tore when twisted or stretched, designed to prevent suicides. The pads and blankets were collected every morning and handed back every evening.

When inmates moved from one place to the other, they were shackled at wrists and ankles, blacked-out ski goggles over their eyes, and sound-deadening muffs covered their ears.

Maj. Dancer designed Camp Echo as a replica of Guantanamo Bay. His only regret was that because he was limited to the existing facility and because of time constraints, the rooms were built from plywood rather than steel shipping containers.

Keep them guessing, uncomfortable, with absolutely no control. That was a lesson learned at Guantanamo. Hot, then cold. Light, then dark. Silent, then loud. All out of their control. Completely dependent on their interrogator. "Womb rooms," the soldiers manning the camp called them. Not cells. Womb rooms cut off from everything. From everybody.

The most important building at Camp Echo was the JIF, the Joint Interrogation Facility. It was constructed from cinderblocks, with sound-deadening vermiculite pellets poured through the holes in the blocks. It, too, had no windows and it, too, was separated into a warren of small rooms accessible only by a single door from the common hallway. Each room had a wall-mounted camera.

Following the pattern created at the interrogation camp established at Bagram Air Base in Afghanistan and continued at Guantanamo Bay, the detainees at Camp Echo were nameless, identified in camp records only by numbers, bestowed on them sequentially in the order in which they were processed. The Nazis used the same procedure at Auschwitz.

Camp Echo's detainees were numbered *00001* to *01657.* There was considerable discussion when the detainee database was first established as to how many digits the numbers should have. Five digits provided for a maximum of 99,999 persons.

"If we need more numbers than that," Maj. Dancer joked, "we'll have bigger problems than reprogramming the database."

Edwards wasn't America's first concentration camp. The Confederacy warehoused 45,000 Union prisoners at Andersonville in Georgia. Some 13,000 died. At the Union prison camp at Elmira, New York, called by its inmates "Hellmira," almost 3,000 of the 12,000 Confederates held there died one winter. Within two months of the Japanese bombing of Pearl Harbor, 120,000 Americans of Japanese ancestry were herded into ten internment camps, some for as long as five years.

Camp Edwards improved on earlier versions.

The interrogation unit remained unused for the first week after the detainees arrived. One day, however, a De Havilland C-7A Caribou transport aircraft bearing no markings but painted in Army olive drab landed at Otis Air Base next to Camp Edwards. Twenty men and women in jeans and T-shirts walked down the stairway rolled up to the twin-engine aircraft. They assembled in the mess hall, which was cleared of both detainees and the Massachusetts National Guards troops who staffed the camp.

Dancer gave a short speech welcoming the young men and women to Camp Edwards, careful to casually drop a reference to his time at Guantanamo to let them know he'd paid his dues.

The next person who stood in front of the group looked decidedly nonmilitary. His posture, his physique, the very way he walked and stood and carried himself showed he spent his days at a desk or, more likely, hunched over a computer. Besides, although he wore a suit and a tie, his shoes looked like they'd last been polished in whatever Chinese shoe factory manufactured them.

"My name is Wilson Harrison," the man said. The twenty men and women were casually draped around wooden chairs dragged into a rough semicircle in front of him.

"I am a deputy United States attorney general. More importantly, I am temporary special legal assistant to the president. I am told that you were each hand-selected from the Military Intelligence Corps, that you are the cream of the crop from Huachuca." He was referring to the Army Intelligence School at Fort Huachuca, Arizona, where Army interrogators were trained.

"You have not been told why you've been brought here, although I suspect you have a good idea, right?" He was met with grins and nods. "Here is what you don't know." He reached into his briefcase and dropped a handful of gold-colored objects on the table behind him, stepping aside so they could be seen.

"These are Israel Defense Forces dog tags. They were found on the bottom of Boston Harbor, directly underneath where the two ships that carried the detainees of this facility were anchored. Somebody from those ships fired rocket-propelled grenades at two United States Coast Guard vessels, sinking both vessels and killing ten people, ten American military personnel.

"We believe that the people who did this wore these dog tags and that they threw them overboard before fleeing from the ships, along with all the other people held at this camp. We've separated all the men and women of military age. They are in this portion of the camp, which we've called Camp Echo." He noticed smiles on several faces and knowing nods on others.

Echo was military slang for an interrogator. Each person in the room was an echo, and they understood that this part of the camp was built for their use.

"Your job is to determine which of the detainees at Camp Echo belong to these dog tags. The president has determined that every detainee at this camp is an enemy combatant. Some of them may hold dual US-Israeli citizenship. That doesn't matter."

Dancer interrupted. The major knew how to address soldiers.

"He means that it don't mean shit if somebody was born in the US of A. We treat 'em all the same. Nobody gets special treatment—that is, unless they earn it. Got that?"

He was met with smiles and a few raised fists, plus a few scattered shouted *HOO-AH*s.

Harrison nodded and continued.

"These detainees, these foreign military personnel, are the first soldiers of any other nation to kill American military personnel on American soil—well, technically on American waters—since the British burned the White House in the War of 1812. The president views this conduct as an act of war, even though the country these people are from no longer technically exists."

He held the dog tags in front of his chest, jingling them. "Your job is to identify these people, these murderers. Once that is done, they will be given hearings and, if you do your jobs properly, will be found guilty."

Again Dancer interrupted. "And shot. Nobody kills American soldiers and lives to brag about it. Right?"

This time every person in the room rose to his or her feet. Fists pumped in the air. "*USA, USA, USA*" broke out. When they returned to their seats, Harrison spoke again.

"There's more. Major, the doors and windows are sealed, correct? The perimeter of this building is patrolled? There is nobody outside the building who can hear what we say, correct?"

"Absolutely, Mr. Harrison. Just as I was ordered to do. This building is tight. What gets said here stays here. And every soldier in this room knows that, knows that damn abso-fucking-lutely. Am I correct?"

This time he was met with stern, serious expressions and a roomful of "yes sirs."

Harrison turned to the soldiers again.

"You have to do more than identify the people who wore these dog tags," he said, now speaking quietly and seriously.

"Once you find them, you must, and I emphasize the word *must*, meaning that you have no choice, you must find out everything they know about another Israeli soldier. This man." He held up the photograph of Chaim Levi.

"His name is Chaim Levi. He is a lieutenant in the Israeli Navy. He made his way into this country. We don't know exactly where he is, although the FBI has determined how he entered this country. It was on a boat, a sailboat that he sailed from somewhere in the Middle East all the way across the ocean to this country, to New England, probably to Maine.

"We don't know who was on this boat with him. Most likely other military personnel were with him, probably a highly trained team. We don't know that, but it only makes sense. We also don't know for certain that this Lt. Levi was coordinating with the military personnel on those freighters, the ones who are among the detainees in this camp. But that, too, only makes sense. Two units from the same country's military are infiltrated into this country at roughly the same time in roughly the same area, both by sea. It only makes sense they are working together. The people on the freighters had military weapons with them and didn't hesitate to use them." Harrison paused again, looking around the room. Every face was staring at him.

"What I am about to tell you is known by only a few people. It will not go beyond you. The consequences of your breaching the confidential nature of this information are most serious."

Dancer interrupted. "That means you tell anybody squat and your ass will fry in the sizzle seat at Leavenworth. And I'll press the button to fry you myself. Is that understood?"

Twenty "yes sirs" rang out.

Dancer turned toward Harrison and said, "Go ahead, tell them the rest. Tell me the rest; nobody else has."

"The president has reason to believe that this Lt. Levi smuggled into this country military weapons," Harrison said. "The president has reason to believe that among those weapons was a quantity of uranium-235. That is a substance that has only one use. That use is to construct atomic bombs.

"We don't know much more than that. We don't know how much U-235 he had. We don't even know whether it was in a functional bomb or just the material itself. We don't know much of anything except that this Lt. Levi sailed a boat containing U-235 and removed that material somewhere along the Maine coast. You are going to wring every bit of information about that material and about this Lt. Levi from every person being held in this camp. The security of this nation depends on your skill in doing this job."

"Are any of you going to let your president down? Are you willing to do *whatever* it takes?" Dancer shouted.

Shouts of "Hoo-ahhh, hoo-ahhh, USA, USA" filled the room.

■ ■ ■

Interrogation was as old as warfare. The Army had a ninety-seven-page interrogation manual and confirmed that the use of torture was prohibited by the Geneva Convention.

President Quaid didn't want to violate the Geneva Convention. But he wanted to come right up to the legal line. Attorney General McQueeney's advice was not what the president wanted to hear.

"America does not use torture, Mr. President," she told him. "That's the law. That's our history. That's what we stand for. You permit torture and you violate the law. It's as simple as that."

"Come on, Queen," President Quaid retorted angrily. "After New York goes up in a radioactive cloud you want me to tell the American people that we could have stopped it from happening but we didn't want to hurt any of the bad guys?"

The attorney general refused to back down.

"I've been offering my resignation for a month now, Mr. President," she said.

"I know, Queen, and I've been refusing it, but maybe it's time for that after all."

"Say the word, and you have my head on a plate, so to speak," she answered.

Carol Cabot, the president's legal counsel, increasingly filled the shoes left vacant by Bob Brown, the former chief of staff. She sided with the congressional leaders urging the president to do whatever it took to protect the nation.

"You have all the power in the world," she'd told the president. "Go ahead and wield it. I'll cover you with the right paper. My job is to protect you, and you can trust me to do that, sir."

Quaid reached Cabot by telephone at her home.

"Carol, sorry to call you this late, but I've made a decision and I want you to make it happen, tomorrow, first thing," he said. "The Queen's been offering to resign and I've been balking at it. Wrong time for that and all. Well, first thing tomorrow you call her and tell her to get her resignation to me, in writing. I want her resignation on my desk by nine, effective immediately. Second thing, those presidential findings and directives you talked about. Do it. I want them by the end of the day tomorrow. Any questions?"

"Well, sir, there is one thing. Who will run the shop at Justice starting tomorrow with the Queen out before a new AG is in?"

"I thought about that, Carol. I like that deputy over there, Harrison. We'll name him interim attorney general for now and decide later whether to send his name to the Senate for the permanent position. Make that happen, too."

CHAPTER 38

Debra Reuben ran to the kitchen window when she heard a car crunch the gravel driveway. The Honda Accord stopped. Levi got out, waving to the driver. Reuben ran to the front door, shoved it open and stopped, catching her breath, ready to scold Levi for not calling. Instead, she opened her arms wide. He walked into her embrace, and as she tilted her head back he placed his lips on hers. They kissed, deeply and long. Neither wanted to be the first to let go. For the minutes they held one another, neither thought of atom bombs, past, present or future.

"I was so worried," Rueben whispered, her lips an inch from his ear. Then she released him, placing her hand on his chest and pushing, not too hard but neither too lightly. "Why didn't you call? Do you have any idea how scared I was? What if you'd been arrested?"

"I'm sorry," Levi said. "I'll tell you everything, but, look, this isn't a good time to be using the telephone. We have to be careful. Things are going on—well, things are about to happen— and we need to talk."

They sat on the living room sofa. Levi told Reuben everything from the past twenty-four hours and everything that was about to happen. He spoke without personal commentary. He wanted to see her reaction before letting her know his feelings about Goldhersh's plans.

When he finished, Levi asked, "So, what do you think?"

"Another bomb," she said flatly.

Reuben stood and walked through the house to the porch overlooking the ocean. She leaned forward against the railing, her arms crossed in front of her chest, staring at the water. Levi trailed behind her and stood silently, watching her back, waiting for her to speak first.

"Chaim, I know I am responsible for terrible things," she said, speaking gently. "While I've been by myself I dared to think about all those poor people in Damascus, all those people who died, and I thought that I am responsible for their deaths and how could my heart, my soul, carry that burden.

"To tell you the truth, I even thought about taking my own life. I thought I could fill my pockets with stones from the shore over there and jump into the water from that rock, jump in from that rock right there." She pointed at a boulder at the water's edge. "I could take one step and sink and all this would be over."

Levi opened his arms. He wanted so much to comfort her, to protect her from her demons. She shook her head and continued speaking, strength in her voice this time.

"Obviously, I didn't do that. I've come to appreciate that I did what had to be done. Not for me. Not for revenge. For Israel. There will come a time, God willing, when there will be another Israel, when Jews will have our land again as our home. And if history is any guide, in that time Israel will have enemies who will swear to drive us into the ocean if they cannot annihilate us first. It has always been that way. Somebody has always sworn to wipe us from the earth.

"I came to understand why the plans were made in the first place. Because when that next time comes, those enemies are going to remember one word, and that word will be *Damascus*. And maybe when they remember that word, just maybe they'll hesitate. And if they do hesitate, if they do step back and another million or more Jews live who they would have killed, well, then those Jews will have lived because of what I did. That was why the plan was made. That is why I followed it.

"So, Chaim, I accept what I did. I can live with it. I'm not a monster. I'm not evil. Shit, Chaim, I'm still just Debbie Reuben from Long Island, just grown up a bit, right? Can you understand that?"

Levi put his arms around her, squeezed her tightly, then lifted her feet from the porch floor and carried her into the house, down the hallway, and into the bedroom, where he placed her gently on the queen-sized bed. He slid on top of her, lowering his mouth over hers, slowly letting his entire weight rest on her, anchoring her, holding her, shielding her from the demons of her past and the demons soon to come.

For now, right now, let's not talk at all, he thought, reaching down to open the buttons on her blouse.

They fell asleep in one another's arms, thoughts of atom bombs and C4 explosive, of FBI agents and detention camps, absent for the day. For the moment, at least.

CHAPTER 39

Ben Shapiro put off visiting Howie Mandelbaum at the Charles Street Jail to deliver the unpleasant news of his meeting with District Attorney Patrick McDonough. It was looking as if Mandelbaum was going to be the only person to face state criminal charges for the Coast Guard deaths. Shapiro had hoped to get the charges dropped, even if it meant Mandelbaum would be shipped to the detention camp on Cape Cod. At least there he would be treated the same as the other detainees.

How bad could that be, Shapiro thought. After all, in the long run they were certain to be found to be nothing but refugees from war, from persecution. This country took such people in every day.

But that was not to be. Instead, Mandelbaum was going to be indicted under state law for murder or conspiracy to commit murder or some such criminal charge, as if he were some gangbanger picked up on the streets. As a result, Shapiro had no choice but to treat this like every other criminal case—build his facts, file some motions, and either plead his client out if he could work a deal or roll the dice in front of a jury. In any event, the wheels of Massachusetts justice turned slowly, and

Mandelbaum was facing at least six months behind bars before anything was likely to happen in court.

Even though Shapiro had visited scores of incarcerated clients, he was stunned by the change in Mandelbaum's appearance from the last time he saw him. All hints of cockiness were gone. Mandelbaum did not walk, but shambled, as if his feet were held together by invisible chains. He looked at the floor, unwilling to make eye contact with anybody—with the guards on either side who brought him to the interview room, or even with Shapiro when the two sat facing each other.

"Howie, what happened to you?" Shapiro asked softly. He'd left their last meeting with a sour feeling about this client. The lack of enthusiasm he felt when he arrived at the jail vanished and his heart went out to the young man, who continued to stare at the floor as if his head were too heavy to lift.

"Are you all right, Howie? Speak to me. Do you remember me, Howie? I'm Ben Shapiro, your lawyer."

The young man continued to look at the floor as he spoke softly, almost too softly for Shapiro to hear him.

"You've got to get me out of this place. Please, please get me out of this place. They'll kill me if I stay here. Get me out. Can you please get me out?" He began quietly crying. Shapiro reached out and placed his hand under the young man's chin, then lifted his face until they were eye to eye with one another.

"What happened, Howie?" Shapiro asked.

"They raped me. Lots of them. Lots of times. And the guards just turned their backs." His sobs grew louder, convulsing his shoulders. "Mr. Shapiro, please help me. They keep talking about Jew this and Jew that, about Jews killing Americans and about setting up camps, camps like the Nazis did. They talk about finishing the job this time. It's hell, Mr. Shapiro. It's goddamn fucking holy-shit hell here."

Mandelbaum wrapped his arms around his chest and rocked in his chair, sobbing louder now, all restraint gone. Shapiro reached out to touch the young man's shoulder. Mandelbaum flinched back from that touch, then looked up at Shapiro, eyes flat. Dead. Cold.

"There's a bunch of them and the guards unlock their cells and unlock my cell and whenever they want they come into my cell. In the middle of the day. The middle of the night. They hold me down. They rape me. They stuff underwear in my mouth so I can't scream. They hold my arms and . . . and, oh God, Mr. Shapiro, I've stopped fighting them because I can't stop them and I just let them do it to me now because I can't stop them."

Mandelbaum's head dropped to the wooden arm of the chair. He lifted his head and slammed it down on the wood surface, his forehead striking with a thud. He lifted his head again and slammed it down, harder. Then again. Shapiro leaped forward and grabbed the young man's head between his hands. Mandelbaum's forehead was red. The skin mangled. Blood oozing.

Shapiro reached into his back pocket, removed a handkerchief and pressed it against the man's forehead. He reached for the man's right hand and brought it, lifeless by now, to the handkerchief.

"Stop that," Shapiro shouted. "Here, hold that, hold that. Get control. We don't have a whole lot of time."

The shouting, or perhaps the stern tone of Shapiro's voice, focused the young man's attention. He looked up, still holding the bloody handkerchief to his forehead.

"I'm sorry. I know you're trying to help me. I apologize," he said. "I can't take any more of this." He sighed deeply. "Okay. What's happening with the case? How much longer do I have to stay here?"

"I'm afraid I don't have very good news for you, Howie," Shapiro said. "I met with the district attorney and got absolutely nowhere. We're going to have to treat this like a criminal case. I'll speak with witnesses and collect evidence and we'll probably be going to trial. I don't see much choice."

"That's okay, Mr. Shapiro. I don't mind going to trial. I didn't do anything, not a thing except push my way onto that boat and then jump in the water when somebody said jump. That's good news. Great. We'll have a trial. Let's go. Can we do it before the end of the week? I'll have to hold out for just a few more days, right?"

Shapiro saw hope brighten the young man's face like a searchlight finding its target. The man's back straightened in the chair. His head lifted.

"It doesn't work quite like that, Howie," Shapiro said softly. "You haven't even been formally indicted yet. The DA has to put your case before the grand jury. I can guarantee they'll indict you. Grand juries always indict. When I was in the DA's office I used to brag that I could get the grand jury to indict a grilled cheese sandwich.

"But that's going to take a while. He's got to get his witnesses lined up. This isn't an ordinary case that goes in with one cop testifying. My guess is you won't be indicted for another month or so. You'll get arraigned before a judge and then the DA will have a while, several months at least, to get his case together. Nothing is happening right away, Howie."

"No, don't say that, Mr. Shapiro," the young man sobbed. "How long is this going to take?"

"I can't say exactly, Howie, but at least six months before trial, maybe twice as long if the DA gets a judge who'll give him that much time. There's nothing we can do about that. From what he told me when we got together, the DA isn't much interested in a plea. It's not like you could give him any information that he needs for another case, he said, since the feds grabbed up everybody else from those ships."

"This isn't fair, Mr. Shapiro. I had nothing to do with anything. It isn't fair. How come they aren't going after the ones who did it, instead of me? This isn't right, you know."

Shapiro looked up from the yellow legal pad on which he'd been making notes.

"Howie, what do you mean about the ones who did it? Do you know who did it, who fired at the Coast Guard?"

"Yeah, sure I do. It was the soldiers, the IDF guys. The guys and that one girl. She and I hung out together on the ship all the way over, sort of had a little thing going, you know."

"Are you telling me there were Israeli soldiers on the ships, that the soldiers were the ones who fired at the Coast Guard?"

"Of course there were soldiers," Mandelbaum said. "Everybody knew who they were. They pretty much organized things, set up the rotation for meals and work and cleanup assignments. They had their own space all the way at the front of the ship. They kept all their shit up there, you know, their army stuff. Nobody was allowed up there unless you were one of them.

"Well, pretty much nobody. There wasn't a whole shitload of privacy on that ship, you know. And when this girl, Dvora her name was, well when Dvora and I needed a little privacy she took me up there when all the others were out organizing stuff. Man, they had some heavy-duty shit there, you know, Uzis and grenades and these rocket things. They were ready for anything, man. I know who they all are, the soldiers. Once I started hanging with Dvora I spent a lot of time with the rest of them, too. Why, can this help me?"

"Maybe, Howie. Let's give this some thought. It at least gives us something to bargain with." Shapiro hesitated. "Howie, how would you feel about identifying these soldiers if it meant they would be charged with pretty heavy crimes, maybe even crimes they could be executed for? Would you do that, Howie? I suppose what I mean is, *could* you do that?"

For the first time in their meeting, the young man looked Shapiro in the eyes.

"Mr. Shapiro, I'm going back to that stinking cell after you leave, and before you are out the front door one of those guys is going to be pumping his cock in my asshole and laughing his head off. And that's if I'm lucky. If I have to spend the next six months here, I'll be dead by the time I go to trial. Are you going to play some morality game on me because I don't want to let that happen? Give me a break. They chose to fire at those boats.

Nobody made them do it. If anybody has to pay the price for that, let it be them, not me."

"Well, I guess that's pretty clear," Shapiro said, rising to his feet. "Let me see what I can do." He reached for the young man's hand. Mandelbaum clung to Shapiro's hand so long the lawyer thought he would have to pry his client's fingers open. As Shapiro walked from the conference room, leaving Mandelbaum sitting in his chair, the young man stood, looked at Shapiro and spoke quietly.

"Mr. Shapiro, I'm not a bad person, you know. When you walk out the front door of this building, think about what they'll be doing to me tonight. I don't deserve that, do I?"

CHAPTER 40

Chaim Levi and Debra Reuben awoke late. Both were exhausted, physically and emotionally, by their lovemaking. Reuben got out of bed first, showered, then went to the kitchen. Levi lay in bed, listening to the rattling of pots and plates and soon smelled onions being sautéed and heard a fork whirling around a bowl, scrambling eggs.

Levi dressed quickly. By the time he got to the kitchen, Reuben was almost finished with Swiss-cheese-and-onion omelets, freshly toasted five-grain bread from the Blue Hill Cooperative market already on the table, and a pitcher of fresh-squeezed orange juice on the counter with two glasses next to it.

"All of a sudden I feel extremely domestic," she said when Levi walked into the kitchen. "I feel like cooking for you. Sit. I'm serving you today. Just for today."

"Sounds good to me," Levi answered. "But after we eat, we need to talk. I didn't tell you before, but Abram said he and Sarah would be coming up here tonight, after dinner, late. We need to make some decisions. Before they get here."

"Decisions about Abram's bomb, you mean?" Reuben asked. "It sounds like he's already made that decision, him and those three boys of his. I don't think we could stop him if we wanted to."

"You're probably right about that," Levi said. "But, of course, he's not the only one with a bomb."

Reuben looked at him quizzically. "You're not going to play some macho game with Abram, are you? Like 'my bomb's bigger than your bomb'?"

"As a matter of fact," Levi said, "my bomb is a hell of a lot bigger than his bomb, not that size matters." He smiled.

Reuben had not reached the point where she could laugh at atom bomb jokes.

"Of course size matters." She saw his face drop. "There's a hell of a difference between a van full of explosives and what's in our cellar. The other thing is," she said with a hint of menace, "we haven't reached the community property stage when it comes to nuclear weapons. That's still my bomb, not yours. I have final say over what happens to it, whether it gets sunk in the ocean or dropped on . . . on wherever. We are still in agreement on that, right?"

"Yes, it's your bomb, not mine," Levi answered quickly. "But, to be perfectly accurate, it isn't your bomb either. That bomb belongs to the State of Israel and it gets used, when it gets used, to protect the State of Israel. You agree to that, don't you?"

"Of course I know that, Lieutenant Levi. Remember which of us has more experience in using these things for the purposes of the State of Israel. Got it?"

"Yes sir, Madam Cabinet Minister. Now that we've got these technical details cleared up, let's talk about whether we tell Abram about our thing in the basement," Levi said. "What do you think?"

"To be honest, the sooner we get rid it, the better I'll feel," she said. "I did some research yesterday on the Internet." She paused when she saw a scowl on Levi's face. "At the library. I walked to the library and used the computer there, okay?"

"Okay, just be careful."

"Do you have any idea whether we are frying our genes being

so close to that thing for so long?" she asked. "Did they give you any training in the navy about how to handle radioactive stuff?"

"No," Levi said. "Remember, the government denied having nuclear weapons, even though everybody knew we had hundreds of them. Everybody knew it was a big lie that we had none."

"As it turned out, not such a big lie, just a little one," Reuben said. "I found out at Dimona we only had a few bombs. The little lie was that we had none. The big lie was that we had hundreds. Anyway, I'll feel better when we turn that thing over to somebody else. But, Chaim, I don't think that somebody is Abram. He's too ready to blow things up. I'd almost rather give it to Sarah; she'd march her feet off first and only use it after everything else failed."

"You can't tell Sarah and expect her to keep it secret from her husband," Levi said.

"I know that. That's why I think we should keep our secret a bit longer."

"I agree," Levi said. "It's only a secret until we tell somebody else. Once we let it loose, who knows what will happen? Let's at least see what happens with Abram and his disciples this weekend."

Reuben was surprised at how much it pleased her to hear Levi speak about keeping secrets using almost the same words her father used. "It sounds as if it will be an interesting weekend in many ways."

"I would probably choose a different word," Levi said. "But you and I will be glued to the TV all weekend, I expect."

■ ■ ■

Sarah and Abram arrived shortly after dinner. They stomped into the house without speaking. Sarah confronted Levi.

"I can't believe you aren't going to stop him from this insanity," Sarah shouted.

Before Levi could answer, Abram spoke, his voice louder

than his wife's.

"Sarah, we've been through this," he said. "It is not Chaim's decision, any more than it is your decision. It is my decision. Well, mine and the men with me. And the decision is made. It is done. Sealed. Finished. Wheels are in motion that cannot be stopped.

"We are all fighting the same fight, all working for one thing—to get the United States government to rescue Eretz Yisrael. You are going to use words. That is legitimate. I respect you for that. A Jew will never tell other Jews not to talk, not to argue, not to use reason and logic to persuade. Okay. Talk yourselves blue. Sing all your songs. Carry your signs. But nothing will come of it. I know that. You know that. I am taking another path to the same goal. My way works. You know it works." Abram glared at his wife.

"So, I'm going to march and you're going to set off bombs and you think that together something will change?" Sarah said. "I think your bombs may counteract my peaceful demonstration, that's what I think."

"Maybe. Maybe not," Abram said. "Sarah, I love you. You know that. But you cannot convince me I am wrong on this. However, perhaps fortunately for you, it turns out I don't have the final word on this. There are some, well, some people in Boston, people I respect in the movement, the old movement and the present one. They are not so sure I know what I am doing with this stuff that I have. They want to hear from our explosives expert before giving final approval."

Levi looked surprised.

"I told them about you in general, only in general terms. No name, no identification, no exact location. They want to see you. Tomorrow afternoon in Boston. I wrote directions for you. They're in the car."

"We drove up in two cars," Sarah said. "We're leaving in the morning, back to Portland. You can drive to Boston in the Honda later in the day."

"You want me to drive to Boston alone?" Levi asked. "Can't one of you come along?"

"No, I have to supervise putting all my little bits and pieces together," Abram said.

"And I have signs to paint," Sarah said. "And a speech to write. A short speech, but a good one."

"All right," Levi said reluctantly. "I'll go. I don't know what I can contribute, but it beats staying here and watching TV."

Reuben looked horrified. "How can you leave again, Chaim?" she asked. "I thought I'd stop breathing when you went to Portland."

"Stop worrying. Nobody even knows we exist," Levi said. "I'm more worried about where I can stay in Boston. It sounds like I'll be away overnight again."

"Stay in Portland with us," Sarah said. "You can spend the night at our house. It's only two hours from Boston."

"You can help me with some heavy lifting in the morning. We'll be loading the van," Abram added. "Bring work gloves."

"And after that you'll come right home. And you'll be very, very careful," Reuben said.

CHAPTER 41

The Echo Team at the detention camp had a surprisingly easy time identifying more than 800 detainees as members of the Israel Defense Forces. After that, however, the interrogations ran into a brick wall. They did not appreciate how deeply the military was involved in Israeli life—far more so than in the US. In contrast to the States' struggle to maintain an all-volunteer army by offering richer and richer incentives to recruits, service in the Israeli military had been compulsory for every eighteen-year-old in the small nation, with only few exceptions. After their compulsory service—three years for men, two for women—service in the active reserve up to age fifty was compulsory.

One result of this deep penetration by the military into civilian society was that Israeli soldiers did not look like the soldiers the American interrogators were used to seeing. A forty-five-year-old woman with an attractive teenage daughter could be a commander of a reserve tank battalion. The teenage daughter could be in the infantry.

What this meant for the Echo Team interrogators was that just about every detainee, both at Camp Echo and in the less strict portions of the base, at one time or another served in the

IDF. Almost all the men, and most of the women, were still reservists.

The Israeli military was particularly sensitive to the risks its soldiers faced if they were captured. In the US military, advanced SERE training—survival, evasion, resistance, and escape—was provided only for specialized units such as Army Rangers, Navy SEALS and fighter pilots likely to be shot down behind enemy lines. SERE training included undergoing hours of mock interrogations and advanced sessions learning how to deflect interrogation techniques.

Because Israeli soldiers captured by Arab and Palestinian forces could expect to be tortured, or worse, such advanced counter-interrogation practice was part of routine training for virtually all members of the IDF. In fact, Israeli interrogators helped the US Air Force design the first formal American SERE training after the Korean War.

The young American Echo Team members were not trained for this kind of job. After a week of round-the-clock tag-team interrogation sessions of the entire Camp Echo population, they had made no progress in identifying the twenty soldiers whose dog tags were recovered from Boston Harbor.

"We pretty much know who was in the IDF," Maj. Dancer, the camp commander, told Homeland Security director Paterson and Acting Attorney General Harrison when they visited the camp for a progress report. "Just about everybody we've got, that's who. And we know there was a discreet military unit on the two ships, one on each ship, in fact, because the divers found their equipment and lots of gear.

"But picking out who was in those units and who was just some forty-year-old reservist, well, we've gotten nowhere with that. These people are tough, strictly name, rank and serial number types, and they lie about that. We know they're giving phony names. That's all we get—that and demands to see their lawyers. Goddamn Jews and their lawyers," he laughed.

"Those results are not acceptable, Major." General Paterson

was not used to subordinates reporting their failures to him. "We could wake up any morning and learn that Chicago or Tampa or Seattle is a pile of radioactive rubble. If this interrogation team is not up to the job, we'll bring in a new team. One that can get the information the president insists we get. Is that understood, Major?"

"Understood, General," he answered. "In all fairness to the Echo Team, though, sir, the problem is not the personnel. The problem is that their hands are tied. It's all those laws that were passed after Guantanamo, sir, those 'we don't use torture' laws. These men and women have been trained not to even look cross-eyed at anybody they're interrogating. As you know, sir, I was at Guantanamo, back during the Iraq War—the Afghanistan War, whatever we're calling it now."

General Paterson nodded.

"We were able to make our own rules then, sir," the major continued. "We were told the Geneva Convention didn't apply to those detainees. For a little while we had all those lawyers coming down representing our detainees there, but Congress put an end to that when they suspended habeas corpus for Guantanamo detainees. Once the lawyers were stopped, and once the detainees couldn't go to court anymore, well, sir, all of a sudden people started talking. By that time we'd been holding them for five or six years, so they didn't have any fresh information to give us. But they broke. And we learned an awful lot about how to break them. Pretty quickly, too, if we're allowed to do so."

"I understand all that, Major, but that was then. We have laws on the books now that out and out say we can't use torture, no matter what. Isn't that right, Mr. Attorney General?" Gen. Paterson turned to Harrison, who stood silently to the side during the conversation, smiling slightly to himself. He stepped in front of the two military men as if he were about to address a class, then gestured toward his briefcase on the table behind the men.

"The president and I discussed this very situation," he said. "I have a document, a presidential directive, in my briefcase that should be of assistance to your Echo Team. I'll read it to you, then you can read it verbatim to the team members.

"'By the authority vested in me by Article II of the United States Constitution as commander in chief of the military forces of the United States of America, I find that this nation is faced with an extraordinary military threat to national security posed by the Armed Forces of the (former) State of Israel.

"'I hereby order and direct that all military forces subject to my ultimate command are authorized to use whatever means are necessary and effective to defend the United States of America for so long as this crisis continues. In furtherance of this defense, I find that all laws, statutes, regulations and directives limiting the use, threat or application of coercive force, both physical and psychological, against enemy combatants, short of the application of torture, are hereby waived and suspended to the extent necessary to fully and adequately protect and promote the national interest. Signed, Lawrence Quaid, President.' What do you think of that, gentlemen?" Harrison asked. He was beaming. "The president signed this yesterday. Actually, I drafted it."

"Well, that should help," Maj. Dancer said. "But run that part about 'short of torture' by me again, will you? I don't understand that part."

"To be completely honest with you, Major, President Quaid inserted those words into my draft. I'm not quite sure what it means, either," Harrison sighed. "Sometimes the president has difficulty fully committing himself. But that's just my guess. Anyway, I had legal research done on that point. Here's some guidance for your boys."

Harrison removed another document from his briefcase. This was several pages long. Gen. Paterson flipped through it, then he frowned.

"Our interrogators are soldiers, not lawyers," he said. "This looks like it was written for a judge." He tossed the document onto the table. "So, what do we tell them they can and can't do?"

"My assistant is setting up a laptop and projector in the mess hall right now," he said. "I had a little PowerPoint presentation put together. Let me summarize it for you. First thing, the president said we can use force but we can't torture. No big deal, right? America doesn't torture anybody, right? We didn't use torture before Congress banned it. We haven't tortured anybody since that ban. The president says we won't torture anybody in the future."

"That's clear enough," Maj. Dancer said. "The team's already had that drilled into them. No torture. Use torture during an interrogation and you've bought yourself a ticket to Leavenworth, right?"

"Uh, not quite right, Major," Harrison said. "It turns out that torture, like beauty, is in the eye of the beholder." He chuckled. "We aren't the first White House team to try to define torture, of course. I—sorry, the president and I, after much thought, have decided to adopt a definition of torture with historical precedence. It was first prepared during the administration of the second President Bush. Prepared, in fact, by a man who went on to hold the same position I now hold, Attorney General Alberto Gonzalez. This is in my PowerPoint for your men, of course. It's called the Bybee memo. Let me quote for you."

Harrison scanned through the legal memo he'd taken from the table, turning pages until almost the end. "Here it is," he said. "For an act to constitute torture, it must inflict pain that is difficult to endure. Physical pain amounting to torture must be equivalent in intensity to the pain accompanying serious physical injury, such as major organ failure, impairment of bodily function, or even death. For purely mental pain or suffering to amount to torture, it must result in significant psychological harm of significant duration, e.g., lasting for months or even years."

Maj. Dancer whistled softly. "So, anything short of causing failure of a major organ is kosher, right? That's what you're saying? We can do anything that doesn't leave major permanent damage, right?"

"Even more important," Gen. Paterson interrupted, "that's what the president is saying? That is what you are telling us?"

Harrison nodded. "President Quaid saw and approved the same PowerPoint presentation," he said. "Between his directive and this legal memo, your men ought to be able to do their jobs. And one final note, gentlemen, in case anybody has any misgivings about this. Keep in mind that we aren't plowing new ground with any of this. Major, these are the same operational guidelines as were used at Guantanamo, correct?"

Maj. Dancer nodded.

"I'll let you two brief your Echo Team," Gen. Paterson said. "And I understand you've brought in some specialized personnel. Let's hope they make a difference. I'm heading back to Washington. I want results. Soon. The president's patience is getting thin."

■ ■ ■

Dr. Bayard was six feet two inches tall, plus another three inches of hair of some indeterminate brownish-grayish color piled in a mound on her head. She tended to pause at odd moments, mid-sentence, as if listening to a hidden earpiece for guidance.

She could not have appeared less military if she'd led a cavalry charge on a tricycle. The young Echo Team members clung to her every word as if she held the secret psychological key they'd need to open the locks behind which their subjects held their secrets. She was a "Biscuit"—head of a behavioral science consultation team, or BSCT. The young interrogators looked at each other and nodded, smiles on their faces. Biscuits were viewed among interrogators as having almost mystical powers. They were usually PhD psychologists who'd spent their careers studying means of programming animals, and people, to do and say just about anything.

Biscuits had great success at Guantanamo.

The Echo Team members were told that at least one Biscuit would be present for all interrogations. Suggestions from the Biscuit were to be followed as orders.

The first interrogation that afternoon was of a twenty-four-year-old woman who gave her name as Dvora Yaron, her rank as *Segen Mishne*, the equivalent of a second lieutenant, and her unit as *Sayerot Mat'kal*. She provided no other information to interrogators. However, her unit designation drew the attention of a National Security Agency analyst, an Israeli specialist who was assigned to aid the Echo Team.

Sayerot Mat'kal was also known as General Staff Reconnaissance Unit 269, he told the interrogator first assigned to Yaron. Unit 269 was one of Israel's prime special forces units. The Echo Team interrogators did not believe a *Sayerot* officer, even a low-ranking one, could be a simple political refugee.

Dr. Bayard spent a half hour studying the report of Dvora Yaron's first interrogation, shaking her head and making odd chucking noises as she read.

"This woman has received training in counter-interrogation techniques," Dr. Bayard commented. "Well, we have a few *techniques* of our own."

The young Israeli woman appeared cocky as she was led into the windowless interrogation cell by two US soldiers. She walked slowly, almost seductively, between the two Americans, sneaking smiles at her captors, enticing them to smile back. The cell was lit by a single fluorescent fixture. The red light of a video camera blinked from a corner of the ceiling.

The soldiers held the woman's arms gently. She was attractive, thin as a fashion model but revealing surprising strength when they took her arms. Her face was darkly tanned. Her straight black hair was tied back into a ponytail.

She looked surprised to see Dr. Bayard in the cell with her former interrogator. The young woman's eyes took in the stethoscope draped over Bayard's shoulder. Instead of the plain wooden chair in which she'd been seated for her previous interrogation, a steel desk was in the room. The surface of the desk was empty except for a six-by-two-foot wooden plank.

The two soldiers who brought Yaron to the windowless interrogation cell remained in the room, together with the Echo Team interrogator and Dr. Bayard. The doctor was obviously in charge this time.

"Tape her to the board, tightly," Dr. Bayard barked. "No need to be too gentle. Make sure she can't slip free."

The young woman's eyes opened wide with the first sign of fear when the two soldiers lifted her onto her back on top of the wooden board. She tried to roll from side to side—as she'd been trained—when they wrapped two rolls of duct tape round and round her body and around the board to hold her immobile to the wooden surface. After a few attempts to flex her arms, the woman stopped struggling.

She knew what was coming. Waterboarding. A washcloth would be placed over her mouth and water would be poured on it. She would feel as if she were drowning. But she'd been trained to resist. It would only feel as if she were drowning. They would stop. She would not drown. Americans did not kill their interrogation subjects.

Dr. Bayard walked around the desk so that she was standing behind Dvora's head. She leaned far forward, looking down at the woman, knowing that she would appear to be upside down to the frightened Israeli—one more effort at disconcerting her. She spoke softly, almost in a whisper, leaning closer to her face, six inches away.

"Dvora, they tell me you've been a very bad girl," Bayard whispered, as if the three men weren't in the room with the two women. "I'm going to ask you one question, one time. If I'm not pleased with your answer, I'm going to make you exceptionally uncomfortable. I'll do my best not to go too far, but you know, sometimes my best just isn't good enough. Do we understand each other, Dvora? Such a sweet name you have, Dvora."

The young woman inhaled deeply. She was scared. But she gathered her inner strength, prepared to do battle with this strange woman in the white coat. As she'd been trained.

She did not respond to Bayard, giving no indication she even heard her.

"All right, Dvora," Dr. Bayard said. "Let's begin our little session. Dvora, I want to know the name of the Israeli who smuggled the nuclear bomb into the United States. You will tell me his name right now or I will be so unhappy with you. What is the man's name, Dvora? Let's start with just his first name."

All eyes in the room were locked on the young woman taped to the board on top of the table. Her reaction was completely unexpected.

She broke into loud, uncontrolled laughter.

"You people are out of your minds," she said. "I don't know anything about atom bombs or about anything being smuggled anywhere. I got onto that ship to save my ass. That's all I know about anything."

The young woman locked her eyes onto the older woman. Dr. Bayard shook her head slowly.

"You disappoint me, Dvora," she said. "I told you I would not give you a second chance." She turned to one of the soldiers. "Tape her mouth, then bring the equipment in."

The soldier tore a six-inch strip of duct tape and placed it over the young woman's mouth, careful not to cover her nostrils. He went out the door and returned pushing a cart. Bayard took a three-foot, red rubber hose from the cart.

"It hurts me so much to have to do this to you, dear Dvora." The doctor turned to the two soldiers. "Take the cinder block from the cart. Lift the other end of the board and put the cinder block under it. I want her feet elevated. Then come back to this end."

The two soldiers followed her instructions. The young woman's feet were higher than her head as she lay on her back on the wooden board. The rubber hose dangled from Bayard's hands just above the young woman's vision, swinging in front of her face from time to time. All signs of Dvora's cockiness had disappeared. Her eyes opened wide in fear.

Where is the washcloth? she wondered. *This isn't waterboarding.*

"Hold her head tightly," Dr. Bayard barked to the soldiers. She leaned forward, holding one end of the rubber hose and snaked it into the young woman's right nostril, causing the woman to gag as the hose went in at least twelve inches, passing down her throat.

"That wasn't too bad, now was it, Dvora?" Bayard said. Turning to one of the soldiers, she said, "Put that plastic funnel in the end of the hose and hold it up high." To the other soldier she said, "Push the cart over here. Dip me one cup of water, please. We'll start with that."

The soldier dipped a plastic cup into a pail of water on the cart. He went to hand the water to the doctor, thinking she was thirsty. She smiled at him and pointed at the hose.

The soldier poured the water into the funnel, watching as it drained into the young woman's nose and down her throat. Her body spasmed with gasping as her throat filled with water. She was unable to swallow because her head was lowered. She was terrified to inhale, knowing the water would fill her lungs. The tape over her mouth prevented her from spitting the water out. Her eyes went white with terror and she attempted to thrash from side to side but could not move because of the duct tape wound around her and the board.

"Dip me another cup," Dr. Bayard said to the soldier. He again looked to the interrogator, who looked at Dr. Bayard expectantly, then, seeing only impatience, shook his head in the affirmative. The soldier held the cup of water near the funnel, waiting for instructions.

The young woman's eyes began to roll upwards, leaving a startling amount of white showing in her wide-open eyes. Dr. Bayard leaned forward and whispered to the woman again.

"Are you ready to talk with me now, Dvora?" she asked softly.

The young woman reacted with enthusiasm, nodding up and down vigorously, life seeming to return to her, mumbles coming from her sealed mouth.

"Wonderful," Bayard said.

The soldiers lifted the young woman, still taped to the board, off the desk and stood her against the wall. She gasped and coughed, spitting and swallowing water at the same time. When she caught her breath she glared at Bayard.

"I thought you were going to kill me, you bitch," she whispered.

The doctor stepped in front of the young woman, who was still bound to the board leaning against the wall.

"But that's the point of this medical procedure, my dear," she said. "So, tell me, who is this man who brought that big bomb to the United States?"

"The absolute God's honest truth, Doctor, is that I don't know anything about any atom bombs. I really and truly don't. I admit I'm in the army, even in the special forces. I'll tell you all about how we sank those Coast Guard boats. I'll even tell you I fired one of the RPGs. Or all of them. I'll tell you everything I know. But I really and truly don't know anything about atom bombs. I don't. I don't." The woman now looked defiant. "You can pour as much water as you want into me. I can't tell you what I don't know."

Bayard shook her head. "You disappoint Dr. Bayard. Now I am going to have to do that all over again. And you know that this time you will tell me the truth. Please, Dvora, don't make me do this to you again."

The young woman was silent, then she spoke in a voice barely above a whisper. "I can't tell you what I don't know."

"Put her back on the desk," Bayard said to the soldiers as she took the rubber hose in her hand. This time, the young woman did not resist, and before the tape was placed over her mouth, she softly said the first words of the ancient prayer, "*Sh'ma*

Yisrael Adonai Elohaynu . . ."

As before, the young woman gagged and choked when the water entered her throat. Her body jerked against the duct tape. She rocked from side to side on the desktop.

"Pour in another cup, slowly this time," the doctor ordered.

The water drained down the hose but seemed to have no effect on the woman, who went limp, her eyes rolled upwards, only the whites showing.

"Shit," Bayard said as she pulled the stethoscope from over her shoulder, placed the ear cups into her ears and placed the end against the woman's chest. She tore the tape from the woman's mouth. The woman did not move. Dr. Bayard leaned down again, placing her stethoscope on the woman's chest.

"Shit, *shit . . .* she's dead."

The Echo Team interrogator remained alone in the room for several minutes, his mind racing. *Leavenworth,* he thought. Use torture and you'll rot in Leavenworth, he'd been trained.

He walked quickly from the interrogation cell to the Echo Team office. He sat at a computer and found a file labeled *Interrogation Room 3.* He slid a DVD into the computer's drive and copied the interrogation room file onto the DVD, removed it from the computer and placed the DVD in his jacket pocket, then walked to his bunk to lie down and stare at the ceiling.

I won't be the one going to Leavenworth, he thought.

CHAPTER 42

Despite having sailed a small boat across the Atlantic Ocean, despite having escaped from a nuclear disaster in his homeland, Levi was terrified at the thought of driving on American roads to an American city. That he had no US driver's license was the least of his concerns. He'd long since abandoned his Israeli license on the assumption that being caught with no license was safer than being stopped with an Israeli license.

American drivers scared him.

His only experience with American drivers was in occasional trips on the back roads near Brooklin. These roads were narrow, barely wide enough for two cars to pass in either direction, and heavily crowned in the center so snowmelt would run off and not accumulate to freeze when the temperature dropped.

Undeterred, Mainers drove as if they were on eight-lane superhighways, tailgating anybody cautious enough to dawdle within ten miles per hour of the speed limit. He insisted that Reuben accompany him on a test drive before he felt confident enough to take off on his solo odyssey to Boston.

Since they were out of the house anyway, Reuben suggested stopping at the Blue Hill Co-op grocery store in the next town over from Brooklin. Reuben stocked up on organic produce, whole grain bread, and free-range, symphonic-music-listening chickens' eggs while Levi waited in the car, growing increasingly apprehensive about driving to Boston to meet with people he did not know.

When Reuben returned to the car, she offered to drive the ten miles back to Brooklin to let him rest before heading out to Boston. He accepted her offer and sat in the right-hand seat for most of the half hour drive without saying a word, lost in his thoughts.

Levi was jerked from his reverie by Reuben's exclamation.

"Who the hell is that?" she asked as the car slowly drove past the Brooklin Public Library. A black Ford Navigator SUV was parked in front of the library. Two obviously upset men in nearly matching black suits, white shirts, and dark ties walked quickly toward the car. One man reached through the open driver's window and pulled out a microphone on a coiled cord. He spoke into it, then tossed it angrily into the car.

The other man looked up and surveyed the Honda Accord as Levi and Reuben drove slowly past the library. His head swiveled to follow their course.

The two men were so obviously out of place—neither tourists, summer people, nor locals, the only varieties of people to come to Brooklin—that seeing them left Levi unsettled and apprehensive.

Levi had loaded a backpack with clean underwear and a toothbrush before they set out on their drive. Reuben stood outside while Levi retrieved his bag. When he returned, Levi walked up behind, wrapped his arms around her and pressed his chest against her back, pulling her tightly against him. He wiped one hand across her right breast, a privilege he felt he'd recently earned.

She swiveled around in his arms.

"I am so, so tired of worrying about when disaster is going to strike us," she said quietly. "How do I know I'll ever see you again? And those two men at the library. Who do you think they were? They looked so serious, so angry. Chaim, I am so afraid of losing you. I love you so much. Yes, I'll say it even if you won't."

"I love you, too, Debra." He tightened his arms to hold her snugly, bending forward to kiss the top of her head. "I'm not afraid to say it one bit. I love you. And because I love you, I'll be extra careful. Of course I'm coming back to you. I'll be back here tomorrow."

She lifted her face and kissed him on the lips.

"Deal," she said, opening the car door for him. As he was about to get into the driver's seat, Levi sprang out and ran to the basement door.

"Almost forgot," he shouted over his shoulder. "Abram's going to have me do some heavy lifting. He said to bring work gloves." He emerged a moment later with the bright-orange rubber gloves. "Guess these will have to do," he said, tossing the gloves onto the back seat as he got behind the wheel and started the engine.

■ ■ ■

The walk to the library through the chill air and bright sunshine raised Reuben's spirits. By the time she arrived at the white front door with the date *1912* over it, Reuben felt ready to launch herself back into her research project, just as she used to do as an investigative reporter back when the world was sane. She sat at the same computer she'd used the day before and renewed her Internet hunt.

Reuben could not help but overhear the excited conversation the librarian was having with two other women.

"They barged right in and started ordering me around," Jolene Dodge said, her voice infused with enthusiasm. And a tinge of pride. "They waved their wallets at me and kept on saying FBI, FBI, as if I couldn't read. Right, as if a town would have an illiterate librarian, even in Maine."

Reuben perked up. She could barely keep her eyes directed at the screen to conceal her eavesdropping. She didn't want them to move their conversation to someplace more private.

"FBI, well glory be," one of the librarian's audience exclaimed. "What in the world did they want?"

"They came right out and told me what they wanted," the librarian responded. "They damn well wanted everything we have. They pulled out this piece of paper and said it was some sort of Patriot Act warrant and they wanted to search the library's computerized list of books people had checked out, and they wanted to look at our computers, see what people had been looking at on the Internet.

"Well, I laughed right in their faces at that one. Where do you think you are, Bangor? I asked them. We don't have any computerized list of books folks check out." The librarian laughed and looked at a varnished set of oak cabinets containing dozens of small drawers. "I pointed over at those drawers and said, 'That's our computer checkout system, fellas. It was donated by the post office.' I laughed in their faces."

Then the librarian's voice took on a serious tone.

"I asked to see that warrant. I looked at the front. I looked at the back. I kept turning the thing over and all round. Then I handed it back to one of the fellas and said, 'I don't see any judge's signature on that warrant you boys have there.' That's what I said to them, you know."

"Why'dja say that, Jo-lene?" the other woman asked. "How do you know anything about judges' signatures and search warrants?"

"How do I know?" the librarian responded. "I'll tell you just like I told those FBI boys. I told them I'm not just the librarian in this town. I'm part of law enforcement hereabouts. I said right to them that I am the only clam warden between Sedgwick and Blue Hill. When it comes to the clam flats, I am the law around here, more than those sheriff's deputies who'd take an hour and a half to get here if you called and said the library was being robbed. I know all about warrants. They have to be signed by a judge or else they ain't worth—well, ain't worth the time'a day to print 'em up."

"I think the FBI sort of outranks the Brooklin clam warden, dee-yah," the first woman said, guessing, correctly, that the story of the librarian-slash-clam-warden's encounter with the FBI would be told and retold throughout the winter. "Why did you give those gentlemen such a hard time, Jo-lene? You'll give Brooklin a sour name."

"I didn't like their high-and-mighty attitude," she replied. "I told them they could come back with a piece of paper autographed by a judge and I'd show them whatever they wanted to see, but until then, they should mind the step at the front door on the way out."

"Jo-lene, you're going to get into serious trouble for that. You better watch out, you know," the second woman said. Then she laughed and added, "I don't know where you find the gumption to stand up to the FBI that way. I could never do that."

The librarian chuckled. "A couple of city boys in suits."

"Do you think that's the end of them?" one woman asked.

"No," the librarian said. "They made a point of saying they'd be back tomorrow with a warrant. And that they would look through every damn card in our files and check every computer in the building. Oh, but they were a mite upset when they left."

"So, what did you say when they said they'd be back?" the second woman asked, dreading the effect the answer would have on the town's reputation in the nation's capital.

"I looked that black-suit-wearin' fella in the eye and told him he'd be hearing from my lawyer if he wanted to invade my patrons' privacy that way. So he says, 'And who would your lawyer be, lady?' He was only pretending to be polite."

"You don't have any lawyer, Jo-lene, you know that," her questioner interrupted.

"Oh, yes I do," the librarian said. "I told those two men—big men they were too, standing right in front of me like that. I told them my lawyers were with the law firm of A, C, L and U. They just stormed right outta here after that, never saying a please or thank you. But I expect they'll be back."

Reuben stood from her computer, nodded at the three women and walked out the front door. She returned home at a half jog. She ran to the telephone as soon as she returned to the house, dialing frantically.

"Sarah, thank God you're home," Reuben said. "Sarah, you have to come here, right away. Today. I have to get out of here. Please, Sarah, can you come today?"

"Debbie, of course. I understand," Sarah said. "But the march—you know I have to leave for DC tomorrow for the march. But if you tell me to drive up and get you today, of course I will."

"Yes, please, now," said Reuben, calming slightly. "Hurry. The FBI, they're here, in town, in Brooklin. They'll be back soon, and they'll find out who was doing Internet research on safe handling of . . ."

Reuben paused.

"Sarah, we have something very important to discuss when you get here. Please hurry."

"I'm on my way," Sarah said. *Debbie Reuben always panics easily,* Sarah thought, remembering one college ski trip that ended in tears when Debbie realized she'd packed two left gloves as part of her new pink ski ensemble.

CHAPTER 43

"I won't be here when you get back. Neither Adam nor I will be here when you get back."

Sally stood in the bedroom doorway, arms crossed in front of her chest, eyes red from crying, throat sore from screaming at her husband.

"I feel as if I'm living in a dream, or a nightmare. Somebody else's nightmare, actually. I don't care how many times you try to convince me; I know you are wrong, so wrong. How can you abandon me? Not just me, but your son. Can you really abandon Adam? I don't think you can do that. The Ben Shapiro I married couldn't abandon his son."

That was her trump card. But she'd played it before. Day after day that week she'd played one variation or another of that card. And each time, she'd lost, inexplicably but without any question. She'd lost.

Shapiro interrupted his packing—throwing casual clothes and clean socks and underwear into a blue nylon backpack. He spoke softly, evenly, patiently.

"I'm not abandoning anybody," he said to Sally. "I'm not abandoning my son. Apparently, however, either I am abandoning my wife or she is abandoning me; I haven't figured that one out yet. Sally, I've told you over and over. What I am not going to abandon is who I am. Not now. Not when it matters who I am. Sally, I am Jewish. You knew that when we fell in love. You knew that when we got married. And, Sally, my son is Jewish. If that is going to have any meaning, then being a Jew has to remain something that he can be proud of."

"You know," she replied, speaking quickly, "technically he isn't Jewish. You told me that. You can't change that. He has to have a Jewish mother to be a Jew, and he most certainly doesn't have a Jew for a mother."

Shapiro smiled, licked the tip of a finger and drew it downward in front of his face, scoring one hypothetical point for his wife.

"Yes, yes. You are so well versed on Jewish law, Sally. Okay, I agree that, technically, Adam isn't Jewish."

She smiled at that concession.

"But no matter what an Orthodox rabbi might say about Adam, the Nazis would have considered him to be a Jew. That's what matters," Shapiro said. He was startled by the angry expression in his wife's face.

"Don't you start again on the Nazis—the goddamn fucking Nazis. They're long ago and far away, like *Star Wars*. I'm sick and tired of your talk about Nazis. This is America, not Germany."

"The Nazis considered anybody a Jew if he had three Jewish grandparents," Shapiro continued, undeterred. "That would be my father's parents and my mother's parents. Four Jewish grandparents for Adam. There's no way my son isn't a Jew. And, Sally, you know that anybody who goes through life with a name like Adam Shapiro is not going to be confused for an Irish Catholic."

"I kept my last name," she said. "Maybe my son should start using my name rather than yours, if your name is going to be such a burden for him. After all, he's going to be living with me. You understand that much, don't you?"

"I won't discuss that now, Sally," Shapiro said. "I have to leave." He closed the zipper on the bag and lifted it from the bed. "I've told you this time after time," he continued, placing his hands on his wife's shoulders. She shook herself, causing his hands to drop. "I've told you. What is happening now is the most important civil rights event of my lifetime. This country is going down a wrong path. This country is not my America. Sally, it isn't your America either.

"My whole career has been working for civil rights. How in the world can I turn my back on this struggle? Now? Here? I wasn't around when the Indians were massacred. I wasn't born when Japanese were locked up in concentration camps. I was a child during the civil rights marches in the South.

"But I'm an adult now, for this struggle. More than just any adult, Sally. I'm in the center of things, in a position to change things for the better, to stand up to this asinine government and turn it around. I can't say no now. It isn't in me. You wouldn't respect me if I did. Adam wouldn't respect me. Sally, I wouldn't respect myself."

"I don't respect you now," she said. "I don't respect a man who abandons his family, a man who chooses to expose his family to shame, to humiliation, to beatings. You know what's been happening to Adam at school, the way they're teasing him and bullying him for being a Jew, because his father is some big-time Jew.

"I don't respect a man who puts his child through that. Maybe you should think some more about those Nazis you keep talking about. Would you respect a father who sent his son to the concentration camps because he was too proud to let his son call himself anything but a Jew? I don't think so. Having a live Christian son is better than a dead Jewish one. I'm right on that and you know it."

"Well, it hasn't come to that," Shapiro said.

"Not yet," Sally replied. "But Jews killed Americans right here in Boston and, it seems, have gotten away with it. Other

Jews sheltered them and got away with it. More Jews dropped a goddamn atomic bomb on innocent Arabs, and they haven't been caught yet either."

The backpack dropped from Shapiro's hand. For once, he was at a loss for words.

"People aren't too pleased with you Jews these days. Heaven forbid if something more should happen. But I tell you, you may feel you don't have any choice, that you have to hold yourself out as the big public Jew. Well, I do have a choice, and so does Adam. I'm not a Jew. He's not a Jew. And I don't have to be married to a Jew if I don't want to be. I'm telling you, Ben. You walk out that door and drive to Washington and by the time you come back here, I'll be living with my parents and Adam will be with me."

Shapiro left without a word. He did not feel like a hero going off to do battle. It was not the argument with Sally that made him feel a twinge of guilt, however. That last argument was a replay of what they'd been going through for more than a week.

He had not told Sally about Judy Katz, had not told his wife that he would be driving to Washington with an extremely attractive thirty-one-year-old woman and probably spending the next few days, and nights, with her. For that—not for leaving his wife, hardly at all for leaving his son—for that he felt guilty.

But guilt was soon replaced with excitement, at both the prospect of the huge demonstration and at who he was about to share that excitement with.

CHAPTER 44

The two young men had no idea how many sticks of TNT to use for each explosive belt. They decided to use as many as would fit around their waists, carrying the entire case to Sam Abdullah's car. The boys returned to search for blasting caps, the small detonators that set off the explosives. They found them in a locked metal cabinet on the far wall of the shack. They smashed the lock on the cabinet with a hammer, not knowing whether the blows would set off the detonators inside.

They drove back to Sam's house and carried their loot to his room, thankful his parents were gone on a short vacation. Sam regretted not having the opportunity to say goodbye to his parents. *I'll see them again in Paradise,* he thought. *I hope they'll be proud of me.*

Putting the devices together was simple. Their research was limited to looking for the term *explosive belt* in Wikipedia. After that, they'd made a trip to the Eastern Mountain Sports store at the North Shore Mall, Sam's target, where they'd each bought a fancy khaki fisherman's vest covered with pockets across its front and back. Not quite what their Palestinian brothers wore, but it would serve the same purpose.

The Wikipedia article said the real killing power came not from the explosives alone but from the hundreds of small steel balls usually wrapped around the explosives. Finding several thousand steel balls would be no problem. Not in modern America. Not with next-day delivery from Amazon.

"They have everything there," Sam said. "I'll bet there's something we can use."

But searches for ball bearings and steel balls turned up nothing helpful. Then Sam had an idea. "What about that stuff that shotguns shoot? What's that stuff called?" he asked.

"You've got to be kidding. What do shotguns shoot? What color is George Washington's white horse, jerk-off? Shotguns shoot stuff called shot. As in 'shot' gun."

"Oh yeah. I knew that," Sam said sheepishly. "Well, do a search for shot at Amazon."

That worked. They could buy 250 quarter-inch round steel balls for less than four dollars.

"That's a good price. Let's get a lot of them."

They decided it would be less suspicious if they split up their order, so over the course of a few hours they placed five orders for steel shot, alternating their names. They paid extra for overnight FedEx early delivery, knowing this was one Visa bill they'd never pay.

■ ■ ■

Five separate packages arrived the next morning at Sam's house. They divided the balls between their two vests, pouring the balls into the pockets containing the explosives, then duct-taping the tops of the pockets so the balls would not roll out.

Wiring the explosives together and to the detonators was equally simple.

"I've done this lots of times," Al said. "The foreman showed me how to do it when we were blasting ledge for those six houses my dad put up last year. Boy, was my dad pissed when he heard what I'd been doing, but it was real safe and loads of fun. You put a blasting cap on the end of each stick, like this." He demonstrated for his friend, trying his hardest to hide the shaking of his hand. "Then you run the wires from the cap to the detonator, but I'm not gonna do that until we're ready to go for real, okay?"

"Okay with me; show me how."

The construction company used a complicated radio-controlled detonator so the explosives could be set off from a distance. Obviously, that was not needed for the explosive vests. They'd made their own detonator from a doorbell switch and a six-volt lantern battery, both from the hardware store.

"Ring the bell and *BOOM*," Al told his friend.

When the vests were completed, TNT and shot taped tightly into the various pockets, front and back, and all the wires run from the blasting caps to the doorbell buttons in the front right pockets, Al suggested they put them on and take pictures of themselves.

Sam held up his hand. After the excitement of handling the explosives and constructing the devices, his voice suddenly took on a serious tone.

"No, remember, it won't be us doing this," he said. "It's going to be a couple of Jews. The whole thing doesn't work if we do it. It has to be a couple of Jews. We can't leave any photos or make any farewell videos."

"I know, I know," Al replied. "I was just worked up, you know, like I was in the Intifadah or something.

"I thought we'd shout 'Long Live Israel' or something before we set them off. What were you thinking?"

Sam smiled. "That's a good start," he said. "But we only get one shot at this, so let's do the full thing—you know, dress up like those religious-type Jews."

"Okay, do you know what they look like, the real ones?" Al asked. "Hey, let me try something."

He turned back to the computer and typed *Jew picture* into

Google. The screen filled with photographs of men and boys in black coats and hats. Many had curls of hair descending in front of each ear.

"We've gotta do that hair thing," Al said, getting excited. "Nobody but a Jew would do that."

In the end, their costumes were simple. Another trip to the mall got them each a long black overcoat and black hats that looked a bit more stylish than in the photos from the Google search, but not by much. An embarrassing visit to a beauty salon at the mall got them a black wig, from which they extracted enough long hairs to give each a respectable lock, which could be held in place by a bobby pin snatched from Sam's mother's dresser drawer.

They decided fake beards would look too fake.

"Hey, we'll be young Jews, too young to shave," Al joked.

On the way out of the mall they made a final, spontaneous purchase at a pushcart titled Flag Us Down. Abdullah spoke to the store clerk.

"Do you have any Israeli flags? You know, those blue ones with the star on them?" he asked.

Eighteen-year-old Carol Rosenthal, whose mother owned the pushcart, was surprised at the request. She looked at the two young men. *They sort of look Jewish, I guess*, she thought as she rummaged through the cardboard boxes in which her merchandise was stored.

"Here are a couple," she said, lifting the top of a box. "I think these are the last two I have." She looked at the two young men sadly. "I don't think they make these anymore."

"Yes, I know they don't," Abdullah answered. "I doubt if they ever will again."

He paid in cash. They returned to his house, to his room, to examine their purchases and equipment.

When the vests were completed and the costumes ready, the two young men became serious. Deadly serious.

"I think we should pray first," Sam said.

He reached under his bed and unrolled the two prayer rugs he kept there, keeping the second because Al seemed to spend more time at Sam's house than at his own.

They knelt on the rugs and chanted, alternating between leaning with their foreheads on the rug and sitting up straight. After ten minutes they stopped and stood, then helped each other dress.

The vests were heavy to lift but comfortable enough to wear once the weight was carried by their shoulders. They put on white shirts, like in the photos, over the vests, then black pants, black socks and black shoes. They pinned the hair locks on each other, then put on their hats and, finally, the black coats.

Then they stood a few feet apart, staring at each other.

"You look like such a Jew," Sam said, shocked at the transformation of his friend's appearance. "You really do."

Al Farouk, too, was surprised at his friend's appearance. "This is going to work," he said. "People are going to think we're a couple of Jews."

Sam looked at his watch, remembering for a moment that it was a birthday present from his parents.

"It's four thirty now," he said. "We can get to the malls in forty-five minutes. Let's give ourselves a half hour in case there's traffic and to get set up. We blow the bombs at six thirty. The food courts ought to be packed then. We stand on a table, give some speech about Israel, shout out something that sounds like Hebrew and then—"

"And then we find out whether there really is a Paradise," his friend finished for him.

"Well, whether or not there is Paradise," Sam said, "we're sure gonna create some hell for the Jews we leave behind. Let's go, brother."

They walked downstairs and out the front door to their separate cars, each holding his breath when the cars hit bumps in the road.

CHAPTER 45

After circling the same block three times, Ben Shapiro identified Judy Katz's building and spotted her sitting on the stone steps leading to the front door. He honked his horn. She stood, waving.

Katz did not look like the crime-busting prosecutor. Dressed in decidedly unlawyerly jeans and a floppy, bright-yellow cotton tank top, Katz could have passed for one of the college students crammed into luxury apartments in her neighborhood. Her long black hair was in a ponytail sprouting through the hole in the back of her baseball cap, a cap that bore a Star of David on the front, above the words *Camp Tikvah*.

She tossed her L.L.Bean duffel bag into the back and sat in the passenger seat.

"I can't tell you how excited I am about this," she said.

"Well, thanks for coming down a day early," Shapiro said. "I got drafted to stand by in case there are any last-minute legal hassles."

Shapiro smiled. This was something entirely new for him. Despite several temptations, he had never been unfaithful to his wife—a few phone sex sessions and porn films while he was on out-of-town trips, maybe, but that did not count as infidelity in his book. Shapiro didn't know where this escapade with Katz was going to lead, but he was surprised at how easy it was for him to be attracted to this young woman and at how she, for some reason he could not comprehend, seemed to be attracted to him.

The expectation that he would return to an empty house and that this separation was for real did little to hold him back. *This could be the world's fastest rebound romance*, he thought. He didn't realize that, more often than not, such rebounds involved overlaps rather than a gap.

"You look ready for a political demonstration," Shapiro said to Katz. "Did you bring your gas mask?"

A troubled expression clouded her face.

"Was I supposed to?" she asked. "Shit, we had a shelf of them in the tactical room at work, you know. I could have grabbed one."

Shapiro laughed. "No, no, I was kidding. I had one in college, government surplus. It never worked. I became a connoisseur of crowd control gas back then. There was tear gas. You dripped water or Visine in your eyes for that. Pepper gas. Hated that stuff. You never ever rubbed your eyes when they used that stuff. It caused more irritation. And, of course, there was that favorite when the pigs wanted to get nasty with you, CN gas. That made you puke your guts out. Didn't feel much like taking over the dean's office with a face full of CN, I'll tell you."

Shapiro saw the shocked look on the young woman's face.

"Sorry," he said sheepishly. "I've been accused more than once of never outgrowing college. And also of telling far too many stories."

"You're like a living history lesson," Katz said, with a sly grin. "I dressed as a hippie for Halloween once."

"Ouch," Shapiro said, placing his hand over his heart. "That one hurt."

They both laughed. Levi turned the car onto the Massachusetts

Turnpike. "I figure we can get there in about eight hours," he said. "I have an iron bladder, so let me know when you want to stop for a break."

They rode in silence for several minutes. Shapiro glanced at the woman sitting to his right. He smiled at the clichéd thought that she could be his daughter. *But she sure isn't,* he added to himself, noticing a pale, untanned spot high on her left arm. She noticed his glance.

"Laser surgery," she said, tapping the spot with her right hand. "A tattoo. A dare." Katz grinned, staring straight ahead through the windshield.

Much as he wondered about that tattoo, Shapiro lacked the nerve to ask what image could have been so embarrassing to a thirty-one-year-old woman that she'd had it surgically removed.

He tried another topic.

"So, what happened at work? Have you quit, or did Arnie Anderson fire you first?"

"Actually, I haven't officially quit, or been fired yet," she said. "I've been trying to set up a meeting with Arnie for days, but he keeps putting me off. We're scheduled to meet Monday morning. That's when I'll hand in my badge."

"I'd like to be a fly on the wall for that conversation," Shapiro said. "My feeling is that he'll be relieved to have you go. Arnie's not a bad guy, but these cases have put him in a tough situation."

"Tough situation for lots of people," Katz said. "The story is that the Queen quit over these cases."

"Good for her," Shapiro said. "That's half the problem now; people know right from wrong, but when their ass, or their job, is on the line, they follow orders now and hope to justify them later. Be sure and take good notes at that meeting with Arnie. I'll be curious."

They sat in silence as the car roared down the highway. Shapiro, again, was the first to break the silence.

"Damn," he said. "I forgot a phone call I was going to make before I left. You're going to have to pretend you're not here.

This is going to be a confidential discussion. No sneezing or coughing, okay?"

"Cross my heart and hope to die," she said.

When Shapiro pressed the telephone icon on the steering wheel, the navigation screen switched to a telephone dial. He scrolled down his recent call list to Suffolk County district attorney Patrick McDonough.

"Ben, thought you'd be down in DC waving a sign," the district attorney said, laughing. "Aren't you the head Jewish lawyer or something these days?"

"Actually, Pat, I'm in the car on the Mass Pike heading for Washington right now. I wanted to check in with you about that kid I'm representing. Mandelbaum. You said you'd give the idea of turning him over to the feds some thought."

"Oh, I thought about it all right, Ben," McDonough said. "For about five seconds. That kid's a murderer, no two ways about it. I saw how the feds rounded all those people up and then sent them home with a stern lecture. No, Ben, it's not going to work that way on this one. People are dead, ten people. It's too bad he's the only one who's gonna pay, but he's all I've got. I think I'll hang onto him."

"I thought you might say that," Shapiro said. "I've got another proposition for you, Pat."

"I didn't think you were calling to ask me to look up the traffic conditions on the Mass Pike," McDonough said. "Okay, Ben, shoot."

"What if he could identify the Israeli soldiers who sank the Coast Guard boats, the ones who fired the grenades and planned the whole thing?" Shapiro asked in a flat voice. "That would be worth something, right?"

"That would be worth something." McDonough said. "What's the deal you have in mind, Ben?"

"Simple," Shapiro said. "Ten or so Israeli soldiers get ID'd, you bring whatever charges you want, you fight the feds for custody, and my guy gets turned over to the feds to be placed in that camp, all state charges against him nolle prossed."

"You want me to dismiss against him?" McDonough replied. "I can't go that far."

"Yes you can. Call it federal preemption or something," Shapiro said. "You can do it on your own, don't even need a judge's approval. You know, Pat, we go to trial and I might walk this guy. He had nothing to do with anything. All he did was jump in the water and not swim fast enough to get away. A jury could walk him."

"Dream on, Counselor," the district attorney said. "Not with the mood going around today. Not a good time to be a Jew on trial for murder. You know that. Let me give your proposal some thought. Just so I'm clear, you say you can identify Israeli soldiers, active military personnel, right, who fired rocket-propelled grenades and sank the Coast Guard ships?"

"This is just a theoretical discussion for the moment, Pat," Shapiro said. "Let's say that in theory that's true. You get back to me and tell me what you would do in return for that information."

"Hold on, Ben. I trust you. I don't trust the time of day from your client," McDonough said. "Do you personally have this information?"

"Pat, if I did, it would be privileged. Does it make a difference if it comes from me or him?"

"It could make all the difference in the world, Ben."

"If it makes a difference in regard to getting my guy out of Charles Street," Shapiro said, "you can theoretically assume that I can be in a position to share my client's knowledge."

"Good. I've got to check with the feds first. You'll be hearing from me, Ben," McDonough said. "Let's say that I'm intrigued by your proposal."

"Can your guy really do that?" Katz asked seconds after the call ended. "I suppose what I mean is, would your client really do that, turn in Israeli soldiers like that?"

"My guy is presently the best girlfriend of at least six very large, very horny men who seem to be very good friends with the corrections officers who are supposed to be looking out for my guy's safety. He'll do anything to, quite literally, save his ass."

They drove on in silence, only to be interrupted by the cell phone ringing. The caller ID was not the district attorney as Shapiro hoped.

"My wife," he said. "We're on the outs. It's a long story, but I don't think this is a conversation you want to experience. I'll let it ring. I can always talk to her later."

■ ■ ■

Sally was filled with guilt as she sat on the bedroom floor and went through the cardboard banker's box that held the couple's "important papers." Wills and investment statements, old tax returns and the like. She told herself she was not doing anything to feel guilty about. After all, they were her papers as much as they were his. She'd give him copies, or her divorce lawyer would give them to his lawyer.

Her search through the box came to a halt when she opened a well-stuffed manila envelope on which was written, in her handwriting, the words *My Famous Husband*. The envelope was filled with newspaper clippings—stories about cases Ben had handled over the years. He never saved anything about himself. Without telling him that she did so, Sally saved everything.

Memories flooded her mind as she glanced at the yellowing newsprint. Each story was about a case, a triumph, a defeat, a crusade, a financial windfall, a financial disaster of a loss. She dumped the contents of the envelope on the bedroom carpet and started reading through the articles, holding each one as if it were precious and fragile.

I remember this case, she thought. *He sued the state licensing board for race discrimination for that old black man when they wouldn't give him a barber's license.* The memory of sitting at the dinner table as Ben reenacted his devastating cross-examination of the head of the licensing board, waving a chicken leg in the air for emphasis, brought a smile to her face. When he finished his tale she'd asked him to tell her the rest of the story, the part he always held back. He'd smiled and said, "Did I mention that the guy I'm suing for race discrimination is black, too?"

Another article described a case Ben brought and lost in the state supreme court, representing a single mom who worked at a high-tech startup who was fired when she said she had to leave work to spend time with her son on the weekends. *He told me from the start he was going to lose that case*, she remembered, *but he took it to make a point, to give that mother a chance to fight back.*

Sally smiled at that one. *What a knight he is, always rushing off to do battle for the little person. I'm so proud of my husband.*

That thought hit her like a rock to the forehead. *I'm always so proud of my husband. Why am I not proud of him now, now that he is fighting his own fight?* She realized—all of a sudden she realized with crystal clarity—that her husband had no choice about this fight. He couldn't turn his back on a single mother, out of work and living off her unemployment check. He couldn't turn his back on an elderly man who'd learned barbering from his father, rather than from a trade school.

How can I expect him to turn his back on his own people, his own heritage? He not only won't do that, she realized, *he can't do that. It isn't part of the man. And that man is the man I love. I still love.*

Sally sat on the floor and carefully replaced each news story in the envelope, then she collected the pile of important documents and put them, one by one, back into the box.

The fist that had clenched her stomach for weeks loosened. Her shoulders lost the slump into which they'd fallen. She stood. Back straight. Head raised. Relieved. She smiled. "I still love him."

I don't even know where he's staying in Washington, she thought, then decided to try calling his office on the chance that he hadn't left yet. Ben's secretary seemed surprised to hear from Sally and told her Ben was going to DC directly from home.

Sally felt she could not wait another instant to talk to her husband, to tell him she was sorry for what she'd put him through; to tell him that of course she'd be home when he returned and to tell him she knew how important this fight, of all his fights, was to him; to tell him that she'd be there with him, her and Adam, if he wanted them by his side at a march or a rally or a trial.

Maybe I'll drive to Washington and surprise him, she thought. *Imagine his face when he sees me.*

Ben did not usually carry his cell phone, to her frustration, but he enjoyed how the phone connected wirelessly to the voice navigation system in his car. *He so loves his toys,* she thought, smiling. Smiling.

She dialed his cell, jabbing at the tiny number keys in excitement at not getting divorced, at not not loving her husband. *He must be in the car now, on the way to Washington.*

The telephone rang eight times before going to voicemail. *I can't apologize in a voicemail,* she thought and punched the disconnect button.

■ ■ ■

Sally remained energized as she waited to pick Adam up from school later that day.

"I have a treat for you, sweetie," she said to her son as he climbed in the car, slinging his backpack into the back seat. "We're going to the mall to buy Daddy a special present."

"Oh boy, the mall?" Adam crowed. "Can we get Japanese chicken, Japanese chicken, Japanese chicken?"

Sally sighed. "This is a special day, and if you are extra good while I'm shopping for Daddy, we'll get Japanese chicken afterwards. We are going to buy a big surprise for Daddy when he gets home."

"Isn't Dad coming home tonight?" Adam asked. "Where is he?"

"Daddy had to go away for a few days," Sally said. "He had something very important to do, very important for the Jewish people, Adam. He had to say something to the government in Washington for the Jewish people. We should be so proud of him for what he is doing."

Adam noticed his mother crying now, softly at first, but soon her shoulders trembled as a week's, a month's worth of fear and anger escaped.

"Why are you crying, Mom?" Adam asked.

Sally reached into the glove compartment for a tissue, finding only an old Dunkin' Donuts paper napkin to wipe her eyes and blow her nose.

"I'm crying because I'm happy, sweetie, and because I love your daddy, and you, so much."

Adam looked at her with an odd expression.

"You're weird, Mom," he said. "I cry when I'm sad. When I'm happy, I laugh."

Sally laughed.

The North Shore Mall was crowded. They parked in a secondary lot, a ten-minute walk from the main entrance. As they walked into the mall, Sally took her son's hand and warned him, as she always did when they went there, to stay close to her and to ask a sales clerk in any store to take him to mall security if he got lost. For some reason she never understood, malls made her anxious.

Early on in Ben's legal career, she'd created what became a family tradition. When an especially big case came in, she would buy him a new suit. That suit would be his "case suit" for the life of that new case, bringing him good luck when he wore it to court. If the case turned out well, if he won or it settled before trial, the suit remained in his closet for future use. If he lost the case, the suit went to the Salvation Army.

Most of his office clothing came from Brooks Brothers,

which had a large store at that mall. Brooks kept a file on each customer, with all of his various sizes recorded, from shoes to neck size. She'd never had to return a suit she bought for her husband at Brooks.

Adam was getting tired and showing it as Sally finally chose between a gray wool pinstripe that she decided was too conservative even for a lawyer and a solid blue double breasted with pleated pants that she thought sent a stylish, confident message.

She glanced at her watch as they left the store. It was six fifteen already. She considered heading home when a revitalized Adam grabbed her arm.

"Japanese chicken, Japanese chicken now," he begged. "You promised, Mom."

The food court was packed. They had difficulty finding a table, finally having to dash as a mother and daughter stood and left. They barely beat two teenage boys wearing iPod headphones and baggy pants, who gave them killer scowls but let them have the table.

Sally piled her bags on the table and ordered Adam to remain right there without moving an inch while she got his Japanese chicken. He promised to guard their table. Her eyes never left him as she waited in line at the Teriyaki-Chicky booth.

Sally returned five minutes later with a Styrofoam dish overflowing with tiny bits of chicken covered in a brown sauce on top of what looked like a triple serving of brown noodles, a few pieces of broccoli and miniature corn to the side. She handed Adam a plastic knife and fork, which he promptly bent over double trying to cut a piece of chicken. He looked at his mother in confusion.

"Just use your fingers," she said, patience running out as the last of her energy, the last remnant of her overcharged emotional state, dissipated. *I'm feeding him junk food at the mall,* she thought. *Might as well finish being a terrible mother by sitting him in front of the TV when we get home while I take a long, hot soak in the tub.* She could almost feel the warm water supporting her.

"What's that weirdo doing?" Adam asked, pointing at a young man in a long black coat and hat. Sally looked up from her thoughts of the bathtub and turned her head to see what her son was pointing at. Two tables from where they sat, a young man was climbing from his chair to stand on top of the table.

His coat was unbuttoned, revealing black pants and a white shirt beneath. The shirt looked odd, puffy. Sally noticed the black curls descending from beneath the man's hat in front of his ears.

"He's a Hasid, Adam—a very religious Jewish person," she told her son.

He's acting strange, Sally thought, looking around for mall security as heads turned toward the man throughout the food court. By now he was standing on the table, his legs spread. He reached into a bag and removed some white fabric, which he draped over his shoulders.

"Look, Mom," Adam said. "It's a Jewish flag. I know that star. They're fun to make. You do it by drawing two triangles, one right side up and the other upside down."

The man started shouting. Most of what he said was unintelligible, but Sally heard the word *Israel* shouted and something that sounded like a prayer. She heard a yell from across the food court. When she turned, she saw a mall security guard gesturing at the man to climb down from the table.

Sally looked back at the man on the table, standing not more than ten feet from her and Adam. She watched him bring his feet together and stand straight, almost like a soldier at attention. His final words were odd, definitely not English at all, not even sounding like Hebrew but more like he was saying something that began with the word *Allah.*

Sally saw the man's right hand reach inside his shirt, where two buttons were left undone. *Funny,* she thought, *I didn't even notice that his shirt was unbuttoned.*

She was just turning her head to smile at Adam, who was staring in fascination at the man, when seventy-five quarter-inch steel balls tore through her upper body, instantaneously shredding her heart and lungs and smashing her face into a pulp beyond recognition. Adam died beside his mother.

The Israeli flag rose thirty feet over the pandemonium in the food court and then slowly fluttered down to cover a small piece of the carnage.

CHAPTER 46

Ben Shapiro and Judy Katz drove west from Boston, south into Connecticut and across to New York, crossing the Hudson River north of the city, connecting with the Garden State Parkway. Then south through New Jersey. They barely stopped talking for the entire five-hour drive. The radio was off. Shapiro told war stories—legal wars, beginning with college demonstrations and continuing through his entire career.

Katz mostly listened. That was unusual for her. As a federal criminal prosecutor dealing with organized crime, she had her own catalog of stories. At the rare parties she attended, she was used to being the person who entertained others. Her stories were more interesting than what her investment banker and stockbroker friends had to say about their jobs.

It dawned on the young woman, several hours into listening to Shapiro carry on about cases he'd won and cases he'd lost, that while Shapiro liked to hear himself talk about himself, this was also a man who'd enjoyed his career and who did more than just make money with his work. She thought about the momentary heartthrobs during her aborted lunch with Bob Shaw of the antitrust division and realized that Shaw's career highs would coincide with the days on which he made the most money. Shapiro casually mentioned, in the middle of what seemed to be half his stories, that this "wasn't a money case" or that another was done "as a favor" or that a client "won me over against my better financial judgment."

Before she became too enthralled with Shapiro's altruism, Katz reminded herself that they were comfortably driving in his year-old Mercedes. *Doing well and doing good*, she thought. *Not a bad combination.*

Shapiro began running out of stories, or out of energy, as they crossed the Delaware River into Pennsylvania. After a few minutes of silence he asked Katz if she wanted to try the radio. She turned it on and began scanning for stations, pausing on a station halfway through Billy Joel's "Piano Man."

"Cool," she said. "I love oldies."

Shapiro grinned but said nothing.

The song finished with its multiple-chord piano flourish. The announcer came on with "And now for WBEB Fox Action News with Brenda Waters."

"Hundreds of persons are believed dead in two massive, well-coordinated bombings at shopping malls outside of Boston," the newscaster said. "Police report two suicide bombers who appeared to be Orthodox Jews wrapped in what appeared to be Israeli flags blew themselves up in the crowded food courts of the Burlington Mall and North Shore Mall in Burlington and Peabody, Massachusetts."

"This won't be good," Shapiro said. "Damn. The North Shore Mall. I go there. I buy my suits there. I need to call Sally. I need to make sure she and Adam are okay. Do you mind?" Shapiro asked.

"No, go right ahead. I understand."

Shapiro voice-commanded his car phone to call his wife. Her cell went immediately to voicemail.

"She probably blocked," he told Katz. "She's probably at her parents by now. If something was wrong, I would have heard."

"I'm sure they're okay," Katz said reassuringly.

The radio stayed on for the remainder of the drive as Katz hunted from news station to news station. She briefly searched through AM stations, pausing on a Maryland talk radio show in which caller after caller complained that "President Afraid" did nothing after the coastguardsmen were killed, and again after the FBI agents were murdered, sending a message that Jews could get away with anything. After a few minutes of similar calls, Katz returned to FM music stations.

It was getting dark as they approached Washington's suburbs.

"Open the glove compartment, would you?" Shapiro said to Katz. "I printed out an email. It's in there."

She removed a sheet of paper.

"It's from Aaron Hocksberg, a client of mine," he said. "It has his cell phone number. He said to call when I got to DC. He's heading the Massachusetts delegation to the march. Would you dial his number, please?"

The sound of Hocksberg's telephone ringing came through the car's speakers, followed by a voice.

"Aaron Hocksberg speaking."

"Aaron, Ben Shapiro. I'm outside DC. Did you hear about the bombings?"

"Hear about it? It's the only thing people are talking about. We don't know if the president is going to pull the plug on the march. We've been on the phone all afternoon with every congressman we know, all of us here. You wouldn't believe that people who came at us two months ago with their hands out and palms up for campaign checks won't even get on the phone with us today. Ben, where are you staying?"

"Staying?" Shapiro answered. "I never got around to booking anyplace and I expect there isn't a room to be found in the city. Worse comes to worst, I guess I'll camp out in my back seat." He glanced at Katz and saw her smiling.

"No problem, Ben," Hocksberg said. "Stay with us. We've got a big suite at the Renaissance, using it as our base of operations. We're crowded here, but we can squeeze you in. They can roll in a cot. Not a lot of privacy, though. Anyway, it would be good to have you close by, just in case."

"Uh, thanks, Aaron," Shapiro said a bit sheepishly. "Aaron, you ought to know, I'm not quite by myself here."

Katz grinned, enjoying this.

"Fantastic," Hocksberg said. "You talked Sally into coming. Good for her. Can't wait to see her again. It's been a while. Rose is here with me, of course. I expect Sally is used to being the only *shiksa* in the room."

"Aaron, I'm not exactly with Sally at the moment," Shapiro said, thinking how accurate that statement was in so many ways. "I came down with somebody else. I don't think you know her."

Hocksberg was silent for a moment. "Whatever, Ben, whatever," he said. "I'll let Rose know Sally couldn't make it."

"Thanks, Aaron," Shapiro said, not sure why he added "but she's Jewish, at least."

They found the hotel. Katz glanced at the back seat as they were taking their bags from the car.

"I was sort of looking forward to that," she said. "It doesn't sound as if we're going to get much time to ourselves, does it?"

Shapiro looked at the rear seat, surprised at how relieved he was that he'd found such a well-chaperoned place for the two of them to stay. He hadn't yet been unfaithful to his wife, not counting fantasies. As tempting and apparently available as Judy Katz was, Shapiro didn't know whether to be disappointed or relieved by their housing situation. He decided to let events work themselves out over the next few days.

CHAPTER 47

President Quaid called senators Wayne Giddings, the Republican majority leader, and Grant Farrell, the Democratic minority leader, to meet with him at the White House. The president felt isolated, not the least by the almost complete refusal of the First Lady to speak with him on other than ceremonial occasions.

"I'll be up front with both of you," he said. "I am at my wit's end about what to do about this situation. The consequences of making the wrong decision are too scary to think about. I'm ready for firm actions, but I'm not willing to walk out on this limb by myself."

"Mr. President, we backed you before, about taking a firm hand with the Jews on those ships in Boston," Sen. Giddings said. "None of my people bothered you about the way you handled that situation—well, except for Jane Struthers from New York. She has a constituency at home to answer to. You do what you have to do with this situation now, sir; just run it by us first so there are no surprises. I'll tell you up front if I can't back you on something."

"Same goes for me, of course, Mr. President," Sen. Farrell

said. "After all, sir, you might not be the dog I would've picked to head the pack in the first place, but you're still our top dog."

"That's what I expected to hear," Quaid said. "My people prepared this for me to give to you. It's a resolution Congress will pass." He handed each man a one-page document.

Sen. Giddings quickly scanned the page he'd been given. "This language looks familiar," he said. "Where was this cribbed from?"

"Good catch, Wayne," the president said. "It's almost word for word what Congress passed after September 11. This language was broad enough for Bush to do whatever he wanted, from invading Afghanistan and Iraq to listening in on every telephone call any American had with anybody outside the country. One of my legal eagles called it a congressional get-out-of-jail-free card for the White House."

"This language is awfully broad, sir," Sen. Farrell cautioned. He handed the paper back to the president.

"With all due respect, I don't see any limitations in there. It pretty much says you can do anything anywhere to anybody. Am I missing something here, sir?"

"No, Grant, you've nailed it right on the nose. This is what I want. This is what Congress gave W. Bush to fight terrorism. The bombing of those two malls was certainly a terrorist act. Nobody is going to deny that."

Quaid gave the two legislators a somber stare. "From what my people tell me, the timing of the bombings, that degree of coordination, was the work of some big organization, probably even a government. And those bombs were damn sophisticated, they tell me. A government did this. No, my people tell me that the Jews have taken a card from the Palestinians with this suicide bombing. And you know what that means, gentlemen. You both know what happens next, right?"

"Uh, tell us, sir," Sen. Giddings said.

"More suicide bombings, that's what happens next, goddammit," Quaid huffed. "At least we hope that's all that happens next. It isn't shopping-mall bombs that keep me awake at night. There's that other thing floating around, too."

"The nuclear thing, sir?" Sen. Giddings asked. "I was briefed on that, just me and four other senators, including, of course, my Democratic brother here. But there's been nothing for three days. Nothing except rumors."

"Sounds like we didn't appreciate how lucky we were to be facing Muslim terrorists," Sen. Giddings said. "Despite years of trying, they never pulled off anything like this. And here the Israelis manage to get a bomb into this country three months after they get bombed themselves." He paused.

"So, what do you have in mind?" Sen. Farrell said.

"This nation is under attack—attack from forces of a foreign state right in our homeland. For obvious reasons, we can't attack the homeland of the nation that is attacking us. There is no Afghanistan, no Iraq for us to clean out in this war. This time the enemy is among us. That's who is attacking us. This enemy among us. That's who I intend to protect the American people from."

The president continued, his voice rising in volume, speed, pitch.

"It's not what's happened so far that's keeping me awake at night; it's what is going to happen any day now—any day now. Do you understand that? More bombings for sure. More Americans killed. They don't have to smuggle any more soldiers into the country. They have millions of them here right now. Millions. I don't know if I can trust any Jew right now—not one."

The two senators sat stunned.

"Give me that resolution. Bush got it. I want it. I am going to sign that legislation tomorrow."

CHAPTER 48

Hocksberg asked Ben Shapiro to come along to a meeting with Rabbi Garfinkle. Representatives of Jewish organizations from across the country were crowded into the office space when Shapiro and Hocksberg arrived. Rabbi Garfinkle was speaking. Shapiro had never met the man. He'd expected to see an old man with a beard, a stooped back and dark suit.

Instead, the man standing in front of the group of forty or so organizers wore jeans and a corduroy shirt. Brown hair covered his ears and he spoke with a hint of a Southern drawl, but not enough to disguise the serious tone of his voice.

"I just returned from a meeting with a representative from the White House," he said. "Wilson Harrison, the new attorney general."

"Acting attorney general," a voice shouted from a corner of the room. "I know him from law school. He was a jerk then. He's worse now, from what I hear."

Rabbi Garfinkle continued, unperturbed.

"I can't say he was the most pleasant person I've ever dealt with. He was quite emphatic in what he said." The rabbi paused to collect his thoughts. "He said the president wants the march called off. It is too dangerous, he said, too dangerous for a million people to gather in the city at this time."

"What he fears is a million Jews," another voice called out. "That's what he doesn't want to see."

"Please, let me continue," the rabbi said. "Mr. Harrison did not come right out and say it, but he hinted the government has received information about a plot against the marchers, that somebody, he didn't say who, was planning on doing something horrible if the march goes forward."

"What did he say exactly, Rabbi?" a woman in the middle of the room asked.

"He said a national security agency—that's how he described it—a national security agency obtained information that an anti-Jewish organization planned on letting loose some sort of biological agent in the middle of the crowd tomorrow, Friday. That's all he said, except to say that the president was concerned for our safety and that the president begged us to call the march off. So, what do we do?"

"That's a load of bullshit, pardon my Yiddish, Rabbi." A man in the back of the room gently pushed his way forward to stand next to Rabbi Garfinkle.

"Sam Lowenstein. New York. I'm with what used to be the ILGWU." He looked around the room. "That's the International Ladies' Garment Workers' Union, for those of you who were born yesterday."

He smiled.

"We used to be a big-time union. In your grandmother's time. I don't believe one word from that asshole of an attorney general, or from his boss, the former great close friend of Israel, President Quaid. They're scared shitless of having a million Yids camped out in front of the White House, that's what this is all about. And they don't have the political balls to ban us. So they're making up this fairy tale to scare us. They want us to tuck our tails between our legs and go home. Then they'll call us cowards. No way. I'm staying, and so are my people."

Rabbi Garfinkle looked around the room. "Anybody else?" he asked.

A tall woman in a conservatively cut, expensive-looking suit raised her hand.

"May I speak?" she said. "My name is Shirley Zarick. I am the chairman of the Hadassah Chapter for the Jewish Community Federation of Sonoma County; that's near San Francisco, of course.

"I agree with everything the gentleman from New York said, although I might not have put it quite so colorfully. And, as an aside, Mr. Lowenstein, my mother, may she rest in peace, carried her ILGWU card until the day she died. She sang 'Look for the Union Label' to my children when she put them to bed. I agree one hundred percent. They are trying to scare us. Show us proof of this threat. Give us some evidence. If they can't do that, then shame on them for telling lies. That's what I have to say."

"Anybody else?" the rabbi asked.

A man wearing a suit and tie, standing near the doorway, spoke.

"Dan Glickstein. Feldman, Brownstein, Rabinowitz and Stern. We're the law firm that donated this office space. What I want to say is that my partner, Sol Rabinowitz, works pretty much full time as a congressional liaison—you'd call him a lobbyist, I suppose. I had breakfast with Sol this morning. He said the Hill is buzzing with a resolution that Quaid is rushing through the House and Senate today.

"Sol tells me that Quaid is trying to pull a Bush 9/11, that's what it is. Sol says his people tell him they just took the war powers bill passed after 9/11 and changed the dates but nothing else. They're gonna give the president the power to do whatever he wants, no limits, just like Bush got.

"Remember what we got the last time they did that? War in Afghanistan. Everything that happened with Iraq. Syria. Yemen. That concentration camp at Guantanamo. Torture. Secret wiretaps. The damn Patriot Act. Sol tells me it's going to be the same thing all over again. But this time it's not because of the Muslims. This time their tails are on fire because of us. Jews, Jewish bombs, Jewish soldiers, the—pardon the expression—the full megillah. I tell you, this is what scares the daylights out of me, not some made-up story about unnamed anti-Semitic biological weapons."

Rabbi Garfinkle looked around the crowded room. Nobody else made any effort to speak. The rabbi smiled.

"Now that is a minor miracle," he said. "Forty Jews in the same room and nobody wants to say anything. I'll take that as a consensus. The march goes on. I'll get a message to the attorney general expressing our confidence that the police will be able to protect peaceful marchers from any threats.

"For those of you speaking tomorrow, remember, ten minutes each, no more. For the rest of you, I'll see you tomorrow at 10 a.m. To quote one of my favorite Jews from another planet, Mork from Ork, be there or be square."

Shapiro and Aaron Hocksberg returned to the suite at the Renaissance. Shapiro stopped in the hallway to surreptitiously check his cell phone for Sally's message, feeling guilty that he'd ignored her telephone call during his drive to DC. There were two messages from his office, nothing from his wife. *Fuck her*, he thought. *I know she called. If she won't leave a message, I'll be damned if I'll call her again.*

Returning to Hocksberg's suite, Shapiro found Judy Katz on the balcony engaged in conversation with a short woman. Katz's face lit up as she spotted Shapiro. When Shapiro walked up to the two women, Katz placed her hand on his arm and left it there comfortably.

"Ben, this is Sarah Goldberg," she said. "Sarah's from Portland, Maine. She is going to be speaking tomorrow."

Sarah laughed. "I'm only going to be speaking if I can figure out what I'm going to say," she said. "I'd planned on talking about nonviolence. I still could, I suppose. My husband threatened to beat me if I do, though."

She saw the shocked look on Katz's face.

"Kidding, just kidding, that was a joke," she said quickly. "I guess this is no time for jokes. Seriously, my husband was not especially upset by those mall bombings. He's rather, to understate it, rather militant. To tell you the truth, I think he was jealous of the bombers."

Shapiro and Katz were silent, not knowing how to respond. Shapiro spoke. He sounded sad.

"Sarah, I understand where your husband is coming from. Look, I'm a lawyer. I believe in the system of laws. But I'll tell you, I don't believe the legal system, or even the political system, is going to do the right thing now. No judge is going to stand in the way of this political wave."

"Especially this Supreme Court," Katz said. "Most of them have been there since the last time the Republicans ran both the White House and Congress at the same time. They'll be the first ones waving the flag in front of the detention camps, like the Supreme Court gave its stamp of approval when Japanese-Americans were herded into concentration camps."

"I can't disagree with you there," Shapiro said. "The politicians are even worse. We can't find a senator willing to sit on the podium tomorrow, much less vote to intervene to save what is left of Israel. No, it isn't going to happen by either legal or political means. I've been tossing around at night thinking that Israel has been destroyed, that maybe a million Jews are in concentration camps run by Arabs instead of Germans, and that this country isn't lifting a finger to stop it.

"Even worse, what am I doing about it? Filing lawsuits that will get nowhere? Making speeches? As if words are going to save a single life or feed a single child in Israel. No, Sarah, I understand what your husband is saying."

"And just as bad, now we've got our own concentration camp for Jews sitting on Cape Cod," Goldberg added. "And a president who seems to want to leave his name in the history books by stomping on Jews."

Judy Katz, standing between the other two, put an arm on Sarah's shoulder and her other on Shapiro's back, rubbing him lightly, casually, possessively.

"I don't think your speech tomorrow is going to make a whole lot of difference," Katz said. "But why don't we find a place for some lunch and we can work on the speech anyway?"

Shapiro was silent as they rode the elevator to the lobby. He was shocked by his own words. It was the first time he'd expressed out loud a feeling growing in him for several weeks.

If there is no legal solution and if there is no political solution, what course of action is left? If you know a holocaust is coming, what action is justified to try to stop it? Or, he thought, *looked at another way, is there any action that would not be justified if it would help stop a holocaust?*

CHAPTER 49

Debra Reuben missed the quiet house on the water in Brooklin even before she left it. She did not expect to return. Ever. Her greatest concern was how she would get in touch with Levi to warn him not to return either. She would have to depend on Abram to reach Levi.

She'd packed what little she had into a suitcase she'd found in the basement, feeling badly about taking clothing from the anonymous owner of the house. *I'll get it back to her somehow,* she said to herself.

Reuben had made up her mind about what to do with the object in the wine cellar. She feared that if she left it in the basement, it would be found before she could return to collect it. She mentally kicked herself for using the library computer. The FBI agents were certain to return and discover that somebody in sleepy Brooklin had an interest in handling atomic bombs. There could not be many new people in town besides herself and Levi. *The FBI will soon be on the doorstep with a warrant,* she thought. *And handcuffs.*

She looked at the plastic-wrapped cylinder in the wine cellar. *Maybe I should let them have the damn thing,* she thought. *What a relief it would be to just walk away from it.* But she couldn't. The bomb belonged to Israel, which, when reconstituted, might someday need it. If only there was someone she trusted to hand it over to.

Rueben knew she could no longer hide the weapon from Sarah, which also meant that Abram was certain to learn about it. Reuben was disturbed at the thought of Abram Goldhersh and his organization getting the bomb, but she could see no alternative.

She sat on the front porch, waiting for Sarah to arrive, hoping the car that came up the driveway would be Sarah and not the black SUV. While she waited, she sat in a rocking chair and looked at the calm water, an occasional lobster boat roaring by.

I'm going to miss this house so much, she thought. Then she smiled. *This is where Chaim and I fell in love. Someday I'll tell my grandchildren how their grandfather sailed me across the ocean and we lived in a cottage by the sea.*

The sound of a car in the gravel driveway woke her with a start. Heart beating furiously, she leaned her head around the end of the porch to glance at the driveway. *Sarah's car,* she smiled.

Reuben took one step toward her friend, then froze. The *THWAKA-THWAKA-THWAKA* of a helicopter drowned out any greeting she could have shouted. *FBI,* she thought, looking up at the helicopter flying slowly along the shore, seemingly straight toward her. *Same one that's been going back and forth all week.*

The sound of the machine faded. Sarah got out of her car and spotted Reuben coming around the edge of the house from the porch.

"So, Debra, what is this big emergency? I have a speech to write, you know." Her words were angrier than her tone, however, especially when she saw the relief on her friend's face.

"FBI," Reuben blurted out. "The FBI knows we're here, or will know any minute. I have to get away. I have to tell Chaim not to come back here. You have to help me, please."

"FBI? They can't know about you. Believe me, if they knew you were here, you'd be wearing handcuffs by now," Goldberg said. "How could they know about you?"

"We can talk more in the car," Reuben said. "I promise I'll tell you absolutely everything, no secrets, no more secrets. For right now, though, I have something that is going to be difficult for you to hear. Sarah, you know I was in the government, a cabinet minister, over there?" Reuben gestured roughly toward the ocean.

"Of course, culture minister," Sarah said. "Abram said it was a joke, but I was proud of my D-Phi-E sister."

"It was sort of a joke, I know that," Reuben said. "Until the end, that is. As it turned out, as far as anyone knew, I was the last of the government to survive. That was only luck because I happened to be out in the desert instead of in Tel Aviv for the prime minister's birthday party."

Reuben paused, then placed both hands on the other woman's shoulders. She squeezed lightly, as if she did not want Sarah to run away when she heard what Reuben was about to say, or maybe just to provide comfort to her friend.

"Sarah, Damascus, the bomb dropped on Damascus," she said slowly. "The bombs were stored at a place, a place in the desert. I was there. I was the only one left to make the decision."

Sarah's eyes opened wide. "No, Debbie, no, don't tell me," she whispered.

"I ordered them to put the bomb in that plane," Reuben said. "They didn't want to do it. I made them do it. I ordered them to do it. I shook that pilot's hand. I watched him take off. I did it. Me."

Sarah stepped back, paused for thirty seconds, thinking, then held her arms wide and reached out for Reuben, who walked into her friend's comforting embrace. They hugged for several minutes, neither speaking, Sarah repeating quietly, "Poor Debbie, my poor Debbie."

Reuben pushed herself away from her friend.

"There's something else," she said. "Sarah, there's another bomb."

"Another bomb? But only Damascus was bombed. I don't understand."

"Actually," Reuben said, "that is something else entirely, for another time. No, there was another bomb there in the desert, on the ground, a smaller bomb. We didn't put it in any plane. We didn't know what to do with it. But we couldn't let the Arabs get it. So I took it with me."

"Took it where, Debbie?"

Reuben pointed behind her at the house.

"No, Debbie, no."

"We brought it here, Chaim and I, in the boat, the one we had to sink," she said. "We had to sink it because Chaim thought the radiation in the boat might be detected. He thinks these helicopters might be looking for it now, although we don't know why they would be looking. It's in the house, in the basement, the wine cellar."

"What are you going to do with it?" Sarah asked.

"I'm taking it with me," Reuben said. "It's heavy, but you and I can lift it. We'll put it in your car and we'll take it away, and I don't really know what we'll do with it, but it can't stay here. I can't leave it here, Sarah."

Goldberg struggled to speak, finally saying, "You want to put an atom bomb in my car—my new Volvo?" She turned on her heels and walked quickly away from her friend to stand beside her car. She turned back to face Reuben, anger in her voice. "Leave it. Get rid of it. Give the damn thing to the FBI. What do you care?"

"Don't you think I've thought that too, Sarah?" Reuben said softly. "I hate that thing. For all I know, the radiation from it is killing me, and killing Chaim. But, Sarah, as horrible as it might be, it isn't mine to toss away. It doesn't belong to me."

"It certainly seems to be in your possession, doesn't it?" Sarah snapped.

"Not possession, Sarah, custody," Reuben answered. "I'm just its custodian. It belongs to the State of Israel. And Israel might need it someday. I know this isn't an easy decision. Sarah, I've lived with what I did—with . . . with Damascus, since the moment that jet took off. I wish I did not have responsibility for that thing in the basement. But I have no choice. We have no choice. Don't you see that? I had responsibility for the first one and I did what I had to do with it. I have this one now, and I have to do with it what is required of me. This is no time for weakness, Sarah. Please help me carry the bomb to the car."

Goldberg was quiet for several minutes, pacing away from Reuben. When she returned she said, "I understand what you are saying. Let's get it and let's find a place for it. Abram will know what to do with it."

"That's something I'm concerned about," Reuben replied. "But we can talk about that in the car."

■ ■ ■

The two women retrieved the device from the wine cellar. It was still tightly wrapped in the plastic that covered it while it was in the water tank on the sailboat. They secured it in the back of the Volvo and eased along the gravel driveway, nervous and silent.

They stayed off the main highways on the three-hour drive to the Portland suburb where the Goldberg-Goldhershes lived. Reuben felt a tinge of envy when she saw her former roommate's comfortable house, her memory flashing on her own tiny apartment in Jerusalem's Old City. Looking out to the fenced-in back yard, Reuben noticed the swimming pool, its dark-green leaf cover floating over the water's surface. She turned to her friend.

"I know the place for that thing," she said. The two women lugged the bomb to the pool, rolled back the cover over the deep end and dropped the plastic-wrapped package into the water, watching it settle to the bottom of the pool, covered by eight feet of water. They rolled the cover back over the surface, hiding what was beneath.

"Chaim was worried that the bomb could be detected from above," Reuben explained. "That's why he kept it in the wine cellar. I think eight feet of water should block any radiation. Let's hope so."

"Sure, let's hope you and I don't glow in the dark, too," Sarah said. "I can't wait for Abram to get home. He decided to go to that meeting in Boston. He'll bring Levi back here afterwards, he said."

"That's fantastic," Reuben exclaimed, not making any attempt to hide her excitement. She smiled at her friend. "Let me tell you about me and Chaim. It's pretty wonderful, you know."

CHAPTER 50

Levi listened to the news on the car radio as he drove south on the Maine Turnpike, heading for his meeting in Boston.

"More than three hundred people were killed less than ten minutes ago in two synchronized bombings in shopping malls outside of Boston." The announcer struggled to remain calm. "Most of those killed were women and children, hundreds more were wounded, many of them seriously.

"Survivors report the suicide bombers appeared to be Orthodox Jews who wrapped themselves in Israeli flags before detonating their bombs in what was an apparent protest of this country's decision not to intervene in the Middle East.

"A White House spokesman said the president's thoughts and prayers go out to those families who lost loved ones and those survivors who are clinging to life. The president promised to spare no resources to hunt down and apprehend the persons responsible for this cowardly action. Congressional leaders from both parties offered their support to the president in fighting what they characterized as today's new war on terrorism, a war that appears to have its primary battlefield on American soil for the first time since the Civil War."

Levi wondered whether somebody beat Abram to the punch. He wanted nothing more than to turn around and return to Reuben. Despite what lurked in their basement in Brooklin, he felt safely hidden away in that house.

He drove no more than the speed limit. Debra had told him he would not be stopped by police so long as he didn't exceed the speed limit by more than ten miles an hour. Using miles per hour rather than kilometers added to his paranoia. Another oddity was the concept of paying a toll to travel a road. Israel had only once such road and the toll was automated. Here, he had to stop at a tollbooth.

Levi collected his ticket from the machine at the booth when he entered the Maine Turnpike, not quite sure what he was supposed to do with it. He did not see any way of paying any money when he got onto the highway, so he took the ticket, tossed it into the back seat and drove on.

When he reached the toll plaza at the southern terminus of the Maine Turnpike, shortly before the New Hampshire border, Levi stopped and handed a twenty-dollar bill to the collector, assuming that would cover whatever he owed. Instead, the man asked for his ticket, then, seeing Levi's confused expression, explained that he needed the ticket Levi received when he entered the highway. Levi rummaged in the back seat until he found it, as cars behind him honked their horns.

The toll collector took the ticket and the twenty-dollar bill and handed Levi his change, adding a "Welcome to America, you Canuck." Levi had no idea what a Canuck was, but he assumed it was not a friendly greeting.

He told himself he'd have to do better at the next toll plaza, wherever that might be. It came sooner than he'd expected. Five miles after crossing from Maine into New Hampshire a large green signed warned *Hampton Tolls Autos $2.00 One Mile*. Seconds later the traffic came to an abrupt halt and stretched onward around a bend in the road.

Levi spent twenty minutes inching forward the final mile to

the toll plaza. He was baffled by signs over some lanes declaring *EZPass ONLY* and changed lanes to avoid them, staying to the far right, edging forward between two large trucks in front and behind him. A white wooden lift gate swung down to block his exit from the booth.

Levi looked up at the toll collector, not noticing the white metal can with a glass front screwed to the wall above the collector's head, pointed over the man's shoulder toward the open driver's window of cars entering the tollbooth.

He handed the man two one-dollar bills. The man thanked him and turned to look at the truck behind Levi.

The gate remained down. The toll collector stepped on the gate button with his right foot to lift it. It stayed down.

"Dang," the elderly man said. "That's never happened before. Sorry about this."

"No problem," Levi said, waiting patiently, somewhat pleased that even in America machines malfunctioned. Levi leaned forward to adjust the radio. He'd lost the Portland, Maine, station he'd been listening to and didn't know whether he was close enough to Boston to receive a station from there, but he enjoyed the country music he'd been listening to as an alternative to the news.

■ ■ ■

Sitting twenty yards away were FBI agents in SUVs. Earlier in the week, agents hooked up surveillance cameras into each tollbooth. Every face passing through to pay a toll was run through a computer with facial recognition software. Levi's photo had been scanned into the computer.

Just as Levi raised his head from the radio to see whether the gate had lifted, two black SUVs came dashing from both ends of the toll plaza, blocking his exit.

Levi reacted instinctively. He slid the gear selector into reverse and pressed the accelerator to the floor before he could turn to look back. His head slammed against the headrest as his rear bumper rammed into the front of the truck three feet behind him.

The doors in both SUVs flew open and men streamed from the vehicles, each with a handgun out, leaving the doors wide open, running to surround Levi's car.

"Put both hands out the window," one man barked at Levi, pointing his gun straight in through the open driver's window. Levi stared into the gun barrel and slowly took his hands from the steering wheel and held them outside the window. A pair of steel handcuffs snapped around his wrists.

"Now get out of the vehicle, slowly and carefully," the man said, his gun never wavering from Levi's face. "Where's your driver's license, buddy?"

"I must have left it home," Levi said, using his best American accent. "I do that all the time."

"Yeah, right," the man said, calling out to another man who was looking into Levi's car. "This guy says he left his license home."

The agents searched Levi's vehicle car.

Another agent walked up to Levi and removed a sheet of paper from his jacket pocket. He gazed at the paper for a moment, then stared at Levi's face.

"What do you think?" he asked one of the other agents. "I can't tell shit, but the computer sure shouted at us. I think it's him, I really do. Same eyes, nose. Yeah, I'd put money on it being a match."

"One way to find out," the other agent said, turning to Levi. "Hey, buddy, your name Chaim?" He pronounced it like "tame," but with a *ch* sound. "Chaim Levi, right?"

They know my name. Levi was stunned. But only for a moment. He shook his head.

"What kind of name is that?" he asked. "Never heard of that guy, whoever he is."

"Then what's your name?" the man asked dubiously.

Levi pondered for no more than two seconds. *A name, quick,* he thought. Okay. He and Reuben had spent hour after hour watching television.

"My name," he said, "is Homer, Homer Simpson."

"Yeah, right, asshole," the questioner replied. "Don't you move an eyebrow. Just stand there."

Another SUV replaced the truck behind Levi's car, blocking it from leaving the tollbooth in that direction. A man leaped from the passenger seat carrying a metal box, a small object that looked like a microphone attached to it by a thick cable.

The man waved the object around inside Levi's trunk, watching a dial on the metal box. He did the same under the car's hood and shook his head.

The man then opened the rear passenger door and leaned into the car, again moving the object over the car's interior. He quickly pulled back.

"Holy shit," he shouted. "I got a hell of a hot reading on something in there."

"Try again," Levi's questioner said. "I don't want any mistakes."

The man hesitated.

"I don't know, boss," he said. "Something in there is damn radioactive. I don't know if I should be in there without protective gear."

"No time for that," the man in charge said. He looked around the tollbooth and focused on a broom with a long wooden handle. He tossed the broom to the man with the box. "Here, use this. Whatever it is, poke it out with this thing."

The man with the box turned the broom around, holding it by the end with the straw, pointing the wooden handle into the car's rear seat like a sword.

"Open the other rear door," he said. "Do it."

The man pointing his gun at Levi lowered it for the first time and walked to the rear driver's-side door, flinging the door open and leaping back. The man with the broom poked it inside the back seat, moving the wooden handle from side to side like a hockey stick.

"Got it," he shouted.

Two bright-orange rubber gloves fell from the car's rear seat and landed on the pavement with a flop. Levi groaned, remembering that he'd used those gloves to handle the bomb.

Israeli soldiers were trained to avoid capture at all costs. Israelis taken into custody by their Arab enemies were unlikely to be treated in conformance with the Geneva Convention.

Levi's military training kicked in without conscious thought. The man who'd kept his gun on Levi throughout the incident now had his back to him, having just leaped backwards to avoid the rubber gloves as they flew from the car seat. He faced the gloves, staring at them.

Levi saw the two black SUVs in front of the tollbooth, doors still open. He could hear their engines running.

Levi planted his foot firmly on the backside of the man with the gun. He shoved the man forward, causing him to fall onto the pavement, his hands landing on either side of the rubber gloves. His chest against them.

The man screamed as if he'd landed on hot coals. Levi sprinted to the SUVs. He jumped through the open driver's door of one of the vehicles, reached in with his handcuffed hands and dropped the gear lever into drive, simultaneously stamping his foot on the gas pedal. The vehicle shot forward, the momentum slamming all four doors shut.

Levi lifted his hands to the top of the steering wheel. He spotted a pullout area to the right of the plaza. A brick building contained restrooms. A New Hampshire State Police cruiser was parked next to the building. Behind the parking area was a chain-link fence. Behind the fence was a road.

Levi turned the wheel sharply to the right, heading straight for the parking area. He would ram through the fence and escape on back roads. It was not much of a plan, he realized, but it was a plan.

The SUV jumped over the curb separating the parking area from the highway, accelerating as it headed toward the fence. The trooper's eyes opened wide as he saw the black SUV speeding in his direction. He saw the FBI agents running and shouting.

The trooper reached down and drew his .40 caliber Glock, sighted carefully down its extended barrel, focusing. The gun bucked and he immediately returned it to his target. He squeezed again and again and again, placing four shots within a six-inch circle in the middle of Levi's face. The SUV continued through the chain-link fence and slammed into a tree.

A SkyFox25-News traffic helicopter circling overhead to report on the mile-long backup at the Hampton tolls recorded the entire scene, which was forwarded to the television studio within seconds of Chaim Levi's last breath.

CHAPTER 51

It was inevitable that the rally would be called the *Million Jew March*, despite a futile attempt by organizers to brand it as the *Million Mensch March*. It began with an announcement from Rabbi Simon Garfinkle of Congregation Beth Shalom, one of the rare Jewish mega-synagogues, with a congregation of more than 5,000 from northern New Jersey. He'd vowed to bring his entire congregation to the capital to pray for intervention in the Middle East.

Other rabbis pledged to join Rabbi Garfinkle with their congregations. Word about the march spread across the Internet with the instantaneous speed of a new joke or cartoon, emailed from brother to sister to mother to uncle to business partner to college professor to office mates until the question "Are you going?" blanketed the Jewish community.

As momentum built in the week leading up to what was planned as a two-day event, nobody knew how many people to expect. A million marchers was thought to be a conservative prediction. There was little else America's increasingly desperate Jews could do.

Even before the first marcher arrived in the District of

Columbia, the event had achieved one of its goals. Politicians, from all levels of government, were forced to choose sides. Were they with the marchers, prepared to be photographed in the crowd, or even on the podium, or were they going to be conspicuously absent? Invitations to join the marchers were widely distributed.

The response was as disappointing as it was predictable. The mall bombings, after the Coast Guard and FBI murders, tipped America decidedly into an anti-terror, anti-Jew frenzy. First Damascus, then coastguardsmen, then the FBI and, now, hundreds slaughtered by Jewish suicide bombers.

The twenty-two Jewish members of Congress, to a man and woman, agreed to appear. Two senators, one from New York, one from California, said they would be there but they preferred not to speak. One former secretary of defense said yes, but the gossip was that his Jewish wife left him no choice since she would be attending regardless of whether he did or not.

The rest of Washington's elite found reasons to be out of the city or otherwise committed that weekend.

The ad hoc organizing committee struggled to find enough prominent speakers to fill two days, especially speakers who could demonstrate that support for intervention in Israel went beyond Jewish voters. The organizers were disappointed that year after year of Jewish political contributions, millions upon millions of dollars, seemed to have been forgotten. They were equally disappointed that African-American leaders seemed to have forgotten the thousands of Jews who supported the civil rights struggles, with their money, their time and, as demonstrated by the murders of Andrew Goodman and Michael Schwerner in Mississippi, their lives.

■ ■ ■

The march was scheduled for Friday and Saturday so it could include what was predicted to be the largest Sabbath service in history.

A large Washington law firm, whose senior partners were virtually all Jewish, donated office space for the march organizers. On Wednesday of march week, volunteers, mostly college students, struggled to deal with the chaos of constantly ringing office telephones.

"I would like to speak to whoever is in charge of the speakers who will address the march," a caller said. "My name is Catherine Quaid."

"Please hold," a young volunteer said. She answered three other calls and was about to run to the coffee machine when she noticed the light still blinking on her phone. She pressed the button for that line.

"I think that Rabbi Garfinkle is handling all the speakers himself," the volunteer said. "He is so very busy right now I am sure he could not speak with you. Could you leave a phone number, or, even better, an email address, and we will get in touch with you? I know they are sending out thank-yous already."

The woman caller laughed. "So much for international fame," she said. "Maybe if Rabbi Garfinkle can't speak with me, somebody else, somebody in authority, can spare a minute."

"I'm so sorry," the volunteer answered, looking around. "I don't think there is anybody who could speak with you. I'm so busy myself. I really have to go now."

"Wait, don't hang up," the caller said. She took a deep breath, audible over the telephone. "What's your name, dear?"

"Nicole."

"Okay, Nicole. Let's try it this way. Do you know who the president of the United States is?"

"Of course, ma'am, it's President Quaid."

"Good. That's a start. Well, I am Mrs. Quaid. Some call me the First Lady."

"Oh my God. I am so sorry." The young Wesleyan University junior hesitated. "Does your husband know what you are doing?"

Within seconds, Catherine Quaid was patched through.

∎ ∎ ∎

"Joe, may I have a chat with you?"

Catherine Quaid took Joe Bergantina, the head of her Secret Service detail, by the elbow and directed him to the balcony overlooking the Rose Garden behind the White House.

"What is it, ma'am?" Bergantina asked. He liked Catherine Quaid. She had a mind of her own and didn't take shit from anybody, including her husband. *Wouldn't want to be married to her, though,* Bergantina thought.

The First Lady walked casually with the Secret Service agent to the far end of the balcony, then turned and stood in front of him, uncomfortably close. Her voice took on an uncharacteristically venomous tone that sent alarm bells clanging for the agent.

"Joe, you rat on me again and you'll regret it for the rest of your life," she said, glaring, her face inches from his. "What goes on between me and my husband is between me and my husband. You work for me. If you don't want to work for me, fine; tell me, and I'll get you an assignment guarding a bucket of frozen moose shit in Alaska."

The Secret Service agent, trained to throw himself in front of this woman and take an assassin's bullet in his own body, was shaken by her words.

"Do you know what I'm referring to, Joe?" Catherine Quaid asked. "A little matter involving Air Force One? Does that refresh your memory, Joe?"

She poked his chest with one finger.

"Do you get my point, Joe?"

Another poke, harder this time.

He could barely collect himself enough to answer.

"Yes, ma'am, yes, absolutely, ma'am, I understand one hundred percent, ma'am," he stuttered.

"Tell me, Joe, what would they do to a Secret Service agent who copped a feel from the First Lady? It wouldn't be pretty, would it, Joe?"

The poor man's face was ashen.

"That would be an exceptionally ugly scene, ma'am," he said carefully.

"So, Joe, may I assume that we have a clear understanding, you and I? No more whispering to anybody about what I'm doing or who I'm doing it with, right, Joe?"

"Yes, ma'am, yes we certainly do," he answered.

"Wonderful," Catherine Quaid said. "Now, let me tell you where we are going tomorrow."

CHAPTER 52

Sarah Goldberg had met Rabbi Garfinkle two years earlier at a conference on youth aliyah to Israel. *Aliyah*, from the Hebrew word for "ascent," referred to immigration to Israel. Rabbi Garfinkle was impressed with Goldberg. He contacted her within days of first proposing the march, asking her to serve on the steering committee. Sarah acknowledged to her husband that they were trying to get speakers from all around the country and she was probably the only Jewish Mainer Rabbi Garfinkle knew.

Sarah was asked to speak at the event. She had no idea what to say. Recalling the civil rights struggle and Martin Luther King's preaching of nonviolence sounded wishy-washy after news of the mall bombings. In the back of her mind, too, Sarah was aware that Abram was planning some violent action of his own, making her feel hypocritical preaching nonviolence.

Sarah and Debra Rueben sat up late into the night crafting an outline of Sarah's speech. Around eleven that evening, Abram returned from the meeting in Boston. His first words when he entered the house and saw Reuben startled her.

"What happened to Levi?" he asked. "He never showed up.

Never called either."

Reuben's stomach had been twisted in a knot since she watched Levi drive away.

"The man embarrassed me in front of some very important people. I'd built him up as some big new-day Maccabee warrior and then he never shows up. I got the go-ahead for my boys anyway, so I suppose there was no harm done," he said, "but the man let me down. I don't forget that easily."

"I hope he's all right," Reuben said quietly.

Sarah looked at her husband.

"You heard about the mall bombings, I assume?" she asked.

"Heard about it? It's just about all we talked about in Boston," he said excitedly. "This is how the war is going to be fought, mark my words. Not by big, coordinated efforts but by small groups of fighters, each acting independently but all for the same goal.

"Sarah, I know you believe that singing the right songs and waving the cleverest signs will get those Washington nudniks to do the right thing for Israel. You'll see, though, my way works. My way works. Terror works. Nobody wants to admit that, but it is the truth. Terror brings change. We will make life so miserable for these politicians that they will have no choice but to give in; you'll see."

"Is that what your secret big shots in Boston told you, Abram?" Sarah asked.

"It certainly is, and it's what I told them. They had no idea who did those mall bombings, but they were all for them. Sarah, you know what else we talked about?" Abram asked. "We talked about the lesson Israel taught the Arabs with Damascus. They'll think again about the price they'll have to pay for attacking Jews. We don't know who ordered that bombing. Maybe we'll never know. But I'll tell you one thing, Sarah. Whoever did that, it was one Jew with giant balls."

He was puzzled by the knowing looks the two women exchanged. But he was too aroused to stop talking.

"Do you think for one minute the United States would be willing to pay that same price? No way, never. When it comes to a choice between paying a dollar or two more for a gallon of gasoline or losing, say, Chicago or Dallas, don't you think that would be an easy choice for Mr. President Quaid? Bombs send a message. Enough bombs send enough of a message. We certainly sent a loud and clear message to Damascus, didn't we?"

Abram was surprised that neither woman responded. He felt perhaps he'd gone too far with his talk about bombs.

"So, how is the big speech coming?" he asked his wife.

"Nowhere at all is where it's coming," she said dejectedly. "Somehow preaching nonviolence feels foolish, as if a sit-in at the Capitol is going to get any relief supplies, or Marines, to Israel. I'm not quite that naive."

"That's nice to hear," Goldhersh said, smiling. "Has there been anything on the news about who did the mall bombings? My three young friends are going to be excited about the two men—Hassids, I heard—who beat them to the first punch."

Abram walked across the room and picked up the television remote, turning on the TV in the kitchen, where they were sitting at a table. The 11 o'clock news was just beginning.

The screen filled with video obviously filmed from an airplane showing a long traffic backup.

"That's the Hampton Toll Plaza," Sarah said.

"Hush," her husband responded. "Listen."

"Dramatic footage taken from a traffic helicopter shows what the FBI says was a daring escape attempt by a man government sources confirmed was an Israeli military commando," the announcer excitedly intoned. "The man was detained by the FBI on suspicion of smuggling weapons into this country.

"*The New York Times* reported on its website minutes ago that undisclosed sources in the Department of Homeland Security hinted that the Israeli had smuggled weapons of mass destruction into this country. The source did not elaborate about the type of weapons, although the source did say that while a small amount of radioactive material was recovered in the man's car, more of the weapons remain at large."

The aerial camera zoomed in on a Honda Accord crushed against a tree near the tollbooth.

Debra Reuben screamed. "That's the car Chaim was in!"

The television news reader continued, "The terrorist, who has yet to be identified, overpowered two armed FBI agents. He was shot and killed attempting to escape."

"No, no, no, no, no." Reuben's head slumped to the table. Sarah placed an arm around her shoulder. Without removing her arm from her friend, Sarah looked up at her husband. She spoke over Reuben's sobs.

"So much for nonviolence," Sarah said. She paused in thought. "Abram, the car—whose car was he driving? They'll trace the car, won't they?"

The large man did not answer. Despite his career buying and selling death-dealing devices, this was the first violent death that had visited his life, at least so closely. The reality of what he was planning to do settled into his consciousness. But only momentarily. He collected himself quickly and answered, "The car belongs to my Mr. Aleph. It doesn't matter whether they trace it to him or not. He isn't going home again."

Goldhersh glanced at his watch.

"By now, they are on a road trip."

Sarah looked up at her husband in surprise. She spoke in a flat monotone.

"Where are they going, Abram? Tell me."

He smiled. "The same place you are going, dear. To our nation's capital. Just like you, they have a message to deliver. Care to guess whose message will be more persuasive?"

Sarah returned to Reuben, who was moaning, repeating her lover's name. Goldhersh stood by her side, watching the two women, not knowing what to do. He felt badly about criticizing Levi, and angry at what he viewed as Levi's murder.

After several minutes, Reuben lifted her head and rubbed

her eyes. She looked up at Goldhersh. Her face was resolute. She shrugged Sarah's comforting hands from her shoulders and stood up, only to pace back and forth, finally stopping in front of Goldhersh.

"Abram," she said, her voice cold. Goldhersh didn't know it, but this was the same voice that ordered a pilot to fly to Damascus. "We can't let them keep killing us—there, here. Jews don't stand meekly and let the Nazis cart us away anymore."

"I'm glad one of you ladies agrees with me," he replied cautiously, unsure about the sudden change in the woman, and her voice.

"You're not entirely wrong," Reuben said. She knew so few people who'd died in her sheltered life. Nobody had been gunned down in public. Levi's death shocked her, shook her beliefs.

"Abram, you talk about needing a new *Haganah*." Haganah was the underground Jewish military force that fought against the British occupation before Israel gained independence. "Maybe the first member of that Haganah was just murdered."

Goldhersh beamed, looking at the two women.

"Abram, come with me," Reuben said. "I want to show you something in your swimming pool."

■ ■ ■

Debra Reuben and Sarah and Abram Goldhersh sat before the living room TV. Debra Reuben mumbled almost silently, speaking to herself or, perhaps, whispering to Chaim Levi's ghost. Abram Goldhersh thought only of the object at the bottom of his swimming pool. *Can it really be an atomic bomb? An atomic bomb in my swimming pool?* Sarah Goldhersh said nothing, but she recognized that a speech in Washington about nonviolence was simply silly.

Television news buzzed with speculation about the announcement of the president's surprise midnight speech on a topic of "supreme importance." Debra, Sarah and Abram shared one thought. *Can things get any worse?*

Midnight. They would soon find out.

■ ■ ■

The president sat in the Oval Office, an American flag behind him. The camera opened with a tight shot on his face, then zoomed back to show his desk, a pen and two sheets of paper on it. The president gestured, and people walked in from off camera to stand behind him. They included the majority leaders of both parties, Homeland Security director Paterson, the new acting attorney general, and Gen. Cruz, chairman of the Joint Chiefs.

"My fellow Americans," he said. "This nation is at war. Even worse, this nation has already been invaded. I appreciate how shocking that news is. For the past few weeks, I have received information that the State of Israel secretly infiltrated military forces into this country. Some of those forces were responsible for the murder of ten Coast Guard men and women in Boston, as you all know.

"We believe we hold most of that commando unit in custody. We are not certain we have captured all of them, but intense, I repeat, intense interrogations are continuing. We will learn the truth from these people. One way or another.

"Another member of the Israeli military, a man who we have identified as a Lt. Chaim Levi, was shot and killed yesterday as he attempted to flee from FBI agents who captured him."

The president paused and looked directly into the camera as it zoomed to a close shot on his face.

"Our killing of this highly trained special forces operative should be a lesson to others who remain at large. This is a merciful nation, but mercy must be earned. To those of you who threaten America, to those of you who believe that threats, bombings, and acts of violence will force me to take actions that are not in the best interests of the majority, I repeat, the majority of American people, I give you this warning: Threaten us and we will kill you, as we killed your Lt. Levi."

Quaid appeared surprised at the applause from the people standing behind him. He nodded his appreciation, then raised his hand to quiet them.

"Madness is not a word to apply lightly to a national government such as Israel, but madness is the only explanation for what has happened since that first bombing. Madness and treason." Quaid reached down to the desk and picked up a pen.

"I am about to sign a law passed this afternoon by both houses of Congress. The law is virtually identical to that passed by an earlier Congress following a previous heinous attack on this nation, an attack that took place on September 11, 2001. Today's legislation gives me the power to protect America from today's enemies. I sign with pride."

The president signed his name to the bottom of the sheet of paper. The people standing behind him broke into applause. He continued speaking.

"Now for the most difficult information I must give to you today. I have received reliable information that this Israeli lieutenant Levi did not act alone. I have reliable, confirmed information that this terror cell managed to smuggle into this nation a quantity of uranium-235. Uranium-235 is a man-made, extremely radioactive substance. It has only one use. The construction of atomic weapons. At this time, we do not know how much U-235 was smuggled into this country or whether that material is contained in a functioning explosive device. We know that this Lt. Levi was involved in the smuggling, that he was a member of the Israel Defense Forces, that one and possibly two other Israeli special forces teams escaped from the ships in Boston Harbor, and that the Israel Defense Forces had hundreds of nuclear weapons.

"I view this conduct as acts of war against the United States. I am appalled, and saddened, that some Americans, some very few Americans, appear to be supporting this nation's enemies.

"As you know, the FBI rounded up thousands of those people,

the Israeli refugees from the ships, and others, American citizens of the Jewish faith, others who I sadly label with the only word that appropriately describes them. That word is *traitor*. The FBI arrested hundreds of those traitors and they are being dealt with. Other traitors, other Jewish traitors, murdered hundreds of innocent Americans in the two recent shopping mall bombings.

"We would be foolish if we failed to learn a lesson from the conduct of those traitors, a lesson that teaches that for one minority among all Americans, their primary loyalty is not to our nation but to their co-religionists and to a foreign nation.

"I have learned that lesson. I will act on that lesson. The first action is to identify those people who are most likely to be traitors, those people we must all watch diligently, knowing they have declared war on America and, sadly, knowing they have a weapon in their hands of dreadful power. Today, Congress gave me absolute power as commander in chief to protect this nation. I intend to exercise that power."

The president picked up the second document from his desk.

"This document is a presidential finding and declaration. I will read it to you, and then I will sign it before the entire nation. It will go into effect immediately."

He picked up the document and began reading from it.

"The president of the United States finds as follows:

"1. Military forces of the State of Israel have entered the United States illegally and without right.

"2. These forces have taken illegal and violent actions against the United States, including but not limited to killing American military personnel without cause or provocation.

"3. These forces have smuggled into the United States weapons of mass destruction, with the intention of utilizing those weapons against American citizens on American soil.

"4. An unknown but sizable number of American citizens of the Jewish faith have taken violent and illegal actions in support of these foreign military forces. Such violent actions caused the death of American military personnel.

"5. Further sympathizers of the State of Israel, also believed to be American citizens of the Jewish faith, have engaged in violent terrorist actions against innocent American citizens that led to the death of hundreds of such innocent citizens.

"6. Thousands, and as many as one million similar sympathizers, all American citizens of the Jewish faith, intend to descend on the nation's capital for the avowed purpose of compelling the United States government and its president to take actions in support of the former State of Israel that the president has already determined are not in the best interests of the United States.

"Wherefore, the president of the United States hereby declares, pursuant to the powers invested in him by Article Two of the United States Constitution and by the Authorization for the Use of Military and Other Force enacted by Congress on this date, as follows:

"First, all citizens of the United States of Jewish faith or heritage shall report to offices of the Department of Homeland Security, when and where such offices shall be established on an emergency basis, within two weeks from the date of this Declaration.

"Second, at such time as these Jewish citizens so report, they shall surrender their duly issued United States Citizenship Identification Card, otherwise known as the Americard.

"Third, each such citizen of the Jewish faith shall be issued by the Department of Homeland Security a replacement United States Citizenship Identification Card. Such replacement cards shall be colored blue and shall prominently mark the Jewish identity of the bearer.

"Fourth, all United States citizens, including those of the Jewish faith and those not of the Jewish faith, shall henceforth carry and visibly display their United States Citizenship Identification Card. Failure to carry and display such card when in public by a citizen bearing a card other than a blue card shall be punishable by a fine not to exceed two hundred and fifty dollars. Failure to carry and display such card by a citizen who has been issued a blue card shall be punishable by immediate detention for an indeterminate period of time in facilities to be established by the Department of Homeland Security."

The president placed the document on his desk, picked up his pen and signed it, with a flourish. The applause this time was louder and longer. President Quaid did nothing to stop it. When the applause subsided, he looked once again at the camera.

"One final word. This is a free country. We celebrate our fundamental right to freedom of speech, which, of course, includes the right to peacefully express our views on important matters.

"It has been suggested to me that I take steps to prevent the gathering of Jewish citizens who at this very moment are descending on Washington. I will not do that. These citizens retain their constitutional rights to freedom of speech and the right to petition their government, even in the midst of a national crisis. This is not a dictatorship and I will not prevent citizens from saying things with which I disagree. The march may proceed.

"But a word of warning. I would be foolish to turn a blind eye to our current state of affairs. I have requested the assistance of Virginia governor Jim Wheeler, which he graciously consented to. I have activated the 129th Light Infantry Regiment of the Virginia National Guard for deployment in the metropolitan Washington area this weekend. I will not hesitate to order these soldiers to take whatever actions are necessary to restore public peace and order should this so-called march on Washington take a threatening or violent turn.

"In closing, my fellow Americans, I ask you to join me in praying to the God who has protected this great nation from its inception that He protect us through this hour of danger from all enemies, both foreign and domestic. I am confident that with our faith in our God and the skill and bravery of our citizens, we will once again prevail.

"Good night and God bless the United States of America and all of its loyal citizens."

■ ■ ■

Abram Goldhersh picked up the bottle of Anchor Steam ale he'd just finished drinking and threw it against the television screen, which shattered in shards on the floor.

"Nazis," he screamed. "They're Nazis. We won't be intimidated by them."

He looked at Reuben, who remained in her chair, speechless, stunned. He was pleased not to see the tears he expected. Her lover's death had hardened her. She wiped her eyes, expecting tears herself, then she sat up straight. Abram stared at her.

"Debbie," he said angrily, "don't you have anything to say to that?"

Reuben looked at Goldhersh as if she had forgotten he was in the room. Her eyes locked on his. She spoke quietly, more to herself than to the huge man staring at her.

"Never again," she said, almost in a whisper. "Never again, never again. They can't do it again. We can't let it happen again."

CHAPTER 53

During their drive in the National Park Service van from New Jersey to Washington, the three men inside had argued about whether to reconsider their choice of targets. The men agreed that while the old man, Abram Goldhersh, could give them what he considered to be direct commands, this was their operation. Final decisions would be theirs alone.

"It's our asses on the line," Gimel said. "Abram is okay for an older guy, but this is going to be our show. We make the decisions."

The mall bombings changed their plans. Before those bombings, they intended to break up the C4 into smaller packages and place them strategically around Washington, maybe with timers set to go off as close together as they could manage. The bombers would be safely on the road out of the city when the first explosions took place.

"Those two guys, Hassids, right, showed they had the guts to give their lives to send a message. The fucking Palestinians have been blowing themselves up for twenty years. What message do we send if we drop our packages and run away and hide to save our tails? What does that say?"

"It says we're smart," Gimel had answered.

"It says we're cowards," Aleph said quietly. "It says we're afraid to give our lives in the struggle, that we skulk and hide and run away. Not even the Arabs did that."

"That's my point," Bet said. "Our lives won't be worth shit if we get caught after doing this anyway. We'll wind up in some federal prison forever, or worse. Guantanamo. If you ask me, I'd rather die a hero. What do you say?"

The other two men were quiet. Finally, Aleph spoke.

"*Masada*," Aleph said. "*Masada* in DC. That's my vote."

Masada, the ancient fortress on a cliff overlooking the Judean Desert. A thousand Jewish rebels held out there against the Roman Legion. When the fortress walls were breached, the Jewish defenders took their own lives rather than surrender. Israeli Armored Corps recruits scaled Masada to take their oaths. Or they used to do so.

Gimel sighed deeply and nodded. "It will make the detonators easier to rig."

The timing of the Jewish march had to be figured into their plans. The trio did not want to kill Jews, of course. Heaven forbid their work should be misinterpreted as an attack against Jews.

■ ■ ■

It was Thursday morning, the day before the march was to begin in Washington. The men were exhausted. They drove the van to the rear of a Ramada Inn in Rockville, Maryland, a half-hour's drive from Washington.

They took three separate rooms using Aleph's credit card. He'd asked for the motel's best rooms, joking afterwards that it was not as if he'd be around when the credit card bill arrived. The men rested, ate a tremendous dinner, and prayed before going to sleep for what they expected was the last night of their lives.

President Quaid's speech dispelled any doubts the three

young men may have had about the righteousness of their intended action. They gathered in Aleph's motel room early Friday morning and prayed together one final time. They chose to skip breakfast, tacitly acknowledging they were too nervous to eat.

The stolen National Park Service van cruised the streets of Washington. Bet held the printout of the route through the city they'd downloaded from Google Maps before leaving Maine. The radio in the van was tuned to an all-news station.

Reports on the decreased attendance at the march caused by the president's threat to bring in troops pleased the three men. Whatever they did, they did not want to kill Jews. They navigated closer to the target until, after a left turn onto Fifteenth Street, they saw it directly in front of them, thrusting upward, more than 500 feet of granite and marble.

The Washington Monument.

They'd studied the monument as if it were a research project assigned by their high school civics teacher. They'd studied it the only way people of their generation knew how to do research— sitting in front of their home computers. They assumed that every fact they needed was available simply by reading enough web pages returned by Google.

They weren't disappointed by what they learned. The monument was built in the shape of an Egyptian obelisk. The exterior was white marble. The interior was granite. The walls at the base were fifteen feet thick, tapering to a thickness of eighteen inches at the top. At the time of its construction, it was the tallest building in the world. It remained the tallest masonry construction.

An elevator ran up its hollow interior.

The men were especially interested to read about an incident in December 1982 when the monument was held hostage by a nuclear arms protester for ten hours, claiming he had explosives in a van he drove to the monument's base. Police shot the man dead and found his van was empty.

Aleph had discovered a post-9/11 report from the General Accounting Office concerning the security of government buildings. The report, posted online by the GAO, said a seven-pound explosive charge set off inside the hollow core near the top, where the walls were the thinnest, would bring down the monument's entire facade.

That was good news.

■ ■ ■

The van stopped as the towering monument came into full view. The monument was more impressive in the flesh than on the Internet. Aleph, who was driving, turned to the other two men sitting on the bench seat beside him.

"Any doubts, any hesitation?" he asked.

"It's our time," Bet answered.

"If not now, when?" Gimel said.

"Okay then," Aleph said. "One last stop before we go in."

He pulled the van away from the curb and drove for two blocks. There, just as Google Maps had told them it would be, was a Starbucks.

Aleph parked in front of the coffee shop and got out of the van.

"A dozen or so coffees ought to do it, right?" he asked.

"And get pastries, a real mix—donuts, cakes, cookies," Bet said. "There's gonna be a lot of cops, park police, there."

CHAPTER 54

President Quaid's speech convinced at least half the marchers to turn around and go home. Parents who traveled across the country with their children intending to attend a peaceful rally were terrified at the prospect of confronting armed Virginia national guardsmen.

By starting time Friday morning, the crowd filled only the half of the National Mall closest to the Capitol, leaving a half mile of open grass before the Washington Monument. The sixty-foot-wide speaker's platform was in front of the Capitol Reflecting Pool. Rather than the exuberance with which most mass civil rights gatherings began, the mood was cautious.

Rabbi Garfinkle stood at the microphone on the platform for several minutes looking out at the crowd. He'd dressed the part that day, wearing a suit conservative enough for a banker, except for the brightly colored crocheted yarmulke on his head. He lifted both hands high above his head, waited for silence and chanted in Hebrew, *"Sh'ma Yisrael Adonai Elohaynu Adonai Echad.* Hear, Israel, the Lord is our God, the Lord is One."

A murmur went through the crowd as people softly said the traditional response to the most sacred, most fundamental statement of Jewish faith. "*Barukh Shem k'vod malkhuto l'olam va-ed. Blessed be the Name of His glorious kingdom for ever and ever.*"

The rabbi nodded, as if thanking the crowd, the largest audience he was likely to address in his lifetime. He'd struggled over what he would say and was anxious to begin. Before he could say a word, he noticed a disturbance at the edge of the crowd in front of him. Young people pushed through the crowd, carrying handfuls of plastic shopping bags. A young woman burst from the front of the crowd and ran toward the podium. She carried two plastic shopping bags in her right hand.

Rabbi Garfinkle stepped back. *A bomb,* he thought. *She's going to throw a bomb.* She stopped. Stared at him. Smiled and tossed both bags onto the podium.

They landed softly at his feet. He looked out at the crowd, where most people were staring at him expectantly as he spread the top open, looked in, then dropped the bag as if it actually were a bomb. All the color washed from his face.

The rabbi then kneeled on the floor and carefully picked up the bag. He reached in and withdrew a small piece of yellow cloth. Without a word, he walked to the people seated on the platform and distributed the contents of the bag, more pieces of yellow cloth, one at a time to the people to his right and then did the same for the people to his left.

He returned to the microphone and held the yellow fabric straight out in front of him, displaying it to the crowd, then slowly returned his hands to his chest and carefully pinned the yellow, six-pointed Star of David to his chest. In the middle of the star somebody had printed in black Magic Marker *Jude*, the German word for Jew.

Rabbi Garfinkle knew the badge was the same the Nazis forced millions of German, Polish, French, Dutch and Russian Jews to wear. He leaned into the microphone.

"President Quaid," he said, his voice quivering, "you want me to wear a badge saying who I am." His right hand, knotted into a first, pounded against the star, against his chest.

"This is the badge I will wear. This badge at least tells the truth. This badge says what you really mean, Mr. President. You say I cannot be both a Jew and an American. I say you are wrong, Mr. President. But even if you are right, sir, this badge declares who I am.

"Mr. President, I am a Jew.

"Do you truly believe you are the first political leader to tell Jews to stop being Jews? We have such a long history, we Jewish people. We teach our history to our children. We teach our history so that our children will not forget what has happened to us throughout our history, again and again and again.

"And, now, again.

"We teach that because what has happened before can and most likely will happen again, and if it does, when it does, we must prepare for it. We must resist it, using the lessons of our people's history.

"Lawrence Quaid, over and over politicians have forced us to make the same choice you want to force upon us. Are you a Jew or are you an American? We have been asked to choose, sir, are you a Jew or are you a Spaniard. Are you a Jew or are you an Englishman? Are you a Jew or are you a Russian? Or a Pole. Or a Turk, or an Egyptian, or, Mr. President, are you a Jew or are you a good German?

"Mr. President, if you ask that question you will receive the same answer every tyrant throughout history has received. Mr. President, I am an American and I love this country. I am so proud to be an American. But I can give up being an American if I am forced to do so—reluctantly, sadly, but that can be taken from me.

"I will never, I can never, stop being a Jew. And as a Jew, I will say to you the two words you have heard spoken so frequently in recent weeks."

He raised both hands in the air.

"Lawrence Quaid, never again, never again, never again."

The chant echoed from the Capitol building as the crowd's frenzy increased and continued for five full minutes, five minutes of those two words repeated over and over and over. The speaker finally raised his hands and the exhausted crowd settled into silence.

"Mr. President. *Never again* will Jews march meekly to camps, to anybody's camps, even your camps, Mr. President.

"*Never again* will Jews stand by and watch our homeland, the homeland promised to us by God Almighty, be snatched away from us. *Never again*, Mr. President.

"And if you can't accept that, Mr. President, well, all I can say is . . ."

He walked around the microphone and stood on the front edge of the podium, raising both hands over his head.

"*Never again, never again, never again, never again.*"

For fifteen minutes the crowd chanted.

Never again! Never again! Never again!

■ ■ ■

Sarah Goldberg, sitting next to Ben Shapiro at the far left end of the podium, leaned close to him and whispered, "I guess I was right about my speech about peace and love and reconciliation being out of place."

"If this is how the show begins," Shapiro replied, "I can hardly wait to see where we go from here."

■ ■ ■

Quaid turned from the television monitor carrying live coverage of the march. He walked to the window and looked out across the Ellipse to the Washington Monument.

"This is not going well," he said to Acting Attorney General Harrison and Carol Cabot, his legal counsel. Gen. Paterson, his homeland security director, sat on a sofa in front of the television.

"How the hell can they say I'm another Hitler?" Quaid said. "This is about protecting the country from a nuclear attack. Can't they see that? I tell the country we've been invaded, that there is an atom bomb floating around somewhere in New England, and these people call me a Hitler? They're going too far, too far. I won't tolerate this."

"I agree, Mr. President," said Gen. Paterson. "Free speech sucks, sir."

Harrison nodded. "Those yellow stars were a brilliant move. You've got to hand it to whoever came up with that, and so fast. Brilliant," he said.

"What's the status of those troops, the Virginia guardsmen?" Quaid asked.

"They're all set, Mr. President," Gen. Paterson said, "sitting in their trucks, can be at the Mall in fifteen minutes. One thing though, Mr. President—they've got riot gear, shields, helmets, armor, even gas, and they've got their firearms."

"Hold them off for now," the Quaid said. "Only a Hitler would send armed troops against his own people in his nation's capital, right?"

"They're waiting for your command, sir. You and nobody else," the general said. "It will be your call whether to send them in."

"Let's move them a bit closer. Get them into the city but back from the Mall. Keep them in their trucks for now. Maybe we can get through this weekend without giving anything more to complain about. We'll wait and see what happens."

CHAPTER 55

Sarah Goldberg was tentatively scheduled to speak at four, but she was told she might be bumped over to the next day if the speeches ran late the first day. She sat in a gallery of more than seventy seats on the large platform. Ben Shapiro sat next to her.

By noon, after the first four speakers each doubled or tripled his ten-minute quota, Shapiro was getting stiff from sitting. He was pleased when Judy Katz snuck up onto the platform and sat in an empty seat next to him and Sarah.

"Stay up here with us," Sarah told Katz. "We're off on the side anyway, and this is where all the empty seats are. Nobody will care."

"Sure," Katz said, moving her wooden chair a bit closer to Shapiro's. "At least I'm out of the sun."

After a few minutes, Judy snuck her hand onto Shapiro's leg, where she let it lie softly. He placed his hand on top of hers. She turned to him and smiled, then looked back toward the speaker.

Katz, Shapiro and Goldberg were distracted when a tall woman in a wide hat, wearing sunglasses and accompanied by two extremely large men wearing nearly identical dark suits and sunglasses, walked up the steps at the end of the platform and moved along the row of occupied seats, stopping at the vacant one next to Sarah.

"Is that seat available?" the woman asked quietly.

"Yes, it's been empty all day," Sarah answered, turning to look at the woman. There was something familiar about her, despite the sunglasses and hat, which drooped to cover much of her face. The two men stood behind her on either side of her chair.

She's somebody important, Sarah thought. *An actress maybe.* Trying to be as subtle as possible, she elbowed Shapiro, sitting to her right, and nodded to indicate the woman. Shapiro leaned forward to look at her. He nudged Katz, to his right, and pointed toward the woman.

"Holy shit," Katz said. "You're Mrs. Quaid, aren't you? Catherine, Catherine Quaid. The First Lady."

The woman smiled. "As a matter of fact, I am. All of those things," she said. "I volunteered to address the attendees and my offer was graciously accepted. I'm supposed to be speaking shortly."

Sarah was stunned to find herself sitting next to the First Lady. She didn't know what to say, fumbled for words and finally blurted out, "Does your husband know you're here?"

Catherine Quaid smiled again, this time more enthusiastically. "Why does everybody ask me that? No, I didn't feel it necessary to obtain his permission. I'm hoping it will come as a complete surprise to him." She swiveled her head to speak to one of the men behind her. "It will be a surprise to him, won't it be, Joe?"

"I expect you'll get his attention, ma'am," her bodyguard said flatly.

They sat quietly for a moment as the First Lady listened to the speaker, deep in thought. She turned to Sarah.

"These yellow stars," she asked, "are they for all the speakers? May I have one, too?"

"I don't think there's anything formal about the speakers wearing these," Shapiro said, indicating the yellow star pinned to his shirt. "Lots of people in the crowd seem to have them on. You do understand the significance of these stars, don't you?" he asked quietly.

She nodded. "I most certainly do. I'm not ignorant of Holocaust history, you know. In fact, when I heard my husband's speech last night, on television—alone in my bedroom, by the way—the first thought I had when he talked about issuing special Americards to Jewish citizens was that the Nazis did something just like that."

Katz unpinned the star from her blouse.

"Would you like to wear mine?"

Catherine Quaid pinned it to her jacket. "I would be proud to do so. Honored. Thank you so much."

They sat quietly for another few minutes. Shapiro turned to the First Lady and asked, "Do you know about the king of Denmark?"

The surprise on the First Lady's face indicated she had no idea what he was talking about. He continued.

"There is some doubt about whether this story is true or not," Shapiro said. "But Leon Uris put it in his book *Exodus*, so that's as good as being true.

"Anyway, the story goes that when the Germans occupied Denmark, the Danish king, King Christian, rode his horse every day through the streets of Copenhagen, to show that he was still around. The Germans ordered all Danish Jews to wear these same stars, like that one you're wearing. The day after the Germans ordered all the Danish Jews to wear this yellow star, the king himself had one pinned to his arm as he rode through the city. After that, the Germans rescinded their order.

"By the way, did you know that the Danish people managed to smuggle just about every Jew in Denmark out of the country into Sweden?"

"I suppose I am as close as this country has to a queen," she said softly. "Mr. Shapiro, I will be so proud to wear this star when I speak."

Sarah Goldberg turned to Catherine Quaid. "We . . . we all know what your husband has been doing—to Jews, about Jews," she said hesitantly. "We want you to know how much we appreciate what you are doing right now."

"Thank you. You know, when I am faced with a decision, I ask myself what is the right thing to do," she said softly. "And then I do it, always."

She finally managed a broad smile.

"Then I pay the price."

Shapiro nodded.

■ ■ ■

The speaker was just finishing. The next speaker was introduced as the chief rabbi of an Orthodox synagogue in Skokie, Illinois. Shapiro leaned across Goldberg to whisper to the First Lady.

"American Nazis marched in Skokie when I was in law school," he said. "The ACLU represented their right to do so. I've represented Nazis' free speech rights myself. Nazi rights somehow seem different now, though."

The speaker was a fragile, elderly man, assisted to the microphone by a young woman. She pulled a chair next to the microphone. "Papa, sit while you talk," she said softly.

"*Hak mir nisht keyn tshaynik,*" the old man barked at her. Rabbi Garfinkle, who was at the microphone to introduce the man, smiled.

"He told his daughter to stop speaking nonsense," Rabbi Garfinkle said. "And you know what, I have a feeling he's going to say the same thing to President Quaid." The crowd cheered. He placed his arm on the old man's shoulder and drew him close.

"I met Rabbi Yehuda Cohane when I was a rabbinical student. He was my teacher. He still is. I can honestly say that I have never encountered a sharper mind or a person who is less afraid to speak what is on that mind."

Rabbi Cohane braced both hands on the wooden speaker's stand. He stood straight as his twisted back allowed. His daughter and Rabbi Garfinkle stepped back, leaving the elderly man alone at the microphone.

"I listened to President Quaid's talk last night," he said in a voice filled with more strength than his body appeared to possess. "When he was finished, my daughter turned off the television. She was crying. 'Poppa,' she said, 'why do they do this to the Jews?'

"I didn't know how to answer her last night. But I thought about her question all night. That sharp mind they say I have, you know. Sometimes it's so sharp I cut myself with my own thoughts." He laughed at his joke.

"I thought and thought. I thought about Jewish history. I thought about American politics. Most of all, I thought about God. And I came to a conclusion I want to share with you today. They do this to the Jews, time after time throughout our long history, a history longer than most any other people on the plane. They do this to us because we let them do it to us. We let them. Jews let them do this to us. We let them because we don't fight back."

He leaned closer to the microphone, his lips inches from it, and whispered in a voice magnified by the giant speakers.

"And they think we won't fight back this time."

The old man paused, collecting more strength. He spoke again in a loud, full voice, gaining volume as he spoke.

"They're wrong. Sometimes we do fight back. Let me read you something." The old man took a sheet of paper from his pocket. He stared at it for a moment, then pushed it aside and recited slowly from memory.

"It is essential in the present state of world affairs that we prove to the world that our right to a Jewish State is not only an historical and human right but that we are ready and prepared to back it with military force," he said. "Those are old words, not new ones. They are from the June 1939 Declaration of Principles of the IZL, the *Irgun Zvai Leumi*, the Irgun, the Jewish Freedom Fighters; some people called them terrorists. They liberated the Land of Israel from British rule.

"The American president talks about terrorism as if when our people are being murdered, are being herded into concentration camps by their blood enemies, when the land that God himself, blessed be his name, gave to our people is taken from us, when our own country, our America, turns its back on our people, as if terrorism is something to be ashamed of rather than something to be proud of.

"When we celebrate Chanukah, when we tell the story of how Judah Maccabee drove the Roman legions from Israel, we celebrate the victory of terrorism. Jewish terrorism. Were the Jewish heroes who drove the British from Israel, who bombed hotels and police stations, were they terrorists? Of course they were. That didn't stop us from electing them our prime ministers, did it?"

He paused. His daughter walked up and whispered in his ear, but the old man shook his head violently and gestured for her to sit.

"When I finally dozed off last night, I slept as soundly as I have in years. And when I woke this morning, it was with a realization. I realized that while I slept, my mind kept thinking. Thinking about terrorism. And I was stunned at what I had realized the instant I awoke. In my sleep I realized who the greatest terrorist of all is. I lay in my bed and my body shook with the power of that understanding. Shook because I knew I would be coming here to address the largest gathering of Jewish people in the history of this nation at the time of the greatest threat to American Jews. I shook because of the powerful and wonderful and terrible message I knew God gave me to deliver today, the message I will deliver to you today; in fact, not just to you but also, also to Mr. President Lawrence Quaid.

"Here is the message I come to deliver. My message is about *terrorism*. My message is about the greatest terrorist of them all—God, the Lord. He is the greatest terrorist of all time. Let me recite some of his acts of terror when his people were in the most danger. I'll recite them as we do every year at Passover. We dip our finger in the cup of wine and remove one drop for every act of terror."

The rabbi held up an imaginary wine glass with his left hand. He dipped his right forefinger repeatedly into this glass, shaking off an imaginary drop of wine, repeating the Passover Seder ritual.

"He turned their drinking water to blood." Dip, shake. "He infested their land with frogs." Dip, shake. "Then lice, then flies. Their livestock suddenly dropped dead. Then boils broke out on the people's skin." Dip, shake. Dip, shake. Dip, shake. Dip, shake.

The elderly rabbi dropped his hands and looked out at the crowd.

"Tell me, does this sound like terrorism, like maybe biological warfare? God's weapons of mass destruction, maybe? But God was not finished." He raised his imaginary cup again and again dipped his finger in it repeatedly.

"Hailstorms, locusts, darkness. And all those horrible actions were not sufficient to save Israel. So what did God the terrorist do next? Talk about weapons of mass destruction. He killed the firstborn son of every Egyptian family.

"Weren't those all acts of terrorism? Was it speeches or marches or email campaigns that changed Pharaoh's heart, that forced him to free the Children of Israel from bondage? No. It was terror. Acts of terror more terrible than the world has seen since. God used this terror to save the Jewish people long ago. If God could take such actions to save his people then, can't we take such actions to save his people today?"

He turned and gestured to his daughter to come to him. She gently held him by the elbow and they walked back to his seat.

Catherine Quaid turned toward Sarah Goldberg, Ben Shapiro and Judy Katz.

"I'm supposed to speak next," she said. "How in the world do I follow that?"

She paused.

"My husband is going to be very, very pissed."

CHAPTER 56

The grassy area around the Washington Monument was empty. The National Park Service closed all museums and memorials around the Mall as a security precaution for the duration of the march. Casual tourists were scared away.

Four National Park Service police officers were stationed at the base of the monument. They heard the rumble of the loudspeakers a mile away across the length of the mall. The words were too garbled to understand.

The FBI video camera mounted on the observation platform at the top of the monument operated remotely from the FBI headquarters building blocks away. Beside it was a television news camera, also remotely operated. Both cameras had long zoom lenses able to focus on any face on the speaker's platform.

The park service officers shivered as a cool breeze blowing off the Potomac River stirred the grass around them. They'd been there since before sunrise. Cold. Bored. Nothing happened. Nobody approached the monument.

The head of the small detail looked up as a National Park Service van negotiated the maze of barrier walls surrounding the monument, coming to a stop directly in front of two steel bollards blocking the drive. The van's horn beeped. Without a second thought, he told one of the other officers, who stood just outside a small guard kiosk, to hit the button.

The steel bollards lowered into the ground on hydraulic pistons, just as the environmental protection plan for the Washington monument posted online said they would. Finding that website revealed to the three young men the way to get close to the monument.

The van drove over the tops of the bollards, coming to a stop just feet from the white marble wall of the Washington Monument. The driver's window rolled down. A paper tray with Starbucks coffee cups was handed out. The detail head walked briskly to the van.

"Boss felt sorry for you guys," the driver said. "Said to send you some coffee. Got these, too." He indicated two paper sacks filled with pastries.

"I'll carry these to the guys." The officer walked from the van without looking back, a broad smile on his face.

"Cops and donuts, you were right about that," Gimel said to Aleph.

"Let's get lined up," Aleph said nervously. "Show me the map again."

Bet handed him a printout of the National Mall from the National Park Service website. Aleph glanced at the map, then looked around outside the van, orienting himself.

"Okay," he said. "That's the White House straight ahead across all that grass." He looked to the right, out the passenger window. "And there's the Mall that way."

"Yeah," said Gimel, "and it's wide open, no people around, for a good long way." They could see the mass of people on the far end of the Mall, and could make out the raised speakers' platform beyond the crowd, almost at the Capitol.

"Move up a little more," Bet said to Aleph, behind the driver's wheel. "We want to be in the middle of that side facing the Mall. Get my door right up against the side."

The van inched forward, scraping against the marble wall of the Washington Monument.

The windows on both doors were rolled down. The sound of the speaker's voice rumbled across the Mall, as did the cheers of the crowd.

Gimel reached back into the storage area behind the seat. He removed three small squares of unpainted plywood, six inches on a side. Screwed to the top of each square was an ordinary doorbell button. Electrical wires ran from each doorbell button around a set of bolts next to the button. The wires were attached to a battery and trailed through the van to the model rocket engines buried in the C4. Each of the three buttons would trigger the explosives. Even if two men lost their courage, so long as any one of them pressed and held his button, the three steel drums feet behind them would explode simultaneously.

The three men exchanged looks. Gimel, glancing past Bet and out the driver's window, noticed one of the police officers staring at the van, then saw him begin walking quickly toward them, shouting something.

They heard the loudest roar yet from the crowd, loud enough so that even the police officer stopped to look toward the mass of people. Aleph jabbed at the radio in the van, turning the power on. It was still tuned to the all-news station carrying live coverage from the march.

"Wait just one moment," Aleph said. "I want to hear what has them so excited."

The three men sat side by side in the front seat of the van. Their plywood squares in their laps. Fingers hovering over the buttons, waiting to press them at the exact same instant. As they'd planned. Nobody was to jump the gun.

"The greatest terrorist of them all is God, the Lord," the voice said over the radio's speakers. The three men sat as if mesmerized. They listened in silence as the man, they did not know who he was, held them with the logic of his words.

The officer's handgun was now in his right hand as he

shouted for the men to get out of the van. They ignored him, entranced by the words coming from the radio.

"Was it speeches or marches or email campaigns that changed Pharaoh's heart, that forced him to free the Children of Israel from bondage?" the voice asked. "No. It was terror, acts of terror more terrible than the world has seen since. God used this terror to save the Jewish people long ago. If God could take such actions to save his people then, can't we take such actions to save his people today?"

The police officer was stunned that the three men were ignoring him. "Get out of the van now," he shouted. "Get out right now or I'll shoot."

He saw the driver turn his head slowly to look at him, then turn his head toward the two passengers.

"I'll count down from three," Aleph said. "Three. Two. One. Now."

Three thumbs descended on the buttons.

The explosion sent steel shards from the van's thin walls flying in all directions. The three men in the front seat were blown into bloody scraps. The police officer, kneeling on one knee, was decapitated by a spray of flying glass from the van's windshield.

The location of the detonation was on the side of the Washington Monument facing the Mall. The blast tore a deep gash into the base of the monument, leaving only the wall on the side farthest from the explosion site to support the 90,000 tons of the tower.

The monument wavered, leaning precariously toward the nearest building, the National Holocaust Memorial. That motion slowed as the tower ever so gradually twisted left, leaning sideways toward the center of the grass-covered Mall, and, when it was precisely aligned with the Capitol, crashed in one long piece to the ground, lying down the center of the Mall, pointing an accusing finger directly at the home of the US Congress.

The ground shook with a deep basso rumble as the structure hit the ground and bounced thirty feet into the air before landing a second time with a softer thud between the National Holocaust Memorial and the National Museum of American History.

■ ■ ■

A rising dust cloud and the boom froze everyone on the podium. The man standing behind Catherine Quaid shoved Sarah Goldberg, seated next to the First Lady, and stepped between Catherine Quaid and Goldberg. His gun was in his right hand.

The other man, Joe Bergantina, leaped in front of Mrs. Quaid, placed his hands on her shoulders and pushed her facedown to the floor of the platform. He knelt over her while he scanned from side to side, looking for threats.

The Mall erupted with shouts and screams from the crowd. Some people dropped to the grass, thinking a bomb had detonated. Others ran.

Rabbi Garfinkle stood in the middle of the platform. Motionless. Shocked. He walked to the microphone and appealed for calm. His voice could not be heard over the hysteria below.

■ ■ ■

The White House shook as a rumbling sound rose through the floor. The doors to the Oval Office flew open. Secret Service agents rushed in, surrounded the president and ushered him rapidly out the door, lifted off his feet by the nearest men in the ring formed around him.

The people remaining in the Oval Office ran to the window and watched the toppled Washington Monument settle under a cloud of dust. Gen. Paterson walked quickly to the telephone on the president's desk.

"This is General Paterson," he said. "I am speaking with the full authority of President Quaid. Send in the troops. Take everybody they find on the Mall into custody. Hold everyone."

Attorney General Harrison stood at the window, staring into the chaos.

"This changes everything," he said. "Everything."

Within minutes, Virginia guardsmen entered the fray of confused and frightened Jews.

■ ■ ■

The two Secret Service agents rushed Catherine Quaid off the platform to a limousine parked on the grass.

A group of soldiers formed a ring around the speakers' platform, not allowing anybody to exit. A dozen SUVs stopped near the platform. Men in dark suits ran up the steps to the platform and approached Rabbi Garfinkle.

"Mr. Harrison," the rabbi said. "You realize, of course, that we had absolutely nothing to do with that."

"I realize nothing at this point," the attorney general said, "except that ten minutes ago I was standing in the Oval Office with the president and I was an eyewitness to the desecration of one of this country's most sacred symbols. Five seconds after your speaker, a fellow rabbi, orders half a million Jews to go out and commit terrorist acts, five seconds, boom, down goes the Washington Monument. Everybody who is on this platform is coming along with my FBI agents here. Everybody else out there, well, they could have gone home last night, after the president's talk. Those folks out there are the hard core of your movement."

Harrison looked at the microphone and turned to Rabbi Garfinkle.

"I want you to get on that microphone and tell people to cooperate with the soldiers, to go along with them. Peacefully. No resistance. Order your people not to resist. We've got trucks and buses coming to take everybody away. It will be a while, so ask people to be patient. The trucks and buses will be here soon. Do you understand me, Rabbi?"

"Mr. Attorney General," the rabbi said, his voice shaking with rage. "Trucks? Buses? Don't you have freight cars to take us Jews away? You want me to address these people? I am proud to do so."

He walked to the microphone and tapped it three times to make sure it was active. The tapping sound made people throughout the crowd turn their heads toward the platform.

"The attorney general here wants me to order you all to go along peacefully with these soldiers," Rabbi Garfinkle said, speaking slowly, loudly and clearly. He appreciated that this could be his most important, and possibly his final, sermon. "Trucks and buses will take you away, away to someplace where you will be detained. To a camp, perhaps."

His head swiveled to take in the entire crowd of hundreds of thousands of people. His words set off frenzied shouting.

After several minutes, he raised his hands and asked for quiet.

"I refuse to do that. History taught us what happens when Jews allow themselves to be herded by soldiers like sheep, driven off to camps in buses, or in trucks, or . . ." He turned to face Harrison, fuming. "Or in cattle cars. Don't be sheep. Don't make it easy for them to round up Jews. Resist. Fight back. Struggle. *Never again, never again,* say it now, join me, *never again, never again.*"

The chant roared from the crowd.

NEVER AGAIN, NEVER AGAIN, NEVER AGAIN.

The soldiers walked into the crowd, plastic shields held before them, placing plastic handcuffs on everybody within reach. Some people struggled and were beaten to the grass by batons.

While this pandemonium was happening, Judy Katz grabbed Shapiro by the hand and shouted to Sarah Goldberg to stand next to her. Katz ran up to the nearest FBI agent, reaching into her jacket pocket as she approached him. She found her wallet and flipped it open to hold in front of the agent's face.

"Justice Department, Assistant US Attorney," she shouted.

"I'm with him." She pointed at Attorney General Harrison.

The agent nodded and looked at Shapiro and Goldberg.

"They're with me," Katz said quickly. "Please help me. Get us out of here."

"Follow me," he said, pushing people aside to make an opening for the three people following inches behind him.

CHAPTER 57

Two hours after the explosion, President Quaid spoke to the nation from the Oval Office. His message was unscripted.

"I will be brief," he said, looking straight at the camera. "I gave a warning last night. My warning was disregarded. A terrible act of cowardice has taken place not far from where I am sitting."

He gestured to his left and the camera swiveled to reveal a window and the park beyond it. A thirty-foot-tall stub was all that remained of the monument.

"I was standing at that window and watched the Washington Monument, a symbol of our nation's pride in its first president, tumble to the ground. I felt the blast on my own body."

The camera returned to President Quaid.

"I am unharmed. The nation is safe. At my orders, federal agents and the military are arresting and detaining all persons suspected of being complicit in this act of terrorism.

"It is no coincidence that nearly a half million Jewish protesters were near the monument and the National Mall when this brutal act of aggression occurred. They were being incited to act as terrorists by a rabbi minutes before the explosions occurred. These protestors are the hard-core element of what has become a Jewish uprising against our nation.

"The bombing of the Washington Monument was an act of terrorism, an act of war. It is obvious to each of us who witnessed this event that it was carefully coordinated with the demonstration. So, by the authority vested in me by Congress, I have ordered these enemy combatants held by the military authorities. I repeat that. They will be held by military, not by civilian, authorities. They will be detained as other enemy combatants are detained. They will not be charged with civilian crimes. They will not be subject to the civilian criminal justice system.

"Further, pursuant to the specific language of Section Nine of Article One of the United States Constitution, which states that the writ of habeas corpus shall not be suspended unless when in cases of rebellion or invasion the public safety may require it, I am declaring that the actions taken against the United States, including what happened today in the nation's capital, constitute acts of rebellion. I am therefore suspending the right of all such persons in rebellion against this nation to petition in any court for a writ of habeas corpus. I am requesting that Congress immediately enact legislation confirming this suspension.

"None of the people held in military custody as enemy combatants can run into court, seek out a liberal judge, and attempt to escape punishment. There will be no lawsuits and no lawyers. This is a military matter and it will be handled by the military as the military, and myself as commander in chief, determine to be in the best interest of the American people."

President Quaid leaned forward and glared into the camera.

"Finally, this is far from the end. As I told you last night, our enemy holds weapons of mass destruction. We continue to search for these weapons. I promise we will find them. When we do, we will deal with the evil persons who threaten us from within our own borders with such cowardly weapons."

The camera zoomed closely into the president's face.

"We know who you are. You know that we know who you are. You cannot escape. We will capture you, as they used to say in the Old West, dead or alive. I don't particularly care which. My fellow Americans. God bless the United States of America and all of her loyal citizens."

■ ■ ■

Abram Goldhersh and Rueben watched the events unfold on a small TV in his bedroom, waiting for Sarah's speech.

The other TV was shattered in the living room from the night before when Goldhersh smashed it in rage over the president's address. Now he sat on the edge of his bed stunned, knowing he was responsible in part for an act of terror that set in motion the arrests of tens of thousands of American Jews. He leaned forward and put his head in his hands. He sobbed.

"Sarah. They're taking my Sarah to a concentration camp," the man wailed.

■ ■ ■

Shapiro, Sarah Goldberg and Judy Katz struggled to walk rather than run as they negotiated the ten blocks to the Renaissance Hotel to retrieve Shapiro's car. The only tense moment was when they started to cross K Street but darted back to the sidewalk as a parade of Army trucks, led and trailed by a phalanx of Humvees, shot down the street, sirens blaring. Shapiro and Sarah ducked into a doorway. Katz stood on the sidewalk, frozen, staring at the Army trucks, unable to move.

They were afraid to go to the hotel room for their bags, concerned that since the room had been used as an office for march organizers, police might be waiting to nab anybody who showed up there. Shapiro's heart pounded as he handed the hotel doorman the receipt for his car and asked for it to be brought to the front of the hotel. He hoped the five twenty-dollar bills he gave the doorman would smooth the process.

The two women were at a coffee shop a block from the hotel. Shapiro told them there was no sense risking all three of them getting arrested when he retrieved his car. The car arrived with no problems, however, earning the valet a further twenty-dollar tip. Shapiro stopped quickly in front of the coffee shop and picked up the two women. Judy Katz sat in the front, next to Shapiro. Sarah Goldberg sat in the back seat.

In a matter of minutes, they were on I-95 heading north toward Baltimore, riding in silence, hoping they were ahead of any roadblocks they expected would sprout on roads leaving the capital. Shapiro set the cruise control at nine miles an hour over the speed limit.

Sarah finally broke the silence.

"I don't know how I can thank the two of you for getting me away from there," she said. "Judy, if you hadn't been so quick, and so persuasive, who knows where we would be now? Thank you so much."

"No big deal," Katz replied. "I was lucky my asshole of a boss couldn't find time to meet last week to take my ID. If he had, we'd be heading for military detention right now, all three of us."

The three sat silent, their minds swirling with paranoia. Katz imagined herself in a striped prison suit, her hair shaved off, stick thin, entering the shower building.

She startled Shapiro and Sarah with a scream. "Nana. Nana was supposed to be in Washington. They've taken my nana to a camp."

The sky darkened as they crossed New Jersey and on into Connecticut. Shapiro broke the silence.

"I wonder whether the president was blowing smoke up our asses with that atom bomb talk," he said. "It sure reminded me of another president who told fairy tales about weapons of mass destruction. I can't believe Quaid had the balls to try the same thing."

Sarah Goldberg remained silent throughout this exchange. Finally, she realized that these two people had saved her from being dragged to a concentration camp. They could be trusted.

"Actually, there may be some truth to what the president said," she whispered, hardly believing that she was about to reveal the secret she'd learned only days earlier and sworn to protect.

Both Shapiro and Katz swiveled to look at the woman in the back seat. The car swerved and Shapiro turned back to look at the road.

The tension, fear and anxiety that had built in Sarah Goldberg throughout the day, anxiety first over what she would say when she walked up to the microphone to address half a million people, fear and tension from the events that prevented her from speaking, all let loose in a torrent of words as she spewed forth the story of her friend Debra Reuben, of Lt. Chaim Levi and his death, of the sailboat and, finally, of the atom bomb at the bottom of the swimming pool in her suburban Portland home.

The car was silent when the woman stopped speaking.

"Holy fucking shit," was Shapiro's first comment.

"Mega-dittos, Rush," was all Katz could say as they drove on through the night, heading back to Massachusetts.

Maybe, Katz thought, *there is an alternative to the shower building.*

CHAPTER 58

Shapiro left the two women at Judy Katz's apartment in Boston shortly before midnight. Sarah Goldberg would spend the night there, then take the first Downeaster train in the morning from Boston to Portland. She'd telephoned her husband from a pay phone at a McDonald's in Hartford, Connecticut. Surprisingly, there was no answer at her home. She left a cryptic message assuring Abram she was safe and would be home the following morning.

Shapiro continued driving north of Boston, arriving at his house a little after midnight. He could hear the waves slapping at the dock at the end of the wooden walkway leading to the salt marsh behind the house. The full moon shining on the water brought to mind a memory of a magical high tide night when he and Sally paddled their kayaks over the flooded marsh while the full moon reflected off the water's surface, blurring the line between sea and sky. They felt as if they were gliding through the air.

Shapiro drove down his dead-end street without noticing the dark Ford Crown Victoria parked under a tree blocking the nearest streetlamp. Two men sat in the car, taking turns napping and watching the rearview mirror.

Shapiro pulled into his driveway and was surprised to see a car parked there and a light on in the house.

The television was on in the family room, where he found his wife's mother, Emily Spofford, sleeping on the couch. Shapiro turned off the set, then placed his hand on his mother-in-law's shoulder and shook her. Her eyes opened. She yelped, startled.

"Emily, what are you doing here?" Shapiro said. "Where's Sally? Where's Adam?" He looked toward the stairs leading to his bedroom. "Are they sleeping?"

His mother-in-law whimpered.

"What the hell is going on, Emily?"

"Ben, oh, poor Ben," the woman said, tears now running down her cheeks. "Oh, Ben, they're gone. They're both gone. I'm so sorry for you. Oh, Ben, it's such a tragedy."

"What do you mean, gone? Gone where? Where are they, Emily?"

"Ben," she replied. "They're dead, poor Sally and little Adam. They were at that . . . that mall, that shopping mall when that horrible bomb went off, when that goddamn Jew set off—" She stopped abruptly. "I kept calling the house but she never answered. I called all through the night.

"Then, just yesterday, two police officers came to the house. They asked me if I was Sally Spofford's mother. They asked if I knew where you were and I said I thought you'd gone away for a few days. Sally told me you insisted on going to that Jewish demonstration in Washington. I didn't tell the police that, of course.

"And they showed me Sally's bag, that ugly Betsy Karen bag with the big yellow daisy on it that she bought last year. Ben, it was all torn up. It was horrible, black marks all over it. Then they told me they'd recovered what they believed was her body, at the North Shore Mall, at the food court. Oh, Ben, they said they weren't sure it was her, they couldn't identify the body. They asked me to come to the morgue and I did and it was her— at least I'm pretty sure it was her. I hardly looked."

Shapiro grabbed the woman by the shoulders.

"Adam," he shouted. "What about Adam?"

"Oh, Ben," the woman cried. "I asked them where Adam was. I explained that she had a son. His name was Adam. They told me there were some children they couldn't identify, five children. And Ben, I had to look at all of them, those horrible, broken bodies of children. Adam was the last one they showed me. He looked so beautiful, so peaceful. Then they pulled the cover all the way off his face and, oh, Ben, he had no mouth, no chin."

The woman collapsed onto the sofa. Shapiro stood in front of her, shaking. White spots appeared in front of his eyes, dancing across the surface of his eyeballs. The next thing he knew, he was on the floor in a heap, cold, clammy sweat on his forehead. He sat on the floor, unable to move, his heart about to explode.

Shapiro startled from the sound of somebody pounding on the front door. He stumbled to the door, his knees weak and trembling.

"Who the hell is it?" he yelled.

"FBI, Mr. Shapiro. Open the door."

He turned the porch light on and opened the door. Two men stood there. Without asking, they walked past him into the hall. One man spoke.

"Ben Shapiro," he said, holding a photograph of Shapiro's driver's license. "We've been waiting for you for quite a while, Mr. Shapiro. We need to speak with you. Right away. It's important."

"You might say it's a matter of national security, Mr. Shapiro," the other man said, moving to stand beside Shapiro.

"This is the wrong time for this," he said softly. "My wife and child have been murdered. I can't do this right now."

He reached for the door.

"You have to leave now," he said.

One of the men placed his palm on the door and shoved it closed.

"You don't understand, Mr. Shapiro," he said. "We've been sitting out there all day and halfway through the night. We're not going to do this some other time. We're going to talk now, right now."

The other man placed his hand on Shapiro's upper arm.

Shapiro gestured with his head toward the left, toward the kitchen, away from the family room.

"We can sit in there," he said. "I'll make coffee. I need it."

"Fine," the first agent said. "That's better."

Shapiro turned toward the kitchen, then stopped, frozen. He looked up at the men. FBI, they would know—maybe Sally's mother was wrong. "My wife, my son," he mumbled. "Did they really die?"

The two men glanced at one another, surprised. "We don't know about your wife," one man answered. "But we know all about you."

"We're told, buddy, that you can identify the Israeli soldiers held on Cape Cod," the other agent said. "That is correct?"

Shapiro smiled wearily. "So that's what this is all about," he said, remembering his telephone conversation with the district attorney about his client, Howie Mandelbaum.

"I can't identify anybody," Shapiro said. "I told District Attorney McDonough that my client, Mr. Mandelbaum, theoretically he might be able to identify certain persons who were on those ships who were affiliated with the Israel Defense Forces. Theoretically, I said. And that was in return for consideration concerning the criminal charges. That's what I said. It was all theoretical." His hands placed quotation marks around the last word.

The agent to Shapiro's right pushed him against the wall.

"Cut the crap, asshole," the agent shouted. "We aren't dealing with some state crime shoot-em-up here. This is serious. National security. We aren't playing little plea bargain games, not now. Is that clear? The DA said you could ID these people. Not your client. Or should I say your former client?" He looked across at the other agent.

The agent continued, "Mr. Mandelbaum, most unfortunately

for all of us, took a flyer in the middle of the night last night. He is no longer with us."

"A flyer?" Shapiro said, looking back and forth from one man to the other.

"Yeah, he played Superman," the first agent said. "Off the fifth-tier balcony at Charles Street Jail. Either jumped or was tossed, not that it matters much either way. Broke his neck. Tragic. They say he was buck naked."

"All that matters is that you are the only one who can ID those Jew soldiers who killed the Coasties. Even more than that, we're told those soldiers might know something about the atom bomb the Jews smuggled into this country. You care about this country, don't you, Mr. Shapiro? This is still your country, isn't it?"

"Yes, yes, of course this is my country," Shapiro said quickly, stunned by news of his client's death. Shapiro remembered his last conversation with Mandelbaum. *Maybe he did jump*, he thought.

Sally. Adam. Too much death. His head spun. He sat at the kitchen table.

The second agent moved behind Shapiro. He grabbed the back of Shapiro's chair and yanked it away from the table.

"Enough of this bullshit," he said. "Get up. You're coming with us. You're going to ID those Jew soldiers and you and your buddies are going to tell us everything there is to know about this atom bomb."

"Where are we going?" Shapiro asked. He wanted to close his eyes and find these two men gone. "This is all a mistake," he said quietly. "I have no idea who the Israeli soldiers are. I never said I could pick them out. It was my client. He could do that. And I don't know anything about any bombs, any atom bombs."

The men grabbed his elbows and lifted him to a standing position.

"Where are you taking me?" Shapiro asked.

One of the agents grabbed Shapiro by the upper arm. "We're going for a drive down to the cape. Camp Edwards. Look, buddy, we're just the delivery guys. All we do is pick you up and drop you off for the experts down there. The experts are the ones who'll be chatting with you."

"Experts?" Shapiro asked.

"Yeah, the experts, the interrogators. Military interrogators. You heard the president, didn't you? You're an enemy combatant, buddy. We turn you over to the military and they make you talk. That's how it works."

"They make everybody talk," the other agent smirked. "You know, like the car dealer, everybody talks."

"And nobody walks," his partner finished for him with a matching smile.

"Especially about bombs, like that one that took down the Washington Monument, and the atom bomb, the one you don't know anything about. You'll puke your guts out once the military guys work on you."

Shapiro was suddenly silent. *Atom bomb?* He remembered what Sarah Goldberg said about what lay at the deep end of her swimming pool. *Oh my God,* Shapiro thought. *Oh my God. I do know something. They'll get me to tell them, too.* He had no pretensions about what the government would do to him to discover information about a terrorist bomb plot.

I have to get away, he thought.

One man still gripped Shapiro's arm. The other agent stood in the doorway leading to the front hall. Shapiro thought rapidly.

"Okay. I understand. I'll be glad to help," he said. "I don't know much about anything, but I'll tell everything I know."

"Fine, wonderful, now let's go," the man holding his arm said, not relaxing his grip.

"Look, can I change my clothes first, real quick?" Shapiro asked. "I've been wearing this for two days now. Hey, let me get on some clean underwear and socks and I'll talk my head off." He smiled. "My bedroom's upstairs. Just give me thirty seconds."

The men looked at one another. The man by the door spoke.

"All right," he said. "We'll check it out first, though."

The three men went up the stairs to Shapiro's bedroom.

"Any chance of a bit of privacy?" he asked.

Before answering, the two agents glanced around the room. One man went to the bedroom window, lifted it and looked around outside, seeing that the room was on the second floor and that no trees were within reach. It was a twenty-five-foot drop to the gravel pathway below the window. The other man threw drawers open and searched quickly.

"Okay, we'll be right outside the door," he said to Shapiro, gesturing to his partner. The men walked out the bedroom door, leaving it ajar.

Shapiro dropped the clean clothes on the floor and quickly stepped to the window, which the agent had left open. Shapiro lifted the hinged lid on the upholstered chest in front of the window and removed a white plastic box with bright-red words: *Fire Friend.* From inside the box he pulled a length of yellow rope with white plastic steps at intervals. Two shiny steel hooks were attached to the ends of the two parallel lengths of rope. Shapiro shoved the chest away from the wall and snapped the steel hooks onto two steel eyebolts sunk into the wall, near the floor. He threw the yellow rope out the window.

All this took no more than five seconds. He'd practiced doing just that, years before. Before Adam was born.

"Thank you, Sally," he muttered. *Thank you for being so afraid of fire, so afraid of being trapped in our second-floor bedroom by a fire on the stairs.*

Shapiro climbed out the window and made his way down the swaying ladder. Just before he reached the ground a head appeared in the window.

"Shit," the FBI agent shouted. The head retracted. Shapiro heard a shout through the open window. "Get downstairs. Now. He's bogeying."

Shapiro dropped to the ground, thinking quickly. He glanced at the driveway and saw a black sedan parked directly behind his Mercedes, blocking it from backing out the driveway. He looked around frantically, then spotted the wooden walkway leading to the dock on the salt marsh.

The full moon showed the flood tide just ebbing, draining the water out to the nearby ocean.

Shapiro sprinted down the walkway to the end of the dock. Resting upside down in a crooked frame he'd constructed from graying two-by-fours was Shapiro's red fiberglass kayak, eighteen sleek feet long. A double-bladed paddle was jammed inside the boat.

Shapiro hefted the forty-five-pound boat off the storage rack and dropped it in the water at the end of the dock. He sat on the edge of the dock and held the boat in place with his right foot. He heard shouts coming from the house.

"He's by the fucking water," a voice shouted. "This way. Hustle!"

Shapiro lowered himself from the dock into the kayak's cockpit, holding the long paddle in his left hand while he held onto the dock to steady himself with his right hand. He heard footsteps pounding down the wooden walkway as he shoved off from the dock and began paddling furiously away from the house, out into the marsh, toward the ocean a half mile away.

When fifty feet of water—which Shapiro knew to be only inches deep as the flood tide covered the top of the grass that made up the salt marsh—separated him from the shore, he glanced back and saw the two FBI agents standing on the end of the dock. Both held handguns.

"Come back here or we'll shoot, asshole," one man shouted.

The other agent shoved the man's arm aside. "Can't interrogate a corpse, dummy," he said. "Get back to the car and get on the radio. Call, I don't know, the Coast Guard or somebody."

■ ■ ■

There was a marina at the mouth of the river that the marsh

fed into. The marina would be closed, but there was a telephone booth there.

He paddled quickly. *One step at a time,* he thought, ignoring the breathtaking beauty of gliding over the shallow water with the reflection of the full moon breaking into kaleidoscopic sparkles from the ripples on the surface. Sally had talked about that magic night on the water so many times. He choked. *Adam. Adam. Why would they kill you?*

The telephone booth next to the gas pump at the marina was brightly lit. *Who do I call,* Shapiro wondered. *Not my law partners. They wouldn't let me run from the FBI.*

He reached into his pocket. It was still there, the yellow post-it note on which Judy Katz had written her home telephone number before getting out of Shapiro's car earlier that night.

It took three tries before Shapiro managed to punch in the correct set of numbers to charge the call to his credit card. A sleepy voice answered on the sixth ring.

"Judy, it's Ben," he whispered. "I need you to come get me right now. I'll explain when you get here."

He gave her directions to Pavilion Beach, a rocky stretch a half mile from the marina.

"Judy," Shapiro said before hanging up, "you'd better bring Sarah with you. I don't think we'll be going back to your place—not for a while."

CHAPTER 59

The eight-foot-tall solid oak door to the Lincoln bedroom flew open with such force that its door handle dented the horsehair plaster wall. Catherine Quaid was so startled she dropped the towel she had just wrapped around her dripping body after stepping from the bathtub.

Lawrence Quaid stomped into the bedroom and stared at his now-naked wife. He hesitated. It was some time since he'd seen Catherine naked.

"What the hell did you think you were doing?" he screamed. She stepped back. "Catherine, don't you realize that I am in the crisis that will define my presidency? There is an atom bomb loose somewhere in the country. It's in the hands of madmen. They've shown us they're willing to do anything to intimidate us, to intimidate me. I'm trying to galvanize the country and protect it, and there you are on the podium at an anarchist rally."

He walked toward the door but turned before leaving the room. "Don't you have anything to say?"

Catherine Quaid reached for a bathrobe, drew in a deep breath, collecting her thoughts, trying to control the angry words that were fighting to fly from her. She spoke softly.

"I think, Lawrence, that you need to worry less about history and more about what you are doing to good people in America right now," she said. "The wonderful man I've loved and admired all these years would not create—there is no other word for it, Lawrence—would not create concentration camps, would not tolerate torture, would not do away with laws that for hundreds of years have been the foundation for liberty and freedom.

"Lawrence, I know you don't think of yourself as a bad man. But—and I hate to use the analogy, but it is the only one that comes to mind—Lawrence, do you think Adolph Hitler thought of himself as bad either? Can't you take a step back and look at what you are doing? Forget about history. Just do the right thing now. History will write itself."

Quaid's head snapped back as if he'd been punched. His wife had equated him to the most evil man of the twentieth century. He felt wounded, shaken. Pundits could criticize him, but his wife, his most trusted advisor, his biggest supporter? He'd trusted her judgment throughout every moment of his political career. It occurred to him more than once that she would have made a better president than he could ever be.

As Quaid paused in the doorway to the Lincoln bedroom, the image of the Washington Monument surrounded by a cloud of dust, tilting at an impossible angle, then falling like a timbered tree filled his mind.

"Catherine, I'm no Hitler, and I resent the implication. It's hurtful and it's wrong. My job is to protect this country, to keep it safe. And, whether you want to believe this or not, our nation is under attack. This is not about persecuting Jews. It's about saving America. The people at that march were hard-core and anti-American. They were being incited to commit violence—and they did."

■ ■ ■

Quaid strode from the East Wing and into the West, settling

into his office and asking for an update from the march. Within minutes, key members of his administration were in the conference room.

The final count on detainees from the march was around 420,000 people, the president was told. Seventy-four people taken into custody from the speakers' platform were driven to nearby Bolling Air Force Base, near Reagan National Airport, and flown to Otis Air Force Base on Cape Cod. The assumption was that the people on the platform were organizers who could provide information about the coordination between the march and the bombing of the Washington Monument, and about the missing atomic bomb.

On arrival at Cape Cod, they were turned over to the Echo Team interrogators.

The big issue facing Quaid was what to do with 420,000 detainees. The Cape Cod facility, even crowded far beyond its holding capacity, could take no more than 25,000 people. Neither the Federal Bureau of Prisons nor the immigration service, two agencies holding the majority of federal detainees, could cope with an immediate population increase of that magnitude. Besides, this wasn't a civilian problem. The marchers were military detainees, and Quaid wanted them held as war criminals.

Even Guantanamo was briefly considered. And rejected. Too small.

"What are we going to do with them?" Quaid asked. "We don't even have a stadium large enough to hold this many people. If they start dying from dysentery or God knows what, we'll have a humanitarian crisis on our hands. We need a solution."

Harry Wade, the Federal Emergency Management Agency director, leaped at this problem.

"We're clearing out all our mobile home parks from the hurricanes," he said. "Take the trailers. String some razor wire around 'em, throw up some guard towers and you're all set."

The last Hurricane Jack and Jill refugees were in the process of moving out of FEMA-provided travel trailers and emergency mobile home parks throughout Florida, Georgia, Alabama and Mississippi.

"I can stuff 400,000 people into these trailer parks," Wade told the president. "We've had more than 200,000 living in them for the past ten months, and they were comfortable. No problem doubling up. Just bring in a couple hundred thousand cots—no problem finding 'em—and we'll have plenty of capacity."

The camps would be operating within days while the Jewish detainees and their sympathizers were transported there.

"Do it," Quaid ordered. "I'll call the House and Senate leaders and get emergency funding. We're at war."

Next, Quaid asked for his daily briefing on the Israelis held in New England.

"Anything new?" he asked.

■ ■ ■

The Echo Team interrogators were producing results. Few people could tolerate more than a week of high stress confinement. The detention cells were isolated from all outside contacts. The fluorescent ceiling lights were always on. The ceiling-mounted speakers were never silent; in fact, they were rarely at any volume less than that of a lawnmower. Music selections were at the option of each interrogator.

Other techniques included forcing a detainee to maintain what was referred to as a "stress position" for hours at a time, positions such as holding arms straight out from the body. A favorite was to have a detainee squat on the floor while his wrists and ankles were chained to a ring bolted between his feet, his urine and excrement accumulating around him. More aggressive interrogation methods included the revived use of waterboarding and electric shocks to men's genitals and women's nipples.

Detainees quickly disclosed the identities of the Israel Defense Force teams on the two ships. The soldiers said there was no central planning effort to place them on the ships. Each person said he or she made their own way to the docks and boarded the ships with whatever weapons they'd managed to save from their military units. As the interrogations intensified, detailed descriptions of vast hordes of nuclear devices, including mind-boggling killing machines and vast stores of chemical and biological weapons, were all disclosed.

"Unfortunately, sir, some of the people we interrogated died," the homeland security chief said.

"Casualties of war," Quaid responded.

The briefing on the interrogations did nothing to calm Quaid's concerns about the still-undiscovered nuclear device. Reports of stores of anthrax grenades and nerve gas agents in Israel's arsenal created new nightmares for him. The scope of the Israeli weapons of mass destruction arsenal disclosed to the interrogators, except for the previously known nuclear weapons, was a complete surprise to the American military intelligence community.

Detainees' talk about Israeli atomic machine gun bullets, anthrax spread by pressurized hair spray containers, and laser machine guns began to sound far too Buck Rogers to be believed. Eventually, all such information squeezed from detainees after torture sessions was discarded as fabrication.

The government was left with its only credible information being what it knew almost from the beginning. Israel had smuggled some amount of U-235 into New England in a sailboat. Where that material was, who had the material, and whether it already formed the core of an operable bomb was still all unknown.

CHAPTER 60

The first night at the Portland house, Sarah let Shapiro and Katz decide sleeping arrangements. Shapiro said he'd be fine on the living room sofa. Katz settled into the guest bedroom.

Katz lay in bed, stunned by the sudden turn her life had taken. Just a few weeks earlier she was happily chasing gangsters. Now she was hiding from her own government, hiding with a group of strangers who seemed unlike any criminals she had ever encountered.

Worst of all, there was no answer at her grandmother's house. She tried calling the few friends she knew her grandmother had. Nobody answered. Of course, her nana's few friends were all Jews, all part of what they called their Canasta Crew. They'd all gone to Washington. It had been an adventure for them, chaperoned by their rabbi, joined by their entire congregation of elderly Jews.

There was no word from them now. *The Canasta Crew is in a concentration camp,* Judy Katz thought. *Where does that leave me? I'm an American. My government is doing this. Shit, a week ago I worked for that government.*

Katz thought about reporting back to work to help the office get through this emergency. Then she remembered the secret meetings before the arrests, the meetings she was excluded from. She lay in bed, eyes closed. She saw an image of her grandmother standing behind a wire fence, thin fingers poking through holes in the wire mesh, staring at her, wondering when her Judilah would take her away from this oh-so-familiar hell, a hell from her darkest, oldest memories.

Downstairs, Shapiro didn't know what to make of the other woman he was introduced to at the house in Portland—Debra Reuben, the Israeli cabinet member. She seemed to live in a void filled by staring out the window at the busy street, and by alcohol.

Shapiro quickly recognized in Reuben an emptiness that he shared. She, too, seemed to be waiting to see somebody walk through the front door, somebody her conscious mind knew would never arrive—somebody her emotions had not yet accepted as gone forever.

■ ■ ■

The second night after his arrival, Shapiro sat on the living room sofa late into the evening, alone in the room with Debra Reuben. Earlier, Shapiro and Abram Goldhersh had worked their way through the remaining half bottle of Lagavulin. Shapiro enjoyed the warm feeling good single malt left him with, crediting the distillers on the long ago and far away island of Islay off Scotland's foul southwest coast for the magical effect of their concoction.

Sarah and Abram Goldhersh had long since gone to bed, as had Katz, leaving Shapiro and Reuben in the living room, him on the sofa, her in an overstuffed armchair.

"My wife used to tease me for being a Pollyanna," Shapiro said, trying not to let any hint of a slur slip into his speech, despite the Scotch warming his stomach like a peat fire. "That's what I would always say—don't worry, it will turn out for the best. That was me. 'Pollyanna Shapiro' she used to call me. She should hear me now. I don't see any hope, any way this situation is going to turn out for the best."

Reuben had taken an instant liking to this attorney. Hearing how he escaped from the FBI agents at his home, she'd sensed the same self-confidence that had attracted her to Levi. Ben Shapiro did not seem like a man who would give up easily. That he sounded so despondent now was either an indication of the desperation of the situation or a result of his tragic loss, she concluded.

"My whole life has been devoted to solving problems—other peoples' problems, sure, but taking on what they thought were impossible battles and fighting them. Sometimes I won." He looked up, directly into her eyes. Smiled. "I won a lot more than I lost, you know. I was pretty good. I was a damned good trial lawyer.

"I believed in the system, the legal system, even the political system. The Rule of Law, that's what they called it in law school. This country is built on the Rule of Law, the professors told us. I used to believe that, you know.

"I believed in the first ten amendments to the Constitution a lot more than I believed in the Ten Commandments. And I even believed that politics was like a pendulum. Sometimes it swung my way, sometimes the other way. But it always swung back, and always toward the center, never too far one way or the other."

"And now, what do you believe now?" Reuben asked, drawn into his story as he'd drawn so many hundreds of jurors into his way of seeing the facts of a case.

"You heard him on TV, didn't you?" Shapiro said, angry. "You know, I voted for the guy, Quaid. I liked him—moderate, not too liberal to get elected. Never in a million years would I have expected him to give in to . . . to . . . I don't know, to the dark side this way."

Reuben unconsciously echoed his emotions, angry when he

was angry, smiling when he smiled. That was the effect a good trial lawyer giving a good closing argument hoped for from a jury.

"I can't accept that all those people, all those hundreds of thousands of people who stood and sat and cheered and clapped right in front of me in Washington, all those people are now behind barbed wire in some sort of American concentration camps. The man has lost his mind."

"But don't you think there are people who will stop him?" Reuben asked. "There are people in the Senate, in Congress, who won't stand for this, aren't there?

"Evidently not," he replied bitterly. "You saw on TV, you saw what Congress did. Suspended habeas corpus. My God, maybe because I'm a lawyer, but I know what that means. It means they locked the doors to the courthouses and handed Quaid the keys."

They sat silently in the living room, Shapiro exhausted both by the Scotch and the depth of his despondency.

"I know what you mean. I've lost my country, too," Reuben said softly. "Both countries, actually, but especially my adopted home. My friends, my neighbors, the baker I bought my loaf of bread from every few days, the librarian who put each new Creighton book aside for me. All those people. I don't know if they're dead or alive. Maybe some of them are in camps, detention camps over there. I don't know which would be worse. Maybe a quick death would be more merciful."

She looked up from the floor, where she directed her words, and noticed that Shapiro's eyes welled with tears.

"I hoped coming here I could change things. I hoped Chaim and I could make it better. Now he's gone and my hope is gone, too."

"You came to America with more than hope," he said. "You brought something with you." He gestured toward the window. Outside was the swimming pool, its cover still in place. "You must have had something in mind when you brought that."

"Honestly, I didn't have any plans for it," she said. "At first, all we knew was that we had to get it out of the country. We couldn't let the Arabs get their hands on it. That was reason enough. Later, once I got it away from Israel and the boat took me to Spain, I wasn't prepared to dispose of it. It's not something that you can leave in a trash can, is it?"

"I suppose not," Shapiro said.

"I wanted to get back to America. That was all I knew then—as much planning as I was able to do. I found Levi and that boat he had and it made sense to bring the thing with me. I even thought I might turn it over to the government for safekeeping. Once we got here, though, and I saw that America was not going to be Israel's white knight, that America was not going to make everything better again, I realized that maybe I was here, with what I had with me here, for a purpose. You know, Ben, I truly believe that there is a reason why I'm here, why all of us are where we are right now, and that reason also includes what we have out there in the pool."

"Have you thought of what that one bomb can do?" Shapiro asked.

Reuben did not answer. Instead, she stood up slowly from the chair and took a step toward the sofa. She leaned down toward him and softly kissed him on the right cheek.

"I hurt too much to talk about the bomb now. Good night, Ben," she said. "I enjoyed talking with you. I think we'll both sleep better tonight."

She took two steps toward the stairs, then stopped and turned toward him.

"Ben," she said, a new sadness coming to her voice. "Ben, I know better than anybody else in the whole world what that bomb can do. I've lived, in a way, with what that bomb can do. You're right, it would change everything. Everything. I just don't know how it would change—if one more bomb, a third bomb, can possibly make better what the first two bombs made so terribly wrong. All I know is that what is happening in this country has to be stopped. I have no doubts about that. And I suspect that it is us"—she gestured upstairs, toward where Judy Katz, where

Abram and Sarah Goldberg-Goldhersh were sleeping. "It is this group who will be making that happen."

"If they don't arrest us first," Shapiro said flatly, aware they were in the house of a woman who'd been on the speakers' list for the march, a woman the government knew had escaped that day.

"Yes, that clock is ticking isn't it?" she answered, then walked up the stairs. Shapiro laid his head back against the pillow and, fully dressed, without bothering with sheets or blanket, fell instantly into a deep, healing sleep.

■ ■ ■

Shapiro prepared omelets for the collection of former strangers sitting at the kitchen table— Katz, Reuben, Abram and Sarah Goldhersh. *I didn't know any of them a month ago,* he thought. *Now they are all I have left.*

"I'm going back to Boston," Katz announced. "They have no idea I'm involved with anything. I'll be safe. Besides, I'm the only defense committee lawyer with a security clearance, so I'm the only one who can visit our clients on the cape." She gave Shapiro a probing look. "Somebody still has to act like a lawyer, right, Ben?"

"Judy, as soon as I show my face you'd be visiting me at that camp," Shapiro said. "I didn't please those FBI agents. But if you feel you can still play at being an attorney, well, go for it." He paused. Looked at the floor. "Those days are over for me."

"I'm not going to play at being a lawyer, Ben. I still am a lawyer." Katz was angry. There was no need for him to put her down. "Look, Ben, I understand your pain. No, I know I can't begin to understand your pain, but I recognize that horrible things have happened to you. But, Ben, I'm in pain, too. We all are. My grandmother, my nana, is in some detention camp somewhere since that march. So why do you have to act like an asshole now?"

"I'm sorry," he mumbled. "I apologize. Tell us what you have in mind."

"I missed my meeting with my boss, my farewell meeting. I want to see him face-to-face, see what he'll say to me," she said. "I have loose ends to tie up. I have to find my nana. Somebody has to get down to that camp to find out what's happening there. That's still important, isn't it?"

"Do you really think they'll let you into that camp, Judy?" Sarah asked.

"They have to. I'm the lawyer for the organization that represents the detainees," she said. "I may have to get a court order, but they have to let me in. These people have a right to be represented by an attorney, don't they? They have rights. Don't they?"

"Do they?" Shapiro made a show of noisily rising from the table and walking from the room.

Katz left to pack the few things she'd brought when she and Sarah left her apartment to meet Shapiro at the beach. She came down the stairs after several minutes. Shapiro asked her to step outside. He took her hand.

"Judy, I'm worried about you," he said. "The world's gone crazy. It's not like it was just a month ago. You push them now and they'll lock you up. I'm worried that if you push too hard to get into that camp, you'll get in, but you won't get out."

She squeezed his hand, then threw her arms around him and drew him close. He stiffened. Then relaxed. His arms hung limply, wanting to hug her but unable to do so. After an awkward moment he stepped back and attempted to smile at her.

"I have to try, don't I, Ben?" she asked. "We can't just stop trying. When we do that, they win. Right? Then they win?" She tried to smile.

"Okay, be the lawyer," he said. "Use my office. Tell my partners I'm off on a secret case. They'll want to know more, but they won't be surprised. One last thing, Judy. Be a lawyer, Judy. Sue the bastards." He grinned for the first time since he arrived home from Washington.

"I'll sue their asses off, Ben," Katz said. "I'll do good, you'll see." She held both his hands in hers. "Ben, I haven't been able to find words to tell you how horrible I feel about your son, and your wife. I know I wouldn't have been her favorite person if she'd known about me, but they didn't deserve what happened to them. To think that Jews did that. Ben, does that make you wonder what else we might do—who else will be hurt?"

He did not respond.

"Ben, what those people did at the mall, what Abram's people did in Washington, how is that any different from what has been happening between Jews and Arabs for a thousand years?"

"I haven't stopped wondering about that, Judy," he said quietly. "But what happens if we do nothing? They've shut off all our other options. All my life I've used the courts, the laws, to find justice. Now they say we can't get into the courthouse. Congressmen, our so-called friends in Congress, won't return phone calls. When the law won't protect us, when the government turns on us, what options do we have? That's what scares me the most. I know there is one thing we absolutely cannot do, Judy. We can't do nothing. We can't simply submit. That's been tried. It didn't work. We can't do that."

He held a fist in the air, smiling.

"Never again. Never again. Right?"

She raised her face, leaned forward and placed her lips gently on his, then circled him with her arms and held him tightly. This time he gave in to his body's need for comfort, his need to touch and be touched. The kiss deepened as they held each other tightly, their bodies merging, pain and comfort flowing from one to the other and back again.

Finally, Katz stepped back. She gave Shapiro a light punch in the chest and walked to her car.

■ ■ ■

Debra Reuben watched through the living room window. *He just lost his wife, his son*, she thought. *How could he do that?* The outrage she tried to summon refused to respond, replaced by another thought. *He's so alone. I just lost my Chaim. I wish somebody could hold me right now, could reassure me that Chaim died for a purpose, that it is going to be better.*

Shapiro returned to the house. Abram Goldhersh placed a huge arm over Shapiro's shoulder and marched him to the living room. Debra and Sarah were sitting on the sofa.

"Can we trust her?" Abram asked. "She knows everything, and until last week, she worked for the government."

"She's a bit confused," Shapiro said. "It might be my fault, or some of it. She might think I led her on about, well, about my feelings. I might even have led myself on, come to think of it. But after what happened to Sally, to Adam . . ." His voice trailed off.

"She's angry and she's frightened," Reuben said. "She told me about her dreams; they're all nightmares. She's in a camp, hair shaved, striped clothes. Did you know her grandparents were in Warsaw? Her father was actually born in the Ghetto during the Uprising. She won't let that happen, not again, she said." She turned to speak directly to Ben Shapiro.

"Ben, don't compliment yourself that it's all about you not sleeping with Judy. She's a Jew. Like the rest of us, she had to decide for herself what that means. She's decided. She'll be all right. We've been doing a lot of talking, Judy and I. Trust me, she's okay. There's a reason each of us is here, including Judy. Including you, Ben. Including you. Just give her a little time."

"A little time is all we have," Abram murmured. "Nonetheless, can we agree to keep an eye on our own federal prosecutor while we decide what to do with our own atomic bomb?"

■ ■ ■

Katz had told them about the data mining capabilities of the National Security Agency. She scared the group so sufficiently that they agreed no telephone calls would be made or answered, not from any phone in the house, not from any cell phone, not even from a pay phone. As Katz described to them, the NSA did not tap individual phone lines. Instead, it monitored every telephone switching center, every location in the country through which every telephone call traveled.

"They have unlimited money behind them," Katz had warned. "The bottom line is that these programs work. I know. We found bad guys based on leads from the NSA—bad guys we had no idea were even bad."

Nonetheless, Shapiro called her cell phone the day after Katz left, worried whether she had arrived safely.

"Where are you calling from, Ben?" she asked. When he told her he was using the Goldberg's phone she immediately hung up.

Her warning forced them to become electronically isolated. No email. No telephone. Not even any Internet browsing. The result was that this group of two men and three women was cut off from all contact with the greater Jewish community. Perhaps their isolation protected them from discovery, but it also left them with an operable nuclear weapon in their possession and nobody but themselves in a position to decide what to do with it.

Days passed. They watched news coverage of emergency evacuations of Akron, then San Diego, after what turned out to be false threats to detonate nuclear bombs. Dozens of people died in those frantic evacuations.

The government tried to calm the nation by reporting extensive efforts to locate the bomb—roadblocks, SWAT team raids on suspected Jewish terrorist cells, airborne radiation monitoring. Those reports may or may not have made the general public feel better. They terrified the four people huddled in the house in Portland.

"It's only a matter of time before they find us," Abram said after dinner one night. They were gathered in front of the tiny television brought down to the living room. CNN murmured in the background. "They'll find us. Judy knows everything. She'll talk, or they'll capture her and make her talk."

The others nodded. They'd discussed this. They all heard the same clock ticking. They all waited for the doors to be knocked down, for the SWAT team to storm the house.

"One phrase keeps running through my head," Abram continued. "One of those 1950s sayings about the Cold War. You know what it is. I'll tell you what it is. *Use it or lose it*. Get it? Use the bomb or lose the bomb. Back then it meant that America had to strike the Russians first because if the Russians hit us first, they'd wipe out our bombers and missiles on the ground.

"I stay awake at night picturing the SWAT team kicking in our doors and them carting off our bomb in a big truck. That's what will happen soon. They'll find it. They have ways. They'll get more and more desperate. They have ways that they'll be willing to use."

No one doubted that.

"Use it or lose it," Abram intoned. "We'd better use what we've got or we won't have it anymore. We may be Israel's last hope. Think about that, will you?"

Reuben nodded in agreement. *Like the Maccabees*, she thought, *Israel's first terrorists, we may be Israel's last defenders. Abram is right; he's so right. What choice do we really have? They killed Chaim. They killed Ben's wife and son. They've locked up Judy's nana. They want to kill us.*

"I hear the same clock ticking," she said. "I agree we can't wait forever. I say we issue a threat, make a demand, do something. Something besides sitting here watching television, for God's sake. At least let's do that much."

"Use it or lose it, Abram?" Shapiro asked, shaking his head in disbelief. "You sound like the Jewish Barry Goldwater, or was he Jewish? Are we going to kill thousands of people because of a slogan?"

Shapiro turned to Debra.

"Tell me, Debbie. Is that the same level of reasoning that went on in that bunker in the desert? Did you and the generals kill a hundred thousand Syrians, Syrians we now know were totally innocent, because you had to use your bomb or you feared you would lose it?"

Her eyes widened as her cheeks were drawn in. They could see Reuben struggling to hold her composure, not to answer his accusation with tears. She struggled, but lost. Instead of crying, Reuben stood and walked quickly from the room. The sound of her pouring something into a glass could be heard, followed by the clunk of ice cubes. Shapiro turned to face Abram.

"Make a threat? And if they call our bluff?" Shapiro asked. "What do we do if they call our bluff?"

Debra Reuben returned to the room, drink in hand.

"What bluff is that, Ben?" she asked.

CHAPTER 61

"**M**r. President, I have some good news, sir," Attorney General Harrison said. "I would like to come right over and show you something."

"Be here in thirty minutes. The Saudi ambassador can cool his heels a bit. I'm getting awfully tired of his pep talks to stand firm about not intervening in the Middle East. Don't give in to the terrorists, he tells me. Don't be intimidated by threats, he says. As if his country's threat to pull the plug on oil isn't intimidation. I don't dare tell him that it isn't his oil that's keeping our troops home. I just don't know that I could persuade our boys and girls to board the planes to fly over there and get blown to pieces by one army or the other. American parents are not in the mood to let their children die defending Jews."

"Yes, sir." Harrison did not know how to respond. The president sounded as if he was badly in need of good news. "I'm on my way as we speak."

Harrison stepped into the Oval Office without a word and placed a large manila folder on the president's desk.

"Cut the guessing games," President Quaid said wearily. "If you have something to show me, then show me, dammit."

"Yes, sir." Harrison removed a set of eight-by-ten photographs. The first photograph showed an attractive young woman wearing short white pants and boat shoes. Her thick Patagonia fleece sweater seemed out of place. She stood on a wooden dock. Dozens of sailboats were behind her, some sailing, most tied to moorings or at anchor.

"Okay, she's a babe," President Quaid said dryly. "Are you engaged? Congratulations. Now get back to work."

"Uh, no, sir, no, I don't know the woman." He glanced at the photo. "Wouldn't mind meeting her. But that's not the point. Sir, this photo was taken six weeks ago. In Maine. Brooklin, Maine. A harbor where a magazine is published. The FBI flooded the area with agents after coming up with suspicious activity, Internet searches, at the local library.

"They can be awfully thorough, the FBI, sir. Turns out that boat magazine runs a boat school. People come for a week and do boat stuff. All very obscure. Not the way I'd want to spend my summer vacation, sir. Seems the agents got a list of everybody who attended the school that summer, then searched for personal websites for each of them. Lots of them had little postings about 'How I Spent My Summer Vacation,' complete with photographs. This photograph was posted on one of those sites, sir."

"Get to the point or send in somebody who can."

"Yes, sir." Harrison placed the photo on the desk. He removed a pen from his jacket pocket and pointed at a sailboat tied to a mooring float. It was to the right of the smiling woman's shining blonde hair. A man and a woman were in a rubber dinghy, rowing away from the boat.

"See that sailboat, sir? The FBI identified it. It's a kind of boat called a Hinckley Bermuda 40 yawl. Expensive boat. Supposed to be pretty nice, if you're into boats." Harrison removed another photo and placed it on the desk. "If you look closely at this photo, sir, you can read the boat's name. It's painted on the back of the boat."

"Why don't you just tell me what it says."

"The boat is named *Swift*, sir. Is that at all familiar, sir?" he asked.

President Quaid drummed his fingers on his desktop.

"Sir, the boat the Coast Guard recovered about thirty miles from where this photo was taken, the boat with the hidden storage compartment, the compartment that screamed of radiation from U-235. That boat was a Hinckley Bermuda 40. It was named *Swift*. This is a photo of the same boat, sir."

"So? We've assumed that before the boat sank, it was able to float, haven't we?"

"Yes, sir. I'll get to the real news."

Harrison placed another photo to the side of the others stretching across Quaid's desk. It was an enlargement of the dinghy. The faces, although somewhat distorted, were recognizable. Harrison pointed his pen at the man rowing the boat.

"That is Lt. Chaim Levi, Israeli Navy lieutenant, sir. The guy we shot in New Hampshire." He placed one final photo on the desk, an enlargement of the woman at the back of the dinghy, facing Levi.

"The FBI identified her, sir. Debra Reuben. The name ring any bells, sir? No? Not for me, either. She used to be a local newscaster, television, in New York City."

The president was clearly interested now.

"She left New York and moved to Israel—Tel Aviv, Israel. She did quite well there, too. Became a well-known television personality for a while, sir."

"And then?"

"And then she joined the government. She was a member of the prime minister's cabinet of the last government to govern the State of Israel. As far as we can tell, sir, if Debra Reuben survived, as she apparently did, she is the most senior living member of the Israeli government. And she was in Maine on the sailboat that carried the bomb. And the strangest thing is she seems to be keeping her presence a secret. Her mother thinks she's traveling around Europe with a new boyfriend. I strongly suspect that if we find Debra Reuben, we'll find that bomb."

"Good work, Harrison. Now go find that terrorist."

■ ■ ■

The trailer park detention camps deteriorated rapidly. And the military was going broke maintaining them. Guantanamo Bay, at its maximum, held 775 enemy combatants. It cost the military $900,000 per year. For *each* detainee. The entire federal prison system held 216,000 people. It cost $7 billion per year. Holding more than 400,000 American Jews, and adding more every day, was an impossible task.

"Mr. President, something—something else—has to be done with these people," General Cruz said at a hastily called cabinet meeting. "We can't continue to hold this many people in giant trailer parks. We can't feed them, and clothe them, and provide medical care for them, for old women, infants, school-age children. Here's a fact for you. I was told to expect thirteen births every day among the people we're holding. This can't continue."

"We're not releasing one of them," President Quaid said. "Who knows what they'd do. Suggestions?"

Attorney General Harrison broke the uncomfortable pause.

"We can do with them what we did with every other criminal group we didn't want. We deported Mexicans, South Americans, Chinese, Africans. Even illegal Irish. Trump deported babies. So deport the Jews. All of them."

The suggestion was met by silence. No objections. Just silence.

"But these are American citizens. How can I deport them? And where would we send them?" President Quaid asked.

"Citizens, yes, but they are enemy combatants, sir. Each and every one of them. You declared them to be enemy combatants and you were fully in your power to do so. Plenty of precedent for making US citizens enemy combatants."

"Don't they still have rights? Wouldn't some judge stop us from deporting them?"

"Can't happen," Harrison said. "Enemy combatants have no right to go to any court in the country. You make somebody an enemy combatant and no judge has jurisdiction to even hear a legal complaint from him. That's the law. It's a pretty slick legal doctrine."

"Where would we deport them to? I'm not turning 400,000 American Jews over to the Palestinians."

Gen. Cruz interrupted. "Had the same problem with Guantanamo. Even when we wanted to release people, we worked our tails off finding countries to take them. Had to twist a lot of arms. Spend a lot of money. But it worked."

Harry Wade, the FEMA head who came up with the trailer scheme, recognized a problem to solve. And he solved it.

"Africa," Wade said. "Between AIDS and Ebola, Africa lost 25 percent of its population. We can send our Jews to Africa. Grease the skids with a few billion dollars to a dozen countries there. Problem solved. The Brits came up with a scheme to relocate their Jews to Uganda a hundred years ago. Too bad they didn't do it. Jews would be running the place by now. Our Jews will probably take over and make their fortunes in Africa."

"Deport America's Jews to Africa," President Quaid said to himself, testing the concept. "It would solve our problem, for sure."

"Lots of problems," Harrison said.

CHAPTER 62

Judy Katz drove her battered green Honda Civic up to the gatehouse at Camp Edwards, wondering if she would be turned around and headed home within minutes. The guard at the camp gate didn't know what to do when she flashed her Massachusetts Board of Bar Overseers registration card and said she was an attorney representing detainees and she intended to meet with her clients.

It took almost an hour for a sergeant in a Humvee to drive up. He told her to park her car in a lot next to the gatehouse, then had her sit in the Humvee's front seat.

Katz spent another forty-five minutes in a wooden chair outside a door marked *Commander*. Eventually, the door opened and a soldier ushered her in. An officer sat behind a wooden desk. Two men stood with their backs against a wall. One wore a uniform, the other jeans and a T-shirt.

"Major Ted Dancer, ma'am. You've thrown us for something of a loop here. Nobody told us you'd be coming down, you see, and, well, as you can imagine, we're not much used to lawyers coming to visit our guests. In fact, you're the first one. It's a total surprise that such a thing could even happen."

He smiled smugly at the young woman sitting demurely, knees together, in front of his desk, like a student called to the principal's office for a chat.

"Save the bullshit for somebody else, Major," she said. "Ted Dancer? You're the same Ted Dancer who was adjutant commander at Guantanamo, right? The same Guantanamo that played host to what, about two hundred lawyers visiting their clients, right? So, get me an escort and a room and take me to my clients. Now, if you please."

"Lieutenant, escort the young lady around, would you please?" he said, then looked Katz directly in the eyes while he continued speaking to the soldier. "Listen to the rules first and make sure she complies. If she doesn't go along with these rules, drive her to the gate."

The man stood at attention and saluted, a smile on his face. The major glanced at a paper on his desk and then spoke to Katz.

"First, you don't get to speak with anybody, no detainees—not until somebody who outranks me tells me that you do. Understand?" he barked at her as if he were her drill instructor. He guessed correctly that she'd never done time in uniform, at least not since Girl Scouts.

"Next, we'll give you a drive around so you can see that people are being cared for humanely. We'll show you the dining hall, a barracks, the recreation area. You can look into the school, hell, sit in on a class if you want. We're treating these people pretty damn good if you ask me. I don't mind showing that off a bit.

"Finally, we've got a high-security section, Camp Echo. Troublemakers in every group of people, you know. You won't be going anywhere near there. Now, if you agree with all that, we'll give you the tour. If you don't agree, we'll show you the gate. Your choice, ma'am. What'll it be?"

Katz realized she had no bargaining chips. She did what lawyers do reflexively.

"I'll go to court," she said. "I'll get an order from a judge ordering you to let me meet with my clients."

"I'm sure you will, ma'am," Maj. Dancer replied, confident that for today, at least, he held all the cards. "And when you do, I'll do whatever I am ordered to do. But for today, what's your choice? My way or the gate?"

She knew she'd lost this round. Katz stood, hoisted her briefcase strap on one shoulder, her laptop strap on the other.

"Let's start the tour, for today," she said.

The uniformed man sprang from standing at attention and raced for the office door, holding it open for her. Before she could leave the office, however, the other man, the one in jeans, cleared his throat loudly.

"Major, what we discussed?" he said.

"Right. Forgot," Maj. Dancer said. Looking at Katz, he said, "Ma'am, no electronic devices, cell phones, cameras, cell phones with cameras, tape recorders or"—he looked at the black nylon bag with Katz's laptop computer—"computers. Security, you know. Captain Howard here will take all that from you for safekeeping." He nodded to the man in jeans. "And of course you'll be searched, thoroughly. We'll try to find a female to do the search, if we can."

Katz looked at the man skeptically, then handed over her computer and, reaching in her briefcase, extracted a cell phone.

"Want to check my shoes for hidden cameras?" she asked the man.

"Already did, ma'am, already did. Passed with flying colors," he said with a grin. He reached for her bag and phone and took them from her. Katz and the uniformed soldier left the room.

"Good thinking there," Major Dancer said to the man after the door closed. "You Echoes do have your tricks, don't you? So what's your plan for that?"

"First thing, I'll do a mirror image of the hard drive," he said. "Whatever's on the computer will be captured in the image. Then I'll download the memory from the phone. Should give us every number she's dialed and every number that called her, at least in the last few months—depends on how much memory the phone has."

"Nothing like having a good lawyer around," Maj. Dancer laughed. "And a good interrogator, too, I suppose. Take care of her things, now."

The interrogator carried Katz's phone and computer to the Echo office, located behind the internal razor wire enclosure at Camp Echo. He linked Katz's laptop to a powerful HP server and started the mirroring of her hard drive, creating an identical copy of every keystroke on the laptop.

Just as he was finishing, and before he could work on her cell phone, the telephone on his desk rang.

"Echo office," he said tersely.

"Lieutenant Williams here, sir," the voice on the phone said. "Major Dancer said I should let you know. This lawyer woman. Seems like she's had enough. She's pretty pissed at being given the celebrity tour. She's pulling the plug. Wants her stuff back. Major said to get it all back to HQ now, sir."

"Thanks for the call. Tell the major I'm on my way."

The interrogator disconnected the cable from the laptop to the server, checking to make sure the download had completed. Before shutting the power off on Katz's computer, however, he walked to the office door and looked down the empty hallway.

Returning to the desk, he pressed the keyboard button marked *Eject* on the laptop and waited for the compact disc drive door to open and the disc carrier to slowly slide out.

The man then walked to a rust-colored canvas barn jacket hanging from a peg on the wall. He reached into one of the pockets and withdrew an unmarked, gold-colored compact disc, which he placed carefully on the disc carrier on Katz's computer. He pressed the *Eject* button once again and watched as the carrier withdrew into the computer, taking the CD with it.

CHAPTER 63

"That's me. Oh my God, that's my picture. Turn up the sound," Debra Reuben shrieked, pointing at the small television.

Shapiro was closest and jabbed at the volume button.

"Debra Reuben," the voice on the television said, "the highest-ranking surviving member of the Israeli government, is believed to have secretly entered the United States more than a month ago and conducted a covert rendezvous with the special forces team that smuggled an Israeli nuclear bomb into this country.

"President Quaid directed Attorney General Harrison to spare no effort to locate Reuben. The FBI announced that capturing Debra Reuben shares top priority with its efforts to locate the Israeli nuclear weapon. Hundreds of agents were reassigned to locating the woman. Find Reuben and you'll find the bomb, President Quaid is reported to have told the attorney general."

The television image shifted to a bullet-riddled windshield of an automobile, a man slumped forward against the steering wheel.

"Reuben is believed to have met along the coast of Maine with Lt. Chaim Levi, the Israeli special forces genius who captained the stolen sailing vessel used to sneak the bomb past a Coast Guard cordon. Levi was shot dead by police while attempting to run a security roadblock in New Hampshire."

"Turn that thing off," Reuben screamed. "I can't look at that picture of Chaim."

Nobody spoke.

Sarah rose from her chair and stood behind Reuben, bending forward to place her arms around the immobile woman.

"I'm so sorry, Debbie," Sarah said. "For everything, for Chaim, and now that they have that picture of you."

Sarah looked at the others, still seated around the table.

"Well?" she asked.

"Debra, you can't go outside, not at all. Is that understood?" Shapiro was frightened. The FBI was looking for her, now, in addition to him.

All eyes focused on Abram Goldhersh. He sat, shaking his head.

"Use it or lose, that's all I have to say. We use it or we lose it, damn soon, too. They're closing in on us." He walked to the living room.

Sarah followed her husband out of the kitchen. She stopped in the doorway.

"We need to talk. Talk more. Talk enough to reach a decision," she said. "My husband, in his own stubborn way, makes a convincing argument."

Shapiro and Reuben sat on either end of the living room sofa, Sarah on the recliner. Abram Goldhersh stood, facing the others. He spoke as if he were delivering a lecture.

"I say the time has come. We either dump the thing in the ocean, which in my mind would be a sin, a sin to God, a betrayal of Israel and of every Jew on the face of the planet, but that's my opinion."

"In your humble opinion, that is," Shapiro interrupted. "Sorry. Go on, Abram."

"We either dump it in the ocean or we use it in whatever way we all decide is best for the Jewish people. That's what I say. No more waiting. That time has ended."

"Can't we threaten to use it, Abram? We don't really want to kill people, do we?" Sarah said, sadness in her voice. "I say we threaten to use it unless the United States frees Israel, or . . . or something."

"That's a little vague, Sarah," Reuben said. "I think we need to make a specific demand, something they can do right away and then, well, we'll make another demand, and then another."

"This is a bomb, Debra," Shapiro said, "not a magic wand. We'll be lucky if this works once. I'm skeptical that Quaid will give in to a threat, even a real one like this. I think the man has lost his sense of reality. There's something missing from him."

"Yeah, like a sense of right and wrong," Sarah said. "And to believe I voted for the man."

The debate dragged on past midnight. Eventually, though, a consensus was reached. Something had to be done, but they would not use the bomb without fair warning.

They would make a demand first that would be most likely to persuade the United States to support the reestablishment of the State of Israel.

They argued about the demand until they reached agreement. Next, they discussed how to deliver their demand. Their decision on that was to use the simplest method.

"We mail a letter to the president. Mail it from far away. Wear gloves when we touch anything. Remember after 9/11 there were all those anthrax letters? They never found out who mailed them. They can't trace mail."

"My cousin Maurice, in Seattle. He can drop it in a mailbox," Abram said.

"We'll send it to him by FedEx. Now, what do we say in the letter?"

The final version of the note, printed in block letters on the elderly HP 1200 laser printer attached to Abram's computer, was simple and straightforward.

We are the people who have the bomb. This is a real threat. You will close every camp. Every person will be released by noon Friday. There will be no repercussions against any person held at the camps. You hold almost 500,000 innocent Jews. That is the population of St. Louis. If you do not comply with this demand, St. Louis will be destroyed by midnight Friday.

How do you know we are telling the truth? The name of the sailboat that brought the bomb into this country was Swift. *You kept it secret for a reason. This is the reason.*

■ ■ ■

President Quaid gripped the plastic-wrapped sheet of paper in his hand, holding it away from his chest as if the paper itself were radioactive rather than just its message.

"Do we know this is the real thing?" he asked, looking around the table at the same team that met after Levi's death. The president knew this group would not have been called together if the FBI had any doubt about the authenticity of the letter.

"We purposely kept the name of the sailboat confidential," Attorney General Harrison said. "I hadn't realized before, but it's standard operating procedure to keep secret information that only a perpetrator would know. To tell you the truth, sir, even I didn't know the name of the boat until I saw those photographs. I doubt if you did either, sir."

"It never mattered to me," President Quaid said. He scratched at his forehead. People around the table looked aside. The falling hair was noticeable. Even more than the falling hair, the dark rings under his eyes evidenced the sleepless, lonely nights he'd been suffering for weeks.

"Where do we go from here?" He looked around the table, daring somebody to speak.

"As I see it, sir, we have two choices," General Paterson said. "We either give them what they want, set everybody loose, or we evacuate St. Louis and try our damnedest to catch them."

"NO FUCKING WAY." The president's shout stunned every person sitting at the long table.

Carol Cabot turned and whispered in Quaid's ear, patting his left hand gently. She gestured to an aide standing against the wall. The young man poured a glass of water and placed it in front of the president. Cabot again whispered to him and he obediently sipped the water.

"Sorry about that," President Quaid said. "Let me make something clear. I don't give in to threats. Never have. Never will. We will not give these people what they want. I don't want to hear one more word about giving in. Won't happen. Is that clear to everybody here? Damned Israelis never negotiated with terrorists. We won't either."

He looked around the table and was met with grim nods.

"Number two, we will not evacuate St. Louis. There have been enough evacuations already. Makes us look weak, turning and running away every time somebody threatens to pop us one in the nose. Americans don't run. We fight. No more running. So, where does that leave us? I'll entertain suggestions."

Quaid sat back in his chair and turned his head briefly to look at Carol Cabot. She stared at him in admiration and clapped her hands lightly together.

"Well, sir, we can keep them out of St. Louis, for a while at least," Gen. Cruz, chairman of the Joint Chiefs of Staff said. "We can ring the city with troops so tight that a snail couldn't crawl through. We can provide enough air cover that no plane will get anywhere near the city. We can keep that up for as long as you say so, sir, for what it's worth. But you know, sir, there would be nothing to stop them from sending another note, this time for Philadelphia or Detroit. We can only button down so many cities, sir."

"I understand that, General," Quaid said, not especially pleased with the response he'd received. "Make it happen. I want nothing to get into that city that we don't want in, on the ground, in the air or on water. St. Louis is on the water, isn't it?"

"The Mississippi River, Mr. President," Harrison said.

"I know that, Harrison. Keep the damned boats away, too."

He looked around the table.

"Am I understood?"

Without a word, everybody nodded.

"We need to teach these people a lesson. As you said, General, they can do this again and again. We've got to give them a reason not to do that."

He turned to Attorney General Harrison sitting directly across from him.

"You seem to know all about St. Louis. I assume there are Jews living there, right?"

"I assume so sir," he said. "I'm under the impression there are Jews pretty much everywhere in the country, sir."

"I share that assumption," Quid said. "Okay. Arrest them— every damned one of them. Take them to a camp. Today. I want it done today. They give us another letter about another city, we'll lock those Jews up, too. It shouldn't take long for them to get our point, now should it?"

Again, he glared around the room.

"Any questions?" Nobody responded.

As people began to rise from their chairs, Quaid said, "Harrison. One last thing. When you ship them south, no buses, no fucking Greyhounds. Send them by train. In freight cars."

CHAPTER 64

The roundup of the 60,000 Jews living in St. Louis did not go smoothly. President Quaid's insistence that it begin immediately limited the advance planning. Warnings about soldiers arresting Jews spread instantly over the Internet and cell phones, triggering a mass exodus from the city before roadblocks could be fully set up or airports, bus and train stations shut down.

Television news and website videos showed Americans who looked as ordinary as everyone's neighbors being placed in trucks and buses, to be driven to train stations. Breathless broadcasts showed cars being checked at roadblocks, and the occasional attempt to speed away stopped by hails of bullets.

The four people huddling in the house in Portland were despondent. They sat in the living room, Abram punching at the TV to switch from one news report to another, searching for some word of the carefully written demand letter and the reasons for the government's actions.

Finally, he threw the remote across the room and turned to face the others.

"So much for demands," he said. "I've said it before. I'll say it one more time. Use it or lose it. I'm not ready to lose it. God gave us this thing for a reason. The time has come."

Suddenly, there was pounding at the front door and a muffled voice shouting, "Let me in, let me in."

Sarah screamed. Debra Reuben rose and stared toward the front door, ready to meet whatever was on the other side. Ready to accept whatever punishment was coming to her.

Only Shapiro reacted quickly. He ran to the door, checked to make sure it was locked, then stepped to the side to look through a window to see who was outside. He threw the door open.

A hysterical Judy Katz ran in, babbling.

"I've never driven so fast in my life but I was afraid the police would stop me and that couldn't happen because you have to see this you just have to see it." The words shot from her mouth with no spaces between them.

Shapiro put his hands on her shoulders and shook her.

"Judy, stop it," he said. "What happened? Tell us what happened."

She walked into the living room and dropped the black nylon carrying case for her laptop on the coffee table.

"You have to see this," she said. "Somebody, somebody at the camp must have put it in my computer. Here, look. It's horrible."

She removed the computer from the case as she spoke, lifted the screen and pressed the power button.

"I went to the camp," she said. "I didn't see much, but when I got home I was so angry. I took a shower. Searched the fridge. Then sat at the table to check email. When I turned on the computer, there was an icon on the screen that said *Untitled CD*. I hadn't put any CD in the computer. I hardly use that drive. So I clicked on it and, and, this happened."

She slid her forefinger around the mouse pad and tapped twice. A video began to play.

It was shot from above, looking down onto a desk. A young woman lay on top of a board on the desk, wrapped like a mummy in gray tape. An older woman in a white coat stood at the young woman's head. Three men, two in uniform, stood around the desk.

Katz pointed at the third man, wearing jeans, who stood at the young woman's feet.

"I saw him at the camp," she said. "He took my computer. I wasn't allowed to carry it there. I think he put the disc in it."

She glanced at the screen, then turned away.

"I've seen it twice," she said. "I can't look again.

The sound was fuzzy, but the words could be made out.

The brief video ended with the young woman's body being carried from the room. The man in civilian clothes was left alone. The last scene showed him glance up at the camera, then walk quickly from the room.

Katz closed the lid on the laptop computer.

"*Mengele*," Abram whispered, as if speaking to himself. "*Mengele*."

Katz's face was white, her eyes wide, darting to her computer. "You . . . you don't think this doctor is doing experiments, do you?" she stuttered.

"No, not experiments. Interrogation," Shapiro said coldly.

Abram pounded his hand against the wall to get their attention.

"Enough. How much more do we have to see? Did you hear the question that woman, that Mengele asked?" Abram's voice was strained, his throat tight. "She asked about the bomb, the bomb that God put in our hands. They'll do anything until they find it. I tell you, use it or lose it."

"God didn't give you that bomb," Reuben retorted. "I did. I got that thing out of the desert. I found a boat to take it to Spain. Chaim and I brought it here. Chaim gave his life to bring that thing here. It was Chaim, not God, who brought that bomb to this country."

"God directed him," Abram said calmly. "It was God's will that it come here. How could it have happened if it were not

God's will?"

Abram looked at the others.

"The Arabs used their bomb. It worked. They won. They wiped away Israel and its people. Now we use our bomb to save what's left of our people. It will work. Quaid will have to give in. He doesn't know how many bombs we have. Simple."

"Enough talk," Shapiro interrupted. "We have to make a decision. I've thought about this long and hard. I've come to my peace. Here's what I think. America should be ashamed of itself. This was a great country. They said they wanted to make America great again, but it only got worse."

"Much worse," Reuben mumbled.

"America is far from great now," Shapiro said. "Not today. Not with what is happening here; in fact, not for a long while now. America once held itself out an example to the world. Now what are we an example of? We've lost our way. Just like the Roman Empire. Just like the British Empire. Just like every great power in history. America's time has passed."

He paused, the enormity of what he'd said striking him momentarily speechless.

"There is a right course for America to take and a wrong course. Standing by and watching Israel die is wrong. Standing up to intimidation, saving people herded into concentration camps, reestablishing the State of Israel as a Jewish homeland, those are the right things to do. I'm ready to send a message to America that there is a price to pay for doing nothing in the face of injustice. I'm with Abram. We use it or we lose it."

He'd risen to his feet, an old habit of a trial lawyer who never addressed a judge and certainly never addressed a jury while seated.

"Debra," he said. "You brought us this thing. What do you think?"

"I already had to make this decision once. Damascus. It's the same decision. Why should it be more difficult to kill innocent Americans than it was to kill innocent Syrians?

They're all human beings."

"And they're all innocent," Sarah interjected.

"They're all innocent, I agree," Reuben said. "I say we use the bomb. Harry Truman dropped two bombs. You don't burn longer in hell for a second bomb, do you?"

"We gave them a choice," Sarah said. "They could have released the people; they could have done that. What would be the harm from setting innocent people free? I don't understand them. I hate it. I absolutely hate it, but I understand why we have no choice now. I agree."

She turned to her husband. "We all know what your position is, Abram."

"Use it or lose it, and teach that Quaid a lesson."

Katz leaped to her feet and ran from the room, her feet pounding on the stairs up to her room.

"I'll talk with her," Reuben said. She followed Katz up the stairs.

Abram looked at the stairs, then back to the others.

"Let's make plans," he said.

■ ■ ■

Not even Reuben knew much about the workings of the bomb. None of them had any idea how powerful it was, except that it was atomic. They assumed, since it was designed to be carried by a person rather than placed on top of a missile or dropped from an aircraft, that it was a relatively small atomic bomb.

But that was like confronting a small elephant. You wouldn't want it to sit on your lap.

Reuben went to her room and came back with a Chemical Bank of New York Visa credit card. She passed it around to the people sitting at the kitchen table. Katz had joined them.

"Are you going to do some shopping before we start World War III, Debbie?" Katz asked.

Reuben explained how the card was used to arm the detonator. She had debated with herself whether to disclose the arming code to be punched into the bomb's keypad after the card was read. She decided these were the only people she could trust. Besides, should something happen to her before she gave them the password, the bomb would be useless to them.

"It's *0-9-1-1*," she said to their shocked faces.

"That is so inappropriate, Debbie," Katz said.

"It seemed like a good idea at the time," Reuben said. "Remember, when we set the code I expected that America was going to be Israel's savior. Back then—God, it seems so long ago—back then the Arabs were the only bad guys. Besides, I thought it would be an easy number to remember."

She explained how the detonator could be set for a time delay anywhere from instantaneous to twenty-four hours. That left them considerable discretion in their planning.

Their first decision was the target. Sarah made a tentative proposal.

"Look," she said. "They can't be sure how many bombs we have. What if we put it in a boat and set it off on the ocean, close enough so they can see it from shore but far enough so nobody gets hurt. Don't you think that would scare them enough to change their minds about Israel, or at least about closing those damned camps?"

"Quaid hasn't shown any interest in giving in to our threats," Shapiro said. "Besides, I don't think they have any doubts about whether we have a bomb. It isn't like this is a secret from them and we have to convince them that we can do what we threaten to do. Besides, this is the only bomb we've got. To paraphrase Abram, once we use it, we lose it."

"I know all that, Ben," Sarah said softly. "I'm struggling with this. I thought I could try something that didn't involve killing people."

"I love you for your gentleness," Abram said. "But sometimes killing people is what it takes to change minds. Terror is all about killing people. As you've heard me say enough times to make you sick, terror works. Always has. Always will.

"You'll see. We'll use this bomb and things will change. Americans won't have the stomach for what we will be feeding them. With that thought in mind, let me say out loud what we all know is the only logical target. Washington. That's where Quaid is. That's where Congress is."

"I was waiting for you to say that," Shapiro said. "I suppose the other reason for choosing Washington is that it is a relatively small city, at least compared to, say, New York or LA. If what we have is a small bomb, we'd do better picking a smaller target. DC has my vote. What about the rest of you?"

Reuben raised her hand, as if waiting to be called on in class.

"Washington will be the hardest city to get the bomb into," Reuben said. "Don't you think they'll know that would be our first target? Don't you think the roads are filled with those detectors that find radiation. And whatever else they have. They were able to find Chaim with just a pair of radioactive gloves in his car. I'm afraid they'll find us if we try to drive into Washington with the bomb."

"I agree that the roads are too dangerous," Abram said. "But what about a boat? There's a river there, the Potomac."

"River won't work," Shapiro said. "It's not like what Debra and Chaim did, smuggling something into a 2,000-mile-long coast filled with coves and harbors. The Coast Guard will have the Potomac bottled up tight. We wouldn't be able to get in with even a kayak, and don't think I didn't consider that."

They sat glumly in the living room, each holding his and her own thoughts.

"Aren't you some sort of a pilot, Ben?" Katz finally asked. "Didn't you say something about your airplane when we were driving down to DC?"

Abram looked at Shapiro in astonishment. Suddenly angry.

"You're a pilot, Ben, and you own an airplane and you never told us? I have trouble understanding that, Ben," Goldhersh said.

"Hold on, Abram, calm down," Shapiro said quickly. "Do you know what a sailplane is?"

"An airplane with sails on it?" he replied. "No, I never heard of such a thing."

"How about a glider," Shapiro asked. "Do you know about gliders?"

"You mean a plane with no engine? I've heard about them. Never seen one," he said. "Do they still have them? I thought that was something they used to invade Normandy on D-Day. Why, is that the kind of pilot you are?"

Shapiro reached into his back pocket and removed his wallet. He shuffled through his credit cards, his driver's license and his Massachusetts Board of Bar Overseers lawyer's registration card. Finally, he removed a dog-eared rectangle of white paper.

"Here it is," he said, showing it to the others. The paper, the size of a credit card, said Federal Aviation Administration across the top. Below that was printed *Private Pilot's License*, then Shapiro's name and a set of numbers. Prominently printed under the heading *Restrictions* were the words *aero tow only*.

"That's my glider pilot's license," he said. "And I happen to own one of the best gliders in the world, but like just about all other gliders, the only way to get it off the ground is to pull it up with a rope tied to a plane that has an engine."

"So what does this glider look like?" Abram asked. "Wings and a tail and stuff like a real plane?"

"Just like a real plane, Abram," Shapiro said. "Only much sleeker. If things were different, I'd be pleased to strap you into the rear seat and take you around for a few hours."

Goldhersh rose from the table and walked away from the others, pacing back and forth.

"Ben, this glider, you say it has a back seat?"

"Yes."

"Big enough to hold the bomb?" Abram asked.

Shapiro considered for a moment. "Debra, how much does that thing weigh?"

"I don't know, Ben," she answered. "But Sarah and I were able to carry it from the basement out to her car."

"I can put two hundred pounds in that seat with no problem," Shapiro said. "Let me think for a minute."

Shapiro left the table and went into the living room. He returned several minutes later carrying a National Geographic atlas. It was opened to a map of Maryland.

"This could work," he said.

Shapiro lectured about gliders. They had long, thin wings that generated tremendous amounts of lift, he said, enough to allow the planes to fly in tight circles within thermals—rising columns of warm air that went thousands of feet into the air.

But the best soaring, he told them, came along mountain ridges where prevailing winds hit the face of a ridge and were deflected upwards.

"You can ride a ridge for hundreds of miles, one wingtip just a few feet out from the trees, flying in lift the entire way," he told them. "I'd lock into rising air and fly for hours." His mind drifted as easily as his sailplane traveled from cloud to cloud. His days of hopping into the glider to shed stress from time in court seemed like another life. *They were another life*, he realized with a jolt. *My life with a family, with a wife, with the best kid in the world.*

The reality struck Shapiro that he was not planning a personal-best cross-country flight. He was going on a bombing mission. And while nobody came out and said it, it was a one-way mission.

Shapiro needed time alone. He told the others he wanted to access the Internet. They argued about that for a while but then consented after he said he would be looking only at gliding websites and would stay away from anything suspicious. He used Goldhersh's computer, located in the enlarged closet space he called his office.

It took Shapiro less than an hour to become confident he could do what he proposed. The first problem was finding a place where he could get his glider towed into the air. That meant either a commercial glider field or a club. It was common for pilots to show up with gliders in their specially designed trailers. Many glider clubs supported themselves on the tow charges visiting pilots paid.

The countryside north and west of Washington provided some of the best soaring east of the Rockies. Long lines of ridges stretched from central Pennsylvania almost to the Florida border. Record-distance flights followed that route, which took the planes a few dozen miles from Washington.

"One record flight of almost nine hundred miles has stood since 1994," Shapiro said after he returned to the living room to speak with the anxious people waiting there. "He left from Pennsylvania and flew almost to Florida. And that was in a much smaller plane than my beauty."

Shapiro reported that he'd found a glider field about sixty miles west of Washington. He could launch from there.

"Sixty miles in an airplane without an engine?" Sarah asked. "Is that really possible?"

Shapiro laughed.

"Sixty miles is a training flight," he said. "I do that before breakfast. Speaking of which, we've been at this all night. Let's go to bed and sleep on this decision. We need to have another long, serious talk. We'll talk over breakfast."

The others went up to bed, leaving Shapiro in the living room for another night on the sofa.

Shapiro was surprised to see Katz sitting on the sofa when he returned from the bathroom. He sat next to her.

"Ben, are we doing the right thing? Is it even a sane thing?" she asked, keeping her voice down so none of the others, upstairs, could hear. "Everything happened so fast. It seems out of control. I can't believe what we're talking about doing. How do you feel about it?"

He took both her hands in his. They were ice cold. He lifted his right arm and invited her to snuggle against him, lifting the blanket from the sofa to cover both of them. She rested her head on his shoulder. He inhaled the clean fragrance of her hair.

"Judy, that's why I went into the other room. I knew all about flying in Pennsylvania and Maryland. I've gone there on glider vacations. It really is the best gliding around. I needed some space to think, that's why I went away for a bit." She snuggled closer to him.

The two sat quietly, immersed in their thoughts and fears but relishing the comfort of each other. Shapiro pulled her closer; her body felt warm and he began to stir. But a chill quickly overcame him—a chill from fear. A chill from knowing that his future was likely to be short; a chill at the loss of his wife and child. He wondered whether his determination to go through with the plan would survive the night.

"Ben," she whispered. "Do you mind if I stay here tonight? We can just cuddle if that's all you want. I'd rather not be alone."

He hesitated, sorting his thoughts. Since learning of his wife's death, he had not so much as looked at Katz with the admiring eyes he'd devoured her with from the first time they met for lunch. It felt more like cheating to be holding her now, so soon after Sally's death, than it would have seemed when they were on the brink of a divorce.

On the other hand, I don't know how many nights I have left, he thought.

As he was about to let his body win its struggle with his mind, he heard the first of a series of tiny snores on his shoulder. He did not move until his right arm was entirely numb. Then he slipped it from under her head carefully, slowly, so as not to wake her. He lowered her gently onto the sofa and covered her with the blanket.

Shapiro slept on the floor next to the sofa, his hand resting on her hand where it dangled from the couch.

■ ■ ■

They refined the plan in the morning. They had considered taking two cars—one to drive the bomb to Maryland, Shapiro towing the glider with the other. In the end, they decided that only doubled the chances of getting caught.

Shapiro would drive from Maine to Plymouth, Massachusetts, to retrieve his sailplane. Abram's Nissan Pathfinder could tow the glider trailer. Shapiro would return to Portland where he'd back the trailer into the Goldberg-Goldhershes' driveway. After dark, they'd retrieve the bomb from the pool and strap it into the plane's rear seat.

Reuben would drill him in how to work the bomb's detonator and, if she had the nerve, would take him through a dry run arming and disarming the device. Then he would say goodbye and get on the road, driving straight through to Maryland. They plotted a route that avoided all cities, keeping him entirely on secondary roads.

They debated whether to issue a warning.

"No, they had their chance," Abram barked. "We warn them, and Quaid escapes. Would you have warned Hitler?"

Katz filled a paper shopping bag with enough sandwiches, apples, and granola bars to feed Shapiro for a week. She smiled when he walked into the kitchen. They did not discuss what had happened, or not happened, the previous night.

The drive from Portland to Plymouth was the least risky leg for Shapiro. Nonetheless, he stayed off the interstates, doubling his travel time. It was late afternoon when he pulled into the familiar grounds of the Plymouth Soaring Society, parking next to the hanger where the towplane was stored.

His glider was where he'd left it, inside the enclosed trailer, its wings removed and resting in padded cradles on either side of the fuselage. The plane's tail extended through the covered slot in the trailer roof.

Shapiro hoped to hitch the Nissan to the trailer and depart without seeing anyone. He'd finished attaching the safety chains from the trailer to the Pathfinder's towing hitch when he heard his name called out.

"Willy, you dog," Shapiro said. "How ya doin', buddy?"

"I'm doing fine," the tow pilot said. "Haven't seen you in weeks. I thought maybe you'd took up golf or something."

Willy looked around Shapiro's shoulder at the trailer attached to the Pathfinder SUV.

"Leaving us for good, or going on vacation?" he asked.

"I'd never leave you, Willy," Shapiro said, smiling. "No, I've been working my butt off. Finally finished up and thought I'd head up to Sugarbush for a week. I'll send you a postcard."

"Yeah, sure, I'll look out for it," Willy replied. "And the box of chocolates." The old tow pilot looked at Shapiro strangely. The humor left his voice as he spoke quietly, almost in a whisper. "Ben, we go back a ways. I gotta tell you this. There were some guys asking about you. FBI, they said. Just routine, they said. I didn't tell 'em squat, Ben. But I thought you should know."

Shapiro placed an arm on his friend's shoulder. "Thanks for the news, Willy," he said. "I appreciate it, and I appreciate all you've done for me over the years."

The return drive to Portland was as slow as the drive down to Plymouth, again avoiding highways. It was close to midnight when Shapiro backed the glider trailer up the driveway. He locked the SUV and walked into the darkened house, careful not to wake anyone.

Shapiro half expected—half hoped—that Judy would be on the sofa when he arrived. It was empty. He was so tired from the drive he simply lay down fully clothed. He was asleep within minutes.

His last waking thought was to wonder how many nights he had left.

CHAPTER 65

President Quaid was surprised when the door to his bedroom slowly opened. The reading light on the headboard of the presidential bed was on, but the novel he had tried to read lay facedown on the blanket. Quaid was on top of the blanket, staring up at the ceiling, eyes wide open, legs spread, arms out at his sides.

"Are we making snow angels?" a familiar voice said. Quaid, startled, turned his head. His wife stood in the open doorway. A black negligee was visible beneath her white terry bathrobe.

"Come in, come in." Quaid's legs came together. He pushed himself to a sitting position and smiled. "You haven't been in this room in months, Catherine. What's the occasion?"

He smiled again, his campaign smile this time—the 600-watt smile he flashed when he wanted to move the masses.

She sat in a lotus position, legs crossed, facing her husband. They looked at one another, each waiting for the other to speak.

Damn, she looks good, Quaid thought. *The woman never ages.* He recalled their private joke about Catherine having a portrait of herself locked in a closet, a portrait that aged rather than she. *She's doing better than I am.* He scratched unconsciously at the top of his head, knowing that with each scratch more hairs fell out. The inside of his cheeks were raw from his constant chewing.

Finally, Catherine reached out for her husband's hand and sandwiched it between hers.

"Lawrence, this has to stop," she said.

"This. What do you mean by *this*?" he asked.

"This, everything, all that you are doing, Lawrence." Her voice was choked. She struggled for control. "The camps, Lawrence. You're locking Americans into concentration camps. The identification cards. Lawrence, this has to stop.

"The violence, Lawrence. It just breeds more violence. Didn't the Israelis learn that lesson? Bombs and retaliation didn't cure anything; they just led to bigger bombs and more retaliation. That will happen here, Lawrence. That's what you are inviting into this country. Bigger bombs. More retaliation. The man I love, who I still love, that man knows what is right and what is wrong. Lawrence, all this, what you are doing, it's wrong. So wrong."

"Goddamn it, Catherine." Each word was louder than the one before. "I don't need some Jiminy Cricket conscience. I need a wife who supports me. Your job is to back me up. I need you to do your goddamn job right now. That's what I need, Catherine.

"This country is under attack. Foreign soldiers. And Americans. I've got six million so-called Americans who chose sides, chose sides against the rest of us. They made their decision. I made mine. I'll lock every damn Jew up if they make me do it, by God I will."

Catherine uncoiled her legs and swung them off the bed. She stood facing her husband, pulling her robe tightly around her. She'd struggled all day about how to approach her husband. Evidently, she'd failed.

"Some people won't stand for this, Lawrence," she said calmly. "I won't stand for this."

He sat in the bed, saying nothing.

"You know, Lawrence, I was going to give a speech at that march asking people to understand you, to support you, asking them to appeal to the good and kind man I married. That speech is in the trash now, Lawrence. Wait until you hear the new speech. Because you know what, Lawrence, you know what?" Her voice rose to match her husband's.

"What?" he responded, his anger at this woman mixing with the desire he still felt for her, had felt every day of his presidency, and well before. "Tell me what."

"When you hear my new speech, Lawrence, you are going to be so, so pissed."

She turned quickly. If she'd been wearing a long dress rather than a terry bathrobe, the dress would have swirled in a circle around her. She walked from the presidential bedroom, leaving the door open.

■ ■ ■

The next morning, President Quaid summoned Carol Cabot to the family dining room, where he sat at a table picking at an omelet. He barely turned his head to acknowledge her.

"Carol, the First Lady is ill, or tired, or something," he said without looking at the woman. "She should go to Camp David, to rest. Seclusion. She needs seclusion." He paused for a few seconds. "She may not agree, but make sure she goes anyway."

Cabot wrestled against the tiny facial muscles that struggled to lift the ends of her mouth into a smile.

"I understand, sir," she said. "When should she leave?"

Quaid sat back in the chair, pulled it closer to the table, lifted his coffee cup and sipped, then replaced it gently on the table. "Right away, Carol," he said. "This morning. Make it happen."

An hour later, Quaid heard the sound of Marine One, the huge presidential helicopter, landing on the South Lawn. He walked to the window and watched as Catherine Quaid marched across the grass to the waiting machine, surrounded by what looked like an honor guard of six Secret Service agents. She walked up the steps into the helicopter.

The president stared at his wife. Suddenly, he noticed an object on her arm.

He balled his right hand into a fist, drew back his arm and punched with all his weight straight at the center of the window, then screamed in pain. Not even a rifle bullet traveling at supersonic speed could pierce that glass.

Cradling his hand, blood starting to ooze from the bruised and torn knuckles, he muttered softly, "That bitch, that fucking ungrateful bitch."

He looked out the window one final time and saw Catherine at the top of the steps. She turned and waved to the perpetual crowd of tourists that clung to the far side of the iron fence surrounding the White House, snapping photos.

Those tourists with the sharpest eyesight or longest telephoto camera lenses saw a yellow, six-pointed star pinned to her left sleeve.

CHAPTER 66

Ben and Abram rose before dawn. Wearing bathing suits, they jumped into the chilly pool and pulled themselves around the edge of the water to the deep end. Shapiro took a breath, then dove to the bottom. The bomb was surprisingly light in the water.

They carried the bomb to the glider, still inside its enclosed trailer, hitched to the Pathfinder. It settled into the plane's rear seat. Shapiro buckled the five-point safety harness around the cylinder, snugging it into place.

Goldhersh ran to the garage, saying over his shoulder that he had a surprise for Shapiro. He came back staggering under a weight that was heavy even for him, carrying what appeared to be small, vinyl-covered blankets.

"My cousin Herman," Abram said as he dropped the blankets on the ground with a thud. "He's in the dental supply business. I thought of these."

He lifted one blanket from the pile and handed it to Shapiro, who bent his knees under the surprising weight.

"For when you get X-rays," Abram said. "You know, they go over your lap so you don't fry your balls with the radiation. I told

Herman not to ask any questions. He said to make sure he got them back. Guess I'll have to write him a check."

They draped the heavy blankets around the bomb, covering it as best they could.

"Maybe that will help hide the radiation," Abram said to Shapiro. "I figured it couldn't hurt."

The men went inside to join the others, gathered around the kitchen table, their morning ritual. Sarah puttered at the stove, serving coffee, carrying fruit and cereal to the table. Abram Goldhersh was fidgety as a ten-year-old the morning he was to pitch his first Little League game. He sat. He jumped from his chair to look out the window. He sat and shoveled Cheerios from his bowl into his mouth.

"I was up all night," he said, speaking to Shapiro. "I decided. I'm going with you."

"We went through this, Abram. No."

Sarah opened her mouth. Her husband silenced her with a stare. He spoke to Ben.

"I went through everything in my mind, every step. Tell me, can you put the wings on your plane by yourself?"

Shapiro opened his mouth to speak, then stopped. There had always been somebody to help put the plane together—a tow pilot, another glider pilot. There wasn't much involved in getting the plane ready for flight, just mounting the wings and the tail surface.

In the past, when Shapiro traveled with the plane, somebody always showed up to help, and if nobody was available, he waited. He pictured himself parked at the small field he'd selected, home to the Mid-Maryland Soaring Society. Glider in its trailer. A surly tow pilot standing with his arms crossed saying he didn't do heavy lifting.

And an atom bomb sitting in the rear cockpit, with every cop in the country searching for it.

Not a moment for patience, Shapiro thought.

"Okay," he said. "You can come, then drive the car home.

Make us harder to trace, I suppose." Shapiro lowered his voice so only the burly man sitting to his right could hear. "You do know, Abram, that there's no room in the glider for you. You wouldn't fit, not with the bomb, even if I agreed to take you."

"I know that, but I want to be there to watch you fly into the sky."

Reuben was all business. "You're sure you can get pulled into the air, or whatever?" she asked Shapiro.

"No problem. I called them yesterday, the glider club there. Their towplane flies every day and they said weekdays are dead slow this time of year. They'll welcome my tow fee."

"And flying to Washington, that's something you can do from the middle of Maryland? I still don't understand how the glider plane works. What if the wind stops blowing?" Reuben asked.

"I've been through this," Shapiro said, slightly annoyed. "From five thousand feet, where he'll drop me off, I could fall asleep in the cockpit and the plane would land on the White House lawn. I've flown this plane hundreds of miles in one flight. This is nothing."

Sarah looked over her shoulder at the three people at the table, then glanced at the kitchen door. "Has Judy been down yet?" she asked. "I haven't heard her."

Abram shot to his feet. "I'm going to check on her," he said. "Why isn't she here with us?"

They listened to Abram clomp up the stairs to the guest room. His footsteps running down the stairs made the house rattle.

He stood in the doorway, his face flushed.

"She's gone," he said flatly. "I'll check the driveway. Her car."

He stamped to the front door. A minute later he returned, hands waving in the air.

"Car's gone," he shouted. "She knows everything. She's a government agent. I knew it. I told you we had to watch her. They'll be here any minute. Go. Now. We have to go now."

He locked eyes with his wife.

"I'll be back tomorrow," he said, his voice suddenly calm. "I promise, Sarah."

Sarah fought against tears. *Oh my God, this is really happening.*

Abram grabbed Shapiro's elbow, pulling him toward the front door. The man was frantic, barely in control.

"Go. Now. Now. No time. They'll come for us."

Shapiro allowed himself to be dragged to the front door. He stopped there, letting Reuben and Sarah catch up. Both gave him quick hugs, hardly holding him at all. Afraid of touching a ghost.

Reuben, however, whispered in his ear. "Don't worry about Judy," she said softly. "She told me she felt so sad she wouldn't be here to say goodbye. She couldn't watch you leave, she said, knowing it would be the last time. She . . . she said to let you know she loves you, Ben, and that she respects you so much. Ben, we each have a role to play, each of us, including Judy."

She stepped back from him. Her face clouded as she searched for words. "Ben, sometimes good people have to do horrible things. I know that. Better than anybody alive today I know that. I still think of myself as a good person, even after what I had to do."

She struggled against tears, then threw her arms around Shapiro again, this time holding him tightly. She whispered into his ear so softly only he could hear. "It will be a blessing not to have to live after what you are about to do. A sweet blessing, Ben. Take that thought with you. From me."

Shapiro sat in the driver's seat of the SUV, where Abram was waiting. He started the engine and drove from the driveway. The glider in its trailer was behind him. As was his entire life.

■ ■ ■

Shapiro and Goldhersh made random, futile efforts at conversation as the car drove south toward Maryland. Goldhersh navigated, running his finger over the fistful of maps they'd gathered, charting a course that took them through a hundred downtowns, avoiding interstates and toll plazas.

Shapiro grunted in reply to directions. His only conversation was the continuous one inside his head. During the hours of silence he heard a barely audible murmuring from the large man in the passenger seat, snatches of what sounded like Hebrew, in the singsong of Jewish prayers.

Only after they'd crossed into Maryland, just after midnight, were the two men able to touch on the purpose of their trip.

"I would change places with you if I could. You know that, don't you?" Goldhersh said. It was easier, safer, speaking in the dark, speaking without having to look at the other person.

"I know that." Shapiro almost laughed. "If we could change places, I'd probably let you. I've pictured myself doing many things with my life, but never anything like this. If there were another option, I'd take it; I'd try anything before this."

Goldhersh waved his hands in the air, interrupting. His hours of silent prayer had placed him in an Old Testament state of mind. "Times come that call for drastic action, Ben. A time for Samson to destroy the temple. A time for God to flood the earth. A time to slay the tyrant," Abram said, passion in his voice, sounding the biblical prophet he resembled.

"I know, I know, we've been through this," Shapiro said. "It's just that, well, that I'm a rational man about to commit what the whole world will know is an irrational act, an act of a madman, a monster." He thought he'd convinced himself, intellectually, analytically that he was making the right decision. He was surprised at the doubt he heard himself expressing.

Am I afraid? he thought. He smiled to himself in the dark. *Damn straight I'm scared. I'm about to kill myself.*

"Ben, Israel is depending on you."

"Don't worry, Abram. I won't back out. I made my decision. We all made a decision. It's the right decision. I know that. Fight evil. Do right. If not now, when. Use it or lose it. Shit. A stitch in time saves nine. I know."

The glider club's website said it began tow operations at ten in the morning. They would arrive well before then. They found an all-night truck stop at which they could pull between large semitrailers. They had three hours to spend there and did not want their unusual trailer, with the airplane's tail jutting up at the rear, to attract attention.

The truck stop neon flashed *Breakfast All Day Always Open.*

Goldhersh was surprised that Shapiro ate only two slices of rye toast. No butter. He looked at the lawyer quizzically as the waitress walked away after taking their orders.

"Not to make light of it, but that isn't much of a last meal," the huge man said.

"Can't eat before flying," Shapiro replied. "You know on an airliner when the pilot comes on and warns that things could get bumpy? That's the kind of turbulence gliders need to stay in the air. It gets awfully bouncy in my little airplane."

He saw the skeptical expression on the other man's face.

"Abram, I'm not getting cold feet."

Goldhersh didn't answer.

Shapiro finished his toast and two cups of coffee. Goldhersh called the waitress over every half hour to order more food for himself, and more coffee, to justify their three-hour sojourn in the vinyl booth.

Finally, Shapiro looked at his watch and gestured for the waitress. She totaled the bill and dropped it on the table.

"Sure you boys don't want to wait around for lunch, now?" she said with a grin.

Goldhersh reached for the check, only to have Shapiro drop two twenty-dollar bills on the table.

"My treat," he said with a smile. "I've always been such a cheapskate of a tipper. Last chance to make it up."

He tossed another twenty on the table and stood.

In ten miles they reached a neatly painted white sign that said *Mid-Maryland Soaring Society.* The airfield was a wide grass strip with a sheet-metal hanger next to a small wood building. A high-winged single engine airplane, a tail-dragger with two wheels under the wings and a small wheel resting under the tail, the towplane, sat next to the building.

They drove down the dirt road and parked next to a sign saying *Visiting Pilots Welcome Aboard.*

CHAPTER 67

Judy Katz ran up the stairs to her third-floor apartment, searching through her bag for her keys. The backpack she'd borrowed from Reuben was heavy. She was breathing hard by the time she reached her door.

Some clothes, not much, and my passport, she thought. *Where the hell did I leave my passport?*

The passport from her teenage years, the one filled with stamps from an eight-week If-It's-Tuesday-This-Must-Be-Belgium American Youth Hostels summer vacation, was long expired. Her rapid-fire legal career did not leave time for vacations. She'd obtained a new passport a few years back, though, after she and a boyfriend-of-the-moment talked about how much fun it would be to take off on a last-minute weekend to Paris. She'd realized her ability to be spontaneous would take advance planning, the first action being getting a current passport. The boyfriend went south before the two of them flew east. She was ashamed the passport was as pristine as the day she'd received it.

Where did I hide that thing?

She turned the key and slowly opened the door, half expecting a crowd of the FBI agents she used to direct, but the apartment was empty, as quiet and lonely as it had been when she fled to Maine after discovering the DVD in her laptop.

She pulled clothes from drawers as if she were conducting a search, which, she realized, she was. Who knew what the weather was like where she was going. Warm, for sure. Hot? She didn't know.

All she knew for certain was that she had to leave, had to get out of the country, soon, today if possible. Before tomorrow for sure. Everything would change tomorrow.

At the top of the heap in her junk drawer was a small blue booklet with the familiar seal of the United States on the cover— her passport.

She grinned, grabbed it and raced across the room to her bed. The passport went into her pocketbook. The clothes, and the manila folder, were stuffed into a nylon suitcase. With a final glance around the room, she walked out the door and down the steps, taking them two at a time despite the weight of the suitcase in one hand and the heavy backpack over her other shoulder.

Her car was parked halfway down the block. *Shouldn't use my own car,* she thought. *Call a cab? Shouldn't use my cell phone.*

Fuck it. She raced to the car. Fumbling with her car keys, she unlocked the trunk and tossed her suitcase in. The backpack went on the passenger seat.

Now where? Abram would know. Wish I could have asked him. Downtown. There's a place downtown.

She drove quickly, following the Boston traffic rule of "green light means go, yellow means go faster." Passing Boston Common, she turned down a side street and pulled to the curb next to a *Loading Zone No Parking* sign. "Screw it," she said.

Locking the car, leaving the suitcase behind, she hefted the backpack over one shoulder and walked to the corner. *Washington Street. Where the hell is that building. Left? Right?* She looked both ways to orient herself. *Left. Maybe.*

She walked down the crowded sidewalk, so distracted she couldn't deal with people walking toward her, doing a dance with a man in a blue suit, carrying a briefcase, cell phone to his ear, walking directly toward her. She moved right, he moved the same way, she moved left, he moved the same way. They smiled at one another in embarrassed annoyance and passed.

Her eyes were on the old brick buildings lining the street. *Which one is it?* A doorway with a sign over the top brought her a sigh of relief. *Boston Jewelers Building.*

She'd been there once before, a Friday afternoon she'd left work early after turning down an invitation to join "the guys" at a bar in Southie to tie one on. She went to look at rings, hoping, fantasizing that one day she'd be engaged. *Where is my life going*, she'd thought, wallowing in self-pity at approaching what she considered to be middle age with no husband, no family, no prospects of a husband or family. *Nana was so right,* she'd thought.

Katz took the elevator to the third floor. She didn't remember the name of the shop, but she did recall the sign on the front door. Beneath the word *Diamonds* it said, *Gold Bought and Sold.*

She tried the door handle. Locked. Looking through the glass door she saw a man behind the counter. He looked up as she pressed the button next to the door handle. She smiled. He smiled and nodded. A buzz. She turned the handle and the door opened.

"Ready for that diamond now, sweetie?" the man asked. Seeing the startled look on her face, he smiled broadly. "My father taught me. Never forget a customer. Especially such a pretty one. If this man doesn't work out for you, there'll be another. I knew it all along. So, *sheyna velle*, bright eyes, are you ready for your diamond?"

Katz lifted her backpack onto the glass counter, plunking it down with such a thunk she was afraid she'd break the glass. The man raised his eyebrows quizzically.

She reached to the bottom of the bag with both hands and

deposited a mound of glistening gold coins on the glass.

"I want to sell these," she said, hiding, hopefully, the nervousness in her voice.

The man picked one coin up and glanced at it quickly.

"Krugerrands," he said, spitting the word out as if it were an obscenity.

"I want cash for these. How much are they worth?" Katz asked.

Without saying a word, the man began counting the coins, sliding them one at a time across the counter as he did so. "Ten, eleven, twelve."

"I have more," Katz said quietly. "But I'm going to take some with me. How much can I get for these?"

The man walked to the far end of the counter where a computer that looked as if it had been purchased during the Eisenhower administration sat, orange characters appearing on a black screen. He pecked at the keys with one extended figure. Rows of numbers filled the screen.

He walked back to Katz with a look of sadness, almost of despondency.

"Gold is down," he said. "Keep them. Sell them some other time." He saw the shocked expression on her face.

"You know I'll just take them someplace else," she said, desperate. "I need the money today, right now."

"No, *tottala*, no," he said softly. "Whatever is troubling you, it will get better. Trust me. I've seen bad in my life. It gets better."

He saw the desperation in her eyes. He made a decision.

"So, sometimes getting better takes some help. All right then. They have a face value of $1,346. I'll give you . . ." He paused, his eyes turned to the ceiling, going distant for a moment, then returning. "I'll give you $1,200 each. Nobody else will give that much. They'd steal them from you, the *gonifs*, thieves."

"I'll take it," Katz blurted. "Thank you so much, so much." She pushed the coins toward the man. "Can I have large bills, please?"

"Oh no, sweetie. I don't keep that kind of cash here. They'd beat me over the head."

He opened a drawer and removed a large leather binder. Inside was a spiral-bound check register.

"I have to have cash," she said flatly, sadly.

The man calculated rapidly in his head and began writing a check.

"You can take this across the street." He pointed out the window. A sign said *Bank of America*. "They'll give you cash for this. I need your name, dear."

"Judith Katz."

"Katz?" He smiled. "A Katz. Not related to Hyman and Myrna are you? No. Of course not. They had no children." He signed the check as carefully as if he were stitching a wound. He waved it in the air to dry the ink, then handed the check to Katz.

"Things will get better. Trust me."

She looked at the man kindly, sighed deeply, relieved by the prospect of completing the first step of her mission.

"But first," she said, "first it is going to get much, much worse."

She left the building with the check clutched in her hand, afraid that if it went into her bag, some thief's radar would be alerted and the bag would be snatched.

Across the street, the bank teller looked at the check Judith handed him, then at the driver's license presented with it, punched keys on a keyboard, looked at a screen and asked, with no hint that anything unusual was taking place, "How would you like this?"

Katz walked two blocks to the American Express travel office next to her dry cleaner. The office was empty except for two bored-looking employees sitting at separate desks.

"I want to book a flight," Katz said.

The travel agent looked more like a bicycle messenger, both of her earlobes riddled with rings, both nostrils pierced, as was one eyebrow.

When she spoke, a glint of gold showed in the middle of her tongue.

She looked surprised. No one Katz's age used travel agents. Most customers looked more like the travel agent's grandparents, and even her grandmother booked her flights back and forth from Florida on Travelocity.

"That's what I'm here for," the woman said cheerily. "Vacation? Got some good packages in the islands."

"Africa," Katz said, no hint of excitement in her voice at uttering such an exotic destination. "I want to go to Africa, Eastern Africa."

She saw the surprise on the agent's face.

"Is there a flight today?"

CHAPTER 68

Goldhersh waited outside while Shapiro went into the small metal building declaring itself to be *Office Mid-Maryland Soaring Society*. Inside were a counter and a coffee table with three ratty rattan chairs. Dog-eared copies of the *Soaring Society of America* journal covered the table. A large erasable calendar hung on the wall behind the counter.

A large-boned woman wearing age-faded jeans walked through a door at the side of the counter. A black plastic tag pinned over her left shirt pocket said *TAMMY*.

"Howdy," Shapiro said, hoping to hide his relief. "I just drove down from Massachusetts. I thought I'd get in some ridge flying." He was met with a blank stare. "I called a few days ago," he added.

"I remember," she replied. "Looks like a sunny day? Whatcha flyin'?" The woman looked out at the Pathfinder and trailer.

"A Grob 103, two place. I thought I'd fly the ridge today. I'd like to get up this morning, if possible."

"Said that already."

"So, how do I make arrangements? Is the tow pilot around? I'd like to speak with him and see about getting a nice high tow, five thousand feet or so. Give me a chance to familiarize myself with the area."

The woman gave Shapiro a blank stare.

"Is the tow pilot here?"

The woman walked around the counter to stand next to Shapiro.

"You're looking at him?" she said. "Why don't you get that fancy plane stuck together and we'll talk about that tow?"

As Shapiro turned to leave, the woman spoke again.

"One thing. Gotta see your pilot's license. New reg. FAA says so?"

I never heard of that regulation, Shapiro thought suspiciously. "Sure thing," he said. "It's in the car. I'll show it to you when the plane's assembled."

"No prob. Don't forget. New reg."

Shapiro said nothing to Goldhersh about any suspicions. He backed the glider trailer onto the grass in front of the club building. The cover slid easily off the trailer, revealing the long white fuselage of the glider, the vertical tail rising at one end, the bulge of the cockpit at the front reminding Shapiro, as usual, of the time a waitress near a glider contest asked him if he flew one of "them flyin' sperm things." The cockpit was topped with a long Plexiglas cover, hinged at one side. The plane's wings were stored on edge along both sides of the body.

The two men lifted the wings and laid them on the grass. They slid the airplane backwards from the trailer, rolling on the single rubber wheel protruding from underneath the cockpit.

With Goldhersh holding the end, Shapiro carefully guided a wing into the narrow opening on the side of the fuselage. A long steel bar at the inner end of the wing slipped into a slot behind the rear seat. They did the same with the other wing.

Shapiro opened the clear canopy and leaned into the far rear of the cockpit, where the ends of the wings were visible. He inserted steel safety pins into holes in the wing ends, then spun locking nuts over the pins, finally inserting cotter pins into holes in the pins to ensure the nuts could not loosen.

He counted the threads exposed on the pins above the nuts. Standard procedure.

All that remained was to carry the horizontal tail section to the rear of the plane and lower it over the flat top of the vertical tail. Locking pins held it in place.

The plane was ready. It had taken only fifteen minutes.

Before returning to the club building, Shapiro conducted his preflight inspection, walking slowly around the airplane, testing the flight controls to ensure that the wing flaps responded to movement of the control stick in the cockpit and that the tail surfaces moved in the correct directions.

Finally, he walked to one wing tip, the wing that jutted into the air while the other wing rested on the grass. He reached up for the wing tip above his head and shook it. Hard. The flexible wing moved in a wave from the tip to the body. He walked to the other wing tip, lifted it and shook it.

Satisfied that the plane was flight ready, he called to Goldhersh, who stood watching this ritual silently. Shapiro glanced at the large man from time to time and noticed his lips continuing to move soundlessly, without stop, as his prayers continued.

Can't hurt, Shapiro thought.

The familiar routine of attaching the wings and tail surface and conducting the preflight inspection settled Shapiro's thoughts. Over the years little could distract him from absolute attention to the details of those rituals; the counting of the threads was as close to a sacrament as Shapiro believed in.

The final step in the preflight brought him back to reality. Rather than buckling the rear safety belts around the cockpit cushions, Shapiro was confronted with the steel cylinder, still wrapped in blue vinyl dental blankets.

He called to Goldhersh.

"Abram, let's put these things in the car." He lifted one of the heavy blankets and staggered as he carried the armload of blue blankets to the SUV. He dropped them on the grass behind the tailgate, lifted it, and placed each of the blankets in the rear of the car.

Shapiro noticed Tammy standing at the window. Her eyes were on the large man at the rear of the SUV.

The door opened and the woman came out. She glanced at his airplane and nodded.

"You said five thousand feet?" she asked.

"That's right. Like to have some time to get situated before hitting the ridge," Shapiro said. That was an exceptionally high tow, twice as high as was necessary to get to the nearby ridgeline. "Can we get started soon?"

"Want me to tell ya 'bout the landin' pattern before ya take off, or ya gonna wait till yer on the way down?" she asked.

"Woops, sorry," Shapiro said, trying to conceal his nervousness. "Run me through it."

The woman described the flight pattern at the field, pointing to the wind sock hanging from the hanger roof, telling Shapiro where the interception point, the beginning of the landing pattern, was located. The familiar right-turn-right-turn landing pattern.

Shapiro only half-listened to her as the reality of what was about to happen surfaced.

I won't need that information, he thought. *One-way trip.*

He noticed the quizzical look on the woman's face. She'd turned to walk to the towplane, then stopped and suddenly walked back to face Shapiro.

"Almost forgot," she said. "Gotta check yer license?" She held her hand out.

Shapiro reached into his back pocket for his wallet and extracted his dog-eared pilot's license. The woman examined it closely, as if it were a winning lottery card.

"Shapira. That's a Jew name, ain't it?" she asked, sounding more curious than anything else.

"Yes, I am Jewish. Why?"

"No reason. FBI been talking to some of the Jew power pilots, that's all. Just wonderin'?" She paused as if trying to remember something, then swung her head to look at Shapiro. "Ready to go?"

She walked across the grass to the towplane, started its engine and waited for it to warm up.

After glancing at the towplane to make sure the pilot was still there, Shapiro lifted the canopy over the glider's cockpit and leaned into the rear seat. He removed the Chemical Bank of New York credit card from his wallet and swiped it through the card reader on top of the bomb.

LED lights lit on the keypad. Shapiro carefully, as carefully as he'd counted threads on the safety pin, pushed keys. *0-9-1-1*. The numbers appeared on a small screen.

The keypad beeped.

Hebrew letters glowed on the small screen. *SET DELAY*, they said, Debra had told him.

Shapiro looked at Goldhersh. This time, the man was praying out loud. "*Sh'ma Yisrael Adonai Elohaynu Adonai Echad.*"

Shapiro pushed the *0* key.

The device beeped.

He looked at the red plastic cover, hinged at one end. Five Hebrew letters were on top of the cover. Reuben had told him they spelled the word for *ACTIVATE*. He left the cover down.

The towplane taxied to a position a hundred feet in front of Shapiro's aircraft. Shapiro climbed into the glider's front seat. Goldhersh stood over him.

The two men did not speak. Shapiro slowly buckled his safety straps, snapping each end into the circular metal buckle that lay on his chest, pulling them tight. He reached forward between his legs and found the end of the aerobatic strap, pulled it up over his crotch and snapped it into the buckle.

Goldhersh reached into the rear seat, doing something Shapiro couldn't see.

A long rope was attached to the back of the towplane, above

the rear wheel. The pilot got out of the plane, walked to the far end of the rope and dragged it to the front of Shapiro's plane.

The cockpit canopy was still open.

"Five-thousand feet, right?" the woman said to Shapiro. His heart stopped as he saw her eyes glance toward the rear cockpit and hesitate. Her eyes widened. She stared at Shapiro for a moment, debating what to say. "Ya might want to strap that down so it don't come loose," she said. "Want to do a release test first?"

"Yes, yes." Shapiro could barely speak. He waited for the woman to bend down to attach the end of the towrope to the release hook at the front of the glider before he turned his head to glance at the back seat.

A jacket, Goldhersh's large jacket, covered the bomb.

They went through the routine release test. She pulled the rope. He pulled the release knob on his panel. The rope released from the glider's nose. When they finished, the woman reattached the rope, gave it a tug, then walked to the towplane and climbed in. Shapiro shoved first his right foot down, then his left foot, wiggling the plane's rudder from side to side, indicating to the pilot that he was ready.

The towplane's engine roared. The two aircraft rolled down the grass airstrip. After thirty seconds, Shapiro pulled back on the stick and felt his glider rise into the air. He maintained his altitude of five feet above the grass until he saw the towplane lift, then he followed directly behind it, banking his wings as the towplane banked its wings.

He heard his takeoff mantra as if somebody else in the cockpit were speaking. *Stick forward, land straight ahead, stick forward, land straight ahead.*

The towplane leveled off as Shapiro's altimeter crossed five thousand feet. His left hand reached for the yellow release knob on the center of the panel, then stopped. His hand hovered over the knob. The towplane continued flying straight and level, buzzing onward.

Two inches separated his left hand from the release knob. He looked at the hand, then at the towplane, continuing to fly past the release point, still straight and level.

Shapiro was shocked to hear a voice over the VHF cockpit radio.

"Everything okay back there, Mr. Shapira?"

Without a word, Shapiro grasped the yellow knob and pulled it. Then pulled it again, just in case it hadn't released the first time. That was procedure.

The glider banked to the right, the towplane to the left.

Shapiro pushed a small button on the GPS chart plotter on the instrument panel, a button marked *Follow Route*.

He'd input his course before leaving Portland—a course that took him from Central Maryland sixty-five miles to Washington, directly over the White House.

■ ■ ■

Tammy was agitated the entire flight back to the airstrip.

"Somethin' off about that guy with him. He looked like a Jew, too. Why go to five thousand feet for a ridge ride?" she said aloud. She dialed her cell as soon as she landed. "Hello, FAA, this here's Tammy Beaujot at the Mid-Maryland Soaring Society, over in Gathistown? No, jerkball, that's Bu Jot, like it's spelled, not Bu Joe, like that fancy wine."

Enough of trying to get these idiots to pronounce her name the way her daddy taught her to say it. She wouldn't give her name.

The woman was in telephone hell for twenty minutes, handed off from one bureaucrat to the next at the FAA regional office in Baltimore.

Five more minutes of listening to instrumental music.

Finally an intelligent-sounding voice, a woman, came on the phone. "Regional security, Rivkin here."

"Look, Rivkin here, I run the glider operation? At Mid-

Maryland Soaring? At Gathistown? Maryland, 'bout sixty miles west'a DC, you know?"

"How can I help you, Mizz . . . sorry, I didn't catch your name."

"Ya didn't catch it cause I didn't toss it. Look, ma name don't matter none. I gotta tell ya 'bout somethin' fishy what just happened."

"I need your name to complete my report, ma'am. It's regulations."

"Well, I don't wanna give ya ma name. It ain't none'a yer bizness. Do ya wanna hear what I gotta say or not?"

"I can't take a report without a name. I'm sorry, I must insist on a name. That's regulation, ma'am."

CLICK.

CHAPTER 69

Air parted around Shapiro's sailplane as easily as water around a fish, causing almost no sound. The Maryland countryside flowed beneath the thin white wings, curved gently upward at their tips from supporting the weight of the aircraft. Sunlight shining through the clear canopy warmed Shapiro's chest.

He glanced at the GPS, displaying a map of the area between his position and downtown Washington. Digital readouts flanked the map. *Distance to Waypoint 59.4 miles. Altitude 4,890 feet.*

He glanced at the variometer, the sensitive rate-of-climb indicator that showed whether the glider was rising or falling. The horizontal needle was barely below level. The aircraft sank as slowly as a feather fluttering in the breeze.

Shapiro planned his flight with the glider pilot motto in mind: *Get High and Stay High.* At 4,000 feet he'd look for lift to boost him back to 5,000 feet, or higher. Until he sank to 4,000 feet, he'd fly straight toward his destination—the White House.

The whistle of air flowing smoothly around the plane removed him from a suicide mission and returned him to his personal place of comfort, calming Shapiro almost to the point of dozing. His head dropped to his chest, then jerked upward with a start.

Stop that, he scolded. *Stay sharp, for God's sake.*

He looked at the instruments. *Distance: 55.2 miles. Altitude: 4,755 feet.*

Shapiro looked over the sailplane's nose, struggling to see the nation's capital through the haze hovering on the horizon. He could only make out farmland, crossed by roads, highways and scattered buildings, fading into the distance.

Soon enough, he thought. He flew onward in silence, senses heightened.

Instrument panel. *Distance: 41.8 miles. Altitude: 4,022 feet.*

Time to take the elevator up a few floors, he thought, looking around. A mile or so off to the right he spotted a shopping mall, a central building covered by a black, tarred roof surrounded by acres of paved parking area, partially filled with cars. Just downwind from the mall but a mile and a half above it, Shapiro saw wisps of white cloud in the sky. He smiled.

The morning sun shone on the asphalt, the cars and the tarred roof, heating them, creating bubbles of warm, moist air that rose through the cooler air from the surrounding fields. Glider pilots searched for these columns of lift and attempted to center in them, flying in tight circles with wingtips pointed almost straight down, circling within the rising air like hawks.

Strong lift, such as that generated by the shopping mall, could raise a lightweight sailplane faster than an elevator in a skyscraper.

Shapiro banked his plane to the right, then flew directly over the shopping mall. He felt the airplane bounce, the indicator of entering lift. Suddenly the right wing rose, as if a giant were crouched outside the plane lifting the wingtip with both hands. Instinctively, Shapiro threw the control stick to the right, lowering the right wing, moving his feet in and out to control the rudder, maintaining a smooth circling turn.

The familiar feeling of locking his glider into the center of a column of rising air swept over him. This was the seat-of-the-pants flying he loved so much. He felt pressure against his bottom as the plane was lifted into the sky, the rate-of-climb indicator pegged in the upward position.

After a few minutes of spiraling flight, Shapiro looked up through the canopy, straight above the aircraft, and saw the bottom of the forming cloud less than a hundred feet above him. He leveled the plane's wings and flew out of the column of lift.

Glancing at the GPS and instrument panel, Shapiro grinned to see that he'd ridden the lift to 6,755 feet. He checked his heading and turned the plane's nose slightly to the left. Back on course. *Distance: 47.8 miles.*

That's all the height I need to get there, he thought, calculating the plane's rate-of-sink against the distance to go. *I can fly straight there and arrive with half a mile of altitude. Piece of cake.*

That realization, that all he had to do now was fly straight and level, focused his thoughts on his destination and his conversation with Goldhersh on the drive from Maryland.

He thinks I'll back out, Shapiro thought. *It's not too late to do that. I could land just about anywhere.* He looked at the ground below, studded with farms. What appeared to be a school, with athletic fields beside it, was ahead to his left. *I could land there. On the football field. Sideslip in. Point a wingtip down the field. Drop like a stone. Piece of cake.*

He flew on, straight, level, on course.

Distance: 28.9 miles. Altitude: 4,948 feet. There it is.

He saw highways ringing the city and clusters of buildings within the ring, the Potomac River on one side. A cloud of haze rested a thousand feet above the city. He was still too far to make out individual buildings.

An image struck him. *The Flying Tzadik. That's who I am, a Jew on a mission. A righteous mission. A tzadik. A righteous man.*

A tzadik, he'd learned, was not a perfect man but rather one who wrestled with the effort to do what was right even when faced with the temptation and opportunity to do wrong. It became his goal throughout adult life.

The still, small voice that lurked in his mind in all but occasional silence whispered to him. He listened closely, his mind wandering from his flying.

Righteous, or self-righteous, the voice hissed. *Are you righteous or self-righteous?*

He cupped a mental hand to his inner ear, straining to make out what the voice was saying.

Heroic or ego-driven, the voice said. *Who are you to think you can change the world?* Shapiro's eyes spotted another farm field below the glider. *I could put it down there,* he thought. *Easy. Piece-of-cake landing.*

No! The camps. That man, Quaid, putting American Jews in goddamn concentration camps. All those people who cheered at the march. In camps.

The image of the young Israeli woman, strapped to the wooden board by duct tape, red rubber hose jammed into her nose, writhing against her bonds, came to mind. *How many others are they doing that to? I can stop that from happening.*

Without conscious thought, as the glider flew over the farm field, Shapiro felt the stick jerk to the right as the sailplane circled the field.

"No," he said, softly, no audience except himself to hear. He leveled the wings, checked the course heading and flew on. Straight and level.

Distance: 19.2 miles. Altitude: 4,135 feet.

Less than twenty miles. He calculated quickly—about twelve minutes.

He felt a cold sweat on his forehead. He twisted his head to glance back at the bomb. It looked larger than before. That was impossible, he knew, but it seemed to him the machine was aware it was about to be called to life.

He looked forward toward the horizon and felt the same thrill at seeing Washington that he had on every visit since his eighth-grade field trip. His eyes sought out the monuments.

He could see the grassy mall with the Capitol dome at one end, flanked by buildings on either side. And that—that must be the White House.

His breath sucked in when he saw the stub of the Washington Monument. *They removed the pieces pretty quickly,* he thought.

He looked at the GPS.

Ten minutes to destination.

■ ■ ■

The skies over Washington crackled with electronic beams from dozens of radars. When one of these signals encountered a metallic object, it bounced back, like a wave striking the side of a swimming pool, reflecting an echo that was picked up by the receiving antenna. These invisible electronic signals created an impenetrable defensive wall mightier than any surrounding a medieval castle.

Jet fighters at nearby Bolling Air Force Base stood on constant alert, armed with missiles and cannon. Armed with orders to turn away errant pilots, orders to shoot down any plane that failed to instantly obey.

However, just as the air parted smoothly around the glider, the electronic waves from the search radars passed through the plastic skin of the sailplane as easily as light penetrates window glass. Shapiro entered the capital city's airspace undetected.

He could see the White House straight ahead, off in the distance. At just more than 3,000 feet altitude, he was well above the highest buildings, but close enough to the ground to begin to attract attention.

A few people pointed at the strange aircraft, its long thin wings distinguishing it from any other type of airplane except, oddly enough, from Cold War U-2 spy planes, which had been nothing more than jet-powered sailplanes. The silent flight of the glider allowed it to slip over most people unnoticed, however.

Calm enveloped Ben—the calm he felt as he rose from the

attorney's table in court to give his closing argument to a jury. Too late for doubts in the righteousness of his client's cause by then. It was all a matter of winning.

Or losing.

This time, though, doubts persisted. *Has there ever been a bomb-throwing tzadik?* he wondered.

He could make out individual cars, people below him. *They have less than ten minutes to live,* he thought. *I'm going to kill a lot of children.*

Like Adam.

Adam. Tears filled his eyes. He wiped them abruptly. *Not now. Focus.* He turned his head to glance again at the bomb. He'd yanked Goldhersh's jacket off the device. The cold, shiny cylinder was bathed in sunlight coming through the canopy, illuminating the cover over the final button. The red plastic pulsed in the sunlight.

A panicked thought. *I haven't made sure I can reach the button.*

Ben twisted his body and strained behind him in the narrow cockpit. His right hand stopped six inches from the red cover. He slapped his left hand to the round buckle on his chest holding the ends of the safety straps and gave it a savage twist, freeing the straps.

His right hand rested on the red cover. He lifted it slowly.

Strange, he thought. *The button is red, too.*

He carefully lowered the cover over the button and twisted back into his seat, then reattached all the safety straps. He could no more fly an airplane with his straps unbuckled than he could drive a car without a seat belt. That was not procedure.

Another thought came. *I should have worn a yellow star.*

He pictured Lawrence Quaid, a brush of a Hitler mustache under his nose. *I'm going to kill today's Hitler. Stop today's Holocaust.*

That picture was replaced by a memory of Catherine Quaid pinning a yellow Star of David to her blouse. He smiled as he recalled telling her about the king of Denmark.

She is a tzadik, he thought. *She knew right from wrong. She did right, rather than wrong. There's a person who took a personal risk for a cause in which she believed. She's probably in the White House now.*

Am I a tzadik if I kill a tzadik?

He looked at the ground. This low, the plane's speed was exhilarating. He liked flying low and fast. *Nobody is looking up at me,* he thought. *They don't know I'm here. Nobody knows what I'm carrying. The Angel of Death is passing over their houses and they don't know it.*

The Angel of Death. Like in Egypt. At Passover.

Can the Angel of Death be a tzadik?

The Angel of Death freed the Jewish people from slavery in Egypt. That was the Passover story. That rabbi, at the march, had said that God sent the Angel of Death to slay the enemies of Israel. The Angel of Death, or God himself, was the world's greatest terrorist, the rabbi said.

Is that what I am, the world's greatest terrorist?

And after the slaying, enemies always struck again. In seventy-five years of Israel's existence, how many times did Israelis attack Palestinians? Who then retaliated against Israel. Which retaliated against Palestine.

Which then struck back. All in God's name. *Everybody killing in God's name,* Shapiro thought. *So, now I'm doing God's work, igniting an atom bomb over the nation's capital, the capital of the country in which I was raised?*

He wondered whether it was the same God who kept the Red Sox from winning the World Series when he was a kid, the God who let awful things happen to good people. Like Sally. Like Adam.

Did the man who killed Sally believe he was doing a righteous deed? Did he believe he was doing God's work, Israel's work? Or did he follow some other God and do that God's work? Did he care that he was going to kill innocent people?

And children.

Adam. I'm fighting back for Adam's sake, in Adam's memory. Right? Did Adam's murderer, too, think of himself as a righteous man?

He thought about the children in Damascus. *How many children died from that bomb?*

How will their fathers retaliate?

Ben flew the glider without conscious thought. His mind spinning. Thoughts racing. Then calm.

Like sunlight breaking between parting clouds, the realization struck Shapiro that he was just another bomber. Just one bounce of a ping-pong ball of perpetual retaliation in a match that had been playing for centuries. Longer.

I'm not a hero executing Hitler. I'm going to kill some other man's wife, some other father's son.

A coward murdered Sally and Adam. Not a hero. Not a tzadik.

Ben stared straight ahead over the airplane's rounded nose. There was the White House.

Men on the roof spotted the glider.

Suddenly a streak of white smoke rose from the White House roof and flew directly toward the glider, then another streak next to it. Then another. And another.

They're shooting missiles at me, he realized, strangely surprised. *Will the bomb go off if a missile hits it?*

The white trails behind the ground-to-air Stinger missiles twisted into corkscrews as the heat-seeking electronics in their noses searched ahead of the missiles for hot engine exhaust.

The sailplane, of course, had no exhaust.

Instead, the missiles locked onto the hottest object in the sky, turned upward, and climbed toward the sun, falling to the ground when their fuel was exhausted.

Ben pictured Catherine Quaid standing at one of the second-floor windows, staring at the strange airplane flying toward her.

Catherine Quaid. America's royalty. America's version of

the king of Denmark, he thought. *I can't kill Catherine Quaid.*

I can't kill other fathers' Adams. I can't do this thing. I won't. I can't.

Break the chain; stop the ping-pong match.

He pictured Catherine Quaid smiling at him.

The White House seemed to rush toward him, rather than he toward it. The National Mall was to his right, 2,500 feet below.

"Enough," he said out loud. "Stop it."

I promised I would do this, he thought. *People are depending on me. Now is the time.* He reached for the safety-belt buckle. Time for the bomb.

No, he thought.

"No," he shouted. "I can't do this. It isn't right. It isn't right."

The red button remained covered.

He moved the control stick as far to the right as it would go, dropping the plane's right wing toward the ground. His left leg straightened, swinging the plane's nose to the left.

A perfect sideslip. *Wish Willy could see this.*

Ben turned his head, staring out across the length of the right wing, pointing toward the center of the Mall and the Capitol building.

Instantly, the silent flight was broken by the noise of air battering the side of the plane. The controls, the stick and rudder pedals, rattled. The glider dropped from the sky toward the grass below, flying wingtip first, sideways to the air.

At fifty feet above the ground, he swung the stick to the left and straightened his right leg, depressing the right rudder pedal. The wings leveled. The plane's nose pivoted quickly to the right and pointed straight ahead, straight down the grassy Mall, straight at the spot where Shapiro had sat so recently facing a crowd of half a million people.

He skimmed just feet above the grass now. People turned and pointed. People directly in front of the plane threw themselves flat on the ground and felt the breeze from his wings on their backs.

He thrust the stick fully forward and felt the single wheel

bounce onto the grass. He reached down with his left hand for the wheel brake and lifted it, pulling hard.

The plane slowed to a halt. The left wing dropped to the grass, the right wing pointed at the sky.

Shapiro reached for the lever that unlocked the canopy, then lifted the clear plastic over his head and swung it open. He twisted the round buckle on his chest to release the ends of the safety belts, then used both hands to lift himself from the seat and climb out of the glider.

He stood on the grass, next to his sailplane, next to an atom bomb, and slowly raised both hands over his head, watching as a park service police officer cautiously walked toward him, gun in hand.

Shapiro smiled. Content. Proud. *I just saved the lives of a million people. I'm a hero,* he thought. *A tzadik. A righteous man.*

EPILOGUE

Abram Goldhersh drove the Nissan Pathfinder into his driveway in Portland. Exhausted. Emotionally drained. Dejected. He'd driven from the glider field due east, toward Washington, waiting to see the flash.

It never came.

He listened on the radio for news of the bomb.

He heard nothing.

Fox Radio News reported that a glider landed on the National Mall in Washington. Nothing was known about the pilot, the reporter said. Park police and the Secret Service had surrounded the plane and quickly removed it, saying nothing about it.

That was all he learned.

He parked the SUV and entered his house. It was after eleven. Sarah ran to the door. She opened her arms for her husband and attempted to surround the huge man with herself, unsuccessfully. Home, with his wife, he finally let loose. Sarah felt his body shaking and heard his sobs. After five minutes of silently holding her husband, she released him and walked him into the living room.

"He lost his nerve," Abram said. "He let us down. He let

Israel down. Why does God do this to us?"

Sarah led him into the living room.

"Abram," Sarah said to him. "Debbie has something to tell you."

"I don't want to hear anything more. Israel is lost. Who knows when there will be another chance like this one?"

Reuben stood in the living room, next to the fireplace, watching him and Sarah. He looked at her sadly, the tracks of tears still on his face. He looked at her and said nothing.

"Abram," Reuben said, sounding excited rather than despondent. "There's another bomb, Abram. A bigger bomb. In Africa. In Ethiopia. I sent the other pilot there to wait.

"Judy is going to the pilot. She had to get away from what we were doing. I told her to take a message to him. But I didn't tell her about the other bomb—just to find the pilot and deliver my message. That's why she left."

Reuben walked to the table where she'd left her drink, poured more vodka into the glass and downed it in a long, desperate gulp.

Goldhersh stared at the woman for a long moment, smiled, then walked to the closet he used as an office. He powered up his computer and started typing.

"Dear President Quaid," he wrote. "We showed we can deliver a bomb to your doorstep. Now let me tell you about our other bombs."

AUTHOR'S NOTE

Never Again came about as a result of my visit to the detention camp at Guantanamo Bay, Cuba, where I represented two young Saudi Arabian men. I interviewed them while they were shackled to a ring on the floor. I heard screams from the next room, but my clients comforted me it was just a recording meant to intimidate me. Or them. Guantanamo shocked me to the core (although it didn't stop me from buying Gitmo T-shirts, refrigerator magnets and coffee mugs at the gift shop. I did wonder whether Dachau, too, had a gift shop or whether that was just an American thing.)

I flew home through Miami, where I visited my father. He had been captured two weeks after landing on Omaha Beach and held in a German prisoner-of-war camp. After I described Guantanamo to him he was silent, then said, "Imagine that, Americans are treating their boys worse than the Nazis treated me, a Jew."

Imagine that. Americans acting worse than Nazis. My father's comment inspired me to come up with a plausible scenario in which something like the Holocaust could happen in the United States. Thus, Never Again.

I'm not saying these events *would* happen in these circumstances, only that, you know, they *could* happen.

After all, ask yourself, if I were a character in this book, what would I do? Would I do nothing? How far would I go? There's no right answer, I know. But there are right questions to be asked.

HARVEY SCHWARTZ
Ipswich, Massachusetts